Lazarus frowned. "Viktor, what happened to the woman?"

Viktor wrung his hands together as he said, "I'm not really sure. After Jake shot her with a dart, we shifted to the hanger with her. He said the mission specs were to remove the target. So, we dumped her body into a sea far, far away from here."

"You what?!" Tanner exploded.

"We dumped her... on Ardus."

"Ardus," Lazarus said, shocked.

Tanner squeezed his hands into tight fists as he glared at Viktor. "You dumped her unconscious into water? She'll drown. You bastard, you killed her," he ground out through his clenched teeth.

"I know. That's what I can't get out of my head."

"No. You don't understand. You killed one of our own," he growled.

"I did? No. No," Viktor groaned. "I knew something was wrong. I knew it. Who? Who did I kill?" he said, holding his hands up in protest.

"Sharra Lane, damn you!" Tanner shouted, and hurled himself at the giant.

VAULT AGENCY SERIES:

SHIFTERS

ARDUS

THE VAULT

ARDUS

A Vault Agency Novel: Book Two

BY

JEAN GILBERT

ARDUS. Copyright __ 2015 by Jean Gilbert

A catalogue record for this book is available from the National Library of New Zealand.

ISBN 978-0-473-31390-6

Published by Rogue House Publishing
Cover design by Getty Creations

This book is dedicated

To my beautiful daughters,

Leia, Nicci, and Sam.

PART ONE

THE VAULT

Chapter One

The Vault

Time had no master. Not even death could defeat it. The charred remains on the table attested to that fact.

The white sheet was pulled back over the corpse's chest. It stood out like fresh snow against the backdrop of blackened flesh that was uncovered. What was once healthy skin had bubbled and peeled away from the chest of the man. The exposed crisscross of muscle was no longer red and healthy. Now it was charred like meat left too long over a hot fire. From it, pieces of shattered rib bones poked out as if a giant hand had squeezed him.

The face looked no better off. Naked eyeballs stared out from lidless sockets among the twisted wreckage that had once been a face. Below the half exposed bone of the nose, the soft tissue of the lips had curled away, revealing a perfect set of teeth left in a twisted smile that was anything but happy.

The cold air hung with the sickening smell of seared flesh. Jake Byson held his breath as he stared down in distain at what was left of J.D. Dash.

The corpse leered back.

"What a waste," Jake said wrinkling his nose as he took a breath.

"Was he a friend of yours?" Cam, the chief medic said.

Jake draped the sheet back over the dead agent's face. He couldn't stand to look at it anymore. J.D. had had his bad points like they all had, yet he didn't deserve this.

"No." He lied. "It's just that it's not every day one of us gets to meet our maker. Kind of a novelty, you know, like a freak show."

The doctor slid the metal slab back into the cooler. It clanked into place. The door was latched, shutting the smell behind the thick metal of the refrigeration unit.

"The word is going around that he suffered a Brain Shift, that at the end he was spouting some lunacy about the Vault holding us here against our will, and blaming Maitland for it. I don't know. I wasn't there. I'm not one to judge, but it sounds like he went crazy to me," Jake said with a shrug of his shoulders.

"The analysis of J.D. Dash's brain has not yet been completed. Brain Shifting does happen on a rare occasion. We are still collecting data to determine what triggers it. The variables of the human brain are endless, and so it makes for a difficult study. The one factor we do know that stays constant in the equation is this: an aggressive shifting pattern. The records will show that he had over-shifted for far too long. The other factor or factors will be somewhere in the analysis."

"So, what happens to the body?" Jake asked.

"After the agrylium is removed, we will send him back to his timeline for a proper burial."

"What a waste."

"Losing an agent is always hard," Cam said. "We can fix most anything, but not this. His timeline is set, it cannot be changed."

But that wasn't what Jake was thinking. He didn't want to fix the dead man. Dash had been a bad choice from the beginning. He realized that now. No, what bothered Jake was the waste of his time. All he had wanted was for J.D. to dissuade Sharra Lane from joining the Agency. That was it, plain and simple. He should've known the man was useless after the first few bungled attempts. Murder had been a last measure, and the man couldn't even do that right. And now, look where he was- back to square one.

He growled in frustration forgetting where he was.

"Are you alright?" Cam asked.

No, he wasn't all right. Sharra Lane was still in his way.

"Yes, yes," he said. "It's just something I need to work through, on my own."

"If you need to talk…"

Jake waved the doctor's concern aside. J.D. Dash had been a loose canon from the beginning. He wouldn't be so careless next time. He needed a new puppet- someone weak, someone he could control… someone in the good graces of the Head Director. Someone who wouldn't lose his mind.

Sharra was getting more popular every day. The Vault was supposed to be his world, not hers. She didn't belong there. He didn't care who she was. She had to go.

Chapter Two

Sharra Lane sat straight up, knocking the sleeping cat from her side with the bedcovers. Through a haze of white, she stared wide-eyed into the darkness of her bedroom as she gasped for air. The figure of a man was still right in front of her. She tried to wipe him from her mind. Yet the distorted face, the sadistic laughter... the hands that tightened around her neck clung fast, searing her mind in white heat as it did every night since the incident a month ago in the Vault.

With a fierceness born from desperation, she blinked the images away, until all that remained was the churning mass of energy behind her eyes. With a mental push, she told it to desist. It obeyed. The light faded from her eyes as it returned to its hiding place between the agrylium threads in her brain.

"Lights." Her voice shook as she activated the room's Personal Voice Control System.

Soft light illuminated the bedroom, dispelling the remnants of the dream that lingered in the dark. Raising a trembling hand, she checked her throat. The swelling was gone, along with the bruises. But she couldn't help herself. She pushed her auburn hair out of her face and looked around. Amadeus blinked up at her with his vibrant blue eyes and meowed a protest at the sudden disturbance of his sleep.

"Sorry, Amadeus. I did it again, didn't I."

He meowed back. She sighed, protesting the loss of sleep as much as he did. It was getting to be a problem- the nightmares.

"Time, please."

"It is eighteen minutes after four in the morning," said the calm female voice of her PVC system.

Sharra sighed again. "I may as well get up.

A few minutes later she was out the door with a swimsuit on and a towel draped over her shoulder. Her feet padded silently down the hallway past several residential apartments before hitting the communal lounge and the lifts on the other side. All was quiet. Even the administration offices on the other side of the lifts were devoid of life, not that she thought Lazarus worked this early in the morning. After all, he was human, too, and needed sleep like the rest of them. And if there were any agents around, they sure wouldn't be up yet. No, they would be tucked in their beds like sensible people.

She stepped inside the lift. The metal door swished shut behind her.

"Main floor.

A few seconds later, she stepped out of the elevator

into a small elegant foyer. On both sides branched out more residential flats. They, too, were quiet. Leaving them and the plush carpet behind, she headed straight down the main hallway of the ground floor until it branched again. After turning right, she worked her way through the sprawling complex, twisting and turning until she came to the doors to the pool.

The smell of the chlorinated water beckoned her forward like the smell of coffee first thing in the morning. She dropped her towel at the edge and without hesitation, dove in, letting the water wash away the remnants of the dream from her skin in one quick rush. Popping up for a breath, she began to swim across the pool in strong even strokes, reaching the far side in little time. Gracefully she somersaulted underneath the water and pushed off the side, and started another lap, keeping a steady rhythm as she swam. The cool water rushed by, soothing her soul as her legs kicked effortlessly.

The dream was always the same.

It began the night after the fateful day when she had confronted J.D. Dash in the Vault chamber in a fight to save not only her new friends, but also the Vault, and all who lived there. Only by a freak accident was she saved.

J.D. was not so lucky.

Thrown into the path of the powerful pylons in the center of the Vault chamber, J.D. had been pulled up between them by invisible hands, and... electrocuted. The scene still haunted her. The stink of his burnt flesh, the sight of his mutilated body at her feet flashed before her eyes at unguarded moments. She knew deep down why it wouldn't go away. It was because she had killed him. She knew it even if the others denied it. If only she had kept her mental shield around her, and not exposed her body to the power of the Vault, then maybe… just maybe, she could have prevented his death, and her conscience wouldn't torment her so. Yet it was out of her hands. Her timeline had been set the moment the agrylium metal had been poured into her brain and made her a shifter. With it set, she couldn't change the past no matter how badly she wanted to.

They called her a hero.

She wasn't a hero.

A hero would tell them the truth. She couldn't, not yet… for who would believe her. What's more her mind reminded her every night like clockwork. In her dreams it was always the same: the energy called out to her, entered her, filled her, became one with her where it wasn't her body anymore but the Vault's. Because she had cried for help, it had listened and had done the despicable. She knew it wasn't just a dream. The alien presence had entered her when she was in the Vault fighting for her life. Weakened she had dropped her mental shield too close to the pylons, not knowing that the cloudmass of energy at their feet was alive, and that they would enter her body. She felt its strange presence even now, churning under the confines of her mental shield.

The alien energy cunningly hid its activities from the others who were gathered in the Vault chamber by wrapping her and J.D. Dash within the folds of the thick cloudmass that clung to the massive electrical pylons. Only Lazarus, the Head Director, knew more than he was letting on about the whole affair, and yet he remained as closed-mouth about it as she did.

That happened a month ago. Since then, she hasn't been able to go anywhere near the Vault chamber for fear of being taken over by the concealed power hidden within the white cloudmass. It was only a matter of time before she would receive her next assignment. And then what? She couldn't hide from it forever.

"For the betterment of mankind," she said, echoing Lazarus's famous words.

She took a breath and dipped beneath the water, swimming to the bottom to kneel on the rough surface to think. Thick strands of hair floated around her head like dark satin seaweed as she settled in the dense quiet to enjoy the thirty seconds or so of blue solitude that her breath allowed. The complete silence soothed her troubled heart for there was no one there to judge her but herself. Yet the feeling was short-lived for as soon as she touched the bottom an unexplained chill ran up her body, as if someone was watching her.

Conscious of the pressure building in her lungs, she did a quick swivel from where she rested just above the floor of the pool to have a look around. Out of the corner of her eye she caught a flash of color in the deep end of the pool. Brushing her hair out of the way, she blinked through the sting of the chlorinated water, not quite trusting her blurring eyes or her vivid imagination. Yet the vision remained where it was against the wall a half a dozen yards away from where she knelt- a pale human-like form.

Bubbles escaped through her tight lips as she questioned her sanity. The ghostly figure remained. It floated gracefully under the water as if waiting for her to make up her mind. Finally it's slim arms spread out from its body. Long webbed hands opened in peace as its webbed feet slowly stroked the water. A shaft of light from the ceiling above broke through the rippling surface of the pool and found its way to the ethereal creature. It caressed its pearl-like skin, illuminating its naked form to a soft brilliance for a moment before the beam of light was lost again to the ripples above.

But it was enough for her to see the creature in its entirety.

A torrent of bubbles burst out of her mouth as she screeched. Kicking off the floor, she raced to the surface, and pulled her body out of the water as if a shark were on her trail. She flopped onto the cold tile, uncaring of the sodden mess she was making as she struggled to get out of the water and away from the thing in the pool.

Chapter Three

A head popped out from the water, and called out to her from across the pool.

"Sharra wait! Do not be afraid. It is I, Araylai."

"Araylai?"

Clutching the edge of the pool, Sharra peered over the water at the head swimming towards her, expecting to see the alien creature from underneath. When she saw that it was human, she breathed a sigh of relief, and kicked herself for her over-active imagination.

"Yes. I am a fellow agent. We have not met yet," said the pale woman. Golden-blond hair surrounded her face. It floated in the water like silken strands of finely spun gold as she glided forward. "Please, let me explain."

Sharra sucked in her breath. The simple request from the woman flowed through Sharra like no voice had ever done before. Like the call of the ancient sirens of the sea that drew men to their watery deaths, the bell-like voice called to her. In that moment she would have followed this woman anywhere if asked.

It was the first time Sharra had come face to face with the beautiful agent. The Vault was full of talk about her. Most of it wasn't nice. Some of it was strange.

Now she understood the other agents when they talked in hushed whispers about the elusive woman. Many derided her odd behavior, labeling her as an eccentric recluse. Yet it was excused because she was beautiful and had built up an excellent reputation as an elite agent. That being the case, her idiosyncrasies were… for the most part… tolerated. They said that Araylai knew the effect she had on others, and so kept away as much as she could, furthering the rumors that surrounded her.

Sharra swallowed and squashed the strange feeling away with great effort.

"How long have you been down there?" she asked.

Araylai stopped a few feet from the edge of the pool where Sharra crouched. Slender arms gracefully paddled the water as she treaded in place. The swell of her small breasts could just be seen above the waterline as she held her body partway out of the water with ease. The long tresses of her hair spilled over her shoulders, hiding her naked form as if designed by nature itself. Two amber eyes stared solemnly out of her oblong face as the woman contemplated how to answer what should have been a simple question.

Sharra shifted uncomfortably in her crouch. Cold and wet, with water dripping down her back from her soaked hair, she waited, thinking the woman would never answer. Finally Araylai's eyelids swept down over her strange eyes in one slow deliberate blink. Sharra shivered. She didn't know if it was because of her wet body, or because of the oddness of the woman's behavior.

Maybe, it was both.

"I have been under for a while. I do not keep count of the time. Like you, I find peace there," she said as she waved her arms in a lazy motion just under the surface of the water.

Araylai's slow speech washed over Sharra like a lover's caress. She fought to control her reaction, finding the first rush of surpassing beauty difficult to brush aside. With effort she shook herself free of the effect and tried to concentrate on the words instead. When it finally sunk in what Araylai had implied, she couldn't believe it. Araylai couldn't have been under all that time. No person can hold his or her breath that long. And yet her eyes had just before beheld a creature with pearl-like skin and amber eyes watching her from beneath the water.

"I must still be dreaming," she said with a frown. "That's it. I'm still in bed, and this isn't happening."

"No, your eyes did not deceive you," Araylai said. "I shall share a secret with you."

Sharra sighed. Another secret. The Vault thrived on secrets as she was slowly learning. Either that, or she was a magnet that drew them out of the woodwork for some unexplained reason. What was one more secret to add to her growing pile?

"A secret? Why me?"

"I have watched you. I trust you."

"Thank you," Sharra said, still not understanding.

Araylai floated a little closer. "You are different than the others. I am lonely. You are lonely, too. And you love the water."

"And that is important to you."

"Yes. I am different."

That's an understatement Sharra thought.

"…Not like your kind."

"Not like my kind… " Sharra repeated, wondering where the conversation was leading to.

"I trust you. I will show you, and you will understand."

As soon as the bell-like words left the woman's mouth, the air touching her flesh shimmered as the minute particles of matter that made up her body shifted and changed. Losing their solidness, the atoms of her flesh broke apart from their natural state and commenced to rearrange before Sharra's startled eyes.

In a matter of seconds the long golden tresses melted away as the agent's pearl-like skin began to shimmer with greater luminance. It thickened and changed, losing all body hair, until it was smooth as silk. Her already slim figure shifted to become more streamlined than before. Free of her glorious locks, her oblong face altered with the streamlining of her body. Above her high cheekbones, her skull shifted beneath her skin, pushing her huge oval eyes a little off to the sides of the center of her face. Her forehead narrowed a fraction more, giving her an almost fish-like look. The bridge of her nose was left as a pointed ridge, flattening her nostrils at the end into long slits. Her wide mouth spread across the new curve of her face, stretching her full lips to fit the new dimensions in perfect proportion to the rest of her transforming face. Below on both sides of her neck appeared curved vertical slits spaced close together, barely visible on her smooth flesh.

Sharra's mouth dropped opened and her eyes bulged as she watched transfixed by the impossibility of the scene. As the seconds sped by, so did the transformation. Atoms regrouped and solidified in a phenomenal way, destroying one form while creating another.

From the crown of Araylai's head to her tailbone sprung out a long dorsal-like fin in a sheet of golden-spun silk, supported by flexible spines. The first spine was three inches long. It held the fin up at her forehead. Two more that were taller jutted out a few inches behind the first. The three spines held the delicate membrane up like a headdress upon the top of her head between her flattened ears. At the low back of her skull were two more with another smaller one centered between her shoulder blades as the fin carried on down her back. Gradually it tapered away to end at her tailbone. It looked like silk. Flashes of blues, greens and browns were woven in thin streaks of brilliant color thru-out the golden gossamer fin as if created with the finest of threads.

Under the water, Sharra just could make out another fin between her buttock cheeks, swirling in the water, holding the creature steady.

In a matter of seconds all traces of the human woman were gone.

Fully transformed the sea creature floated in the

water in front of Sharra. Her webbed fingers caressing the water in idle detachment as if nothing had happened. The flexible spines collapsed against her flesh. The long dorsal fin snapped down her back like an accordion. Not a ripple of emotion marred the porcelain surface of the fish-like face. Yet, her huge eyes told a different story. Hope and fear warred within their amber depths as she stared up at Sharra, and waited patiently for judgment to be passed.

Silence boomed loud in the room with unspoken tension as the two women stared at each other, each fighting their own internal battle. Sharra tried hard to understand what had just happened, but her brain was not cooperating. She let go of her breath, not realizing that she had been holding it until the noisy rush of escaping air broke the silence. After a few calming breaths, she finally got up the nerve to speak.

"Araylai?" she asked, questioning if the vision before her was real, and not some chlorine induced mirage.

The spines of the gossamer headpiece flicked on the creatures head.

"Yes." Amber eyes stared up at her from the strange yet familiar face.

Sharra sat down heavily onto her backside as she tried to get a grip on the situation. No one had prepared her for this. The Agency's Guidebook hadn't mentioned anything about aliens being involved. It was only filled with regulation upon regulation about time travel and related subjects dealing with the particulars. That's all. She planned to have a word with Lazarus, the Head Director of Vault Agency, about the omission.

"Just wait a minute. What are you? Who are you?" Sharra said as she cautiously scooted closer to the edge of the pool to get a better look at the creature.

"I am Araylai... the same."

With that, the air shimmered around the sea creature. Her slim shape altered in a matter of seconds back into the human woman that had been there before.

"See? The same," she said before changing back to the sea creature once again.

Araylai blinked her slow blink as she watched Sharra's eyes widen in understanding.

"I thought shape-shifters were only make-believe," Sharra said in awe.

"I am no shape-shifter. I am one of the Arderie people, from the water world of Ardus. Like the small chameleon lizard of your world, we can adapt our form to blend in with your race. But it is difficult, and takes much energy to hold, and so I come here to rest."

"The Arderie." Sharra tested the foreign word on her lips.

"Yes," Araylai said with a regal nod. "Your world has much dry land. On Ardus, beneath the blue waters it all lies: mountains, valleys, and plains, all of it. That is where my people dwell."

"Then how did you get here in the Vault? Do the others know about you?"

"Lazarus knows. He is the one who found me... saved me from a horrible fate. Through my own stupidity, I was netted on the surface by smugglers and shipped off world to be sold on the slave market."

"That's horrible," Sharra said. It seemed that the Head Director had a knack for saving people, she thought as flashes of her first interview with the charismatic man popped up from her memory as if it was just yesterday.

"Lazarus is a good man," Araylai said, as if reading her mind. "He said the Vault needed me, and kindly offered me a place here. So I came."

"Why not go back home, to Ardus, to your own people?"

"I can not," Araylai said in a sad whisper.

Amber eyes stared back at Sharra and waited patiently as the air stilled between them once again. Sharra didn't know what to do with the revelation before her. It seemed so farfetched, like out of some science fiction novel. But wasn't time travel just as farfetched an idea? And yet she had accepted it with hardly a blink of an eye. Now she was sitting at the edge of the pool, shivering on the cold tiles, confronted with the reality of the presence of an alien life-form, and she was baulking at the possibility. She almost laughed out loud at the irony of it all.

"So," she finally said, breaking the awkward silence, "you must be from the future, because where I come from, there are no aliens present." Under her breath she mumbled," that I know of."

Araylai nodded once, confirming what Sharra had guessed.

"There is one other from my time period here, Viktor, the Mechanic. He does not know about me... about who I really am. Only Lazarus knows... and now you. I *sense* the truth in you."

"Sense?" Sharra said, picking up on the slight inflection in Araylai's voice.

"I feel your loneliness." Araylai eyes met hers.

"Excuse me?"

"Humans give off strong emotional impulses that are easy for my people to read. That is how I can tell what people are thinking. I have learned that this makes your kind uncomfortable. You are different, though. Your mind is not like theirs. Yours is stronger."

"What do you mean?"

"With you, I can 'sense' the minute intricacies within your emotional responses as if you are speaking actual words to me. I thought only my people had that ability. It is how we communicate when under the water. I have not met another human that could do this, until you."

Sharra froze. Araylai knew her secret, the one caused by the extra agrylium infused into her brain at assimilation. Not even Lazarus knew of her ability to read the thoughts of others. But Araylai, with her uncanny alien senses, had easily detected it. What was she to do? She had worked so hard to keep it hidden from the rest of her fellow agents.

Since her assimilation, she had been caught out too many times accidentally invading the privacy of other people's thoughts to her own embarrassment. She had learned the hard way that it was best that she didn't know what was going on inside their heads, and so had disciplined herself to keep the mental shield in place as much as possible until it became second nature to her.

Now though, it seemed that there was a use for the gift after all.

She didn't need to be told what the woman wanted. The green-rimmed amber eyes beseeching her said it all.

How could she reject such an offer of friendship, especially when Araylai trusted her enough to take the risk of revealing her true self? Sharra couldn't deny her. How could she, for Araylai was right, she was lonely, too.

Araylai treaded the water a few feet away from where Sharra sat at the edge of the pool... waiting.

A quick thought released the shield, freeing Sharra's mind from its protective cover. Reading human minds had been easy. There she knew what to expect, the grounds familiar. Reading an alien mind was a bit more daunting, like traveling into the unknown for the first time. It took courage and faith, things she was learning to build.

With a tentative brush of her thoughts, Sharra reached out and touched the alien mind, expecting to find a wall. Finding no resistance, she pushed ahead into the mental folds, inserting her presence into the foreign mind with more confidence than she felt.

Feeling the soft questing touch, Araylai's mind opened before her in welcome abandonment like the petals of a flower opening to the morning sun after a dark night. As she did so, a soft yellow aura appeared around her body.

Yellow. Sharra couldn't help but think it. Not the vibrant yellow of a canary, but more gentle, like the soft touch of silk laced with the powder of crushed pearls.

Beautiful.

Alluring.

Once the connection was made Araylai wasted no time in bridging the distance between them. Along the open line flowed back a tidal wave of intricate colored electrical impulses, somehow making words form out of the kaleidoscope of emotional chaos.

You honor me. Thank you, Araylai said in the words that weren't words. Around her the aura changed to tangerine.

Sharra felt the words as if she had been punched in the gut. It was as if hearing 'thank you' for the first time, and understanding the true meaning behind those simple words... the sincerity... the truth. It almost made her cry.

Thank you for your trust in me, Sharra said in all seriousness, marveling at the gift that had been handed to her. Without hesitating, she offered without reserve what they both needed. *Friends?*

Sharra stuck out her hand, extending it over the pool, leaving her mind open for Araylai to read. The truth was there. No lies. No deceptions. Only honest friendship, the kind that two strangers brought together through even stranger means could understand and want.

A slow beautiful smile broke the porcelain mask that was Araylai's alien face. The tangerine of her aura melted into the green of new grass. Sharra felt the color more than saw it. The meaning was clear. The word that followed confirmed it.

Friends.

Araylai raised her hand out of the water and wrapped her webbed fingers around the offered hand, palm to palm. As they touched the sleeping ball of energy in Sharra's head awoke with a flash of white light. Before she could stop it, it broke up into tiny threads, and left its resting place to speed down her spinal cord to the nerves that ran down her arm. In a millisecond it was at the juncture of their hands. Through the contact of her skin it leached onto Araylai and began to suck up the electromagnetic energy of her aura like a starving animal.

The green aura changed in a flash to deep navy as she gasped and tore her hand away as if hit by a shock of electricity. The green rings around her irises flashed in horror.

With a harsh mental command Sharra pulled the energy back to the safety of her brain, and held it tight with a strong thought. In its hiding place the tiny threads regrouped into its ball, a little bigger and brighter than before.

Her hand tingled. She stared at it in disbelief.

"What was that?" Araylai's voice shook.

She shook her head, as shocked as Araylai. "A leftover gift from my encounter with the cloudmass," she said. "It has never done that before. I'm so sorry. Did I hurt you?"

"It was too brief to do any harm. Does Lazarus know?"

"No. I haven't told anyone. I thought it would go away."

Sharra tested the strength of her grip on the ball. The mental hold felt strong.

"Can we try this again?" she said as she put her hand out. "This time I'll be ready."

Araylai looked at the hand. The dark navy of her aura weakened to a lighter blue as the seconds ticked by. Finally it softened back to green and held.

"You ask for trust?" she said.

"It starts here, for you, and for me."

Araylai lifted a hand out of the water and carefully touched hers. The ball in her head jumped, but Sharra was ready. Holding it fast, she wrapped her fingers around the alien hand and shook it.

When nothing happened, Araylai gripped her hand firmly. A big smile broke across her face as her aura flashed through the spectrum from blue, green, to yellow, and held.

Friends, she said through the link.

Sharra smiled back, and shook the cold wet hand.

Friends, Sharra repeated.

Life had just gotten a little more interesting.

Chapter Four

———

Lazarus Maitland, the Head Director of Vault Agency, had a lot on his mind… and things weren't getting any better. The tiny spitfire of a blond glaring up at him had just made it even worse. He should have run the other way as soon as he caught sight of the expression on her face as she hailed him down in the corridor. He knew that look, and grimaced when he saw it, having dealt with it many times before. She was not an easy woman, but what agent was? Sometimes they expected him to perform miracles for them, like now, but he could only do so much.

"I'll have a chat with Antonio," Lazarus said, trying to calm her down with the promise after listening to her latest complaint.

"And he had better listen this time or… or… I'm

going to do something drastic… like… cut off the part of his body he loves the most," Zoe said in aggravation. "And this time, I mean it."

Lazarus inwardly cringed at the thought, having no doubt that she would do it, given the chance. He actually felt sorry for Tony for once, and that was a new experience. But Tony willingly chose her as his partner, and knew how to handle her aggressive temperament. In fact, they were perfect for each other, each one strong enough to rein the other one in when necessary, like now.

"Try to wait before you do that, Zoe. We can't afford to lose another agent just yet. Let me talk to him."

Zoe stared up at him, her ice-blue eyes shooting sparks of annoyance as she mulled over his request. He waited in the heavy silence as he watched the storm pass from her face. She sighed, and dropped her gaze.

"All right, I'll wait, but only because you asked me to," she said. "Just do something fast. He's getting more difficult with each passing shift. I don't know how much more I can take."

"As soon as he returns from the field, I'll pull him aside, and see what's bothering him."

"All I can say is you had better do something," she said throwing the open threat over her shoulder with the toss of her platinum-blond hair as she turned to leave.

Zoe stormed away leaving Lazarus in the vacuum left by her sudden departure as she headed to the lifts at the end of the hallway. He waited until she had disappeared, putting some distance between himself and the fiery she-devil before heading to the lifts himself, and to the second floor to the quiet of his office.

Where have the good old days gone to, Lazarus thought as he stepped off the lift, and headed to the administration block.

Antonio Rossi had an inborn flare for the dramatic. He couldn't help it. It was like breathing to him, as old as the Italian blood that flowed through his veins. No amount of time had tempered the man. Only Zoe's feisty influence had kept him in check, but now it looked like even that wasn't working anymore.

The discontent was definitely getting worse. At first, nobody had noticed the change, for the agents were, by force of the nature of the job, an arrogant bunch. Disputes were as common as eating. It could be anything: a simple misunderstanding, some jealousy or another, or over-exaggerated egos. Nothing unusual there.

Since the investigation initiated because of the attempts on Sharra Lane's life the month before, there had emerged a pattern that could no longer be ignored as inconsequential. Now it had become an everyday occurrence where he was spending more time as a referee than as a leader.

Since he had recruited Sharra to join their elite group, things seemed to have escalated to a point where even others were starting to notice. The Vault needed her. That much he knew, but not why. He had also been warned that her addition would come at a cost. Was this the cost, the discontent and disharmony? He didn't think so for she had only been there for a few months, not enough time to cause that much trouble.

No... this went back much farther.

Yet, he couldn't help but think that somehow there

was a connection. Trouble seemed to follow her every step. First came the stolen contract, which had since been recovered. Then, on her first training exercise into the field with Tanner, her trainer, they were brutally attacked and Tanner almost lost his life. A month later, it was followed by a second attack when she was most vulnerable, being sent on her first mission back into time alone. Again Tanner shifted in and saved her from the rogue agent, risking his life once more for her. In the end, one of their agents, J.D. Dash, was killed when holding Sharra hostage in the Vault chamber. Dragging her too close to the electrical pylons, he got swept up by the force generated by the tall metal conductors, and was electrocuted to a blackened mass of stinking flesh before their shocked eyes. Lazarus still had a hard time erasing the sight from his mind. Miraculously, the cloud of energy had left Sharra unharmed.

Then there was the mystery surrounding the tampering with the medical equipment that caused the extra agrylium to be pumped into Sharra's brain during her assimilation. It had never happened before. Lazarus had his suspicions, but was impotent to do anything about it.

"Dammed secret," he muttered to himself.

He knew his limitations, and so had called in the Committee members from the field to set up an investigation into the recent events surrounding their newest recruit. It was the Committee who, through their discreet inquiries, had stumbled upon the underlying problem of unexplained unrest and discontent among the agents. Since then, the problem had turned into a stone in his shoe, making its painful presence felt with every executive move he made.

Tanner had it right. If they weren't careful, he would have a mutiny on his hands before he knew it. The unruly behavior had to stop before the Vault disintegrated around them, and their home was no more.

In the meantime, he had to do something about Sharra. Dash's death had not ended her problems as they all thought. He knew there was another agent involved, which meant he needed to get on to it before someone else got hurt, or worse, ended up like Dash- dead.

Making a deal with Faolan seemed like a sensible thing to do at the time. Having someone on the outside watching over Sharra was a sound plan. An extra pair of eyes couldn't hurt, and it'd free him up to work on the other problem. With Faolan a free agent, he could be that ghost in the wall that might tip the scales in their favor. Though Lazarus couldn't do anything about Sharra until his friend showed up again. When that would be, he could only guess. For now, he would get to work on the problem of Tony.

Lazarus reached his office door distracted with thoughts of Zoe's complaints. He opened it and groaned, catching sight of the pile of information chips stacked haphazardly on one corner of his desk. It seemed the work never ended, like a stack of dishes or a pile of laundry that never went down, not that he had to do either anymore, just endless computer work.

Shutting the door, he walked over to his desk, not seeing the man hiding behind the door. Without taking his silvery eyes off of Lazarus's back, the man reached over and clicked the old-fashion lock in place, sealing himself in the room with the Head Director.

At the audible sound of the metal lock, Lazarus's body tensed and whipped around, instinctively taking up a fighting stance, ready to attack. Unafraid, the man smiled and leaned against the locked door with folded arms.

"Lazarus," he said in greeting.

Lazarus visibly relaxed, and shook his head at his long time friend. Faolan had a way of throwing him off his axis. Today was no different.

"Speak of the devil."

"That's no way to greet an old friend," Faolan said, raising an aristocratic eyebrow in surprise.

"I was wondering when you'd show up."

"Missed me, have you?"

Lazarus sent him a look and walked over to the cabinet against the wall next to Faolan, and poured two half glasses of whiskey from the bottle that was waiting there. Faolan eyed him in the uncomfortable silence that ensued as Lazarus watched the golden liquid flow out of the bottle into the glasses.

Faolan waited for an answer, but Lazarus refused to give him one. When nothing came, the younger man said, "I'll have you know that it's not easy sneaking in here. Timing is everything."

"Hmmm, I've been meaning to ask you how you manage to slip into the complex undetected," Lazarus said as he passed him a glass, and raised his own to his lips.

"Now, now, Lazarus. We all have our secrets."

Lazarus's glass stopped in midair as his grey eyes hardened and grew hooded at the insinuation that fell off the younger man's lips. He took a breath and caught himself before he made a snide remark back. Rehashing the old wound that stood between them would serve no purpose. They had other things to discuss that were more important. He took his eyes off Faolan to look at the glass in his hand.

Keep the peace, he reminded himself, as he finished raising it to his lips. He took a deep swig of the smooth whiskey and closed his eyes, savoring the burning trail as it slid down his throat.

———

Faolan watched the drink disappear down his friend's throat and noticed for the first time the blue smudges of fatigue underneath the older man's eyes. He had never seen him this tired before.

"Has it been that bad?" he asked.

"Worse," Lazarus admitted before taking another sip, this time much slower. "It's been a month. What took you so long to return? I need to get this situation with Sharra fixed."

"You know it's not easy for me to get in here undetected. You don't want me to risk blowing my cover, do you?" Lazarus shook his head once. "I thought not. That's why I've waited. Plus I needed the time to think of a plan."

"I take it you've come up with something," Lazarus said as he moved around the desk to sit in his comfortable chair.

"I'll tell you in a minute. First, let me see if I understand things correctly. We need to implant the tag into Sharra without her knowing. And it has to be done under the nose of Tanner, who you inconveniently assigned as her watchdog, without giving the game away to him."

"That's right. So tell me, how do you plan on accomplishing this feat? I assume your brilliant mind has come up with something…"

Faolan took a sip of whisky and left his position at the door to walk over to Lazarus's desk. "I've been studying the list of upcoming missions, and there's one in particular that would suit our purpose, a perfect setting for a game of cat and mouse, something to keep Tanner distracted while I draw Sharra away from his protective eye."

While he was talking he moved around the desk and stopped in front of Lazarus's private monitor. He looked at the darkened screen and then over to Lazarus with a raised eyebrow.

"May I?"

"Please. You've caught my interest," Lazarus said. He rolled his chair in next to Faolan and touched the corner of the screen with the flat of his thumb to unlock it. The screen shot to life as it connected to the huge mainframe of the Vault and its vast store of information. "She's all yours."

Lazarus sat back and watched with keen interest as his friend worked the system with a familiarity that had only come from years of experience. Quickly scanning through Lazarus's private collection of icons that lit the screen, Faolan found the one he was looking for labeled: Unassigned Job file. Without hesitating, he touched the icon. The massive file opened. With a flick of his finger he scrolled down the page, sifting through the endless list of upcoming jobs with a sharp eye. All of a sudden, he stopped the list and tapped on one of the titled files, opening up the main page of the unassigned job.

"This is it," he said. Tapping several boxes, opening them up, he moved them around on the monitor before moving back so that Lazarus could see.

Lazarus leaned in to get a better look. "A fancy Ball in London, England, eighteen twenty-five. How original."

"No, you're not getting it. Look at the nature of the mission. The job is an intervention, to stop a business deal from happening. It's at this ball that the two parties initially meet. If the introductions are never made, then they remain strangers, and a new timeline is created. The bad business deal that did take place will have never happened."

"I don't see what this has to do with Sharra," Lazarus said.

"What better place for her to get lost in than amongst a crush of people in a crowded ballroom," Faolan said with a smile. "Plus, it falls around the time when I first bumped into her."

Lazarus eyes narrowed. "What do you mean 'bumped into' her? I thought you two had never met." He paused and thought back on the possibility with a calculating mind. "Ahhh... the gallant gentleman from her first training mission with Tanner. That was you?"

A cheeky smile spread across Faolan's clean-shaven face in answer.

"You sneaky devil. I should've guessed," Lazarus said with a shake of his head.

"Believe me, it wasn't planned. I just happened to stumble upon her on my way into town. I didn't know she was an agent until I got a good look at the man she was trying to help, and saw that it was Tanner. I couldn't leave them like that, unprotected and hurt. I had to interfere. No, Tanner didn't see me. He was unconscious the whole time."

"And Sharra?"

"To her I was just a local gentleman from that time period offering a helping hand. Besides, it was dark, and the city was covered in a blanket of thick fog. You know how it gets. There's no way she could've seen my face. Anyway, she was too busy worrying about Tanner than to think about me."

Faolan spoke with more confidence than he felt as memories of that foggy night came flooding back. Inside he wasn't so sure if she got a look at his face or not. He had tried to stay in the shadows as much as possible and remain neutral. His involvement could've jeopardized the mission. But once he caught sight of her large frightened eyes, he knew he couldn't leave her.

And then it had happened.

He had touched her. That had been his undoing. The feel of her soft skin as he had wiped the smudges from her cheeks, the smell of her clean hair as he tucked it back under her wig, the shape of her lips as they waited for the kiss that never came; all had captured him as surely as if he was a fish in a net. He was drawn to the girl like a starving man to the feast. The temptation to take her offered lips had stretched his willpower to almost the breaking point. But he had resisted. He kicked himself now for not kissing her when he could have. He was either a saint or the devil himself. He didn't know which. It was eating him alive. He had to see her again.

Lazarus studied him for a long minute with a calculated look. Faolan waited for the questions that hovered behind his eyes, but they didn't come. Instead Lazarus dropped his gaze back to the screen.

"London, England, eighteen twenty-five. So what's this brilliant plan of yours?" Lazarus said.

Faolan relaxed as the weight of those steel-grey eyes left him for the moment. He didn't think he had fooled Lazarus for a second. The man was all too knowing for that.

Tapping a box on the screen, Faolan said, "We send in a team of three: Sharra, Tanner, and another female agent, for etiquette sake. Tanner can shift in ahead of time to set up the Agency's townhouse in preparation for the women, and also to arrange invitations to the ball. Once at the ball, it will be easy to extract Sharra from their side while Tanner and the other agent are concentrating on keeping the target, Lord Pennington, from meeting Lord Darby, our bad guy." He tapped Lord Darby's name in the box, opening up the specifics on the man in question.

"And how do you plan on planting the tag without Sharra knowing?" Lazarus said. "They do bite going in."

"Don't worry. A little distraction is all I'll need. Sharra won't even notice."

Lazarus snorted. "None of your shenanigans, Faolan. We all know of your reputation. She's an agent. I don't want her hurt."

"The only pain she will feel is the prick of the tag. You have my word of honor."

"Hmmm. Your word of honor."

"Yes. I won't do anything to hurt her. From what I understand, she has been through enough pain already."

"Your word of honor then," Lazarus said, finalizing the agreement. "After the tag is in place, you'll need to disappear. She can't know you're involved."

"I realize that," Faolan said a little irritated.

Lazarus ignored the look Faolan shot him. "Good, as long as we understand each other. I'll sleep better at night knowing there'll be an extra pair of eyes watching out for her until the mastermind behind her attacks shows himself, or better yet, is caught."

"We will catch the bastard. He's bound to go after her again."

"That's what I'm afraid of." Lazarus heaved a sigh and rubbed his face between his hands, wiping at the weariness that seemed to cling there. He dropped his hands into his lap, and looked up at Faolan with tired eyes. "I don't want to admit it, but we can't afford another incident right now. Tensions are strung tight as it is. If something were to happen to Sharra, it wouldn't be good for any of us. It might disrupt time itself, as we know it. We can't let that happen."

"We'll get him," Faolan said. He had never seen the Head Director so low. A small ripple of fear hit his heart. It had to be worse then Lazarus was letting on if he let that much slip out. "Together."

A mask of resignation slipped back over Lazarus's face. He picked up his forgotten glass and finished it off in one long gulp.

"Together," he said, setting the empty glass back down on the desk. "Right then, I'll get to work on this right away. Sharra will be pleased to receive notice of an

35

assignment after being held off for so long. Leave it in my hands."

"I'll see her at the ball then."

Faolan tipped the last of his drink down his throat, and headed to the door. He had stayed longer than he deemed it was safe to. It was time to leave. He unlocked the door and cracked it open enough to stick his head out, peering down both lengths of the hallway. Finding it clear, he opened the door to step out, but something made him look back at his friend. Worry hit him as he really looked at Lazarus, seeing the deepening age lines around his mouth and nose. He had never noticed it before. He didn't like it.

"Keep in touch," Lazarus said with a tired smile.

"You take care of yourself. Take a vacation, or something," Faolan said, at a loss of what to do for his friend.

"Sure," Lazarus said.

With a final nod, Faolan slipped out and shut the door with a soft click, leaving Lazarus alone once again with his troubles. He stared at the door thoughtful, and hoped his plan would work. Not just for Sharra, but for Lazarus, too.

Chapter Five

Sharra headed down the long hallway like a man on a mission. The summons couldn't have come any sooner for her liking. She had been meaning to have a word with the Head Director for days. Avoiding him had served its purpose, but now she was done with it, done with being treated like a delicate flower. Besides, it was time to get into the field and earn her keep. Tanner and the other agents involved in catching Dash had all been sent back in the field right after the incident. But not her. She wasn't going to accept another lame excuse from Lazarus, not without a fight, anyway.

Her determined stride pushed her through the residential block and past the communal lounge in no time as she headed towards the administration block located further down the long hallway of the second floor. The elegant lounge was all but empty except for a few agents who were enjoying a quiet drink together. At seeing her, they raised their glasses in greeting over the overstuffed furniture. A wave and a hello was all she could afford to give, which she did. Normally she would've stopped for a chat. Lazarus was expecting her, and she didn't want to keep the busy man waiting. She quickened her pace, leaving them to their drinks as she continued on.

The hallway was empty. In fact, the place was always empty. That's because the other agents were out somewhere in time doing missions like a good agent should be doing.

Sharra fumed invisible steam out her ears to the rhythm of her pounding feet. The coddling was going to end today. She was going to go in and demand a job. And if Lazarus dared to question her again about what happened while she was enwrapped in the cloudmass, well, he had his own explaining to do if he wanted to get her to talk. It looked like he was holding a few secrets of his own, one of which she happened to stumble upon by accident. If he wished to keep it from the others, she didn't see why she should say anything either. She hadn't broken any rules according to the Agency Handbook. In fact, the rulebook was blatantly silent on the subject.

The wooden door of the Head Director's office loomed ahead, looking out of place in the futuristic complex. Maybe Lazarus had it installed on purpose to stand out as different, either that, or to be easily found in a place filled with identical metal doors. She picked it to be the latter.

She stopped in front of the door and knocked

without hesitation- three solid raps. It was so different from the first time she had knocked on his office door. That was back in Charlotte, North Carolina, when she had been naive to the ways of the Vault. This time it was firm, determined, and unafraid of the man behind the door.

"Enter" Lazarus said, his voice muffled by the closed door.

The door opened under the pressure of her hand as she turned the old-fashion handle and pushed it in. Once inside she shut it behind her before striding over to the desk and to the man waiting expectantly there. The air in the room hung heavy with expensive cologne and authority. He wore both with ease as if he were born to the position.

Some of her courage left her when she caught the look in his eyes.

He's only a man, she reminded herself in an attempt to bolster up her courage.

Or was he? Her discovery of Araylai's true nature had tipped her world upside-down. She wasn't so sure of anything anymore.

"Thank you for coming so quickly," Lazarus said, pointing to the chair next to her. "There's something I wanted to talk to you about."

Sharra ignored the invitation to sit. Instead, she remained where she was. "I wanted to talk to you, too."

"Please go first. What's on your mind," he said, forever the diplomat.

Sharra didn't hesitate, but plowed right in before she lost her nerve. "It's like this, I'm an agent. And agents get sent out into the field. It's been two weeks

39

since we sprung the trap, and caught Dash. All the others involved are back on duty, and yet my personal monitor remains blank. There's nothing wrong with me. I've received the okay from Cam ages ago. So why won't you assign me a job? No wait," she said, holding up her palm to stop him before he had a chance to reply. "Let me rephrase that. I want a job. I'm not asking you. I'm telling you. Give me an assignment. Now. Today."

Her finger hit the desk twice emphasizing the last two words as they clipped out of her mouth.

At the surprised expression on his face, she stopped short, and snapped her lips shut in shock as the realization of what she had done sank in. Raising your voice to the most powerful man at the Agency was not a smart thing to do. Her heart froze at the thought. She had gone too far, and she knew it. It was too late to take the words back. She folded her arms, hiding the tiny tremors that began to shake her limbs behind her stiff posture, and waited for the reprimand that was sure to come.

A clocked ticked in the background filling the silence that fell over the room. Lazarus leaned back in his chair, and looked at her with thoughtful eyes while he stroked his trim goatee between his thumb and index finger in contemplation.

"I see you have some backbone after all," he said after a while. "I'm glad to see you exercising it, even if it's at my expense."

A blush of shame stole up her cheeks. "I'm sorry, sir. I meant no disrespect."

"Apology accepted. As a matter of fact, the reason I called you down here was to discuss a mission with you."

"Oh," she said, feeling worse for her tirade, having gotten worked up for nothing.

"I thought I'd go easy on you, just this once, you understand, and give you a rather cushy assignment, something that I thought would be right up your alley."

From off the plasitop surface of the desk, he picked up a slim metal Com-Link and handed it over to her. She touched the screen of the pad and activated the account, opening up the specifications for the job in question. Scrolling down the pad, she read the information with eager eyes. The date, place, and timeline were first. Then came the purpose of the mission.

"If you scroll back to the top and look," Lazarus said, "it calls for a team of three: one male and two females." He waited for her to read over the section. "I thought to send Tanner since you and him work so well together."

"Will he be okay with that?"

"Why do you ask?

"It seems that he's always saving my butt at his expense. I'd hate for him to get hurt again."

"It's a ball. The only way he'd get hurt there is if someone stepped on his feet while dancing. Besides, it'd be good for both of you to have some fun."

"Fun on a mission? That's a new one."

"Not all missions are dangerous. As long as the job is completed, no one says you cannot have fun while you're there. All time periods have their own uniqueness in culture and customs. Why not experience it while you're there. It's one of the perks of the job. Now, as far as a female agent, I thought_"

"Araylai," Sharra said, interrupting him in a flash of

inspiration.

"Araylai?" His fine eyebrows arched in surprise.

"Yes, Araylai," she said. "Pale skin, long blond hair, amber eyes_"

"I know who she is," he said, cutting her off. "I don't know. She usually prefers to work alone."

"I think she might accept this time," she said, sounding more confident than she felt about the idea.

"Araylai it is then… if she agrees."

"Then I accept the assignment," she said, handing the Com-Link back to him.

"Good. Give me a minute, and I'll transfer it over to you right now."

He set the Com-Link aside on the desk, and turned to the monitor. He touched an icon from the many that lit the screen, and flicked it open with practiced fingers, and got to work. His fingers flew over the screen, touching this, moving that, pushing boxes aside with years of familiarity. It wasn't long before he gave a final click to a box and sat back, sending her a smile.

"Done," he said. "The job is yours. Now was there anything else you wished to discuss with me?"

"No, that was it."

"Then you may go. I know you'll be anxious to get started," he said dismissing her.

Sharra headed for the door, ready to escape from his knowing gaze. She had embarrassed herself enough for one day. At the door, he stopped her.

"And Sharra?"

Her hand stilled on the doorknob as she looked back at him. A small tremor of anxiety swept through her. "Yes?"

"One of these days, when you're ready, you and I are going to have a talk about what happened in the Vault chamber."

She dropped her gaze to the floor. Like a stone, the heavy weight of his words settled around her neck, until she remembered that he was hiding his own secrets. How could she have forgotten so quickly? The thought gave her courage.

"Of course," she said with a nod.

Shutting the door behind her, she trotted down the hallway past the lifts and the communal lounge to the row of residential apartments on the other side. As soon as her apartment came into view she sent a command to the metal door.

"Open."

The door slid open just as she reached it. Sharra raced inside, and went directly to her desk. It wasn't long before she had the files of the job opened and the information blocks spread across her screen in orderly chaos that was her fashion. Everything was there that she needed to memorize for the shift: the timeline, the target's name, people and places surrounding the mission, and of course, the purpose of the mission itself. She settled into her chair, and began to devour the information with methodical precision.

It wasn't long before Amadeus wandered out of the bedroom searching for his mistress. With his fluffy tail high in the air, he sauntered across the living room floor, and over to where she sat at the desk. He stopped at her feet and stared up at her with his bright blue eyes, and meowed.

"All right, come here."

She picked him up onto her lap, and settled him in her arms, petting him softly. He looked up at her with adoring eyes as he purred his contentment.

"Spoiled," she said, looking down at him with an indulgent smile.

Over the soft purr of the cat, the words and pictures on the monitor called out to her. She could not ignore them, no matter how much she loved her cat. Her eyes went to the next box on the screen. The faces were new and quickly memorized along with the details of each. The sooner the mass of information was in her head, the sooner she could shift into that timeline and feel useful again.

Going to a ball sounded like fun, much different than anything she had done so far. She had always dreamed of dressing up in fancy clothing, and going to a ball. What girl didn't? At least the job meant that she would be going as a woman for a change.

And then there was Tanner, her former trainer. A few weeks back, when they were alone in the Vault chamber, she had let her guard down to peek into his mind. Her excuse had been to find out what was troubling him and fix it before he shifted out to trap Dash. As soon as she had done it, she had wished she hadn't, for she got more than she had bargained for. So intense were his feelings for her, it nearly knocked her over. Strong, vivid, and real.

He loved her.

She had not been prepared for that. It had taken her totally by surprise.

Even so, it was no excuse. She had to have been completely blind to have not seen the signs. Looking back, if she were to admit it, they had been right in front of her the whole time, as blatant as a neon sign. But she had been too consumed with trying to find her feet at the Agency then to take the time to see that the man was falling in love with her.

She was such an idiot.

What was she to do about him? If only she had controlled her curiosity and not peeked into his mind and seen his thoughts, she wouldn't feel so awkward about it. That's what she gets for snooping where she didn't belong. Her mother had taught her better manners than that. She deserved to squirm.

Tanner was attractive, strong, dependable, funny, and always around when she needed him. Plus, he liked her cat. What more could she ask for in a man? He was perfect for her.

"It's not fair," she said to the screen.

It wasn't Tanner's face she saw in her mind, the man she could see and touch, who resided in her timeline. Instead, there was another man who occupied her mind, a stranger from a distant timeline, a man that she couldn't have. The same rush of attraction swept through her as if she were there again in the darkened garden standing in a pool of light with a gentleman stranger, feeling his fingers brush her cheek as he tenderly tucked her hair away, and the warmth of his breath on her lips as he brought her face close to his. The kiss never came, but it didn't matter for the damage had been done.

"Faolan." His name escaped from her lips on a wispy sigh before she could stop it.

Angry at her foolishness, she shook her head and

45

pushed the images away. It was ridiculous to keep pining for a man she was never going to see again. Tanner was real, and available. She just needed to give him a chance. A ball was a good place to start. Lights, music, dancing, it was a perfect setting for romance. And Tanner was going.

Sharra pressed her lips together, and got back to work. She would do her part. The rest would be up to Tanner.

Chapter Six

In another part of the Vault complex, tucked away in a forgotten conduit room, Jake Byson tapped out the final password, and waited with fingers poised above the flat keyboard of his Com-Link that sat on the narrow ledge of the service area. In the dark room of blinking panels his eyes shone with an eerie light as he stared at the screen. His handsome face was frozen into a mask of concentration, unrecognizable in the ghostly dim light that came from an open panel at his feet. Around him the room hummed like a thousand insects, but he didn't notice the noise. All that mattered to him was the screen.

The seconds seemed like minutes. He frowned at the screen and stared harder, willing it to work with the force of his mind, until finally the pilfered code disappeared, and the screen opened.

He was in.

"Finally," he said, rubbing his hands together. Once inside the mainframe of the vast computer system of the Vault, it didn't take long for him to work his way through the security checks and firewalls, and find the particular connection he was looking for. He typed in a name, her name, and slipped undetected into the agent's personal database.

"Let's see what you've been up to, my dear."

A program was running. A few keystrokes of his fingers, and he was inside it. Words poured out like liquid type onto his screen, filling it from one end to the other. Invisible hands clicked the icons. One by one boxes of assorted pictures, maps, and detailed descriptions opened, and stacked upon the next making a pyramid of information. Like a ghost, he watched what she watched, following the movement of the blocks as they spread across the screen. He knew a mission assignment when he saw one. And this was definitely one.

Anger bubbled up from the deep recesses of his heart. With it came denial. It spewed out like vomit as his fury at what he saw reached his mouth.

"No, no, no, no!"

His breath grew more agitated as he stared at the screen not seeing the words or the pictures. The only thing he saw was her. It killed him. He tried to wipe her face away, but couldn't.

The vein in his right temple began to throb. It wasn't fair. This was supposed to be his domain. And despite all his previous efforts to get rid of her, she was still there sitting somewhere above him in her apartment busy memorizing in total ignorance of his presence.

Jake snatched the computer off the ledge, and flung it above his head, ready to smash it to the floor. The cords that he had painstakingly spliced together inside the hole in the wall were ripped away with the force of his anger. As he held the computer above his head, they dangled down his chest and caught on his shirt. The exposed ends pricked his skin. He flinched at the irritation. The distraction was enough to break the red haze of his anger. He stopped in mid-action. Sweat gathered on his broad forehead as he stood there among the twinkling lights like a madman. In and out he breathed as he fought for control.

"Wait. Wait. We can use this. Yes. Yes. That's right, think."

A drop of sweat trickled into his eye. He blinked it away and looked around. The hum of the room returned to his consciousness. Slowly he lowered the computer and set it back onto the ledge. Winding up the damaged cords, he placed them next to the computer before crouching down to check on the wires sticking out of the opening in the unscrewed panel. The damage looked minimal, nothing he couldn't handle.

With a delicate hand, he began to reattach the wires inside the wall one by one. The worked settled his nerves.

"So Maitland has decided to set you free," he said.

He needed to keep his head. He was going about this all wrong. A new mission was a good thing. It meant that she would be out from under Lazarus's protective eye, and away from the Vault.

"And from your leach of a lover-boy, Tanner," he snorted.

And if she did a few missions without any incidents, well, it might work in his favor, lulling them into thinking her troubles were over. After all, J.D. Dash had to serve some purpose, even if he was a disappointment in the end.

No, it was only a small setback.

A new pawn was already being cultivated. Someone easily manipulated, someone with skills that he could use. The thought made him smile.

Finished with the repairs, Jake gently placed the wires back into the hole, and snapped the panel in place. Though the room was forgotten, he was not taking any chances. He would need the room again, and soon. For he still had an agent to catch.

Chapter Seven

London, England

Eighteen Twenty-Five

Tanner leaned his head out of the door of the borrowed carriage for the third time, and checked the row of waiting vehicles leading up to the shallow steps of the grand house. A quick peek told him all that he needed to know. Shutting the door with a snap, he flipped his tailcoats and eased back onto the squab across from Sharra and Araylai, avoiding the soft material of the girls' gowns as best he could.

"Two more to go, and then it's us," he said.

"What a line up. And I thought Charlotte traffic was bad," Sharra said.

She smoothed the soft pearl satin material of her

gown with her gloved hand in nervous agitation. Her hands itched to pull up the low-pleated neckline of the gown, but settled to fiddling with the antique pearl brooch pinned between her breasts. Grimm had added it at the last minute. "Because the costume needed something more," he had said. She thought the dress was beautiful just as it was.

"Bad traffic is bad traffic, no matter what the century. Only the mode of transportation changes," Tanner said.

"Can't we fix that, put it on our list of things to do?" she said with a wry smile.

"Some things can't be changed, like the weather, or the movement of the earth's crust, or Grimm's bad temper." His voice changed, taking on a gruff Scottish accent. "So help me, if another outfit comes back stained, or torn, or whatever else you can manage to do to them in the short period you wear them, I'll have you whipped and locked in the stocks."

Sharra laughed at the rough impersonation of the Head of Staxx whose gruff ways were legendary though harmless enough. Beside her sat Araylai dressed in a gown the color of soft honey. In the dim light coming from the carriage window, her pearl-like skin glowed with a pale luster above the low neckline of gathered satin. Matching puffed sleeves fell off her smooth shoulders. She returned Sharra's gaze, but said nothing. Only her eyes registered her humor.

Tanner's eyes dropped to her hand on the brooch, and said, "You do realize that the old man has a crush on you."

"Excuse me?"

"The brooch that you're playing with, I saw him give that to you right before we left. Made an ass of himself pinning it to your dress."

She dropped her hand to her lap, and blushed.

"He was just being nice."

"Keep telling yourself that. Araylai, you're a woman. What do you think?"

"I think you are both right."

"Araylai," Sharra said, "you're suppose to be on my side, not his."

"I cannot lie," her friend said with a tiny shrug of her shoulders.

Pulling out an engraved pocket watch, Tanner checked the time before slipping it back into his white embroidered waistcoat.

"We still have a good hour before Lord Darby arrives. That should give us plenty of time to get through the receiving line, and scope out the place. Maybe you can even get a dance or two in and meet some of the local aristocrats. Lady Chadwick has volunteered to take you girls under her wing. I'll find Lord Pennington and renew our acquaintance while you two work your magic."

"You're not going to dance with anyone?" Sharra asked, trying to hide her disappointment. "Not even with your co-agents?"

"Feeling nervous, are you? That's right, I forgot. It's your first ball, kind of like Cinderella. Sure I'll dance with you as long as I can be your handsome prince."

And handsome he was dressed in his eveningwear. All muscles and broad shoulders. They tested the strength of the black fabric that molded around his fit body. His light brown hair no longer sported a military cut, but was grown out and swept back from his high forehead as befit the time period, showing off his fine blue eyes. A pair of curved sideburns accentuated his strong jawline, pointing to his easy smile. He was bound to turn some heads tonight.

"Maybe even steal a kiss before the clock strikes midnight," he whispered with a cheeky smile.

Sharra felt the heat rise into her cheeks again, grateful for the dim light in the carriage. Even though Tanner joked out loud, she knew deep down he was serious. She promised herself to give him a chance, and a dance would be just the thing.

"The carriage has stopped," Araylai said before Sharra could come up with a witty reply, leaving the thought of a kiss hanging in the air between them.

A footman opened the door. The two women gathered their gowns, and waited for Tanner to exit first. He paused at the door, and looked them over with a practiced eye.

"Don't forget to use your pseudo names_" Tanner started to say.

Sharra rested a hand on his arm to stop him. "Tanner, we're big girls. We've got this."

"Right."

He hopped out and lifted his hand to help the women descend to the cobblestones, ignoring the footman who stood holding the door. Once they settled their gowns, he offered each an arm, Sharra on the right and Araylai on the left, and escorted them up the shallow steps and through the entranceway to the reception line situated in the white marbled foyer of the grand mansion. Up ahead the hostess was busy greeting some friends. The line moved along quickly and before they knew it, they were through. They followed the bejeweled ladies and their escorts up one of the curved staircases that went to the second floor and to the ballroom where the guests were gathering. Music drifted down from the chamber above. It mingled with the excited voices of the guests, as the orchestra tuned their instruments in preparation for the first dance of the evening.

Reaching the landing, Tanner guided them through a set of tall doors, past one room filled with mingling guests, and on to the next set of doors. The crowd thickened as they followed the couples ahead of him into the brightly lit room on the other side. Once over the threshold, Sharra took one look around and stopped, halting their procession.

"Oh my," she said in a tiny gasp, squeezing the muscle of Tanner's arm in her excitement.

Long gilded mirrors graced one side of the long room. In them were reflected the lights of a thousand pieces of cut crystal shining down from three huge chandeliers. Held up by strong chains high above the polished hardwood floor, they glittered below a ceiling of murals of clouds framed with ornate plastering. In the clouds, cherubs smiled down upon the gathering like indulgent children. Below, the honey-wood of the floor gleamed as the upper crust of London gathered around the outer edges of the room, preening to see and be seen by their peers. Through the heat of the room wafted a cool breeze, coming from the two sets of open French doors off to the far right. Near them was a set of Grecian pillars set equal distance apart. Tall potted ferns were set next to them as a natural divider to the room.

Above in an alcove off to the left the small orchestra finished tuning their instruments and waited for their cue from the hostess.

Soft-colored silks and satins of the gowns of the young women blended in with the richer shades of the matrons. Their bejeweled images reflected in the long row of mirrors behind them as they stood near the wall gossiping while they waited for a gentleman to take their hand in the first dance. The men stood out among the flashes of color in their dark tailored suits and turned-up white-collared shirts. Some headed towards the ladies, while others headed to the left to the card rooms.

"It's a fairytale come true," Sharra said in awe.

Tanner gently tugged her to the side away from the entrance, letting the other guests spill into the ballroom.

Leaning over, he whispered in her ear, "Close your mouth before you catch a fly. You're supposed to be used to this sort of thing, remember?"

"Pictures just don't prepare you for the real thing. What am I supposed to do?"

"Act."

"Right," she said. "Act."

"Lady Chadwick approaches," Araylai said from his left arm, tilting her head in the direction of the short round older woman making a beeline towards them through the crowd. Dressed in a turquois satin gown and a matching turban hat with peacock feathers floating in the air above she was hard to miss.

"There you are, Mr. Whitley," Lady Chadwick said addressing Tanner, all smiles.

The peacock feathers danced from her turban as she bobbed a curtsey in greeting, making her look like a funny little bird.

"Lady Chadwick," Tanner said, bowing over her plump hand as he raised it to his lips for a light kiss.

"Charming as ever, I see," she said with a giggle. "If only I was twenty years younger... but my time has passed, and it's up to the younger generation to snap you up."

"Now, now, my Lady, I see several pairs of eyes looking this way, checking out the vivacious woman in blue standing before me," he said with a gentle smile.

"It's not me they're looking at, you silly young pup, but Miss Maxwell and Miss Whitley," she said, pointing to Sharra and Araylai respectively. "You're going to have your hands full this evening keeping the wolves at bay."

"That's why I called on your ladyship for help, for I am just a lowly man and need the guidance of an experienced lady such as yourself to venture through this dangerous territory and keep my sister and Miss Maxwell safe."

"It's just a ball, Mr. Whitley, not a battle," Sharra said, while inwardly rolling her eyes to the thick ooze of charm coming from his lips. The poor dear lady didn't stand a chance.

"Don't you worry," Lady Chadwick said, patting his arm in reassurance, "I'll take care of them as if they were my own daughters. Ah, the music is starting, and here come the first set of brave young men right on cue."

Sure enough, a pack of young bucks broke off from the wall and headed straight to them through the gathering couples on the floor, eyeing the girls like fresh meat behind their mask of society politeness. Tanner watched them approach through narrow eyes before his gaze flicked over to where Sharra waited patiently beside him.

"If you will excuse me, Lady Chadwick, I've promised the first dance to Miss Maxwell," he said, offering Sharra his arm. "I'll leave my sister with you."

With that Tanner whisked Sharra away to the middle of the dance floor just as the group of young men stopped before Lady Chadwick to await introductions to the golden beauty left behind. Tanner took Sharra's hand in his and placed his other in the middle of her back as the orchestra struck up a waltz. Before she knew it, she was gliding across the floor in time with the music, following Tanner's lead as if they had danced together for years.

"Have I told you how nice you look tonight?" Tanner said, glancing down at her before returning his gaze to the path of the other dancers.

"Yes, twice," Sharra said with a smile. "Are you trying to turn my head?"

"Is it working?"

Sharra's smile widened, happy to bask under his obvious admiration, remembering the promise she had made to give Tanner a chance.

"You're really good at this," she said as he guided her through a tricky turn.

"You sound surprised."

"I just didn't picture you as the dancing type."

"I see. You thought I'd have two left feet and fall on my face. And you still wanted to dance with me. I don't know if I should feel flattered, or insulted."

"Honestly, Tanner, take it as a compliment, and don't spoil the moment. You're a good dancer, and you know it, otherwise you wouldn't have agreed to dance with me on the chance of making a fool of yourself in front of everyone."

"For you, I just might," he said, letting the meaning behind his words sink in as he stared into her eyes.

Caught up in the blue of his eyes and the unmasked feelings behind them, she missed a step. Quick on his feet, Tanner held her firm in his arms, breaking his gaze to guide her away from a collision course with another couple.

"Sorry."

"No, it's my fault," Tanner said. "I shouldn't have said that. Bad timing. Maybe we should concentrate on the mission."

"Yes, the mission."

They both turned silent as Tanner scanned the crowd around the perimeter of the ballroom, looking for Lord Pennington, one of the two targets of the mission. Catching sight of a familiar face among the overly dressed aristocrats, he swung Sharra around and positioned her so that she could see through the dancers.

"Look who's here," he said, nodding in the gentleman's general direction.

Sharra glanced to the side as they danced passed the three gentlemen standing in front of the potted plants deep in conversation. She studied their faces from underneath her lashes, trying not to look obvious. With a start, she knew whom Tanner had recognized.

"Why it's Lord Hembry, the man I saved in my first

training mission," she said as they danced away from the thin balding man. "He looks quite recovered from his illness."

"Will save," Tanner corrected. "It hasn't happened yet. This is early spring of eighteen twenty-five. The training mission was in late autumn of this same year. So, in this timeline, Lord Hembry's timeline, we've only just arrived."

She glanced over his shoulder to peer at the group of men deep in discussion. Her mind raced with possibilities as she mulled over what he said, remembering the mission. It was as if it were yesterday: the horrible thugs, the knife wounds, the blood, and Tanner unconscious on the ground. Looking back into the face so close to hers, she reached up with gentle fingers to brush the scar half hidden in his hairline.

"Couldn't we somehow warn him already, so that he can avoid what caused the illness? And save you much pain?" she said.

"No," he said, his voice harsh in its suddenness.

She flinched and looked away, setting her hand back onto his shoulder as if she never touched his face.

Realizing what he had done, he pulled her a little closer until the heat of their bodies touched, and softened his next words. "You know that we can't. Rule number three in the Handbook says: 'It is forbidden to change anything from your past timeline.' We've already come to Lord Hembry's future, but it is 'our' past. We cannot warn him and change his future now, negating the need for our mission to save him, without causing a paradox in our timeline."

"You're right," she sighed. "I don't know what I

was thinking. I just don't like you getting hurt."

"Hey, chickadee, don't you let that scar worry you. I'm fine with it." From under his breath, as if he didn't want her to hear, he whispered, "We all have things we wish we could go back and change."

Sharra hated the scar. It was a constant reminder of how close he had come to death. Being an agent wasn't all about glory and honor. Life was at stake.

For the betterment of mankind, she thought, no matter what price had to be paid by the agent.

She was grateful that Lazarus had the foresight to assign her an easy mission, one with no violence attached. She couldn't bear it if Tanner received another scar on her account, or worse, lose his life.

The music continued to swirl around them as they danced in silence each scanning the crush of people for any sign of their two Lords until the orchestra finished the final bar. The dancers bowed to their partners while the room clapped in appreciation. Rising out of her curtsy, Sharra took Tanner's arm and prepared to leave the floor when she spotted the newcomer framed in the entranceway. Long sandy-blond hair tied back outlined the square face of the imposing man. His narrowed blue eyes shone with a hidden agenda above a crooked nose as he searched the crowd, greeting people as an afterthought with a tight smile.

Pasting a smile on her lips, she whispered through her teeth, "Tanner. Lord Darby, to your left, by the entranceway."

"I see him, the weasel. We must've spent longer in the reception line then I thought. He'll head straight to the card rooms, and Lord Pennington. Where's Araylai?"

Sharra searched the crowded ballroom for Araylai as Tanner pulled her along to the side to intercept the blond giant. Like an exotic orchid, Araylai stood out among the field of wildflowers that fritted around chatting and preening, vying to draw attention their way, but it was an impossible fight. Golden, silent, and unconcerned, she stood surrounded by a swarm of black suits, while by her side Lady Chadwick clucked like a mother hen to keep them in control. Remembering the trick in the pool, Sharra raised her mental shield and sent Araylai a silent message, hoping it would work.

Lord Darby has just arrived. Go find Lord Pennington in the card room and keep him occupied elsewhere while we take care of Darby.

Araylai looked across the room and found Sharra through the milling dancers awaiting the next set. Their eyes locked.

Understood, she sent back before breaking the link to say something to Lady Chadwick, pointing to them as she did so.

With a look of relief the round lady patted Araylai's arm, and after a brief apology to the disappointed men, guided her across the floor, leaving Araylai to continue on to the open doors that led to the other part of the grand house as she made a bee-line to catch up to them.

"I signaled Araylai to head to the card room," Sharra said, turning back to Tanner. "She is on her way now, but be prepared. Lady Chadwick is heading our way, and is in full sail."

Tanner took his eyes off his quarry long enough to glance over his shoulder at the approaching lady in blue, and sighed.

"Sharra, you deal with her. I don't want Darby to get away. Ah Lady Chadwick," he said just as the woman reached them. "Perfect timing. I see an old friend I want to catch up with. Miss Maxwell, I'll leave you in the good lady's care now that she's here."

With a slight bow to the ladies, he left them and raced to catch up to the receding back of their target as fast as decorum would allow.

"Humph," Lady Chadwick said with a shake of her feathered head as she watched him disappear across the ballroom. "To the card tables is where that young man is going. I'll never understand men. Trading a beautiful woman for a chance to gamble."

"Maybe they feel it's the safer of the two," Sharra said as she linked arms with the older woman, and followed her through the press of warm bodies and heavy perfumes.

"Never you mind, Miss Maxwell, I was coming to steal you away, anyway, for there's a gentleman of my acquaintance who has asked for an introduction. And if you ask me, and I'm never wrong, Mr. Whitley is going to have some competition, for Mr. Ferguson is quite handsome and has the most arresting of gazes."

"Competition?"

Ignoring her question, Lady Chadwick continued to chatter as they passed Lord Hembry's group still in conversation in front of the greenery by the wide pillar, and moved into the adjoining room where, from the French doors, a cool breeze drifted over the guests that lingered there. Sharra breathed in, grateful for the moments reprise from the overpowering smell of perfume as she listened with half an ear to the dear lady's ramblings. Eyeing the open doorway to the balcony with longing, she watched as other couples took advantage of the calm night, wishing she could slip outside for just a moment. Thus occupied, she did not notice the dark-haired gentleman leave the protection of the potted plants of the other pillar until she realized that they had stopped moving and Lady Chadwick wasn't talking to her anymore, but to someone else.

"There you are, Mr. Ferguson. May I present to you my young friend, Miss Maxwell," she said all smiles.

Lady Chadwick tugged lightly on Sharra's arm to get her attention, but Sharra was already turning by that time. Prepared to act the part of a nineteenth century aristocrat, she painted a polite smile on her lips as she raised her eyes to his face, curious to see whom Lady Chadwick deemed as competition. As soon as her eyes met his, her face drained of color and her knees weakened.

The man smiled as those black-rimmed silver eyes that haunted her dreams for more nights than she cared to remember locked with hers.

Chapter Eight

"It's you," she blurted out before she could stop herself.

The ballroom went quiet as if by magic. In her mind all the guests in their fancy dress had disappeared. Everything stilled. Even the musicians with their instruments had mysteriously vanished, leaving a vacuum of silence behind. All that was left was the two of them. Not a sound could she hear but the beating of her own heart.

She stared into the depths of his silvery eyes and saw the scene in the back of the Monteque house flash before her. Like then, he stood so close that she could smell the clean scent of him. It was the same scent that he had worn that night that Tanner almost died. Her pulse began to quicken. His name came unbidden to her lips. It almost slipped out, but the brogue of his cultured voice broke the spell that she was caught it, and saved her from making a huge blunder.

"Pardon me, but have we met before?" Mr. Ferguson said.

With his voice came crashing back the music, the swish of fabric from the ballroom, and the hum of reality.

Yes, your name is Faolan, she thought, but had the good sense not to go there, for just as with Lord Hembry, it hadn't happened yet in his timeline. Plus to explain the circumstances of their first meeting would be breaking Agency policy, and she wasn't about to anger Lazarus over a crush on a nineteenth century man. No, it was best to leave it alone.

"Mr. Ferguson, you say? No, I don't recollect knowing any Fergusons. Excuse my manners," she said, and curtsied. "It's nice to meet you."

"The pleasure's all mine," he said with a bow, and then looked at her with concern. "Are you feeling unwell, Miss Maxwell?" To Lady Chadwick he said, "What do you think, Lady Chadwick, does she look pale to you? Maybe a stroll around the terrace for some air would be good for her. I'd be happy to offer my services, and escort her, if you agree."

"Tsk, tsk, poor girl. Must be from the heat from the crush of people," Lady Chadwick said, patting Sharra's arm in worry as she studied her face. "Maybe a few minutes of fresh air would be good for you. You go with Mr. Ferguson, but not for too long."

"I'll see that no harm comes to her," he said as he took Sharra's elbow and drew her away from the heat of the ballroom and into the darkness of the terrace.

Only a few other couples were taking advantage of the cool air, for the night was still young, and the dancing had just started.

Once outside, he led her to a protected corner where a stone trellis met the house, and turned her to him, placing his warm hands on the soft flesh of her upper arms. Holding her there he studied her face.

"There, Miss Maxwell, is this better?"

"Yes, thank you." Her voice came out soft. She couldn't help it. The nearness of the man was doing things to her insides, making her pulse quicken, and befuddling her mind.

"Good, for it would be terribly ungentlemanly of me to let a beautiful woman like you faint away from the heat when I can offer my assistance." He touched her cheek, sliding his finger down the line of her jaw, leaving a trail of liquid fire behind.

"Beautiful? Me?"

Sharra stilled under his touch, too stunned by his presence to protest the liberties he was taking. How many nights had she fantasized about him since the training mission six months ago, she couldn't guess. And now, they were together in the dark, something she thought would never happen again. Unknowingly she leaned into his touch. It was all the encouragement the rogue needed.

"Very beautiful." His voice lowered as he touched the curl of auburn hair that rested at the side of her neck, deliberately brushing the pulse that beat there. "Has no one ever told you before?"

A small shake of her head told him everything. He moved in closer, their bodies only inches apart.

"Then let me. You are beautiful, as beautiful as a young doe in a field of wildflowers warmed by the sun, with eyes like the soft green moss that grows in the rich earth of the highland hills," he said running his fingers over her eyelids so that they closed, "and hair made up of thick locks of mixed copper and chestnut that beg for a man to run his hands through it."

He moved to her hair and wove his fingers through the loose ringlets that hung down around her shoulder. Bringing his face close to hers, he brushed his lips over the locks in his hand as he breathed in her clean scent. With her eyes closed she leaned her cheek into his palm as his soft words and heady touch heightened her awareness of him, of the warmth of his breath so close to her lips.

"And your lips," he whispered, "your lips are like the dew gathered on a petal of a red rose, lush and velvety soft, waiting to be tasted."

With that last whispered thought, his lips brushed against hers in a feathery touch as he held her face between his hands. He kissed her for only a moment before he raised his head a fraction, breaking the link. She trembled underneath his hands, wanting more, forgetting all about Tanner and the mission. All that mattered was now, and the man she couldn't let go of.

She didn't have long to wait before his lips descended onto hers again, this time firmer as he explored hers with his own, tasting, insistent, until she finally opened with a soft moan and let him in to discover the warm secrets of her mouth. Once inside, their tongues collided and danced with pent-up need until their starving lungs cried out for air, and they reluctantly broke apart. Still cradling her face, he rested his forehead against hers as they both fought to catch their breath.

"I will not apologize," he whispered as soon as his breath slowed enough to speak.

"I wanted it." *More than you could ever know.*

"You feel it too, the connection. I know you do." Raising his head, he took her hand and placed it inside his waistcoat against the fine white linen of his shirt, and held it there. From under her palm, his heart pounded a wild beat against his chest, matching the beat of her own, confirming his words as true.

"Yes, I feel it," she said in wonder while he kept her hand imprisoned there.

But the feeling of joy did not last long as the reality of the situation sunk in. She was a Vault Agent, only there on Agency business. Her timeline did not run with his. He would be staying behind in this century when she left after the completion of the mission. An unbreakable wall of time would separate them.

It's not fair, she screamed inside, yet she knew what she had to do, no matter how hard it would be.

"We cannot do this," she said, pulling her hand free from his waistcoat. "Time does not allow it."

"Time?"

"Oh, I can't explain it. And if I could, you wouldn't understand. You and I can never be."

"Am I so loathsome to you then?" he said as he released her hand.

"Faolan," she said with raw emotion. Resting her palm on his cheek, she gazed into his eyes, hoping he could see there what she could not say. "I can't.

Please…"

"If this thing you call time weren't in the way, would I have a chance?" he said in earnest.

"Don't ask that of me. You don't even know me."

"Then I should get to work on that," he said as he gathered her in his arms, and swooped down to capture her lips once again, kissing her as if there were no tomorrow.

Crushed to his chest, she wrapped her arms around his neck and gave into the sweet torture of his lips, hot and demanding on hers, until all thoughts of the future melted away, leaving just the two of them in a time warp of her own making. She met him, kiss for kiss, desperate to hang on to him for the little time that was allotted to her, knowing that any moment it would be gone. Lost in the warmth of his embrace, she clung to him, giving him what his lips demanded, only to be jarred back to reality by a sharp prick on the lower slope of her neck.

"Ouch!" she said, breaking the kiss to grab her neck.

"What is it?" Faolan asked. "Did I hurt you?"

"I think I've been stung."

"Let me see." He turned her into the light to check, brushing his hand over the spot where her hand had been, wiping the telltale speck of blood away with a finger as he inspected the area. "I don't see anything. Whatever it was, it's gone now. Does it still hurt?"

"It's getting better," she said as her fingers explored the small bump that was beginning to form under the sting.

The mood was broken, and with it came flooding back her responsibilities to the team and the mission.

She had lingered outside long enough. "I think we should return to the ballroom. My friend, Miss Whitley and her brother will be looking for me."

"Of course," he said, "but before we go, let me just…" He reached over and with gentle hands wound each ringlet around his finger and placed them back against her neck, lingering over her pulse for a tantalizing moment, before stepping back. "Now you look presentable again."

"Thank you," she said as she fought to control the trembling of her limbs from the mere brush of his hand on her flesh.

Think. The mission. The mission, she told herself with a shake as the urge to cry welled up from nowhere. She took his proffered arm. *No time for tears now. Later.*

Shoulders back, head up, she forced a serene smile on her face as he led her back into the heat and light of the ballroom, and back to the mission at hand.

Chapter Nine

Pompeii, Italy

Seventy-Nine a.d.

The day turned to night as the sky thickened with the ash that continued to spew from the top of the mountain in the distance. It fell like heavy clouds, covering everything in a blanket of grey down, from the clay rooftops to the polygonal block roadways, settling without ambiguity on anything and everything, leaving nothing untouched in the great city. Once a busy center of activity, the city lay desolated as the local people hid away in their homes, praying to their pagan gods for protection against the anger of the mountain, while others fled to the waters edge hoping to find salvation there.

Inside a protected alcove of an abandoned home,

Sharra leaned against the warm wall of the stone entryway to catch her breath. Sweat beaded her face and soaked her hair underneath the facemask. The black protective Vault uniform that covered her whole body was no better off. It could only withstand so much, and right now, the tremendous heat from the outside was testing its limits. Even with the protective layer, a constant stream of sweat trickled down her spine and into her fitted boots to collect in pools around her toes, making her more uncomfortable the longer she stood there. The little part of her skin that was exposed to the deadly air shone with a thin covering of moisture, yet the discomfort was nothing compared to what the locals were going through. She didn't want to think about that... about the wave of death that was soon to come.

Reaching up to her head, she adjusted the straps of her breathing apparatus to a tighter fit against the heavy fumes that permeated the air of the city, and checked the readings on the far right of the thin shield of the facemask, noting that the temperature gauge was heading into the red. She couldn't afford to rest any longer.

Leaving the protection of the alcove, she dove into the falling ash, and sprinted north up the deserted street. Wading through the calf-high layer of powdered slag, she took a quick right at the next intersection until she reached a set of columns that marked the entrance to the central bathhouse of the city. Without stopping, she dashed through the tall square archway and into the bathhouse, finding relief from the ash inside the deserted marble structure. Once inside, she slowed down to a jog as she went over the floor plan of the large building. In a matter of seconds the way out the back was mapped out in her mind. In the dim light, she searched for her next landmark.

"There it is," she said, catching sight of the double-arched doorway ahead.

Sharra took it. Inside was the main bathhouse. Just a few days ago they had been teeming with the rich. Now, the marble-tiled pools were abandoned along with the rest of the city. Whatever water had been in them had either been drained or evaporated. Dust filled the air as the filtered light from above worked hard to find its way to the once white stone floor. It covered everything in its path, from the marble statues that stood like guardians over the mosaic tiles, to the many beautiful frescoes that filled the renovated sections of the baths. Only the soles of her small boots marred the blanket of filth concealing the floor. Like the rest of the city, those too would be erased in the ever-falling ash and the destruction that was imminent.

At the back of the baths, Sharra veered into one of the changing rooms. Without stopping she flipped on the mike in her helmet as she jogged to the end of the room, and out the next door into another bathing chamber.

"Tony, where are you? I'm in the bathhouse, heading to the back door."

"I'm heading west on Via di Nola. It's getting heavy out here."

The Italian's voice sounded out of breath. Time was running out.

"How far are you from the engineer's office?" she said as she passed through one bath and into another, not stopping in the dusty light to admire the half-naked frescoes that lined the walls around the large empty marble pools.

"Almost there," he said.

"Hurry."

Sharra picked up her pace and pushed across the last few rooms and out the backdoor of the bathhouse, and onto Via di Nola, and into the never-ending rain of ash. The heat hit her like a brick wall. It told her to hurry. Turning right, she sprinted down the street to the next alley. There she caught site of a dark shadow running towards her in the heavy cloud of ash. Tony stopped in front of her, grabbing her arms to hold his body erect as he fought to catch his breath. Sweat poured down his handsome face from behind his mask as he nodded for her to lead the way, knowing time was of the essence.

They ran into the alley, through the darkening gloom and rising ash, counting the doors as they went until she found the one they were looking for. She didn't knock for she knew that the occupant was already dead. Instead she shoved the door open, and with Tony on her heels, rushed past the main room to the inner chamber to the stack of papyrus rolls that littered the table opposite the thread-worn bed.

"Tony, help me find it," she said as she began to shuffle through the documents, blinking the sweat out of her eyes to read the writing on the outer edge of the scroll before throwing it to the floor and moving on to the next.

They worked in silence all the while aware of their dwindling time, quickly discarding one scroll after another until none were left on the table.

"It's not here," Tony growled in frustration.

"It's got to be," Sharra said. "Look around."

Just then the floor shook as a low rumble came from the northwest. Sharra grabbed the table for support as the small room shuddered and bucked as if they were in a boat on the high seas. It knocked furniture around. Bits of pottery and dishes dashed to the floor. They shattered around their feet. More dust filled the room as the rumble continued to shake the building. After a few more seconds, the earth calmed down, but not the rumble. In the distance it continued to grow louder like a freight train rolling towards them.

"That's our cue," Tony said. "Time to go."

"We have to find it," she said, moving away from the table to search the room. "It's here, I know it is."

"Forget it. I'm not ready to die over a stupid document. The pyroclastic cloud that the mountain just spewed out will be here in less than a minute. If we don't shift now, we'll be history like the rest of Pompeii."

"Shift, then," she said as she scanned the room, catching site of the lone tapestry fluttering against the wall.

She ran over to it and pulled it aside, revealing a hidden recess built into the wall. From it, a hot breeze filtered through the newly made cracks at the back, hitting her shield as she stuck her hands in and pulled out a parcel wrapped in leather, marked with the aqueduct engineer's seal.

"I've got it!" she yelled as she threw it into her backpack.

In a matter of seconds the rumbling grew louder

and the temperature rose to an unbearable heat. Like a wave it came crashing over the city, killing every living thing in its path.

Tony's faceplate warning went off. "Malfunction overload. Please advise. Malfunction overload. Please advise," it repeated over and over again as the rising heat compromised its circuits.

"Sharra!"

Tony raced across the room and grabbed her, his eyes staring at hers through their faceplates in wild desperation. Sharra didn't wait any longer, but sent the command to the Vault's mainframe just as their uniforms began to melt.

"Shift!"

Chapter Ten

———

The Vault

In an instant the unbearable heat from the erupting volcano shut off as Sharra shifted them back to the safety of the Vault with only seconds to spare. Inside the shiftroom, they broke apart, and tore off their faceplates, throwing them to the floor as they gulped in the cool air. Their seared gloves soon followed, landing with a splat onto the pulsing floor.

Sharra wiped the sweat off her face and glared at Tony as she set her backpack onto the floor and started releasing the clasps at her neck and shoulder of her ruined uniform. One by one they snapped free under her angry hands. With a quick pull, she peeled the flexible material away from her throat and over her head, dropping it to the floor with the rest of her gear. Free from the protection of the hood, her ponytail fell back limp as wet as the rest of her.

Fire burned in her eyes, but the man did not notice. Wiping his face, he started to chuckle, shaking his head as he leaned against the wall to strip out of his gear.

"You... are... amazing," Tony said. "I was sure we weren't going to make it. I bet you could stare death in the face and not blink an eye. Cool and collected, that's what you are. No wonder Lazarus paired us together instead of Zoe for this mission. Zoe, well, she's like that mountain, all spitfire and heat." A wide smile crossed his face as he spoke of his partner. "Which I like, don't get me wrong. You, on the other hand... you're something of an enigma."

"How can you be so stupid? Where did you go? We were supposed to stick together!" she said as she attacked the zipper of her uniform. Once the skintight suit was loosened she peeled it down her body and pulled her legs free with a snap. She turned to him and shook the damaged uniform under his nose. "This could have been avoided!"

Without waiting for an answer, she swooped the rest of her gear off the floor and stomped out of the shiftroom. The adrenalin rush of the close call with death was wearing off. Yet her anger towards Tony's carelessness was enough to fuel her forward. Free from the protective suit, the cool air from the vast Vault chamber flowed around her body as the row of massive pylons rotated on their axis in the center of the waking cloudmass. It cooled her skin underneath her soaked tanktop and underwear as she stormed past, brushing the floating tendrils of energy away with impatient fingers.

For once she was too angry to notice their effect on her body.

Tony rushed out of the shiftroom in a soaked t-shirt and briefs. The rest of his gear was tucked under his arm. He caught up to her, matching her steps with his, unaware of her seething emotions.

"Relax. I just needed to pick up something. Couldn't go to a place like Pompeii and not bring back a souvenir. Zoe would never forgive me if I came back empty-handed."

From his backpack he lifted out an oblong package wrapped in purple cloth. After quickly unwinding the cloth, he held it up to show her it with pride. In his hand rested a half-naked woman dressed in a Grecian robe with her slim arms poised above her coifed head, exposing one perfect breast. It was carved of the purest of white marble Sharra had ever seen. It glowed liked crushed opals against the onyx backdrop of the Vault floor, displaying the master craftsmanship of the piece to their eyes.

"Believe me, they won't miss it," he said as he held it up to admire its beauty. "It's one of the perks of the job. We all do it."

Sharra stared at the statuette in shock as her mind registered what Tony had done.

"You jeopardized our lives over a stupid souvenir?" she said, grabbing the statuette out of his hand and brandishing it in his face before swinging around and stomping out of the Vault with it.

"Wait! That's mine!" he said, chasing after her.

"Not any more."

Grabbing the purple cloth out of his hand, she

wrapped the marble statuette in it and slipped it into her backpack next to the scrolled documents, and headed into Staxx. With the precious cargo settled on her shoulder, she leaned over the counter in search of the Head of the storeroom.

"Grimm, we're back," she called as she peered down the aisles between the rows of shelving visible on the other side.

On the counter was a freshly folded pile of period clothing, ready to be picked up.

"Grimm?" she called out again.

"He's not here," Tony said.

She ignored him as she dumped her ruined gear on the counter, and left, grateful Grimm wasn't around to growl at her over the unrepairable state she had brought it back in. Tony did the same, leaving it with hers as he scurried to catch up to her.

"Hey, wait. We're not done yet," he said as he caught up to her in the hallway.

"Yes, we are."

"Give me back the statuette."

"And what would Lazarus say if he knew you almost got us killed because you took a detour for a 'souvenir,' especially on an already dangerous mission like Pompeii where you knew every minute counted?"

"Come on, you're alive, aren't you?"

"Wrong answer."

Tony glanced at her set face and turned quiet. "You aren't going to tell him, are you?"

"I should," she said, and pressed her lips together to think through the red haze of her anger.

They marched the rest of the way in silence as Tony

waited for her to calm down, realizing that she was serious. Neither one cared that they were in their underwear. At the lifts she stopped and turned to him.

"Promise me that you won't ever jeopardize your partner's life over a trinket again."

"I promise," he said, resting his hand upon his heart. "Keep the figurine. It's yours. As a token of my sincerity."

"I intend to keep it, but I won't forget what you did." She entered the lift and stared at him with cold eyes as he remained in the foyer. "Just don't do it again, ever, and this will stay between you and me."

The elevator swished shut on his worried face, leaving her alone in the small space as it shot up to the next floor. Once in her apartment, she set the precious cargo onto the floor and stripped out of her damp underclothes as she headed for the shower to wash the residue of heat and grime of Mount Vesuvius from her skin. A little while later she came out of the bedroom dressed in a long flowing skirt and blouse with her clean hair clipped back behind her ears and a touch of makeup on her face.

The smell of daffodils filled the air reminding her of what still needed to be done. The bright bouquet waited in a vase on the kitchen counter. She had picked them earlier from her hothouse. She closed her eyes and breathed in their fresh scent, clearing her nostrils of any lingering ash smell before tackling the backpack. Amadeus had found it where she had set it on the floor, and was busy sticking his nose into the unzipped compartment and getting leftover ash all over his fur, turning the white parts gray.

"Not now, Amadeus," she said as she set him on the couch.

She lifted the cloth-covered statuette out and set it aside on the cushion. Next came the parcel wrapped in leather. Gently she blew away the remnants of ash off of it to reveal the wax seal, and wondered how the document that lay protected inside would help someone else's future. The novelty of checking timelines had worn off ages ago. Yet, this one interested her for the risk had been greater than usual. Somewhere in another timeline, others would somehow benefit from their efforts.

That's all she knew.

That's all that mattered.

As carefully as if it were the greatest treasure, she wrapped it in a clean cloth and transferred it into a fresh satchel. Slipping the satchel over her shoulder, she plucked the daffodils from their vase, and headed to the door. Amadeus meowed and ran up to her.

She dropped into a crouch, and said as she petted him, "I promise to spend time with you when I get back. I won't be gone long." With a final sweep of his fur, she got to her feet, and left him for the second time that day.

Outside her door, she adjusted the strap of the satchel as she strode down the hall to the administration block. In her other hand, she held the bundle of daffodils like a shield to her chest. In no time she was in front of the heavy wooden door of the Head Director. After knocking, she waited for permission to enter.

Seated behind his desk, Lazarus smiled and waved her forward.

"How did it go?"

"I got you what you asked for." Removing the leather parcel from her satchel, she passed it over to him.

"Ah, the aqueduct notes," he said, setting them on the cabinet behind him with extreme care. "Thank you. I hope you didn't find Pompeii too stressful. It's not easy seeing the disaster first hand, especially knowing you can't change the outcome for the city, nor for its people."

"That I can handle. It's a part of history. But what I can't handle is an unreliable agent."

"Tony," Lazarus said with a sigh.

"Yes, Tony. You need to do something about him. He's out of control."

"Sad to say, yours is not the first complaint. And you're right: it can't be allowed to go on. I'll send him to Cam for a medical check." Lazarus paused and looked her over with a sharp eye, missing nothing as he studied her tight face. "Is there something else bothering you besides Tony's lack of maturity?"

"No, why?"

"You've been shifting nonstop since the Darby/Pennington assignment. Are you sure you're alright?"

"I'm fine," she lied as she tried to suppress the image of a silvery-eyed Scotsman from her mind.

"The Agency doesn't expect you to work so hard," he said. "It's not good for you. Why don't you take a break from shifting, and rest for a bit, spend some time on yourself."

"Maybe I have been a little hard on myself," she said, hating to admit it. She looked at the flowers in her hand and turned quiet before saying, "You're probably right. Amadeus has been missing me."

"Tanner has been asking about you, too. He's worried about you. If you could give him a Link, or meet for drinks and catch up, it'd make him, and me feel better. It's not good for you to be alone."

"I've been busy…"

"A mission does not take the place of real companionship." Lazarus left his desk and came around to face her. Taking her arms, he said, "This can be a lonely job, if you let it be. I care about you, Sharra. I don't want to see you go down that path. I only want you to be happy."

"I am happy." She lied, but kept her eyes glued to his, knowing that if she gave into her feelings she would not be able to hold back from crying. "Really."

Lazarus stared down into her eyes as if gauging the truth in her words and found them wanting. But, to her relief, he didn't push her any further.

"You'll take some time off?"

"Yes, but first I have something I have to do," she said looking at the flowers in her hand.

Reluctantly he let her go. Sharra breathed a sigh of relief as soon as she left the office. He hadn't asked where she was going, though she could tell that he had wanted to. The flowers should have been a dead giveaway. But he was the Head Director for a reason, and discretion was one of them.

Sharra went down to the main floor, and passed through the high archway into the Vault chamber for a second time that day. With her mental shield firmly in place she treaded past the sleeping cloudmass that covered the feet of the nine pylons, hoping to go unnoticed. However, no matter how hard she tried to hide her presence, it always knew. She was sure it had to do something with the small ball of energy in her head. They were connected, the ball and the cloud being of the same source.

The cloud mass began to stir as the silvery conductors started to rotate. With the rotation came the tiny sparks of energy that sped to and fro across the empty spaces between them like dancing lights, stirred up from the stored energy in the cloud below. Long tendrils of mist broke away from the body of the cloud and reached out to her as she hurried across the floor. It called to the tiny ball of light imprisoned in her head, but she didn't give it time to respond. Tightening her shield, she clamped down on the ball and sped up, and entered one of the eight shiftrooms.

As quickly as she could, she gathered her memories and prepared for the shift, sending the information to the agrylium in her head. Down her nerve endings it went and out her body through the pulsing floor to the pylons in the Vault, and on to the mainframe hidden somewhere underneath. Once completed, she gave the command and shifted out with the flowers in hand. This was one appointment she didn't want to miss.

Chapter Eleven

Chicago, Illinois, USA

Nineteen Ninety-Seven

It was an overcast day. The sky was thick with clouds. The smell of rain, exhaust, and rotting garbage hung heavily in the air. Not even the breeze off the lake could dispel the unpleasant smell. Tall brick apartment buildings in disrepair lined the street on both sides, some with bent railings and with windows boarded up, others with small signs of occupancy: a knickknack on the windowsill, mail sticking out of the slots by the door, garbage piling up next to the steps. In the street between them ran an upper railway system supported by heavy cement pillars. Most of the street was unused, for Chicago City Roadworks had sometime in the past decided to use it for storage. Row upon row of concrete barriers and some old rusty bulldozers filled the area under the railway, blocking the middle section to traffic, not that it mattered. Broken glass littered both sides of the streets. It gathered alongside anything it smashed against, from fire hydrants, to lamp-poles, to the stored barriers, and all along the broken down curb.

Sharra had forgotten what Chicago was like until she took that first breath in, and coughed, wrinkling her nose at the mixture of overripe garbage and neglect that hung over the neighborhood. She pushed it aside, for other things were on her mind. As soon as she shifted in, she dashed to the barriers. Shattered glass was everywhere. More had collected since last year. Picking her way through it, she slid behind the nearest cement support pillar. Tucking her body in against its rough surface, she scanned up and down the street to see whether anyone had seen her odd arrival.

Nothing moved.

A mangy orange cat washed itself on the roof of an abandoned old car that sat half-covered in weeds in the empty lot across the street. Next to the car was an old green dumpster. With its peeling paint and rusted hinges, it was an eyesore, as was the car. Filled with rotted bags of trash, Sharra was sure the horrific smell was coming from there. The buzz of flies that feasted on its contents could be heard over the sounds of the city. Even so, the neighborhood did not stir. Not even a flutter of a curtain moved in any of the windows overlooking the spot on the street where she had appeared.

In the sky above the railway the electrical wires that ran the system came alive, signaling the approach of a train. She craned her neck to see it in the distance coming from the south end of town. Three cars she counted. Louder and louder it got as it came closer. The wires buzzed and crackled. Under her hand, the pillar trembled under the weight from above until the last car passed by with a clickity-clack. It slowed down and stopped at the station a few blocks away. Its stop was brief, a few minutes at most before it took off to the center of town. The noise faded away into the city.

A dog barked somewhere off to the right followed by some loud cursing, but Sharra ignored it, for the sounds came from within one of the apartments too far away to have seen her. Overhead the dark clouds thickened as more moved in from the lake to cover the midday sun. She looked up at the oppressive sky and frowned.

Gloomy and restless, just like her mood.

Perfect, she thought.

Clutching the flowers in her hand, she stepped around the pillar to the front. Unlike the other pillars, this one showed signs of old damage. Chunks of cement from eye level down had broken off sometime in the past. The holes were deep. Whatever had hit it, had hit with such force that it caused the pillar to fracture and crumble in places. A dark-grey smudge covered the pillar and ran up to the underbelly of the overpass, remnants of the fireball from the accident.

She looked across the street to the gaping hole between the long lines of apartment buildings. Once it had been all connected, but the fire had spread across the street. The building was gone, cleared away by the city years ago. An abandoned lot remained behind. Now, scraps of metal and strips of old plastic poked through the weeds that covered the rocky ground and hid the trash underneath. Near the sidewalk, the old car sat rusting in the weeds next to the forgotten commercial garbage dumpster. Its windows had been smashed out years ago, its interior ripped to shreds and full of trash.

Not much had changed in the last year.

She had shifted in not five feet from the pillar. It was perfect in her estimate. And it should be. Just like the smudge marks incinerated permanently on the pillar and underbelly of the railway, so, too, was this spot burned into her memory.

Ten years.

She stared at the spot, not seeing the broken cement or the black marks. Instead the loving faces of her parents filled her mind as they were when they had kissed her goodbye before they went out to dinner that night ten years ago. She and her older brother, Greyson, had been home when the police had stopped by later that night to give them the devastating news. Greyson had answered the doorbell, expecting one of his friends from work, but instead was greeted by two local officers. At seeing the lights of the police car out front, Sharra had figured that Greyson had gotten into trouble again. If only that was it. Leaving her schoolwork on the couch, she had gotten up and reached the hallway in time to hear the male officer give Greyson the bad news.

"Are you sure?" Greyson asked, stiff with shock.

"I'm sorry for your loss," the officer said, holding his hat between his hands.

Sharra sank down to the floor and burst into tears, hugging her legs tight to her body as she hid her face in her knees.

"Is there someone we can call," the female officer said, "a relative, a grandparent, or a close friend of the family? You shouldn't be alone tonight."

Greyson looked over to where his sister was curled up on the floor, crying into her hands. "Our grandparents are dead."

"Aunts, uncles?"

"There are only the two of us. Maybe one of my mom's friends?"

And that was that.

Sharra didn't know who had arranged the funeral, or who had handled her parent's financial affairs, assuming it had been Greyson. All she knew was that the only two people who had ever loved her were gone, leaving her lost and alone in the care of her selfish brother for four long years.

A tear flowed down one cheek, escaping from her lashes to lay a cold trail to her chin. She brushed it away along with the memory of that fateful night, and focused again on the pillar in front of her, remembering the flowers clutched in her hand. Crouching down, she brushed the shattered glass away from the edge of the pillar with careful hands until a clean patch of concrete was exposed. There she laid the bunch of daffodils, arranging the blooms against the grey pavement with tender care.

"I love you, Mom and Dad," she whispered as she stared at the bright yellow flowers, and brushed another tear away.

The first sound of thunder rumbled in the distance somewhere over Lake Michigan. Wiping her eyes,

Sharra stood up and examined the dark sky over the row of decrepit apartments, wishing she had the foresight to have worn a jacket, or brought an umbrella. It was Chicago, after all.

It was then as she was looking at the sky that something stung her on the neck, right below her ear.

"Ouch!"

Without thinking, she slapped it, smashing the tiny assailant underneath her fingers, and plucked it off her neck. When she pulled her hand away to look at it, it wasn't a bug that rested there, but a small dart the size of her thumbnail.

"What in the world?" she said as she stared at the miniature weapon, forgetting all about her parent's death and the imminent threat of rain as her brain tried to register what had just happened.

Within seconds a wave of dizziness hit her. Her vision blurred. A second wave hit, making her stomach turn as she rocked on her feet from the sudden assault on her senses. Dropping the dart, she grabbed the pillar for support and fought for control as her legs wobbled. Fog rolled in and darkened her mind, making it hard for her to think. She shook her head to clear the fuzziness away, but it only made her dizzier. As the seconds passed, her strength drained out of her body along with the will to fight. Her vision closed in on itself until the pinpoints of light disappeared. Weakened beyond help, she gave in, and fell to the ground.

———

From his hiding place behind the dumpster across the street, Jake Byson smiled and lowered the slim dart gun to his side as he watched the woman sink to the ground, landing in a heap next to the concrete barrier.

"Did you hit the target?" Viktor said from his crouched position.

Jake looked down at the big blond agent at his feet and raised an eyebrow. "What do you think?" he said with a curl of his lip. "Of course, I hit her. Now wait here until I give you the signal."

He peered over the top of the dumpster, and glanced up and down the street. Nothing stirred except the constant hum of the city in the background. Slipping the gun back into the holster at his hip, he left their hiding place and crossed the street, holding his long canvas jacket tight to his body as he jogged over to where the woman had fallen on the bed of broken glass. Hunching down over the body, he brushed her hair out of the way to get a good look at her pale face, and smiled a tight smile.

"So predictable," he said as he stared at her face, brushing her cheek in a loving caress. "You make this too easy for me. Where's the fun in that, my dear?"

His fingers stilled over her face as a new thought entered his mind. He pressed his fingers to her neck and felt a weak pulse. "You had better not die on me, not this way, not until I want you to."

Reaching behind her left ear, he removed the Link, and stuffed it into his shirt pocket. From one of the deep pockets of his coat he pulled out a black sack and shoved it over her head and down her shoulders, hiding her face and her hair from sight, and waved Viktor over.

Waiting for his cue, Viktor bounded across the street and hunkered down next to Jake to get a look at the woman.

"Who is it?" Viktor said.

"Our target. Who do you think?"

"I know that, but who is she?"

"She's just another thorn in the order of time, I suspect, causing enough pain in someone's neck to merit her removal."

"Why did you put a sack on her?"

"Orders of the mission. I don't question them. I just do them, and you should too."

"About that," Viktor said with a frown. His eyes narrowed. "It seems odd that I wasn't allowed access to the file of this mission. I'm flying in the dark here. It doesn't feel right. I think_"

"You're not here to think," Jake barked, the words leaving his lips before he could stop them. He took a deep breath and held onto his temper before he continued in a calmer tone, "The orders were specific. We were to come in as unobtrusively as possible, and remove the target. Now pick her up, and let's get out of here before we're seen."

Mollified, Viktor scooped the unconscious woman into his beefy arms as if she weighed no more than a child, and followed Jake across the street to their hiding place behind the stinking dumpster in the vacant lot. Once there, Jake grabbed the other agent's bicep as they prepared to shift.

"You know where you're going, right?" Jake said.

Viktor nodded over the limp woman. "Transport is ready and waiting."

"Good. Let's go."

Jake held tight to Viktor as he waited for the shift.

The big man signaled his readiness.

"Shift."

The two men and the woman blinked out, leaving the city behind. A second later they reappeared inside a large shiftroom the size of a small aircraft hanger. Inside the hanger, underneath the bright illumination of the surrounding walls sat a sleek shuttlecraft on four metal feet. Its wings were extended as if prepared for flight, half-hiding the pulsing silver design etched into the smooth floor of the hangar.

Jake let go of Viktor's arm and looked around at the bright walls and pulsing floor, and whistled in appreciation.

"Impressive," he said. "I wonder what else Maitland is hiding. How did you stumble upon this treasure?"

"I didn't stumble upon it," Viktor said as he strode to the shuttle cradling the woman in his arms. "It's always been here, though we don't use it very often. Mostly when larger gear is needed, or some sort of transport. I'm here more often than not. I use the space to fix things. Lazarus doesn't like to use it much for shifting, for it complicates missions more than it helps."

"Does anyone else know about the hangar?" Jake said, trying to keep his excitement at the discovery in check.

"Not many. Max. Grimm, of course. I think maybe, Tatiana. The assignments were all solo jobs, except for today's."

"Well, I won't tell," Jake said with a smile. *Another secret. Interesting.* "Where is it? Must be close to the main Vault."

"It is."

Viktor ducked under the wing of the shuttle and stopped in front of the hatch door. Shifting the limp body over his shoulder to free his arm, he reached over and typed in a sequence of numbers into the pad next to the door. Once the code was accepted, the lock released and the hatch door slid open into the bulk of the craft. A short set of steps unfolded to the ground. The blond agent settled the woman back into his arms and climbed into the small cargo bay.

"Set her on the floor," Jake said from behind. "You go start this thing, while I make her comfortable."

After setting his burden on the floor as gently as he could, Viktor headed to the narrow opening in the front of the cargo bay, and squeezed his bulk through. On the other side was the cockpit. He slipped into one of the bucket seats and began the preflight check; pressing buttons, activating screens, all the while shooting commands to the PVC of the craft. Gone was the stumbling giant. In his place was a man of confidence born from experience.

Inside the cargo bay, Jake dropped down next to the woman. Through the narrow opening that separated the cargo bay from the cockpit, he could see Viktor busy with the preflight check. Keeping one eye on the giant he slipped a narrow box out of a deep pocket of his coat and set it on the floor next to the woman's head. The lid clicked open under the pressure of his fingers. His eyes flew back to Viktor, but the big man was engrossed in the preflight check to have heard the small noise. From the box, he pulled out a wand on a long cord and plugged it into the unit before switching it on. The box hummed to life, but the noise of the craft warming up hid it.

"How's it going up there?" he called to the front.

"Almost done," Viktor said. "Just a few more checks."

With Viktor busy, Jake turned to the woman. Tearing off the cover from her head, he checked her pulse.

The beat was stronger than before, but it didn't matter to him.

"Sorry it had to come to this," he whispered as he stared down into her pale face. "You should've stayed away."

As he watched, her eyelids fluttered opened, revealing the hazel eyes that he hated so much. Their drugged-clouded depths were filled with confusion as she tried to focus.

"Greyson?" she said as she latched onto his face, but that was all he let her say.

"Oh no you don't," he said and punched her in the jaw, one quick hard hit to silence her, knocking her back into dark oblivion.

Small beads of sweat broke out on his brow as he whipped around to see whether her voice had carried into the cockpit, but Viktor continued deaf to what was going on in the cargo bay.

Satisfied that he was safe, Jake turned back to the unconscious woman and pushed her hair out of the way to expose the twin silver markings behind her ears. Picking up the wand, he held her head to the side and touched the heated end to the first tattoo. Under the hot tip of the wand the silver metal bubbled and sizzled. The tattoo melted as the metal boiled and ran together into a solid disc, burning the flesh around its edges. He turned her head and did the same with the other side, filling the air with the smell of burnt flesh as he worked. When it was done, he turned the machine off and shoved the cover over her head. Quickly, he hid the box back inside his coat.

"Is everything okay back there? Smells like something's burning," Viktor said as he poked his head through the opening.

Jake jumped at the sound of Viktor's voice, but composed his features as his mind raced for an explanation. Standing up from his crouch, he headed to the doorway and pushed the big man back in as he slid into the other seat in the cockpit.

"Just a loose wire. I've already fixed it. What's our status?"

"All systems go," Viktor said as he settled back into his seat and slipped his arms through the shoulder harness, buckling it at his waist. "Ready when you are."

As he strapped himself in, Jake looked out the cockpit window to the bright walls of the shiftroom. "So, how does this work?"

"I don't know. It just does," Viktor said as he switched the engines on.

From behind the craft, the engines rumbled as they flared to life, filling the hangar with their high-pitched sound. Jake froze in his chair and searched the shiftroom through the glass shield, waiting for Lazarus to come charging in, but as the seconds passed, no one came, and he relaxed.

Grabbing the control yoke, Viktor eased the aircraft

off the floor with the skill learned from years of practice. Once in the air, he activated the stabilizers with a voice command so that the ship hovered in midair in the hanger.

"She's ready."

"Do your thing then," Jake said, clutching the straps at his chest in a death-grip.

Holding the ship steady, Viktor closed his eyes as he prepared for the shift. Jake waited as the agent gathered the information blocks stored in his mind of their destination, organizing them to send along the invisible connection to the interfacing engraved into the floor below, and then onto the mainframe. He hated not being in control, but Viktor was his only way to the future, and to the place he had picked for the dump.

It was by mistake that Viktor had let that bit of information leak out, not realizing that Jake had manipulated him to reveal the secret of Ardus, and how to get there. Jake smiled inside at how easy it had been to manipulate the big lug. He may be a genius with machines, but not when it came to people. From the beginning, Viktor had been ripe for the picking. Jake had no qualms about using him for his own purposes, disguising it as friendship when in fact he couldn't stand the man.

Viktor opened his eyes, and nodded to Jake, signaling he was ready. Jake nodded back. "Do it."

"Shift," Viktor said.

With engines running and wingtips out, they disappeared from the hangar.

PART TWO

———————————

ARDUS

Chapter Twelve

Ardus

Twenty-One Fifty-Three

Ardus sparkled like a round sapphire as it reflected the light from the medium size star in the center of its solar system. From afar the planet rotated in a lazy spin, peaceful and serene, a jewel shining in the black sea of space like a prized treasure. What made it a jewel was the blueness of the planet. No brown or green of any landmasses broke the tranquility of its surface. Only one substance dominated it.

Water.

Above the vast expanse of endless water, two satellite moons watched over the planet. Calo, the larger, dominated the northern skies while its brother, Laluma, sat meekly off in the southeast. Though thought of as the lesser, Laluma had great control over its brother, causing havoc with the weather patterns when their orbital paths brought them in alignment once a month. The two moons constantly were at war over Ardus, pulling tides this way and that, like two children fighting over the same toy. Not only did it cause currents to fluctuate from their normal courses by miles, it also produced massive upheavals in the weather.

Today though the moons were at peace and the sky was calm. A few cloud formations drifted in the planetary air like fluffy white balls of cotton. In the northern hemisphere, the clouds were heavier. As they blew across the great expanse of water they grew with moisture, and darkened, until the weight was too much and they released the storehouse of water back to the waters below in an endless cycle of life.

Into the upper region of the stratosphere of the planet popped a tiny winged shuttle. It bounced and shuttered as it hit the thin air. Inside the cockpit, Viktor held tightly to the control yoke, and pulled it to him as he engaged the engines, sending the ship forward at a thirty-degree angle down towards the planet while he fought to steady the ship.

"Thrusters to starboard," he commanded as he struggled with the controls. "Adjust port wing stabilizers by eight degrees south."

Out his window Jake watched the thrusters flare to life in the dark sky of the stratosphere as they worked to push the wing up into balance, while the other wing compensated for the shift by swooping down. His stomached flip-flopped at the motion. Gripping the armrests, he held his throat closed against the rising bile that crept up from his stomach. Finally the swaying stopped as Viktor gained control, and leveled the shuttle. With the wings steady, he started their descent to the planet's surface.

"Cut thrusters and hold position," Viktor commanded.

From the side panel, he took out a headphone, and clipped it to his ear, and flicked a lever on the switch panel above his head, turning on the receiver before settling more comfortably in his seat.

Once they were flying level, Jake pushed against the restraints of his harness to get a good look at the planet that Viktor had whispered about. His eyes widened in awe at his first glimpse of outer space and the blue jewel under his feet, but he didn't look for long, for the mission came first. Time was not a luxury on this trip. Pushing his curiosity aside, he sat back into his seat and got down to business.

"Bring us down close to the surface," he said, eyeing the watery depths below.

"Entering the troposphere now," Viktor said as the sky lightened around them, "heading southeast towards the equator. Still no signals from any watercrafts. Do you have the coordinates for the rendezvous point? I could really use them now."

"Get below the clouds first."

Viktor frowned, but didn't say anything more. Instead, he pressed his lips together and stared out the forward window as he prepared to enter the thick cloud below them. Adjusting the angle of the ship, he pressed the yoke towards the control panel and eased them down into the clouds. The pale blue sky turned into a mass of fine mist too thick to see through as the cloud engulfed the aircraft.

Jake watched it pass by and gather on his window as they descended, happy for the silence that had fallen over the cockpit. Keeping Viktor in the dark was more difficult than he thought it would've been, and the worst bit was yet to come. He needed the reprieve to plan his next move, but as soon as they broke out of the cloud, Viktor was back at it.

"You do realize that the Federation has made Ardus a natural reserve, and has declared it off-limits. We could get into deep trouble if we're caught anywhere near here."

Jake gnashed his teeth together and suppressed a growl as he kept his gaze focused on the approaching surface, and said, "We won't be here long enough for anyone to notice, so stop worrying."

"Fine. But, if you're looking for any dry land, you won't find it here, only miles and miles of the wet stuff. That's all. Watercrafts are only allowed by special permits. And their whereabouts are strictly monitored." Viktor glanced down at one of the screens. "The radar is showing nothing below us. I'll need the coordinates for the rendezvous point."

Jake stared at his reflection in the side window and smiled a secret smile. "Bring the shuttle down to twelve feet above the waves, and hover there."

"But there's no-one down there, unless they're cloaked, which doesn't make sense." The harness strained around the big blond giant as he leaned over to look out his window for a ship.

A deep sigh escaped from Jake. "There is... no... rendezvous point, okay? We were to remove the target from her timeline, and make her disappear. That's it."

"But it will kill her if we leave her here! I can't see Maitland agreeing to this. It goes against all that we stand for. Doesn't feel right."

"Shut up, and just do it! Maitland knows about the mission," he lied, "otherwise, how could I have gotten the file. These are the orders, and that should be enough."

Jake glared at Viktor as they locked eyes in a battle of wills. After a heated moment of silence, it was Viktor who gave in first. With his lips pressed tight together and his brow furrowed with suppressed anger, he broke away to glare out the window as he obeyed the plan of the mission. Carefully he maneuvered the ship closer to the churning surface, drawing it level above the waves as Jake had instructed.

"Good man," Jake said, slapping Viktor's shoulder as he threw off his harness and slipped past him through the narrow opening to the cargo bay.

Wasting no time, Jake punched in the code to the hatch door, and stood aside as it slid into the wall. Through the open door a warm breeze blew in from under the wing, and filled the cargo bay with the scent of salt and warm water, washing away the remnants of burnt flesh that lingered in the compartment. The fresh air blew over him, whipping his short soft-brown hair around his head. His long coat flapped behind him as he clutched the edge of the door to look down at the waves below.

Perfect, he thought with a slap of his hand against

the side of the shuttle.

He left the spot and went over to the woman, and dragged her across the metal floor to the edge of the opening.

"If you want it done right, you have to do it yourself," he said as he shoved her limp body parallel with the doorway.

Kneeling down next to her, he stared at the cloth that covered her head. Not a flicker of emotion crossed his face, for his heart had turned cold years ago. Whatever good had come his way had been overshadowed by her needs. Her sweet nature. Her goodness. Always doing for others. Blah blah blah. It sickened him. It had made his life miserable. Yes, it was all her fault. He had to be free. It was the only way. She had to go. That was all he could think about. He put his hands on her body and rolled her out without another thought, and watched her drop to the water. The body hit the surface with a splash, and sank underneath the next wave.

"Bye, bye, Sharra," he said as she disappeared under the water.

Slapping the control panel, he shut the hatch, watching the spot in the water until the door blocked his view.

"Get us out of here" he said to Viktor as he climbed into his seat and buckled up.

Face as hard as granite Viktor rammed the controls to his chest, forcing them back into their seats as they climbed above the clouds to the upper atmosphere in a matter of seconds. Jake held on for dear life as the pressure battered his chest and pulled at his face, making it hard to breathe. With a mad jerk against the throttle, they leveled out in the dark upper layer. Viktor said nothing as he initiated the thrusters and set the stabilizers to hover the craft. Jake held onto his stomach, ready to give the big agent a tongue lashing, but Viktor showed no mercy. Giving Jake no time to recuperate from the quick ascent, Viktor prepared for the shift. Without any warning, he gave the command, and the shuttle disappeared out of the sky.

Chapter Thirteen

The slap of her body hitting the water woke Sharra instantly. In a flash, the water engulfed her as she sank below the surface. It surged through the black cloth of the sack covering her head, knocking the drug-induced cobwebs from her mind as quick as a slap to the face. She shut her lips and held her breath, not thinking about where she was, or how she'd gotten there, only thinking about the nightmare around her and her next breath of air and where it was going to come from. Arms and legs flailing, she kicked out in fear, losing one shoe, and then the next. Her legs tangled in her skirt. Panic set in. She struggled to see through the sack without understanding what was in the way. Finally she reached up and ripped it off, and got her first glimpse of the watery nightmare that she was unceremoniously dumped into.

Blue water sparkled around her as the rays of the

sun filtered down through the water to where she ended up somewhere underneath. The black sack floated nearby like a strange fish. It caught the attention of some tiny fishlike creatures as they swam closer to inspect the foreign object. But she hardly noticed, for her lungs burned with a great need. Finding the surface was all she could think about, and air, glorious air. She blinked through the burning salt of the water, searching for a lighter shade of blue that would indicate the right direction to swim in, knowing that if she chose the wrong way that it would mean her death.

There it was. A shimmer of a sunbeam broke through the water overhead. With all the strength she could muster, she kicked towards it in desperation. With a whoosh of water, she broke through the surface and into the air. A great gasp filled her mouth as she gulped in the air into her starving lungs, again and again, until the immediate fear of drowning left her.

The sea rolled in gentle swells as the sun disappeared behind a huge white cloud. The sound of an engine came from close by. A light warm breeze blew across Sharra as she treaded in the waves choking and sputtering through her hair to see it. Right above her, a shuttle roared to life as it angled up and away. Soon it was in the first layer of clouds. The blue-white engines flared hot as it sped up. She pushed the strands of wet hair out of the way and treaded harder to raise her body further out, and waved her hands above her head as she tried to get their attention.

"Hey! I'm here! Help! Help!" she yelled.

Although the shuttle soon reappeared on the other side of the clouds, it did not turn around. Instead, it continued on its upward climb, getting smaller and smaller as she watched, until it winked out from sight.

She sank back into the water numb with shock. It was only when her body started to shiver that reason set in.

"Stupid," she said to herself. "I can shift."

The blocks to the Vault chamber were quickly assembled in her mind. Closing her eyes, she pictured the white walls of the shiftroom as she pushed the blocks to the agrylium in her head. But the blocks didn't move. Like a small pyramid they remained stacked where she had gathered them.

She tried again, and still they didn't budge.

It was then that her mind registered the pain behind her ears. She touched the agrylium tattoos expecting to find the familiar silver pattern underneath her fingers, but they were no longer there. Her breath hitched as she searched the outline of raised skin, hoping beyond hope that her fingers were lying to her, but all that was left were two smooth round coins of metal. She lowered her hands back into the water in despair.

"No. It can't be. It just can't be."

The warm waves rolled around her as she bobbed in the water, and fought down the panic that swelled up in her chest and gathered in her throat. With her mode of transportation to safety taken away, she was on her own. There wasn't going to be a rescue this time. Whoever did this had made sure of that. She was dumped there for a purpose and that was to die. No Tanner, no Lazarus, and no Vault to save her, just her and the endless sea.

"Get a grip on yourself, and think," she told herself. "You can beat this. There has to be land somewhere out there."

On the crest of the next wave, she spun around and searched the horizon for any signs of land. All that greeted her eyes was an ocean of endless blue, blue sky and blue water. Not one smudge of a landmass of any sort marked the horizon. Her options were limited.

"Follow the current, and hope it brings me close to land, or lay down and give up to the sea."

The breeze carried her voice away, leaving her empty. It was the sea that decided for her. It tugged at her, pulling her along on a gentle current of warm water, giving her the encouragement to go on. Besides, giving up was not in her genes.

With a growl, she undid her long skirt, and tied it around her waist. Next came off her stockings. She tucked them into the belt of her skirt, freeing up her legs for the swim ahead. Marking her position with the slant of the sun, she began to swim, stroke after stroke, her movements fluid from years of practice as the current propelled her along to an unknown destination.

The sun traveled across the sky as the day wore on and yet she continued to swim, resting now and then on her back before flipping over to carry on, not caring to think about what might be lurking underneath her in the deep, or of the coming night. Finally her arms gave out. She turned onto her back for the last time, and let her waterlogged body float free upon the quieting waves as she breathed deep to feed her starving muscles. As she floated the waves vanished and the sea turned to glass, giving her a much-needed reprise. She licked her lips, thirsty for water, and tasted the ever-present salt that burned in the cracks that had formed there. With the stillness of the sea came the thoughts she had pushed aside while she swam. Now, though, there was nothing to hinder them.

She had thought her troubles were over with the death of J.D. Dash. Now it looked like he was just a henchman, doing someone else's dirty work. He had almost succeeded, too, before he had been caught.

She touched the swelling on her jaw, and felt the soreness deep inside. Whoever it had been that had hit her had meant to hurt her. No, it was worse than that. He wanted her dead. Why else would he have dumped her in the sea without remorse. She tried to remember the face that had hovered above hers for that hazy moment when the drug had worn off enough for her to regain consciousness. On a blank page in her mind she drew the set of his jaw, the curve of his lips, the familiar color of his eyes, until it formed into a face she knew all too well, as if it were her own... for in some ways it was.

"Greyson," she gasped in disbelief. Tears came unbidden to her eyes as memories of her brother flashed up in her mind. "Why? What have I done to deserve this?"

The tears slipped out and ran down the side of her face to mingle with the sea. She had always known that he didn't love her, but this was beyond imagining. To be betrayed by family, the last of her family...

Deep in her chest her heart weighed heavy with hurt, and she cried for the loss. If it weren't for her new friends at Vault Agency she would be truly alone in the world. Even now she doubted she would see them or the Vault again.

The Vault!

Her mind spun with another kind of fear.

How could she have forgotten so quickly the secret she held in her head in the form of a tiny ball of energy, alien energy. Did Greyson know about it, too? Was that why he wanted her dead? She wiped her tears away, and tried to think.

Something wasn't right.

Lazarus had never mentioned that her brother had joined the Agency. He must have known that someday they were bound to run into each other. There weren't that many agents working there. So, why keep it a secret? She could've told them from the beginning that Greyson was nothing but trouble.

It didn't make sense. Lazarus was smarter than that. And yet, now that she had seen Greyson, there was no doubt in her mind that he was the one stirring up the discord thru-out the Vault. She didn't have a clue why. She must tell Lazarus.

They needed to be warned, she thought.

But how could she when she was left for dead, floating who knows where, and still with no land in sight.

On the horizon the clouds turned pink, then to purple, and on to deep midnight blue as the sun swung low and dipped out of sight beyond the water's edge. One by one the stars began to wink alive as the light faded from the sky, and the night heavens took over. Soon a thousand stars filled the dark canopy above her head. A half-moon lifted slowly above the edge of the water to reflect like a nightlight over the calm sea.

Exhausted beyond measure, she watched the moon slowly rise into the night sky, and came to terms with her life, of the regrets and lost opportunities, of lost loves and life, knowing that there would be no tomorrow for her. Her hope dwindled away along with the last of her strength, and she closed her eyes.

"I'm so sorry, Tanner," she whispered through her cracked lips, sad for the wasted chance to be loved. "Take care of Amadeus for me, and maybe, once in a while, think of me when you pet him."

Underneath her the water stirred, but she had no strength left to fight whatever creature was swimming there. In fact, she welcomed a quick death. Exhausted she gave up and let her body sink below the water, and waited for the teeth to rip into her flesh. Yet the bite never came. Instead, she hit a shelf of soft flesh like a smooth sheet of rubber. It caught her and lifted her up out of the water into the warm night air, and held her suspended upon a blanket of heat. She didn't know why and didn't care. From deep within its body vibrated two loud honks as if it were calling out to someone. It did it again and again. After a while, she stopped noticing it. Cushioned by its slick body, she gave into the exhaustion, and slept.

The dawn came, and with it the stirring of the sea. She awoke with the rolling of her makeshift bed as the sea creature shifted upon the returning waves. Underneath her head her pillow vibrated as it emitted its honks, waking her from a nightmarish dream of endless sea and thirst. The early morning sun touched her damaged skin, rekindling the heat from the sunburn from the day before, reminding her of where she was. Her thirst grew with a vengeance as her body craved the much-needed water. She licked her lips at the thought, but her swollen tongue was as dry as a desert, and she soon gave up. A light breeze tugged at her dried hair and tickled her face like an annoying fly. She swatted at it, her hand heavy on her face as she pushed the hair away, and opened her eyes to the morning sky and the sound of moving water.

With a groan she rolled onto her side, and sat up using an arm to hold her weakened body steady. The weight of her body pressed onto her hand, sinking it into the charcoal flesh of the sea creature she had slept on. It didn't seem to mind, and she was too disorientated to care. The creature floated on the waves like a large piece of carpet, thick and sleek. Large flaps of skin were extended out like wings. They were stretched taunt, holding her weight out of the water as its wingtips bent stiff to the sky.

The wind swept her tangled hair around her neck as she moved to her knees and searched the sea around them, hoping for land, but the horizon remained untouched. Nothing had changed from yesterday. She sank back down onto the cushion of flesh, at a loss of what to do. Her stomach grumbled. She pressed her fist to it, to ease the pain, and tried to remember the last time she had eaten.

"It must have been before Pompeii," she whispered, "a lifetime ago."

Below her the creature honked again, and stirred, its muscles rippling under her legs. She hunkered down in the center, and held her breath. It was probably as hungry as she was, having sat all night on the surface of the water holding her up. And now she sat like a tasty snack, helpless to do anything about it. Images of large teeth and separated limbs filled her mind. Drowning was looking better all the time.

While she was contemplating becoming the creatures breakfast, a presence slipped into her mind, foreign, yet slightly familiar.

Holy Sea Mother of us all, it said.

A flash of red colored the exclamation, and then it was gone.

What is it, Nayada? Another one said, orange with curiosity.

A landwalker, the first one said. *Female by her aura.*

"Hello? Who's there?" Sharra said as she whipped around, searching for the sources of the voices in her head.

Did she hear us? How is that possible?

Floating in the water at the edge of the sea creature were four sets of eyes. They stared up at her from identical oblong faces. On the back of their heads, the delicate webbing of their dorsal fin flicked partially open in alarm. She had seen that fin and face before, on Araylai. She rubbed her eyes and blinked to clear her vision as she tried to bring the four into one being, but it didn't work.

"Araylai?" She had to ask, not knowing if her eyes were telling the truth or if the lack of water was finally screwing with her brain.

The dorsal fin of the one in front unfurled like a sail as the long spine above her forehead stiffened in surprise. Eyes so like Araylai's stared back at her for a second more, and then the alien sank back into the water, followed one by one by her comrades until Sharra was left alone in the morning breeze.

"Wait!" she cried out, as she scurried as close to the edge, and watched as the last one disappeared underneath the waves.

———

Hidden below the white underbelly of the bladderbird, Nayada tucked the blue worry of her thoughts away with tight control, covering it with the orange shade of command, and waited for her Umbra scouts to join her. They floated down and took their positions in order of rank in front of her. Their minds whirled with different shades of curiosity as they waited in deference for their captain to speak.

Calyx, her Right Pectoral and closest friend drifted closer to her side and sent her a silent message, *be careful*, before propelling back to join the two male scouts.

Nayada didn't need the warning, knowing full well that what sat above in the open air was going to cause them trouble no matter what decision she made. Either way, Caetus, her guardian and mentor who waited at the outpost for news, would not be pleased, for it meant attention from their Queen, and that was something they both didn't want. No one did.

Opening a wide channel she linked their minds together in the common space between them, and spoke.

This was not what any of us had expected when Loch heard the distress call of the bladderbird, she said, waving a webbed hand at the underbelly of the sea creature. *By the way, good ears, Loch. Twenty miles. That must be a record. I will add it to my report.*

The blue rings surrounding the yellow eyes of the tall male flashed bright at the praise as a smile stretched his firm lips.

Thank you, Pod Leader. I am Arderie, and my only aim is to serve with honor and humility.

Quit sucking up, Loch, Cael said, the male on her left. *We are all Arderie. Anyway, it is a known fact that your senses are better than ours. No need to rub it in.*

As Caudal to this pod, it is my duty to be better than you, Loch said. *Or would you like to exchange positions? I would be happy to be Left Pectoral and let you take over the tail.*

No thanks. I like my fins, Cael said with a twitch of his lips.

Bulls, Calyx ordered, her mind tinged with streaks of red annoyance. *You are wasting Nayada's time with your male preening. You should be more concerned with what a landwalker is doing in the open water.*

Calyx and Cael turned as one, eye rings flashing bright in the water as they waited for their leader to answer, but it was Loch who spoke first.

If I may, he said to Nayada, who then motioned permission with a wave of her hand. *I think the bigger question is how does the landwalker know of Araylai, the Queen's daughter?*

Sssss, Calyx hissed blowing bubbles as she grasped the bone handle of the dagger strapped to her outer thigh. *Do not utter that name. The Queen_*

We are deep in the open waters, who is to hear it? The waves? Loch said.

The sea has long ears, even this far from the reef. You of all people should be careful, Cael said.

Loch's aura flared brown with anger at the reminder, but held himself in check, his voice in stark contrast to the obvious color of his mind.

I am well aware of the treacherous nature of the court. I need no reminder. But this is big and you know it. The landwalker not only heard our link, but also knows of the Queen's daughter. We need to ask how this is possible.

Loch is right, Nayada said, breaking into their thoughts. *These questions need to be answered. It could be important to the investigation.*

What are we to do with her? The bladder bird can only last so long on the surface before it will tire out. She will die if we do not help, Cael said.

She will just bring us trouble for sure, Calyx said. *I say let the sea claim her, and be done with it.*

No, Nayada said, keeping her aura in check. Yet her crest flicked in agitation, giving her away. *The Queen's daughter has been missing for over a year and a half. This is the first news we have had in a long time. We cannot brush this off so easily. The creature might be able to tell us something. We need proof that Ara... that she is innocent, and not the traitor the Queen has decreed.*

Landwalkers are nothing but lying treacherous creatures, Loch said. *How do we know that this one is no different?*

It is a chance we have to take. Anyway, she cannot stay forever on the bladderbird.

But she is an air-dweller, Calyx said. *They are forbidden to enter the water, let alone the city.*

Subdue your thoughts, you two, Nayada said to the

scouts. *Where has your training gone? Your auras give you away. You must control it if you want to remain in my pod. As for the landwalker, I am the lead Umbra of this pod, and I will decide her fate. Loch, speak to the bladderbird and prepare it to take in the landwalker, while I take Calyx and Cael up to meet our guest.*

Loch gave her a nod and went to the front of the huge beast as Nayada led the rest of her team to the surface. Without a sound, they broke through the waves and swam to the fat end of the wing of the bladderbird, and rested their webbed-hands on the edge. In the open air, the female landwalker huddled half-naked in a ball in the center of the bladderbird, with her arms wrapped around her knees and her head bent low. The brownish-red silk strings that covered her head blew around in the breeze, hiding her alien face from them.

How do we get her attention? Calyx asked in the silent link between them.

I think that did it, Cael said as a pair of strange hazel eyes whipped around to stare at them.

"Please, don't leave me," the landwalker said out loud as she scooted over the rubbery hide to where they bobbed in the water. "I need your help."

"What are you doing here on Ardus?" Nayada said speaking the words out loud in her bell-like voice.

"Ardus? Is that where I am?" the female creature said, sinking back down onto her knees with a thunk. The landwalker turned pale under the pink of her flesh as she stared out over the water. "Then there is no land…"

"You do not belong here," Cael said.

The landwalker's strange eyes turned from the sea to look at him. "Believe me, I know. I'm tired, and thirsty, and want to go home, but I can't. Araylai_"

"Sssss, silence, landwalker" Nayada commanded her with a wave of her webbed hand. "Answer my question. Why are you here?"

"I don't know what I'm doing on your world, or how I even got here. All I know is that whoever dumped me into the water wants me dead," she said.

She tells the truth. The color of her thoughts cannot lie, Calyx said through their link. *There is no harm or hidden deceit in her aura.*

Then, we shall proceed, Nayada said in the link to her team. To the landwalker she said, "What is your name?"

"Sharra."

"I am Nayada, Umbra of the Arderie, keeper of this water. I hear your plea, and so act on your behalf. My honor is now bound with yours. Do not defile what I freely give."

"Thank you."

"Do not thank me yet. It may be a kinder fate to leave you on the surface," Nayada said.

As she spoke, she thumped the beast with her fist and pushed off, and led her guards a safe distance away as the bladderbird sank underneath the waves, leaving the landwalker treading water. Down swam the great beast, moving farther and farther away as it spread its wings in glorious freedom. Gracefully it turned on a wingtip and headed back to where they waited, building speed as its wide wings beat the water. Faster and faster it came, until it burst through the waves and cleared the surface close to the alien female. Once in the air, it's cavernous mouth opened and billowed out, filling with air like a balloon as it twisted its body in a graceful arch and fell back to the water with a crash, swallowing the landwalker whole.

Chapter Fourteen

The Vault

"What do you mean she's missing?"

Lazarus shot out of his chair, and shut the door behind Faolan, who had rushed into his office, forgetting all about stealth and secrecy in his mad dash through the door with the news.

"Taken. She's been taken," Faolan said, his Scottish brogue thickening with worry. "I'm telling you, Lazarus, it's like she's been wiped off the face of the earth. Her tag just stopped transmitting."

"How long ago? No, never mind. It's irrelevant," Lazarus said.

"I've lost her," Faolan said, rubbing his face between his hands.

"Damn it! I sent you out there to keep tabs on her."

"I know, I know. Do you think I'm happy about it? Believe me, it's eating me alive."

"Sit down, Faolan. I need you to focus," Lazarus said. At his desk, he pulled up the mission records with a flick of his wrist, and scrolled down until he came to Sharra's name. "It looks like Pompeii was her last mission. That was two days ago."

"I was there at the blasted infernal. Hot as hell. Fortunately, Sharra and Tony didn't stay long."

"That's the last of the recorded shifts."

"Not according to the tag receiver."

"What do you mean?"

"Look here." Faolan pulled out a small electronic device from his pocket and passed it over. "Chicago USA nineteen ninety-six. You can read it for yourself."

Lazarus read the information on the receiver with alarm. "That's her original timeline. What was she doing there, and in that part of the city?"

"I don't know, but by the time I caught up with her, she was gone. No reading from the tag. No nothing. It's like she just vanished."

Lazarus handed the tagfinder back, and looked at his friend, understanding the deep worry lines on his face at the implications. "She should have shifted back by now."

"That's what gets me worried," Faolan said. "If she was there, here, or anywhere on earth, the tag would have registered."

"Are you sure she was taken?"

Faolan's eyes flashed. "I'm sure of it. Did some door knocking at the last place the tag registered. Unsavory neighborhood. No one wanted to open their door to me. Almost gave up until I finally got an old woman to talk. Told her I was looking for my sister. She took me to her window, and pointed to a burnt support pillar across the way, and said she saw a woman staring at it and thought it was odd, a white woman, alone and unprotected in the neighborhood. And then she told me she saw the woman faint, and two white men go over, pick her up, and take her away."

"Any descriptions of the men?"

"Too far away for her old eyes, just that they were white folk, one large, like a bull, and one like a cigarette. Those were her words."

"I guess that's better than nothing," Lazarus said. "Two men this time. And we can't track her. They must have found the tag, and destroyed it, or…" He couldn't continue. If they had killed her… no, he wasn't going to think that.

"I'm not giving up on her, Lazarus. I can't explain it, but my gut tells me she's still alive."

Lazarus rubbed his goatee as he struggled with the new complication, hiding his frown behind his hand. It didn't make any sense. He couldn't understand why the Vault would recruit someone of alleged great value, only for her to die at the hands of one of their own. There had to be more to it. He was missing something.

"We need more information," he said, speaking his thoughts out loud.

"I agree, but from where? Here?" Faolan said. "You know I'm taking a risk each time I come. There's no way I can investigate inside the Vault without being caught."

"I'm not asking you to expose your cover. I need

you on the outside. No, I have someone else in mind for the job." Lazarus activated the Link behind his ear with a thought and spoke into the thin wire next to his chin. "Tanner, I'd like to see you in my office."

As clear as if he was standing there, Tanner's voice rang in his ear, "Right now? I'm kind of in the middle of something."

"Yes. Now."

"Yes, sir. Be right there."

Lazarus broke the connection and turned back to Faolan who stared at him with eyebrows raised.

"Are you sure that's wise?" Faolan asked.

"Tanner has had more contact with Sharra than anyone else. He may know something that we don't, plus he's well liked among the agents. We can use that."

"What about my cover?"

"We'll deal with that when the time comes."

A few minutes later came a knock on the door. Lazarus pointed to the far wall and gestured for Faolan to move out of sight.

"Enter," he called out.

Faolan ducked behind the door and flattened his body against the wall, just as it swung open on the heels of the trainer.

"That was quick," Lazarus said as Tanner stepped up to the desk out of breath.

"It sounded important. What's up?"

Lazarus hesitated as he studied the ex-military man, unsure if it was a wise choice to include him or not. He had become too good at reading people, and it was times like this that it got in the way. Even though Tanner tried to keep his feelings for Sharra hidden, the signs were there, if one looked hard enough. Yet, it was that emotional connection with her that they needed, for at this point, that's all they had.

"When was the last time you saw Sharra?" Lazarus said.

"Couple of days ago. Why? Is she in trouble again?"

Behind them Faolan shut the door with a soft click, but it was enough for Tanner to hear. He whipped around, and came face to face with the man he hadn't seen in years.

"Faolan," he said in surprise, and then his eyes narrowed in suspicion as he turned back to Lazarus. "What's he doing here?"

"Hello, Tanner," Faolan said as he sauntered over to the desk and sat on the edge. Folding his arms across his chest, he smiled. "Nice to see you, too."

Tanner glared at him through narrowed eyelids. "Right," he said before turning to the Head Director. "Lazarus? You care to explain?"

"Faolan has been working for me undercover, someone off the radar to watch over Sharra."

"Watch over her…" Tanner said, repeating the words. "I thought we took care of it with Dash."

"There has been a… complication," Faolan said, and stopped.

"Well?" Tanner asked, looking from one to the other as he waited for an answer. "What is it?"

Finally Lazarus spoke, "Sharra is missing."

"What do you mean, she's missing?" Tanner said, echoing Lazarus's earlier words.

"Keep your voice down," Lazarus said. "Dash was

only a puppet. Someone else was behind Sharra's attacks, using Dash as his front man. And with Dash dead, we knew that it was only a matter of time before he struck again. That's why I had Faolan keep an eye on her, just in case they made another move."

"If she's missing, why hasn't she shifted back yet?" Tanner said, asking the obvious. He looked back and forth between the two men, waiting for an answer, but none came. And then it sunk in. "Are you saying she's_?"

"No!" Faolan shot out.

"Relax, Tanner," Lazarus said. "We still have time. That's why you're here. We need to find out where she is."

"Why wasn't I informed about this from the beginning? I could have made excuses to stay close to her and guard her."

"You would've been too obvious," Faolan said.

"Like you did a good job," Tanner growled back.

Faolan stood up at the challenge, his eyes blazing with anger. They glared at each other, eyes locked in battle like two elks in rut. Neither one was willing to back down as the testosterone built in their blood. Between them flared an unspoken challenge of possession, as jaws clenched and fists tightened, until the air was thick with pent up tension.

"That's enough, you two," Lazarus said. "Your behavior isn't helping Sharra one bit, and we have work to do. So get it together."

The truth of his statement reached their ears at the same time, but it was Tanner who broke away first to turn back to Lazarus, and ask, "What can I do?"

Faolan relaxed back onto the desk and folded his arms, though he kept one eye on the trainer as he waited for Lazarus to speak.

"All we have right now is a vague description of the men involved. One described as a bull, the other as thin, like a cigarette. Both Caucasian. It's not much, but we can use that as a start."

As he spoke, he fiddled with the screen of his monitor until he found what he was looking for, and opened the file. He gestured the two men over to have a look. On the screen was a list of all the agents registered with the Vault, each with a photo next to their name. They started from the top, picture-by-picture, male and female alike, and searched for any similarities among the forty or more agents using the vague description of the two men as a guideline. Before they knew it they had accumulated a small list of potential suspects.

"That's the last of us," Lazarus said as he closed the program, and sent the list of suspects to their personal Com-Links. "Tanner, you're well-liked among our crew. I want you to use that, and see what you can pick up: any odd behavior, talk, boasts, and the like, concentrating on the agents on the list for starters, and working out from there. If you tell them you've been grounded, then that'll give you a reason to be around. You'll need to come up with an excuse as to why, though."

"That should be easy enough. What about him?" Tanner said, pointing a thumb back at Faolan.

"I'll go back to Chicago, and see if I can charm anything else out of the locals that will be useful," Faolan said.

"And the Committee?" Tanner asked.

Lazarus stood, and walked Tanner to the door. "No need to involve them yet. We don't want any of this getting out, so the less they know, the better. When the time comes, I will inform them. And that goes with Faolan's involvement, too. Not a word from you, Tanner. I'm trusting you with this."

"I may not like it, or understand it, but you're my friend, and I trust you," Tanner said, ignoring the smile on Faolan's face as he walked with Lazarus to the door.

"Thank you," Lazarus said as he rested a hand on the taller man's shoulder. "Keep me posted. Good hunting."

The door shut, leaving the two alone again. Faolan stood up and prepared to leave. "I hope you haven't jeopardized my position."

"He'll keep quiet."

"Let's hope so."

With those final words, Faolan slipped out the door and disappeared down the hallway, leaving Lazarus to shut the door behind him. Alone in his office, Lazarus slumped against the door and shut his eyes. His mind felt heavy with this new burden. He had hoped with Faolan's help he could have kept Sharra safe, but even his best tracker had been caught out. Now things were worse than before, and he wasn't so sure if any of their efforts would make a difference.

Right now, he didn't need this complication. Morale was already at an all time low.

He prayed that Tanner came up with something, and quick.

He needed a drink.

Chapter Fifteen

One day turned into two, and still no word from Faolan or Tanner to ease his mind. Lazarus picked up another disk from the dwindling pile and slipped it into the slot in his desk. A fresh icon appeared on the screen of his monitor. With a sigh he touched it and braced himself for the next complaint in the never-ending clutter of personal discs that ended up on his desk. The words spilled out of the page, angry and agitated, no different than the others in the read stack off to the side. Who it came from was inconsequential, for the gist of the message remained the same- discontent. And that spelled disaster for such a small community as theirs.

No longer was it just one or two agents, like Tony and Zoe. That he could handle. No, the list of grievances was only getting worse with each passing day. It was as if it was in the air, and spread with each breath they took. He didn't want to admit it, but he could feel it too.

And now this thing with Sharra. It didn't help matters. He had hoped to have news by now.

He pushed the stack of discs away, and went over to the bottle of whisky and poured himself a drink. In one quick gulp he drained the liquid, before pouring another shot into the glass and downed it with the other. His eyes stared at the painting of the Maitland Manor hanging on the wall, not really seeing anything at all.

A knock sounded on the door, bringing him back into the room. It could have been seconds, or minutes that he was gone, he didn't know. All he knew was that he was grateful for the interruption.

"Come in," he said, setting the empty glass down with a last look of longing before turning to see Tanner walk in with a frown on his face.

"What's going on?" Tanner said. "It's turned into a ghost town in the Vault. What's the use of being grounded if no one is around to get chummy with?"

"Nothing yet?" Lazarus said. "It's been two days… wait." He held up his hand, stopping the response that was ready to fall from Tanner's lips. "I've got Katherine coming in on the Link."

His gaze turned inward as he activated the Link and listened to his daughter for a few seconds before directing her to his office. At the end of the conversation his focus reverted back to the room, and to Tanner. The light dimmed in his grey eyes as he struggled to control his features.

"Trouble?" Tanner said.

"More of the same," Lazarus said, sighing as he sat down. "I had hoped that Katherine would have more sense than the rest."

"She's only human, no matter what you'd like to think. Do you want me to go?"

"No. Just make yourself small while I deal with this," Lazarus said, gesturing to the couch.

"You want me to look small," Tanner said with a snort as he settled into the corner of the couch as best as his muscular frame would let him.

They didn't have long to wait, for soon after, Katie burst in towing a reluctant Viktor behind her. Her tiny hand pulled the giant along with a gentle force as she drew him to the desk. Lazarus watched with hidden amusement at the antics of his daughter. Why she had taken it upon herself to be the advocate of the big man, he couldn't guess. Unafraid of his size and strength, she managed him like a mother hen managed a brood of chicks. Her sweet nature was enough to calm the wildest of beasts. Though Viktor was larger than anyone else at the Vault, he was no beast, but as gentle a giant as there ever was.

She let go of him, and turned him to face Lazarus with gentle hands, leaving them on the bulge of his bicep as she stood by his side.

"Viktor has something he wants to tell you, Father," she said, before turning back to look up into Viktor's worried face. "It's okay. I'm right here. You can tell him."

In front of him, Viktor stood with eyes lowered. His hands were grasped together tight at his belly, knuckles white. Worry lines creased his broad forehead, as he stood silent beside Katie, the words locked behind the fear in his eyes. She squeezed his arm encouragingly, but still he struggled to speak.

Losing patience, Lazarus said, "Viktor? You have something you wanted to say?"

"Yes, Sir," Viktor said in a small voice as he looked down at Katie. She gave him a nod, and another squeeze of her hand. He cleared his throat, and directed his gaze over the desk to the Head Director. "I think I may have helped kill someone. A woman."

Ears perked at the quiet admission. Tanner jerked up from the corner of the couch and came to stand beside the desk, his eyes blazing with unspoken anger. Lazarus understood the emotions for it struck a nerve of unease in his own heart. He shook his head at Tanner, and frowned, sending him a clear message. He didn't need the trainer jumping in and scaring Viktor, for they needed to keep him talking.

"Go on. A woman, you were saying?"

Encouraged by the calm voice of the Head Director, Viktor continued to explain. "Yes. She was drugged. I never got to see her face, though. It felt wrong at the time, but my partner, Jake, said it was all part of the terms of the mission. So I didn't question it any further."

"Jake? Jake who? And when does an agent not know his target?" Tanner asked, disgusted.

"That's what I kept telling myself," Viktor said, his face full of animation as the words spilled out, "but Jake, you know, Jacob Byson, he seemed to know what he was doing. So I went along with it. Yet after we were back, I kept thinking about it, how Jake was acting all odd like from the beginning: keeping me in the dark, ordering me around like I'm an idiot... not knowing the target. It didn't sit right. So, Katie here convinced me I'd feel better if I talked to you about it, to see if you could check back on the mission file for me. Sir, it'd ease my mind if you would."

After the last request came out, he stopped and waited, breathing heavy from the exertion of the speech as he looked anxiously at the Head Director.

In the quiet that followed, Tanner said, "Jacob Byson, you said. I don't recognize that name."

"Neither do I," Lazarus said as he typed Jacob Byson into the Vault data system. "There aren't that many agents to forget a name."

The screen remained black. He tried again, and still the system spit out no stats. As the seconds sped by and the page remained empty, his alarm grew. The Vault data system couldn't lie. Either the information had been erased, or the man didn't exist. Both cases were alarming. He was missing something, and that was not like him.

"Can you describe him for me?" he said to Victor.

"About six feet tall, thin, brown hair, hazel eyes, American. He talks about you all the time. I figured you two had to be close."

"And you say he's an agent... here... at the Vault," Lazarus said.

"Yes, I'm sure of it. I worked with him in the field a few times now."

"He can shift."

"Uh-huh. Has the agrylium mark behind his ear. I've seen it."

Lazarus turned to Katie and asked, "Do you know him?"

She shook her head, shrugging her shoulders.

He looked up at Tanner who was hovering beside him and in an undertone said, "This Jacob Byson is not in the system. No stats, no recorded mission notes, no nothing. It's as if he doesn't exist. Yet, I believe Viktor is telling us the truth. I don't know how it's possible that we have an agent we don't know about, but I'm going to find out. But first, does Viktor's description of our mystery agent remind you of anyone? Thin, like a cigarette?"

"The man from Chicago. Hey, Viktor, did this mission that has you all worried happen to take you to Chicago nineteen ninety-six?"

"Yes. How did you know?"

Tanner leaned down to Lazarus and said with a nod in Viktor's direction, "One man large like a bull, wasn't that the other description?"

Lazarus frowned. "Viktor, what happened to the woman?"

Viktor wrung his hands together as he said, "I'm not really sure. After Jake shot her with a dart, we shifted to the hangar with her. He said the mission specs were to remove the target. So, we dumped her body into a sea far far away from here."

"You what?!" Tanner exploded.

"We dumped her…"

Tanner squeezed his hands into tight fists as he glared at Viktor. "You dumped her unconscious into water? She'll drown. You bastard, you killed her," he ground out through his clenched teeth.

"I know. That's what I can't get out of my head."

"No. You don't understand. You killed one of our own," he growled.

"I did? No. No," he groaned. "I knew something was wrong. I knew it. Who? Who did I kill?" Viktor said, holding his hands up in protest.

"Sharra Lane, damn you!" Tanner shouted, and hurled himself at the giant.

Caught by surprise, Viktor didn't stand a chance as Tanner hit him straight in the chest and overpowered him, knocking him to the floor. Landing on top of Viktor, he wrapped his hands around his neck and began to squeeze in earnest, giving the man no time to recover from the attack.

"You killed her, you bastard," Tanner said, his face contorted with rage as he held him in a death grip.

Viktor struggled to breathe. His face bulged redder and redder as he bucked and twisted underneath the weight of the ex-military man as he grappled with the hands around his neck.

"Stop it!" Katie screamed, and jumped on Tanner's back, but Tanner didn't hear her. With her fists she beat his broad back as hard as she could and continued to scream, "Tanner, stop it! You're killing him! You're killing him!" but her tiny hands made no dent into the madness that filled his face.

Lazarus flew into action. Grabbing Tanner by the hair, he yanked his head back, forcing him to look at him. "Get a hold of yourself, Agent. He knows where Sharra is. We can still save her."

"Save her? She's dead. Didn't you hear him? How can we save her?" Tanner rasped.

"If we shift in time, we can get to her, and save her," Lazarus said, his voice hard with conviction. "We need Viktor alive. He knows where to go. He can get us there. Listen to me. We still have time."

Lazarus let go of the fistful of hair that held Tanner at bay, and pointed to the hands still wrapped around Viktor's throat.

"Release him."

Tanner glanced down at the red face of the man under his hands. Bending low, he put his face close to Viktor's ear and growled, "You had better deliver."

Viktor gave him a slight nod, understanding the implied threat. Tanner stared him in the eyes as he slowly released the pressure off his neck, and stood up. Gasping for breath, Viktor pressed his hand to his neck as Katie helped him sit up. She wrapped her arms around his shoulders as she crouched next to him, and glared at Tanner.

"How dare you," she said, spitting fire. "There isn't a bad bone in Viktor's body. That's why he came, because he knew something was wrong."

No one denied it. Out of all the agents at the Vault, Viktor was the meekest of them all, even though he had every right to brag about being a genius. Yet he never let his mechanical brilliance overshadow the man he really was, and everyone knew it.

At their feet, he sat hunched over with his arms wrapped around his knees, his breath labored as Katie held him. Tears clouded his eyes as he struggled to speak, "I'm so sorry. I didn't know. She was my friend."

"Then help us," Lazarus said, squatting next to him. "Where did you leave her?"

Viktor raised his head, despair written all over his face as he looked at Lazarus and said, "Ardus. We left her on Ardus."

"Ardus," Lazarus said, shocked.

A tear dropped out of Viktor's eye, and he nodded, confirming what Lazarus feared.

"Ardus?" Tanner said. "Where the hell is Ardus?"

Ignoring Tanner, Lazarus concentrated on the distressed man on the floor, keeping his voice calm when he asked, "Can you get us there, to the spot where you left her?"

"Yes, the coordinates are here," he said, tapping his head, "but I'd need to get my hands on a shuttle again, and that won't be as easy the second time around."

"Where's he going to find a shuttle, Lazarus? NASA?" Tanner said with a sharp laugh. "You can't just walk up to the door and ask for one. And come to think of it, I don't think they've even been invented… yet. Oh, I get it. You're talking about the future, Viktor's future."

Lazarus took Viktor's hand and helped him up. "I'm sure you can handle it… for Sharra's sake. Right, Viktor?"

"You won't find anything," Viktor said sadly.

"Let us worry about that," Lazarus said. "You just get us our ride. Katie, go with him and see if you can help him."

He sent Viktor out of his office, along with Katie. He needed to be alone to plan, and right now his office was feeling a bit crowded. Viktor was only too happy to go and get started on arranging their transportation. Katie gave her father a look, but obediently followed Viktor out of the door. He knew she'd wait and pounce on him later.

It was much harder to get rid of Tanner. As soon as the door shut behind Katie, Tanner let go, firing questions left and right about Ardus, Viktor's involvement, and what the plan was. When Lazarus remained vague about it all, he finally stormed off, slamming the door behind him, leaving Lazarus with the sound echoing in his ears.

Lazarus didn't want to leave his friend in the dark. He knew no good would come from it, especially when Tanner found out that he wasn't included in the rescue team. The less that he knew about Ardus, the better, and that meant keeping their numbers down.

Viktor had to go.

Not only did he have the coordinates to Ardus and the drop-off point to find Sharra, but also he was from that time period. He was the only one who could steal a shuttle and pilot it.

Faolan, on the other hand, controlled the receiver to the tag. They would need that to get a precise reading on the location of her body. There was no way Faolan was going to give up that responsibility. That was his ticket onto the shuttle.

That made three, counting himself.

But there was one other he needed, someone who had an intimate knowledge of the planet and the society that lived underneath its waters. Someone he had promised to keep hidden. Someone who swore she would never go back.

Araylai.

That made four, if she would go.

Chapter Sixteen

Ardus

Twenty-One Fifty-Three

Silence descended upon the Vault as the night settled in. Empty hallways and muted lights marked the lateness of the hour. Faolan was glad for that. Still, he kept a wary eye out for any late night stragglers as he followed Lazarus down to the Vault to the rendezvous point. He wasn't quite ready to have his cover blown wide open. It was bad enough that Tanner and Viktor knew that he was involved. They had better keep their mouths shut that's all he could say. Otherwise, Lazarus had some answering to do.

Up ahead the Staxx doors were wide open. As they passed the Terminus he scanned the room for any waiting agents. It was empty, as was the Vault chamber on the other side. Even the pylons sat silent on their axis that night.

But Staxx was not empty, for inside around the corner hidden from their view waited Araylai, the fourth person of their team. Faolan felt her before he could see her as a tickle of a presence touched his mind, reading him. He slammed his shield down, and kept his face neutral as they entered Staxx. It wouldn't do if she knew that he could read her too. It was one weapon he wanted to keep concealed, just in case. He didn't trust her.

Tanner was there too, dressed in the same skintight Vault uniform they all wore, leaning against the wall with arms crossed next to Araylai. A look of pained resignation was on his face. Faolan frowned and sent Lazarus a quick look that said, what's he doing here, but Lazarus ignored it.

"The shuttle's arrived," Lazarus said. "Sorry for the delay. I hope you weren't kept waiting long."

"Naw, Araylai and I were having a good old chat," Tanner said with a wry twist of his lips. "Couldn't shut her up."

Araylai stared at him, a small smile playing on her lips, but said nothing.

Tanner left the wall and went over to the counter. Leaning over it he pretended to search the tall shelving. "Speaking of shuttles, don't tell me that Grimm has one hiding somewhere in there. Oh, that's right. Viktor. He's the one with the shuttle. And the shuttle is... where?" He looked around, waiting for an answer.

"Lazarus has never told you?" Faolan said finally speaking up.

"Told me what?"

"About the hangar."

"What hangar?"

"I guess he hasn't," Faolan said under his breath.

Though it was said softly, Tanner had heard him. He didn't know why he was goading the man. It's not like Tanner had ever done anything to him. Tanner was a decent agent, trustworthy, and loyal, as far as he could remember. He knew that Lazarus counted on him. That had to stand for something.

"Sorry, Tanner," Lazarus said, "but there's never been a need for you to know about it."

Hurt registered on Tanner's face as he said, "Yet Faolan knows."

"Faolan's been around the Vault a lot longer than you." Lazarus went to the wall where the larger gear was usually left for pickup, and pressed his palm against a spot on one of the panels. "Just think of this as your lucky day."

As he spoke something clicked in the wall. A crack formed at the floor as the wall slowly lifted up into the ceiling with a swish of air. Inside was a huge chamber, big enough to hold a small aircraft with room to spare. Like the eight shiftrooms off the Vault chamber, this one glowed with the same unusual brightness. White seamless walls ran from floor to ceiling. On the floor pulsed the same silvery design only much larger.

In the middle of the hangar-like chamber sat a dirt-encrusted shuttle. Dent marks pocketed one side of its square body, while deep scratches ran the length of the underbelly, mutilating the large white registration number imprinted there. One wing sat tilted off center, as if someone had tried to hammer it straight, but gave up part way through the repair.

Tanner walked up to it and banged his fist against the side, knocking a patch of dirt to the floor.

"You really don't expect us to get in this thing, do you?" he said.

From around the other side, Viktor came over and said, "I know she doesn't look like much, but she'll fly."

"What did you do? Raid the garbage dump?"

"Something like that. I couldn't go back and borrow one too close to the last one I took. It was hard enough to swipe that one as it was. No, this baby still has some life in her," Viktor said, caressing the dented nose of the shuttle. "She'll do just fine."

"I don't know about that," Tanner said as he eyed the warped wings.

"It's okay, Tanner," Lazarus said. "You're not going anyway."

"You can't kick me out. Not on this."

"I need you at the Vault where you can be the most use to Sharra. And right now, that's finding Jacob Byson."

"But_"

"No buts. I need someone here we can trust while we're gone."

Tanner stared daggers at Faolan, and pressed his lips together as Lazarus continued, "In my office I've programmed my monitor so that you have full access to all classified information. Just press your thumb onto the identification icon, and you'll be in. You know your way around the file systems better than anyone I know, save for myself. You can start by digging for any clues on how Byson got in under our noses, and where he's hiding, anything that will help Sharra. Will you do that for me?"

Looking somewhat mollified, Tanner broke his gaze away from Faolan. "You'll let me know as soon as you find her?"

"Of course."

Tanner nodded assent to Lazarus's request as he turned to the others with a hard glint in his eyes. "Well, what are you guys waiting for? Go find her."

The words echoed off the chamber walls, moving Viktor to shoot off around the nose of the shuttle to disappear through the hatch door and into the cockpit. Faolan followed Araylai around the nose after Viktor. On the other side, she grabbed the edge of the hatch door, jumped in, and took a seat. Faolan scrambled in after her, taking one of the seats near the window across from her. Behind him, Lazarus hopped in and slapped the control panel next to the hatch door before slipping into the closest seat and harnessing himself in. With a groan, the door came down and slotted into place, activating the seals with a swish of air.

"Buckle up," Lazarus said.

"Are you expecting a hard ride?" Faolan said as he clicked the harness into the buckle between his legs.

"Rule number nine: always be prepared for the unexpected," he quoted.

"Ah, yes, the handbook. How could I forget."

Up front Viktor's hands flew over the console as he flicked switches and pressed buttons, completing the preflight check before pressing the button to start the dual engines. Behind their backs the engines flared to life with a whine, growing louder as it warmed up, until it reached a high pitch of readiness. Through the shuttle portal, Faolan watched Tanner duck under the hangar door and disappear from sight as the hangar door slid to the floor.

The air in the hangar began to shine brighter. The silvery pattern on the floor pulsed under the legs of the shuttle. Hands on the throttle, Victor eased the shuttle off the floor, adjusting the stabilizers to control the wobble of the wings until they hovered in mid-air.

Holding the throttle steady, Viktor called out over his shoulder, "Hang on to something. It may get a bit bumpy."

Faolan grabbed the harness straps at his chest, and prepared for the shift, hoping that the metal hunk of a spacecraft survived the next bit. Otherwise it was going to be a short ride.

"Shift," Viktor said, calling over the hum of the engine.

The hangar disappeared as the shuttle shifted out.

An instant later they reappeared high above the planet called Ardus. Coming in, they hit the air hard as the cross winds grabbed the shuttle and tossed it around as if it were a feather on the wind. Viktor, tight-lipped, kept a steely grip on the yoke with one hand while his other hand flew over the controls, adjusting the stabilizers and activating the thrusters, as his passengers in the back held on for dear life.

Outside their portals, they watched the wings flex and shudder in the wind as the shuttle danced upon the invisible current. For a few harrowing seconds Faolan thought they were headed for a quick dash to the waters below, but just when he was ready to shift back to the Vault the ship leveled off, and the shaking stopped.

"Everybody okay?" Viktor asked over his shoulder.

Lazarus looked at the other two, and said, "All good back here."

Faolan let go of his grip on his harness and pulled out the tagfinder. His hands shook as he held the sleek case and stared at the blank screen, praying for a signal, any sign that she was there.

"Come on," he grit through his teeth as he willed the machine to work. From out of the blackness, a tiny green dot showed up inside the screen and blinked. His heart jumped in his chest and began to beat rapidly against his ribs.

"She's here," he said.

"Where?" Lazarus said. "Is she alive?"

"Yes." Faolan brought up the stats on the green dot. "She's about thirty-five miles southeast of here, but..."

"Viktor, you got that?" Lazarus said.

Viktor twisted his head around the cockpit divider. "She's alive?"

"Yes. Head southeast, thirty-five miles," Lazarus said.

Relief washed over his face as he turned back to the controls. "Yes, Sir," he said with a lighter spirit.

The engine flared hot exhaust as he pushed on the throttle and swung the shuttle around and headed southeast. Below them the endless water churned as they ate up the miles while Faolan kept an eye on the moving green blip inside the tagfinder. The dot moved closer and closer to the center of the screen until it finally became one with it.

"Viktor, slow down," Faolan said. "We should be right on top of her."

Viktor pulled back on the main power to the engines, and turned the shuttle around back to the spot Faolan had indicated. With the engines on minimum power, he initiated the stabilizers and held the craft hovering a hundred feet above the water. Lazarus slapped the door lock, and opened the hatch. The seals broke with a swish as the door slid up into the body. A rush of warm sea air filled the cabin. Faolan jumped up and joined Lazarus at the open hatch. Together they hung onto the side and leaned out into the wind. Scanning the water below, they searched for any sign of their missing agent. Yet there was nothing to see, only endless sea of blue waves.

"It doesn't make sense." Faolan left the door to recheck the tagfinder, only to shake his head in frustration. "Her stats are transmitting from underneath the water. Deep underneath the water. But that can't be right."

"The reef of Ardere must be below us," Araylai said quietly from her seat. "She is in the city."

Through their turbulent arrival, her eyes had remained glued to the portal, never leaving it as the blue planet rose and dipped while Viktor fought with the winds. Now they turned away and looked unblinking at Lazarus, sending him a message that only he could read.

Faolan saw the exchange and knew she wasn't happy, even though her face showed no expression. He couldn't blame her. Coming back couldn't be easy. From the little Lazarus had told him, Araylai had her reasons for staying away, something to do with pissing off the government, not that he could imagine her being capable of doing something like that, but they all had their demons back in their own timelines. He guessed that she was no exception.

"I was afraid of this," Araylai said.

He looked at her as if she was crazy. "What are you saying, that there is a whole city underneath the water? And that's where she is?"

"Yes."

"What about the pressure?"

"The reef takes care of most of it."

He knew from the briefing that there was no land on Ardus. He had assumed that the indigenous people had built on floating platforms or some other advanced technological material that would be used in the future, and that is where they would find her. He had never dreamed that they had moved to the bottom of the ocean, and she would end up there instead.

"If that's the case," he said, "how are we supposed to get down there without killing ourselves in the process? You know the rules of shifting as well as I do. 'A half-mile radius.' That's our working distance. Drowning won't help anyone."

Lazarus shut the hatch. "Viktor, take us up. We need to get back to the Vault."

"What about Sharra?" he said.

The stabilizers flipped into the wings and the shuttle set off into the sky. Lazarus lurched forward into the seat next to Araylai and leaned closer to the silent beauty. She turned away from the window and looked at him with large eyes, eyes haunted by unseen visions.

"Can you get Faolan inside the city safely?"

Lazarus asked her softly. "I know I had promised you…"

"Yes." Araylai said. "For Sharra I will risk it."

"I wouldn't ask this of you if there was another way. I'm sorry."

"Do not be sorry. You have done so much for me. You rescued me, and gave me a home when I had none. You have always treated me with respect and kept my secret. It is time that I did something for you."

"Thank you."

From out of nowhere came a whining of air. A flash of energy hit the left wing and exploded into a thousand sparks, frying the electrical components inside the wing within a matter of seconds. Without any power to the thrusters on that side, the wing dipped, throwing Lazarus and Faolan to the floor.

"Whoa, what was that?" Faolan said as he jumped up and peered out the portal just as another ray of energy zoomed by.

"We've got company," Viktor shouted from the front.

Grabbing the yoke, he pulled hard and jerked them up into the sky as he adjusted the controls to the right wing to compensate for the loss of the thrusters of left wing. At the same time, he leaned on the power nozzle and gave her all the juice she could take. The engines flared red and the shuttle jumped forward as it picked up speed.

"Can we out-run them?" Lazarus asked as he stood holding onto to the seat.

Before Viktor could answer, another blast sliced the side of the shuttle, sending sparks along the inside wall.

Faolan jumped away as the shuttle bucked under his feet, flinging him across the seats and onto Araylai's lap. Losing his balance, Lazarus landed back in a heap on the floor.

"Viktor, quit running, and shift us out of here," Lazarus yelled as he lifted his body into the nearest seat.

"I can't. We need to be hovering. And right now, that's not an option," he yelled back.

Faolan climbed off of Araylai and into the seat next to her just as the floor tilted at a sharp angle, a quick right than a quick left, as Viktor dodged a ray of energy, pin-balling them between the shoulder brackets of their chairs. Before they could recover, they were slammed back into their seats as Viktor sent the shuttle into a nosedive, twisting and turning the ship in a tactical maneuver as he tried to outrun whoever was behind them.

"I can't shake them," he said.

"This is crazy. We should dump the shuttle, and shift out before we all get killed," Faolan said.

As he spoke, the shuttle bucked as another blast hit them full in the back. The engine screamed in protest. Unable to hold the engorgement of energy the compressors flared and exploded. Dangerous sparks flew everywhere in a beautiful array of color as the blast tore through the engines to the turbines, eating up the fuel lines in a matter of seconds. The heat shot forward into the bulkhead that separated the engines from the rest of the shuttle, melting the first layer away in a sizzle of smoke and fumes. It didn't stop there, but found its way along the conduit lines within the ceiling. It followed it through the cabin and up to the cockpit, to the control panels, melting everything in its path. Within seconds it ate through all the components in the control panel. Viktor fumbled with the panel, but nothing worked.

"Not good. Not good," he muttered as he tried to restart the engines, braving the electrical current that snapped and sparked over the control panel. "We're dead in the air," he yelled.

Sparks flew everywhere as smoke began to seep through the seams along the ceiling. The smell of hot metal and burnt plastic filled the cabin, choking the air with its toxic fumes.

Gagging Faolan threw his shirt over his mouth and nose, and checked on Araylai, who had the smarts to do the same thing. He shot a look at Lazarus through the thickening smoke. "Can we go now?"

"Yes. Go," Lazarus said through his own shirt. Coughing he waved them on.

All of a sudden, the air turned deathly quiet as the shuttle nose tilted down at a dangerous angle, and held there for an infinite second, balancing on an invisible wall, until the force of gravity grabbed it by the wings and dragged it down. Like a millstone they dropped out of the sky, fast and heavy.

"Abandon ship!" Viktor yelled, staring at the fast approaching wall of water.

"Shift! Shift now!" Lazarus yelled.

Faolan didn't wait around, but grabbed Araylai's arm and shifted them out of the shuttle. An instant later inside the shiftroom, he tore his shirt from his mouth and took in a deep breath of cool air, coughing and gagging as he staggered with Araylai to the wall. Beside him, Araylai's body shook as a fit of coughing wracked her lungs. Outside in the vast Vault chamber the pylons awoke within the slumbering cloud of charged particles, and began to rotate as if in answer to the noise of their arrival.

"Are you okay?" Faolan asked as he propped Araylai against the wall.

"Yes," she said, her voice weak with coughing. "Go check on the others."

He raced into the Vault and found Lazarus helping a coughing Viktor out of a shiftroom. His clothes were riddled with burn patches where his body had fitted in the confines of the burning cockpit. Grabbing the other side of the big agent, Faolan helped him out of the Vault and into the Terminus, where they lowered him onto one of the couches.

"Araylai?" Lazarus asked, searching the darkness for the woman.

"I'm here," she said, coming up behind them.

"What in the hell was that?" Faolan said as he flung his hand back in the direction of the Vault.

Viktor stopped slapping the smoking patches on his chest and said, "Must've been smugglers. It's not like Ardus has any air patrol of its own, not that I know of. Nor would the United Federation of Planets fund it, even though they're the ones who made Ardus off limits in the first place. But why shoot us out of the sky? Unless they thought our shuttle had come from an orbiting cruiser. But that would've only drawn attention to themselves. It doesn't make any sense."

"It doesn't matter now. What matter is that we've found Sharra, and that she's still alive," Lazarus said. "You did good, Viktor. Now get yourself to the Ward for a medical check. Make sure Cam dresses those burns."

"What about the mission?"

"Your part is done for the time being. Now, go, and get yourself looked at. When Cam says you're ready, come to my office, and we'll go over the headshots in the files. I need you to identify Jake Byson."

Steel entered Viktor's eyes. "Yes, Sir. I'll find him for you," he said. Pushing up from the couch, he headed back through the Vault chamber to the medical ward doors on the other side.

And that's what they needed, to identify the bastard behind it all. Faolan grit his teeth with hatred. Why would Byson, whoever he was, go to such lengths to get rid of Sharra? The man had to be demented, and someone like that left loose in the Vault was a danger to all of them.

After he left Lazarus turned to Araylai and said softly, "Are you sure you want to do this?"

"I gave you my word."

"In that case, you and Faolan get ready to go. Raid Staxx for supplies. I'll pacify Grimm in the morning. And, try to find some way for Faolan to blend in," Lazarus said.

Araylai flashed him a look. "Blend in. Is that supposed to be humorous?"

Lazarus sighed and said, "No. I'm asking the impossible, I know. It's your world. Do what you can. I don't want to lose any of you."

"We will find her," she said, her eyes solemn with promise as she rested her hand on his arm.

It was a brief touch, more than Faolan had ever seen her give to anyone, but it spoke volumes of her respect for the man. The touch, the way she looked at him, it was something he hadn't expected from the beautiful recluse. He looked at her with new interest, wondering what was between the two of them, but the moment had passed as quickly as it had started. She turned her amber eyes away from Lazarus, and headed to Staxx without a glance in his direction.

"Come on, Faolan," she called over her shoulder. "I'll get you a knife."

"A knife? That's it?" he said as he took off after her.

He would have no problems thrusting a dagger into Byson's cold heart if it came to it, especially after what he has done to Sharra.

Sharra, he thought as a picture of her sweet face filled his vision.

Through impossible odds they had found her, thanks to Viktor's confession. Was it luck? Faolan didn't believe so. They were connected, him and Sharra. He didn't know how he knew it, he just did. They're timelines were now intertwined, and he wasn't about to let her go, not after waiting centuries to find love again.

He hoped Araylai knew what she was doing. To shift under water was unheard of. The half-mile radius was getting wider and wider the more he thought about it. Yet, it was their only hope of finding Sharra and bringing her home. He loved her. He would do anything for her. Anything.

With fresh resolve, he quickened his steps as he followed Araylai into Staxx.

Chapter Seventeen

Ardere, Ardus

Twenty-One Fifty-Three

"Greyson," Sharra said.

Her brother's face hovered over her. His hazel eyes alight with a wicked fire. His thin lips twisted in a cruel smile. She swatted at him, but he caught her arms and squeezed her body in a vice grip. She struggled under the heavy weight of his body and watched in horror as his face started to distort above her. Like a balloon it grew, his mouth stretching with it, spreading wider and wider until it turned into a gaping cavern. It filled his whole face, crowding out his eyes and nose. Human teeth grew razor sharp to fill the whole jaw. She couldn't breathe. All she could do was stare. And when the mouth began to descend, panic set in.

"Greyson," she called, trying to reach the man inside the beast.

It didn't listen. Instead, it swooshed down upon her in one fell swoop, jagged teeth and all, until the black walls of its mouth enclosed around her. She screamed.

"Greyson!"

Sharra sat up in the narrow bed with a start, terrified, and gasping. She filled her lungs with air as though she had been drowning. Her heart pounded loudly in her ears as she stared wildly around panting, but the monstrous mouth was gone. So was the sea. It left the room she found herself in strangely empty.

Now wide awake all her senses returned with a vengeance. Her throat and mouth felt as dry as sandpaper. She tried to swallow, and cringed in pain. A tight pressure pounded in her ears. Even her skin where left exposed to the sun and wind, felt hot and tight.

A cool draft of air caressed her breasts, and she realized she was naked. Grabbing the thin sheet, she covered herself and popped her ears. The relief in her head was instant. She licked her cracked lips and pressed her hand to her aching stomach as she stood up. Under her feet the stone floor felt surprisingly warm. Once wrapped in the sheet, she looked around.

The room was small. A shallow dish of neon light sat on a small side table by the simple bed. Yet, the light wasn't needed for the walls themselves were of a translucent nature, letting in a soft light from some outside source beyond the four walls of the room. No windows, no pictures, no homey touches to say to whom it belonged. Only a large chest made from some lustrous material sat in the corner opposite the bed. If it weren't for that expensive looking box, she would've thought it was a prison cell. Either way, it didn't give her a clue to where she was or who had rescued her.

"It's just a bad dream," she said as she licked her lips again. "Just a dream."

Yet, the aches and pains of her body told her otherwise. Her fingers found one of the scars behind her ears. She traced the flattened metal, and knew. There was no going back. Greyson, if it were Greyson, had made sure of that. He had left her for dead sometime in the future on a water planet, on Ardus. How was anyone from the Vault to find her?

She tried to shift right then and there, but the blocks in the front of her went nowhere.

No one knew about her last shift. No one. She should have told Tanner, or even Lazarus. But she didn't because she knew going to her timeline was against the rules. In her foolishness she had to go and break them. Rules were there for a reason.

How long would it be before they realized something was wrong? A day? A year? A lifetime? Vault Agency wasn't governed by time. They may never know.

Time. What was that?

A harsh laugh fell from her lips at the irony of it all. The sound grated on her ears, and made her feel worse.

At that moment a part of the wall moved as a hand shoved a thin piece of stone open. In the entrance stood an alien woman dressed in a short halter-top tunic of brown kelp. A copper half-circle choker held the halter-top over her small breasts. From there, the material draped tight down her sides, leaving her back open to the small of her waist. Tight fitting shorts hugged the slim curves of her upper thighs. Around the lean muscle of her upper left arm was a band of twisted metal. In the center of it was a medallion made of a thinnest of slices of nautilus shell. The minute details of the graduating support walls were wrought in fine gold. Positioned on top of it was a slender black scepter. Its ends were dipped in gold. A black pearl crowned its top. Sharra knew the armband meant something. It was in the way the woman wore it, like a trophy.

That wasn't the only thing she wore. On the outside of the shin of her right leg was strapped a sheath. A bone-handle dagger stuck out of it, plain but deadly looking all the same. Another longer knife, a dagger, was strapped to outside of her left thigh. A thin woven belt hung low on her hips. Her webbed feet were bare.

In her hand was a tray holding a glass and a carafe made of the same lustrous material as the chest in the corner. Those familiar unblinking eyes in that stony face watched her from the doorway, holding the tray like a shield between them as if she were afraid.

Her pearl-like skin, the soft amber eyes rimmed in deep green, the yellow aura that surrounded her, even the small birthmark on her right palm all bespoke of her friend and fellow shifter. Sharra's heart burst in her chest at the sight of her.

She was rescued.

"Araylai," Sharra said. "Where am I? How did you find me?"

The alien creature's eyes flashed as the web crest on her head flicked open before snapping back against her skull. "Sssss. Do not say that name," she hissed. "Do you want to get us killed? I am not the one you speak of. My name is Nayada, Umbra Scout of the Arderie. We are in Riff, an outpost on the edge of the Arderie reef system. That is all you need to know."

"But you look just like her. You even have the same birthmark," Sharra said. She grabbed Nayada's hand before the creature could stop her, remembering what happened to Araylai when she had left the ball of energy in her head unshielded and they had touched. Cautious, she held it tight so that it couldn't feed on the stranger. She opened her palm and touched the small brown birthmark located on the soft pad below her thumb. "Here… see?"

The Arderie scout snatched her hand away, and tightened it into a fist against her thigh, hiding the telltale mark. "I am not the Queen's daughter. I am Nayada. Do not forget it. Now, please, I have brought you water."

She moved into the room, and set the tray down on the chest, and after filling the glass, she handed it over.

"Drink."

Sharra gulped the water down, not stopping until the glass was empty. "More. Please," she said, holding the glass out.

The alien woman filled it, and gave it back. Sharra took it and attacked it greedily.

"Slow down, or you will make yourself sick," the woman said as she refilled it a third time.

It was hard, but Sharra did as she was told, and drank more slowly, this time savoring the cool liquid as it ran down her parched throat.

Nayada took the cup away, and said, "Why were

you on the waters of Ardus? And how do you, a land-walker, know of the Queen's daughter?"

"I told you before I was swallowed by the floating mattress. Someone is trying to kill me, and figured Ardus was a good place to dump me to die. But I am alive thanks to you," she said feeling the warm solid stone under her feet, and the annoying pressure in her ears.

"You still can die. The Queen's daughter, how do you know of her? Speak truth, for your aura will show if you lie."

Sharra tried to comprehend whom the woman was referring to, until she put two and two together. "Araylai is your queen's daughter? A real live princess. She never mentioned it."

"I said not to speak her name. It is treason."

"Treason. Not Ara… What did she do?" Sharra sank down on the bed, stunned by the news. Not only was her friend a princess, but she was also in deep trouble. That explained why she couldn't come back to her home world.

"I am the one asking the questions. How do you know her? Now."

Sharra adjusted the sheet around her body, stalling for time as her mind frantically worked to formulate an answer that would appease the scout, and yet not jeopardize the Vault and its secrets.

Choosing her words carefully so as to speak only the truth, she said, "I've known her for some time. She is my friend. Believe it or not, we have a lot in common. But she never talks about her past. Sometimes we work as partners. You see, we are a part of an Agency that helps bring about a better future for others, working together to make real changes."

"She works for you hu-mans? Why would she betray her people, and then leave Ardus for land-walkers?"

"She said she didn't leave Ardus of her own free will. She was kidnapped, by smugglers, and sold on the black market as a slave. It was Lazarus Maitland, a human, who saved her, and gave her a life again."

Nayada eyes widened. "Your aura says that you speak the truth. How can this be? It changes everything."

"Changes what?"

Nayada waved the question aside with a brush of her webbed hand. "Let me think."

Sharra didn't want to wait. Instead she reached out with her mind the way Araylai had taught her, hoping to get a glimpse inside the head behind those cool amber eyes to find the answers she was looking for. But as she passed through the layer of yellow that surrounded the scout's inner self, she came to an abrupt stop, hitting a hard mental wall. She pressed against it, but there was no give, not even a lightening shade of its dark surface to indicate a weakness. The mental shield was as impregnable as a stone fortress.

The Arderie scout must have felt her touch, for no sooner had Sharra pressed against the mental shield, then the alien's arm whipped down and grabbed a fistful of her sheet, and hauled her to her feet. Dragging her up face to face, Nayada held the material tight in her fist as she stared deep into her widened eyes.

"Know your place, land-walker," she said, low on her breath.

Only inches separated them, yet the Arderie scout held her there with the strength of a bull. Locked in her unblinking gaze, Sharra waited breathless for the toss of her body that was sure to come. But the Arderie scout had something else in mind.

An alien electrical impulse breached the short distance between them in a flash. It touched her mind, hard and fast. Without any reservations Sharra dropped her mental shield, only leaving it around the tiny white ball of energy that lay lodged in the innermost reaches of her brain. The mad rush into her head turned into a tentative touch when the Arderie scout realized that Sharra made no move to stop her.

You let me in of your own free will, Nayada said in surprise through the link.

It is Araylai who taught me the gift of freeness of mind.

The words evoked a flash of red in the hard armor of the scout's aura, but only for a second before the yellow covered it over. Yet it was enough for Sharra to get a glimpse of the disquieting thoughts behind the mental shield that the woman hid behind. Nayada abruptly let her go as if scorched, and slowly backed away to put some space between them.

She has honored you, she said.

With new insight, Sharra used the knowledge she had extracted in that brief moment to push ahead. *I realize you do not trust me, but Araylai is my friend, and I am honor bound to help her. You cannot deny me this right.*

"What is it that you wish?" Nayada said out loud, breaking the link as she did so.

Sharra's stomach decided then to make its presence heard by letting off a loud gurgle. She couldn't remember the last time she had eaten.

"Food would be nice. And my clothes, unless this is how you wish to keep me," she said, clutching the sheet to her chest.

"I have bound my honor to you. You are my responsibility now. I will see to your needs."

As Nayada turned to leave, Sharra asked, "You are seeking the truth, right?"

Amber eyes turned to look at her, but Sharra was no longer afraid. After the slow nod of agreement came, she plunged ahead with an idea that had been formulating in her mind.

"From where I stand," she said, "it looks like someone wanted the princess out of the way. So, you need to ask yourself, who among your people would want her gone… and why? Once you find the answers to those two questions, the rest should fall into place… and you will have your truth."

"Truth is not always what it seems," Nayada said, and left.

Sharra unlocked her knees and sank onto the bed, weak from hunger. Or was it the stress of the brief encounter with the alien scout? She didn't know. Her stomach growled again. She bent over and pressed her fist against it, and hoped they brought food soon.

It wasn't long after that the door opened to her cell. A male of the species entered followed by the aroma of cooked fish. Like Nayada, he too paused on the threshold and looked her over with a curious light in his deep amber eyes, but Sharra only saw the plate of food that he held in his hand. Seeing the direction of her gaze, he stepped into the room, and handed her the plate of fish. Beside the cooked fish was a row of evenly cut pieces of raw fish.

"Thank you," she said.

She shoved the hot fish into her mouth and swallowed, hardly tasting it before picking up the next piece. All the while the Arderian male watched in avid curiosity as she shoveled mouthful after mouthful in until the plate was empty. Even the raw fish was eaten. With her stomach full she paused to breathe. It was then, after the hunger had abated that she noticed him staring at her. Her cheeks warmed at her lack of control.

"It was very good. Thank you," she said as she handed the plate back sheepishly.

"I am glad you enjoyed it," he said as his lips fought back a smile. "I am Cael, Left Pectoral Scout of Nayada's Pod."

He stood tall before her, wearing the same tight-fitting shorts and nasty daggers as Nayada had on, only his uniform didn't come with a shirt as hers had. Instead, his chest was bare. His iridescent skin showed off the fine definition of the lean stack of muscles underneath. An identical insignia band was wrapped around his upper left arm.

It meant something. She was sure of it.

Sharra studied him for a moment, and said, "You were on the surface with Nayada."

"You recognize me?"

"Yes. It's your eyes. Yours are a deeper shade of amber, almost orange, with a brown ring instead of green like Nayada's. And your skin is more like powdered sand than pearls."

There was a knock on the door. Cael went over and cracked it open. Through the opening an arm passed a bundle to him. He took it, and shut the door.

"A uniform," he said, setting it next to her on the bed, "to replace the clothes that you lost."

"Thank you."

"Nayada has also sent some salve for the wounds we discovered behind your ears." In his hand he held a small alabaster jar. He dipped his finger in and looked at her. "May I? I am qualified to treat all sorts of... creatures."

Sharra pulled her hair away and bent her head to the side to expose an ear, and held the ball of energy in her head tight. "How bad is it?"

With gentle fingers he brushed a few strands of hair off the raw wound.

"It looks like metal."

"It is."

"Why would someone pour hot metal on you?"

"What does it look like?"

"A round disc of... it looks like silver. Very strange. The skin around it has been burned. The salve will help, but I will need to think about how to remove the disc without causing more damage."

"No! Leave them."

"As you wish. But, if you change your mind..."

"I'm okay."

Carefully, he rubbed the salve over the raw edges. Finished with one side he moved to the other, saying nothing as he worked. After the wounds were dressed he stepped away and closed the jar.

"I am curious," he said as he set the jar on the water tray. "Are you not afraid? A creature… a hu-man alone, a stranger in a strange land?"

"I haven't had a family in a long time," she said, pushing her hair out of her face to look at him. "It's only recently that I have become part of one again."

"A new pod? What happened to your first pod?"

"My parents were killed in an accident when I was young. I was left in the care of my older brother, but it was too much for him… and he left me."

The bitter memories of that day popped into her head, along with all the pain of years of loneliness that followed Greyson's abandonment. Those days were over. Now she had a new family that cared for her. She must have transmitted some of her distress, for the Cael's aura went from tangerine to muddy brown in an instant.

"Was he punished for his betrayal?" he asked, the brown ring of his iris flashing bright in anger. "Is that why you had no pod?"

"Punished?" A harsh laugh escaped her lips. "Greyson? He wouldn't know the meaning of the word. No, he's still alive."

A picture of his face leaning over her flashed into her mind.

"If he was an Arderian he would have been executed for his lack of honor."

"Things are done differently where I'm from."

The room turned silent as he struggled to understand the alien concept. It was no different for Sharra. Stuck on a planet she knew very little about, she was in the same predicament. As she watched, Cael calmed himself down, muting his brown aura back to the tangerine that she knew meant curiosity.

When he spoke again, he said, "But this new pod you speak of…"

"Vault Agency."

"They are now your pod, your… family?"

"Yes. Lazarus, the Head Director, the same man who found and saved your princess, also found me and took me in, and gave me a purpose again. Now, I get to travel to the most interesting places, meet new people, and experience new things all the time. It makes me feel alive again, and useful… somewhere I can be myself."

"And the princess. On the surface you spoke her name. Is she happy there?"

"Yes, I would say so. She doesn't say much to the others, but she has told me that she finds the work fascinating, even though it means she has to stay in human form for most of the time. But the Vault has a huge swimming pool that she loves, where she can rest in her true form."

"Your people, they don't mind her_" He stopped in mid-sentenced as if he got cut off. When his eyes went blank, Sharra knew that someone was speaking to him through their alien link. Sure enough, when his eyes focused again, he said, "I am called away. More food will come. Rest and regain your strength. That is all you can do for now."

As he went to the door, Sharra stood clutching the sheet to her chest. "What will you do with me?"

Cael paused to look back at her and said, "That is to be decided yet."

His eyes said nothing. Only his aura changed, and

that told her even less.

Chapter Eighteen

Cael headed down the hallway of sleeping quarters. His bare feet made no sound on the warm stone floor as he hurried along. He passed the communal pool, and looked at it with longing. His skin itched for a dip, but duty called and so he left it behind for later when he had some free time coming to him. It would be crowded by then, but he was used to sharing the water-space with the other guards.

After passing several more closed doors he left the sleeping quarters and met Loch coming toward him from the arched doorway.

"Nayada called you, too," Loch said as he fell in step beside his friend.

"Mmmm... " Cael said, and nothing more.

Loch sent him a look, reading his aura with interest. "What is going on in that crazy head of yours?"

"Nothing."

"Come on. You cannot hide from your aura."

Cael took a few more steps before answering. "Is it strange that I find the hu-man, the land-walker, interesting?"

"Strange? Yes," Loch said. "Can I give you some advice, my friend? Guard your aura. Not everyone would agree with your new fascination with the hu-man."

"What are you afraid of, Loch? Is it the soft stuff on her head, or the lack of webbing that scares you?"

"Neither."

"Ah… Your aura wavers. You sense a change."

"It is not always a good thing, Cael."

"Maybe change comes easier for the Harena. Survival in the kelp fields depends much on my kin being adaptable. It is one of the few advantages we can claim over the upper Houses. I wonder how long you, a nobleman, would survive out there? A week. No, that is too long. You would have been stabbed, and used for fertilizer by then. Noble blood is quite rich. Makes the kelp grow thick."

Cael watched Loch's aura turn pale blue with annoyance as the jab hit home, and smiled. For all his airs of superiority, Loch was an easy target, and Cael found great pleasure in riling him up. As predictable as ever, Loch opened his mouth with a denial, but was stopped before the words came out because, by then, they had passed through the main conclave, and had entered the small conference room. At the end of a table Nayada and Calyx were talking in low tones to a frail-looking elderly Arderian.

Nayada waved them over. "How is the land-walker?"

"She is a strong one," Cael said.

"Has she said anything more about… the princess?" Nayada said.

"No, I did not presume to ask without your permission," Cael said, and no more, keeping his aura of curiosity about the human in tight control.

"I have many questions I wish to ask her." From his seat on a wooden chair made from thick kelp stalks, Caetus, the retired guardsman spoke up. His voice was still strong though his body was bent with age.

Nayada rested a hand on the elderly Arderian's shoulder and said, "No, Caetus. I have already put you in danger by bringing her here. I cannot allow you to be involved. You have done enough in allowing her to stay under your roof."

"You did the right thing, child," he said, resting a hand on top of hers, "but I am stronger than I look. Whatever harm you worry over has already been done. Meeting with the land-walker will not make it any worse. There may be more that she can tell us, and I wish to know."

Nayada's aura turned navy blue with worry as she hovered over her guardian. After a moment of consideration, she backed down and said, "I will bow to your wisdom."

She turned away from Caetus, and left the room, only to return a few minutes later with the land-walker by her side.

The hu-man had put on the brown halter-top uniform of the Umbra that Cael had given her. The slim woven belt was low on her hips. Below the shorts her legs were naked of weapons. Her face, arms, and lower legs radiated red heat where her skin had been exposed to the harsh rays of the sun, drawing lines against the pale parts that the uniform didn't cover, like a funny striped fish. The long reddish-brown strands on her head had been pulled back and tied with a string. Strange and alien she stood in front of them emitting electromagnetic rays of nervousness. Her odd eyes were wide as she looked all around until they settled on Cael. He stared back, keeping his aura under tight control.

Her gaze did not stay on him for long, for her eyes were drawn to the elderly Arderian. With much pain, he lifted his aged body out of the chair and shuffled over to where Nayada stood guard over the land-walker. His aura was bright orange with curiosity as Cael's had been earlier, making Cael feel somewhat better.

"You must excuse our lack of manners," Caetus said with a gracious smile. "It is not often we get visitors here in Riff. Please, what is your name?"

"My name is Sharra. Sharra Lane."

"Sharra," he said, rolling the r's as he tested the foreign sound on his lips. "Pretty. My name is Caetus. I am Nayada's guardian from long ages. I must apologize in advance for any insulting behavior from my young pod friends. None of us have ever expected to have to deal with a... foreigner such as yourself, so they are not quite prepared on proper etiquette, or on how to proceed."

"Please, sir, I can only be grateful to your people for saving my life, and to you for giving me shelter. I've nothing to give you in return. I lost what I had in the water. I only hope that somehow I can repay you for your kindness."

"There is something that you can do, if you wish to repay your debt," he said. "But first, come, stand next to me. I hear you have an interesting tale to tell."

He drew her over to the oblong table and took his seat at the head. Nayada took her place behind him and gestured for her guards to sit.

"Nayada tells me that you know of our princess." Caetus said.

"Yes, she and I are friends." With that she lifted her shield and touched his mind. *I lay my mind open for you. Ask what you will.*

Caetus eye rings flashed in surprise before he could hide his reaction. He reached across the connection in awe. *Holy Sea Mother*, he exclaimed. *Nayada told me of this, but I did not believe. You honor me. Thank you. I wish I could indulge in my own curiosity of your kind that you offer, but I must think of the pod in the room, and the reason you are here.* He broke the link and said out loud, "You have a story to tell. Shall we start at the beginning?"

All eyes turned to Sharra as she began her tale, starting with her recruitment to Vault Agency, the excitement of the missions, and working with a mixed range of agents that included Araylai. At the same time, she spoke highly of the Head Director, Lazarus Maitland, how like a father he takes care of all of them, and how much he had helped her grow as a person. Then came Tanner, the Agency's trainer, and some of the others, of how they had taken her in, and made her feel part of the family, and how she had come to care for them, even with their idiosyncrasies.

From there, she told of the early morning visit to the Agency's private swimming pool where she had come across Araylai in her true form. Around her, the auras in the room brightened with interest as soon as she spoke of the princess, but no one broke her narrative. So she continued to tell of her initial shock and subsequent discovery of how Araylai became a part of the Agency, retelling the conversation in the pool as best as she could from her memory. From that initial revelation they had partnered up on missions. While in private, they'd meet at the pool, where the alien woman could be free to be herself in Sharra's company.

"And by a freak chance I am here on Ardus, her home world. What are the odds of that happening?" Sharra finished.

"All things happen for a reason," Caetus said.

Nayada read his aura with concern. "Is it enough?"

"What Sharra tells us about the princess' disappearance is too important to dismiss as a coincidence," Caetus said. "And for those loyal to the princess, it is just what we need to renew our search for the truth. Yet, with caution we must proceed. The Queen has been quiet for some time. We do not want to give her any reason to look at Riff."

"So, where do we start?" Nayada said.

"Where treachery grows like algae," Caetus said.

"The Queen's court," Loch said quietly from the side.

Nayada gave a slow nod, and spoke, her bell-like voice soft as she came to a decision. "Then that is where we will go."

177

JEAN GILBERT

"Not you," Caetus said. His aura flashed deep blue in alarm. As quickly as it came, it changed to soothing green. "Someone else must go."

"Let me go," Loch said. "I may have been gone for a while, but I still know my way around the court. My presence there will not be questioned."

Nayada agreed. "Take Calyx. That will give you a full set of eyes as back-up."

"Nayada_" Calyx started, but the Head Umbra stopped her with a look.

"I will hear no excuses. You will go with Loch. Stay sharp. I don't want you two to take any chances in drawing the Queen's attention."

"What about me?" Cael said, coming to stand next to his friend.

"You and I will take care of our guest," Nayada said, for the first time smiling at Sharra, who had stepped back as soon as the Arderians had finished with her.

Cael frowned, but nodded, keeping his inner thoughts of pleasure under tight control, and hoped Nayada's piercing eyes didn't see through the mask of annoyance he had pasted on his face as soon as he had heard her answer. Just to throw her off, he concentrated on bad memories of his childhood to change the color of his aura. He knew it would be no good for him if Nayada saw the current of his interest in the hu-man, especially in that she had just afforded him a reason to spend more time in her company.

178

Chapter Nineteen

The air-pressure changed inside Sharra's room, and woke her up, signaling a new day with the shift of the ocean current. Like regular clockwork it beat against the protective wall of transparent rock that covered the main reef system of the Arderian kingdom, coinciding with the motion of the two satellite moons that circled the planet and set the rhythm of the tides of the ocean planet. She knew this because she had asked Cael when he had brought her breakfast the previous day. She yawned and popped her ears, relieving the pressure in her head as she wiped her hair out of her face from another night of tossing and turning.

The blackness of the room turned grey with the dawn as the lichen that grew prolifically on the rock ceilings responded to the rays of the rising sun that broke across the horizon somewhere high above and filtered down to wash the underwater world in early morning light. As the rays grew stronger in the sky with the movement of the sun, so did the living fluorescent light that covered the ceiling, until the room was awash in a warm glow of soft light.

From her narrow cot Sharra watched the phenomenon as she had for the last four mornings, waiting the hour or so for the glow to stabilize before moving to get dressed. In that time the first morning bell rang like it did every morning. Soon after, the patter of feet could be heard through her door as the other occupants of the sleeping quarters hurried to the pool to get ready for the day. Their splashing echoed down the hallway along with their voices as they joked and riled each other in easy comradery. Soon another bell rang, and the patter of feet dwindled away leaving silence behind. She knew another half hour was allocated for breakfast before they disappeared out of the conclave for duty, and she was free to move about.

She sighed and pushed the sheet aside, and took her time putting on the uniform they had given her. After clipping the copper choker of the halter-top around her neck, she slipped into the shorts, setting the belt on her hips before picking up the makeshift brush from the chest and attacking her hair.

The bell rang three short tolls. It was the signal calling the guards to duty. After waiting a few more minutes, she pushed the door aside and padded down the hallway of the sleeping quarters. At the pool, puddles of water covered the floor from the others. She quickly washed her face and hands and followed the trail of wet feet down the hallway. She cracked open the door to the conclave and peeked in. The large common room was empty of Arderian guards. She slipped in and quickly crossed the floor, and entered another hallway to the left that led to Caetus' private quarters, and to the outer wall of the outpost.

Since her arrival five days ago Nayada had kept the guards under her watch busy as much as possible, sending them away on scout missions into the open waters, or assigning them sentry duty along the outside wall of the reef where Riff was located. Besides the original scout party, the only other Arderian that knew she was there was Caetus, the old guardsman. He wanted to keep it that way, until they figured out what to do with her. It was Caetus who gave her some freedom to move around, inviting her to use his personal quarters as a place to stretch her legs after the conclave cleared out each morning.

Sharra opened the door to the room Nayada called the Otior, and entered into a lounge fit for a royal dignitary. In stark contrast to the rest of the outpost, the Otior was filled with soft colors and rich textures, from the woven sea-foam carpet to the piles of colorful plush pillows that littered the floor, to the low-rise divans scattered here and there. Low tables of glass and metal were spread between the cushions and divans. Imbedded in their glass surfaces were etched different designs of intertwining swirls made from fine gold and Paua shell. Delicate carved sea creatures of ivory or greenstone with eyes of precious gems sat on the tables and around the room, each exquisite in detail and interlaid with gold. All was worth a king's ransom.

Though the room held many treasures, it was the far

wall that drew Sharra to the room, for it was like nothing she had ever seen before. Where the rest of the walls of the outpost had been somewhat translucent, the great wall before her was as transparent as glass. Like the outcropping of a rock, the uneven window jutted out into the sea giving a panoramic view of the outside world.

She walked up to the sheer wall, and watched a school of sissorbacks pick at the tiny crustaceans cleaning the glass. Catching sight of her, they stopped and swam closer for a look, moving up the glass to come face to face with her with only the thin transparent wall between them. Her full lips twisted up into a self-depreciating smile.

"Now who's in the aquarium?" she said to the school of small fish. Their red-rimmed eyes watched her through the glass, but soon lost interest and moved back to feeding off the tiny crabs. "So that's what it feels like."

"What 'what feels like'?" Nayada said from the doorway.

Caught off guard, Sharra jumped and spun around as the Arderian woman walked in and set the breakfast tray down on a low table before waving her over to eat. The smell of warmed fish and mashed whiteroot wafted over to her, making her stomach growl.

"How it feels to be the one imprisoned in the glass bowl, and stared at as if you were a pet," Sharra said as she came over and sat down next to her on the pile of cushions.

"I am sorry we cannot give you your freedom," Nayada said, handing her a plate. "It is not safe for you to wander around."

Sharra looked at the food, but couldn't eat. "No, I understand. I am the intruder here. I cannot ask for more than what you have already done. It's just that… what if I'm stuck here forever? What then?"

"Caetus has an idea."

"What is it?"

"If it is true that someone from our city has connections with the poachers that fish our waters illegally, then Caetus thinks we might be able to find a way to get you home through them."

"Aren't they the ones who kidnapped Araylai, and tried to sell her at the slave markets? Then, no thank you. I'd rather stay in hiding," Sharra said, remembering the fear in Araylai's voice when she had told her the story, "even if it means I am stuck in an aquarium for the rest of my life."

"I understand your concern. It is the same as ours. That is why it is just talk for now, until we know more about who was involved in the abduction of the princess, and who their connections were. I know Arderie is not like your Earth, but I promise we will do all in our power to make it work for you as your people have done for Araylai."

At the utterance of the forbidden name, Sharra's eyes widened in surprise and flew to the soft amber eyes that stared unblinking at her. For a second Nayada's defensive wall cracked as a profound sadness filled her eyes, flushing her neutral green aura a deep indigo before she collected herself and slammed her feelings back behind the wall of green. But it was enough for Sharra to see that the hard exterior that the Arderian guard wore was just a guise, and that Araylai meant something to her, something more than she was letting on to the others.

She wanted to say something about it, to question her, but Cael then chose to burst into the room. Nayada rose to her feet to meet her Left Pectoral guard.

"What is it?"

"Loch and Calyx are back in the barracks," he said. "Their auras are tight, but I can tell that they have news."

Nayada turned to Sharra and said, "You will have to excuse me and eat your breakfast alone while I go take care of this. Cael, come."

"Wait. I have told them to meet us here."

"In the Otior?" Nayada said. "That is presumptuous of you."

"Punish me if you must, but Loch requested that Sharra be present, and I know you trust his judgment. So I assumed it would be easier to have them come here then to try to move Sharra to somewhere else in the barracks."

"No, you did right. Let's hope Caetus feels the same."

They didn't have long to wait before the rest of her pod showed up with Caetus, whose aura expressed signs of displeasure at the invasion of his private sanctuary. Loch brushed the old guard's displeasure off as he and Calyx marched up to Nayada.

"This had better be good, Loch," Nayada said, glancing at her old guardian out of the corner of her eye.

"You won't be disappointed," he said with Calyx adding a nod to lend weight to his words. "You were right to look to the court for answers. And the timing could not have been better planned. With the Queen's attention occupied with the uprising in the outer kelp fields, my friends at court were only too happy to entertain us, especially since I have had first hand experience fighting in the skirmishes."

Nayada nodded and said, "Queen Aniani should have learned by now that oppression is not the answer to controlling the people."

"A black aura can see no other way," Caetus said under his breath.

Not hearing the quiet exchange, Loch continued, "And it seems the latest uprising have tipped the scales. It has gone so far that the prominent families, her most loyal supporters, are starting to murmur against her. Too many of the Praemin children are coming back injured, or even worse, dead, with no end in sight, and no honor given."

"That is news," Nayada said. "And what has been the response?"

"If auras are to go by, everyone's color is off. It seems that a few from Queen Aniani's inner circle have let it slip to some in the Praemin court that she had been unhappy with her daughter for some time. It was no secret that the two were as different as day and night, and that Araylai had the support of the people when her mother's was dwindling. The word is that Aniani worried that her daughter was weak, and unfit for the throne. You know what that would have meant. Now there are whispers going around that maybe Araylai was set up, that the Queen feared she would lose in battle if challenged legally."

"Those are only words. That does not prove anything. We need more than that," Caetus said.

"Wait. This is where it gets interesting. At a party the night before last, we happened to overhear a conversation between Praemin Reu and Praemin Minnowmen. I do not know if you remember the scandal with Praemin Reu's youngest son. He had gotten involved with the Grexs a few years back, and paid for it with his life. Almost brought the Reu House down."

"Grexs," Caetus spat out the name with disgust. "They are everywhere. In every House and reef. Their tunnels reach deep wherever there is dirt to be found, and there is plenty of dirt surrounding the throne. The shame is great. I am not surprised to hear those dirty worms are connected."

"Let me tell you the rest. What is interesting is that Reu informed Minnowmen that his son had given him something right before the Queen's Umbra came and took him away. His son told him to hide it deep. It was a document. Reu did not say what it said, only that it could get them killed. It looked like he was trying to pass it on to Minnowmen. We figured it was because Minnowmen is from a lower House and less likely to be in the Queen's eye."

"A document. It could be anything. How do we know if it pertains to the princess?" Caetus asked.

Loch smiled, but it wasn't a friendly smile. "Rue should have had his mental wall tighter. It will surely get him killed. If I could slip in so easily…"

"Come on, Loch, what did it say?" Cael said.

"It was a receipt for services rendered. One Arderian slave to be transported off world, paid with enough money to buy anyone's silence."

As he spoke the auras around the room grew

brighter with excitement as the implications of what he had overheard meant.

"And the Arderian slave? Did it give a name?" Caetus asked his aura bright with hope.

"No, but it does state the slave was a female. And by the amount of money exchanged, who has that much lying around, and for a mere slave? I would bet my life that it was for Araylai.

"Finally, a break," Caetus said. "After months of searching, we have something concrete to work with. Did Minnowmen agree to take it? We need to find out who signed the receipt."

"They were interrupted before he could give an answer, but knowing Minnowmen, he will not risk his House to take it," Loch said.

"Spineless fish," Calyx said in disgust.

Nayada, Loch, and Cael all nodded in agreement.

Caetus said, "We need that document, before it disappears for good. Loch?"

Loch shook his head. "It won't be easy. I will have to gain Praemin Reu's trust. Our families have never been close. May take some time."

"Do it," Caetus said.

Loch turned to leave, but Calyx reached out and grabbed his arm to stop him. She drew him close and asked him, "What about the other rumor, the one that concerns our... guest?"

"Me?" Sharra said.

Nayada's eyes narrowed. "What other rumor?"

Loch turned back to the group. "Some from among the Harena are spreading the tale that a land-walker was spotted with an Arderian in the Sand Markets yesterday afternoon. It is said that they slipped away into the thermal ducts before they could be stopped."

"Another human? Here?" Sharra said. Her heart jumped in her chest as her brother's face flashed before her eyes.

"Can that be possible?" Nayada asked her.

"The only one who knows I'm on Ardus is the one who dumped me here to die. He must have been watching me from his ship, and saw your pod take me under. I don't know who else it could be. It has to be him."

"I don't know," Cael said. "Could it be the Helix juice talking? You know how it can cause some major hallucinations when downed too quickly, and the Harena have been imbibing heavily since the skirmishes have started up again."

Loch didn't look convinced. "A week ago, I would have agreed with you, my friend, but now that we have a hu-man standing in our midst... we cannot deny the possibility that another one could have slipped in."

"But how did he get into the city? If he had come down from the surface, the Umbra would have seen him," Cael said.

Sharra touched one of the ruined agrylium discs behind her ear.

"There are other ways of moving from point a to point b," she said. "The metal behind my ears, if it had not been damaged, it would've taken me home to the Vault in a blink of an eye. If he is from the Vault, which I believe he is, he could have gotten here the same way."

"That means he will be searching for you," Cael said.

Sharra turned pale as she looked at him with big eyes. "He's come to finish the job."

The deep green rings surrounding the amber of Nayada's eyes flashed bright with emotion. "Not if we get to him first. If he is inside the thermal tunnels, it could easily take him days to work his way through the maze of passageways before he found another duct out. We can use that to our advantage. Cael, are you up for a hunt?"

"I never say no to a hunt," Cael said, resting his hand on the handle of his dagger.

"Do not forget that there is an Arderian who is helping him," Loch said.

"Right. Calyx, you are with us," Nayada said to her Right Pectoral. "If there is an Arderian involved, it is probably one of the Grexs."

Nayada headed to the door with her Right and Left Pectoral guards in step behind her, discussing the gear they needed to gather for the hunt, when an important detail came to Sharra's mind.

"Wait," she called out, stopping them at the door. "There's one thing you should know about the human. He can leave at any time as easily as he came. If he feels cornered, he will leave, disappear right before your eyes. So you must catch him by surprise, knock him out, or something, so that he cannot shift."

"Why not just kill him?" Calyx said.

"No!" Sharra said, a little harder than she meant to. "I need to question him. I need to know why."

She bridged the space between them and linked with Nayada, sending her a silent plea. Sharra feared it was her brother, but couldn't say it out loud, or even silently across the connection. She didn't want it to be true. It couldn't be true, but the emotional punch she sent Nayada spoke otherwise.

Nayada sent a questioning pulse back, but Sharra shook her head, not ready to explain it to the Arderian pod leader.

Just bring the man to me, and then I will explain, she said.

We will see if the human cooperates. If he does, then I will honor your request. If he does not... I cannot guarantee you anything, Nayada said.

With those parting words, she and her scouts left to gather their gear and head out for the hunt. Loch left soon after to repack his bags and head back into the city, leaving Sharra alone with the elderly guardsman. She plopped down onto the pile of cushions next to the tray of uneaten food. She had set it down earlier when Cael had burst into the room and had forgotten about it. The smell of the fish turned her stomach. She couldn't eat, not with the thought of her would-be killer lurking somewhere in the city, searching for her. She felt defenseless, even with Caetus to watch over her.

I need a weapon, she thought as she eyed the long knife strapped to the old guardsman's leg.

If Tanner had taught her anything, it was to expect the unexpected, and she didn't want to get caught out again.

Tanner.

Her mind flooded with memories of him, of his charming lop-sided grin, the twinkle in his eyes when he teased her, of the unsaid love that he felt for her. All the time throughout her ordeal with J.D. Dash, he had been her constant rock. Looking back it had been all wasted opportunities. And now... now she had nothing. She blinked away the tears that welled up, hating the weakness, when an idea struck her. She did have a way home, and it was coming right for her. If Nayada didn't catch him, then she had better be ready.

Caetus sat quietly nearby, watching her with keen eyes.

"Caetus, can I borrow a knife?"

A slow smile spread across his face. "I was wondering when you were going to ask."

Chapter Twenty

The bright light of the shiftroom disappeared as Araylai shifted them across space and time to Ardus, into her home city, Ardere, a place Faolan had no idea existed until an hour ago. During the time it had taken to find the knives in the organized chaos of Staxx, strap them to their legs, and head back to the Vault chamber, Araylai had fed him bits and pieces of information, but none of it made much sense. And when he had tried to question her, she had just shrugged her shoulders, and said that he would have to wait and see.

"I will have to aim our shift deep within the city," she said. "It will mean more of a risk of being seen, but given that we want to end up inside the reef where there is air, we have to take that chance."

"Air is good," he said.

She hadn't elaborate on what he was expected to

find, only that he was to follow her lead.

The pulsing floor of the shiftroom was gone. Now under his boots was a floor of hard packed sand. The smell of musty canvas and wet sea filled his nostrils. A quick look around found them in a deep tent stretched over thick wooden poles. A weak light filtered through the canvas material. All around them were piled large wicker baskets brimming with soft sponges of all shapes and sizes, filling the tent, leaving a narrow aisle down the center to the back.

A heavy pressure hit his ears as soon as they shifted in. He moved his jaw to relieve it as he scanned their surroundings, noting the motion of activity at the open end of the tent. Araylai noticed it too, and pushed him to the back of the tent, dragging him down behind a stack of empty baskets before they were seen. Through the canvas walls they could hear the creaks and groans of a wooden cart passing by, followed by the sound of shuffling feet.

"Do you know where we are?" he whispered.

"It smells like the Harena Markets," Araylai whispered back.

"Are you sure?"

She sniffed again, and wrinkled her nose. "Yes. It is a smell that one never forgets. The locals call it the Sand Markets."

The talking up front moved further into the tent as the proprietor searched through his supply of sponges at the insistence of his latest customer. It brought him closer to their hiding place. Araylai stared at Faolan with big eyes and put her fingers to her lips. They waited crouched in the corner, ready to shift away the moment before they were discovered, but the owner never got to them. With a shout of victory, he pulled a sponge from a basket, and scuttled to the front to resume business, but not before Faolan got a good look at his face and the row of fins that ran from the top of his head all the way down his back to the edge of his loose fitting pants.

His brow furrowed as his mouth worked to speak. No words came out. Nor did he trust what his eyes just saw. Araylai saw the expression on his face, and grabbed his arm to hold him down.

"Stay down," she whispered.

He had to know, and so stole a peek over the baskets to the front where the proprietor was busy passing over the sponge to a group of customers whose webbed hands and spiny fins on the crest of their heads flapped in excitement. Araylai jerked him back down.

"Huh. They're not human. Did you know they weren't human? Of course, you knew they weren't human. It's your world," he whispered as he came to the realization that Araylai had left out some important details. "When were you going to tell me?"

"We need to move," she said, avoiding the question.

"And how do you propose we do that? Lose our hair, and grow some fins?"

"For one of us, yes."

Before his eyes the golden trellis of thick hair that fell down her back changed into delicate webbing like the people out front. In a matter of seconds the bone structure in her face altered as she morphed into her true form. Webbing appeared between the fingers that gripped his sleeve. His eyes locked on them.

"Stay here," she said as she let go and ducked out a flap in the back of the tent.

"Wait," he said to the back of the flap, but she was already gone.

He sat back on his haunches and fumed. Then he remembered the small device tucked away in his uniform. He pulled it out, and checked it. A tiny green dot blinked reassuringly inside the top left edge of the screen.

"Sharra," he whispered in relief. "Hold on a little longer. We're coming. We're coming."

He touched the dot, and a set of coordinates came up on the screen pointing northwest. He pressed the coordinates and swept the air with the tagfinder in the general direction of the dot, and brought it back to his chest to read. A three-dimensional hologram layout of connecting tunnels and open spaces rose from the screen and hovered above it. A blue line drew the shortest path to the tag. It was all he needed to find her. Now all he had to do was wait for his partner to come back.

He peeked over the baskets, and studied the alien creatures bickering over the sponges.

Araylai was one of them.

That explained a lot.

Even though he had been gone from the Agency for quite some time, he still remembered the oddities of the woman, how she never quite fit in. He would hide too if he looked like a fish. Poor woman. Why didn't Lazarus say anything? When he got back to the Vault, Lazarus would have some explaining to do. The man sure did love holding onto his secrets.

By the time Araylai returned, he was spitting fire.

"Where have you been?"

"Shhh, here. Put this on," she said, shoving a garment into his hands. "We are too vulnerable in here."

"Really. Do you think," he said as she unrolled her bundle of clothes.

She stopped what she was doing, and looked at him, and then to the bundle in his hands. He got the point.

"Have it your way," he said. "But when we get out of here, you and I are going to have a little talk."

Crouched on the floor, he unrolled the bundle. It was a long tan robe. He threw it over his head, and worked the course material down to cover his uniform as quickly as his awkward position would let him.

Beside him, Araylai took off her ankle-high boots and said, "Yours, too. They will notice."

"Shouldn't you be more concerned about my head?" he huffed as he unbuckled his boots. He pulled them off along with his socks. Bare footed, he leaned up and kept one eye on the front of the tent and one eye on the woman undressing at his feet.

Araylai unsnapped the front of her tight-fitting uniform, and after unzipping it, slipped it off her shoulders, exposing her alien body, fins and all, as she worked it down each of her legs. After tossing it to her feet, she slipped into a plain halter-top dress, and snapped the metal ring around her neck, holding the open-backed garment in place. Grabbing their boots, she tossed them into the empty sack along with her Vault uniform, and handed it to him.

Faolan slid back to the ground with the sack, "Now what?"

"The hood," she said.

He raised the hood of the robe over his head, hiding his human features behind the low rim of the material, and gave her the go ahead.

"Ladies first."

She opened the flap and slipped out into the narrow alleyway formed by the backs of the multitude of stalls. Faolan followed close behind, staying at her back as they worked their way through the forest of tension lines pegged into the sand.

Over the top of the tents loomed a wall of jagged rock, twenty stories high. It arched as it neared the top to form an irregular dome of rock high above their heads. The rock glowed with a strange light. It was too far for him to see what it was, but it was enough to light up the cavern. The sound of falling water came from the far end about a half-a-mile away. Peering at it, he could see a hole high in the wall where a waterfall spilled out from inside the rock. It cascaded in a sheet of white into a holding pool two stories down. From the pool it flowed out into access canals on both sides of the cavern wall before spilling down to the next level and the holding pool there. It did this all the way down, from one pool and access canals to the next, until the tents hid it from view. Open balconies like eyes looked down upon the busy floor of the cavern, some close enough for him to see the sheer material moving in the light breeze that flowed from the north end.

Faolan's eyes darted down the breaks in the tents, catching a glimpse now and then of the local inhabitants as Araylai led him to the end of the row.

Now I know what a fish out of water feels like, he thought, and laughed at his own joke. But it didn't last long before anger set in at the position Lazarus and Araylai put him in. Whatever happened to full disclosure?

They stopped at the end of the row where it came out onto a broad walkway busy with foot traffic. On the other side were more tents.

Faolan pulled out the tagfinder and took a reading. "Sharra is about two miles northwest of us." He passed over the instrument to Araylai. She took it, and studied the hologram.

"The dot puts her in Riff, an old outpost on the outer edge of the reef."

"Do you have any suggestions on the best way to get there? This is your turf, after all. And since I stand out like a sore thumb, I can't go walking around like normal. Why couldn't you have warned me before we left the Vault?"

"How do I explain this?" she said, waving her arms to encompass her world.

"Most people start at the beginning."

"It would have taken too much time."

A bark of sharp laughter escaped from him before he could stop it. "You're worried about time? We had all the time we needed back at the Vault.

"I thought it would be easier if you just saw it. What is the saying? 'A picture paints a thousand words.' Anyway, your feelings pushed me to hurry."

"My feelings?"

Her eyes bored into his, telling him something, but he couldn't read it. In fact, he couldn't get anything off of her since they had arrived. Her mental shield was down tight as a clam.

"Who else knows about you?" he said.

"Sharra. Lazarus. And now…you. Please, can we save this conversation for later? I do not want to be here anymore than you do."

"Fine. But we're not done." He paused to look at the passing cart of covered goods pulled by a burly-looking male. "How long do you think this disguise will work?"

"Not much further than this cave. Slaves wear different clothing depending on class distinction. You will be out of place outside of this sector," she said as she handed back the hologram.

Faolan enlarged the section of the cavern they were in, and studied the far wall of the hologram. "I assume these larger tunnels are roadways through the reef."

"Yes, but they will be crowded this time of day."

"What about these small tunnels underneath?" he said, pointing to the maze of lines running under the main grid of the reef. "They seem to lead everywhere."

"The thermal ducts? No one goes in there."

"Perfect."

"No, you do not understand. It is a maze of intense heat. No water, no relief. The molten core of the planet feeds them. That is what warms the ocean floor and the city of the reef. There is no map of them. Those that dare go in are never seen again."

"Unless there is another way, we don't have much choice."

Araylai sent him another one of her looks. "No."

"We have an advantage. We have our Vault uniforms, and a guide," he said as he studied the layout of the ducts in the hologram. "We can't get lost with this. Unless you have a better idea."

In the end Araylai gave in and picked the duct they would use to enter the maze. "There should be holding pens in this area. We can use them for cover. It looks like there is a duct right behind them."

"Holding pens for what?"

"Slaves," she said. "I will need to get some water. Keep your hood over your face and stay one step behind me. This is what will be expected of you. You are wearing the robe of a slave, my slave. You are the sand beneath my feet. Behave as such, and this might work."

Araylai straightened her back and stepped out into the lane and into the crowd, leaving questions burning on his tongue. Head bent, Faolan took his place behind her and kept his eyes glued on the back of her legs as she worked her way through the throng of people. From somewhere a warm breeze flowed through the tents that lined the lane, flapping the small triangle flags that decorated the fronts of the stalls. Through his hood he caught a whiff of over-ripe seaweed, dung, and other things he didn't recognize. He wrinkled his nose, and wondered how the locals could stand the pungent smell. Maybe they were immune to it, or maybe they couldn't smell at all. They were alien, after all, and he had no idea what they were capable of doing.

The crowd thinned the closer they got to the end of the Harena Market. Soon they left the packed sand of the tent city behind and entered the softer sands that led to the stockyards and to a large archway in the wall beyond. The smell of dung lay heavy in the air as they passed the wooden pens that lined both sides of the road. Sounds of animals hooted and snorted from behind the wooden railings. With his hood down, he stared in frustration at Araylai's legs, deprived of seeing much of her world.

Araylai turned her face to the side and said in a low tone, "The thermal duct is on the far side of the slave pens past the auction block." She pointed with her head over the wooden platform to the row of large metal holding pens that lined the sloping wall of the cavern.

Slave pens. The words made him shudder as an ancient memory surfaced unexpectedly. It was a mission to the Colonies when slavery was at its darkest hour. It had bothered him so much that, after the mission was completed, he had asked Lazarus for a memory block. But Lazarus had told him to wait, that those memories would fade with time. And he had been right. But seeing it again brought it all back.

Faolan pressed his lips together and lifted his head a fraction to scan the road ahead, bracing himself for what he might see. The row of animal pens had ended. In the next section stood a high wooden platform. On the ground in front of it was a group of female Arderians. Dressed in silk and gold they fluttered together like colorful butterflies in conversation too far away for him to hear.

"Praemin buyers," Araylai said, noting the direction of his gaze. "We are beneath their notice."

He switched his gaze over their finned heads to the other side of the auction block to the metal cages that lined the cavern wall, catching a shadow of a movement behind the metal bars. He didn't want to think about who or what were in those cages. He had to keep focused on the mission, on Sharra. At the far end of the cages was the air duct at ground level. So small was it that he had almost missed it.

They entered the small clearing around the auction block just as four bound slaves were dragged up the steps and hauled in a line across the stage. The Praemin, eager for new stock, pressed forward to get a closer look at the latest offerings. A male guard snapped his whip against the floor, and pushed one of the three male slaves up to the front, leaving the female off to the side. The slave stood before the Praemin on trembling legs half-naked as they examined his body as if he were chattel. The auctioneer appeared from the side, and began the bidding.

Faolan followed Araylai around the bidders, keeping his head down. The auction was in full swing. The entrance to the underground maze lay fifty feet on the other side. They were almost around the crowd when Araylai stopped short to stare at something on the stage. He heard her sharp intake of breath, but couldn't see what had caused it, only knowing that when she started to move again they were not heading to the duct.

"Where are you going?" he whispered close to her shoulder, but she said nothing as she led him to the side of the platform, and stopped in front of the female prisoner.

"Immari?" Araylai said.

Hearing the shock in Araylai's voice, Faolan dared a quick glance at the one called Immari, and gasped. The female stood leaning to one side in a tattered knee-length dress. Now several sizes too large it hung off her boney frame like a rag doll. The crested webbing on her head drooped down her back. Her right eye was swollen shut, her lips cracked and bleeding. Fresh welts oozed blood down her arms and legs, half-covering older darker bruises from past lashings.

Immari raised her head and blinked her good eye as if awakening from a trance, and searched the Praemin for the one who called to her. When her eye found Araylai, her body stiffened in shock. She shook her head, sending her a warning, but Araylai ignored it.

"Immari," Araylai groaned. A tear slipped down her cheek as she stared at the tortured creature.

"Araylai," Faolan whispered in warning.

Araylai reached up and swiped the tear off her cheek with an angry hand. Her face tightened as she pressed her lips together and sent a hint of a nod to Immari. Immari saw it and shook her head no, but Araylai had already turned away. With cold eyes, she sought out the auctioneer.

"I will take this one," she shouted, thrusting her arm up to point a long finger at Immari.

Heads turned as her strong demand cut through the crowd. The auctioneer stopped the bidding on the male, and put his hands on his hips. "What is this? Is she so desirable to you that you cannot wait?

"What are you doing?" Faolan whispered through his teeth.

Araylai brushed him off and stared at the auctioneer. "Desirable? Look at her. Her crest droops. The skin is sagging off her bones. There is no life left in her. Yet you parade her around on your stage like she is a prize. Do you insult our intelligence on purpose?"

"No, My Lady. I would never do that." His eyes narrowed as he studied her. "I am only looking to recoup her holding costs."

"You ask much in return for damaged goods. Maybe the council should be informed of your mismanagement…"

"Please, My Lady, we wish to bring no dishonor. This slave has been difficult_"

"Then you should be happy that I am willing to take her off your hands," Araylai said.

Faolan grabbed her arm. "We can't take her. Think of the mission."

A collective gasp rose in the air around him. He followed their gaze to the exposed human hand sticking out of his robe, and knew he was in deep trouble. With a quick flick of his wrist, he shoved it back into the sleeve of his robe, but not before he heard the crack of a whip. A millisecond later a searing pain wrapped itself around his lower leg like a stinging python.

"Aaaaa," he yelled as he grabbed his leg.

"On your knees, slave."

One of the guards strolled closer and yanked on the other end of the whip, jerking Faolan to the ground. He landed hard on his kneecaps with a grunt. Pain throbbed up his calf muscle from the ring of newly formed welts and joined with the pain in his knees, bringing tears to his eyes.

"Stop," Araylai said. "He is mine to punish."

"No. They have witnessed his insolence," the guard said, gesturing to the slaves standing forlornly on the platform. "They need to see what happens to those who do not know their place."

Faolan clenched his teeth and growled low in his throat as he thought of the fresh welts that covered

Immari's body, of the pain she must have suffered under the hands of the guard, making his own pain pale in comparison. He didn't need anything more to act. It was enough.

The pockmarked guard raised the whip in the air to bring it down on his bent back, but he got no further. Before it found its mark, Faolan sprung from the ground and hurled himself at the guard with a growl. The whip dropped to the ground as they both went down in a pile of arms and legs. Faolan didn't wait, but leaped onto the guard's chest and raised his fist. Bam, bam, bam, he slammed it into the ugly alien face, drawing blood.

"That's for assaulting me," he said.

The guard howled and bucked underneath the weight of Faolan's body as he tried to get a hold of him through the heavy folds of the robe that smothered him. Finally, the Arderian found some leverage and grabbed the hood of the robe and yanked it back, exposing the human face for all to see.

A loud gasp went up, followed by whispers of shock.

"A land-walker."

"He must be a spy."

"A spy."

"Kill him."

Silvery-grey eyes narrowed below the shock of unruly black hair. Faolan's lips curled as he sneered into the face of the shocked guard.

"Surprise," he said.

Before the Arderian could recover, Faolan let his fists fly again. Bam, bam, bam. Like bullets he hit the guard's nose and jaw over and over again until he heard the satisfying sound of cracking bones. Blood splattered over his fists and on his robe as the nose on the alien face gave way.

"And that's payback for the slaves," he said, breathing heavy with adrenalin.

The moans of the fallen guard reached the Auctioneer on the platform, breaking him from his stupor. Looking around he called to the others, "Guards, Guards," and jumped down to the ground, pulling his knife from the sheath at his thigh.

Araylai saw it and grabbed Faolan's shoulder as he ready for another punch. "Time to go."

She grabbed her knife and leaped onto the stage. On crouched legs she ran to Immari, and attacked the thick rope around her wrists with the blade.

"We can't take her," Faolan yelled.

The Arderian guard moaned underneath him. With one final act, Faolan stood and slammed his foot down onto the wrist of the whip hand, feeling the bone give way under the weight of his body with a gratifying crunch. The guard screamed in agony as he grabbed his wrist, forgetting all about Faolan.

Araylai looked up from her sawing.

"Behind you!" she yelled as she continued to hack at the rope.

Faolan looked up to see the direction of her gaze and swung around just as the Auctioneer plunged his knife into the folds of his robe. A warm sensation billowed from below his left ribs and spread down the inside of his Vault uniform. The Auctioneer drew the knife out. It gleamed red with blood, his blood. The Auctioneer smiled triumphantly.

Before his blood could drip off the blade, Faolan whipped his leg around and knocked the knife out of the Auctioneer's hand with the side of his foot. The smile left his adversary's face as he watched the long blade arch through the air end-over-end, and land with a thud into the floor of the platform.

Faolan landed on his feet, ignoring the searing pain in his side as he shifted onto the balls of his feet. While the Auctioneer stared at his knife stuck in the floor out of reach, Faolan shot a hand out and jabbed him in the neck, crushing his esophagus with a quick thrust. The Arderian stumbled back as he grabbed his neck, and dropped to his knees. Gurgling and gasping, he said nothing as his lips moved soundlessly below his protruding eyes.

On the platform, Araylai tore the last of the ropes from Immari's arms. "Faolan! More guards! To your right!"

Faolan twisted to the right and spotted a squad of guards working their way through the circle of excited Praemin.

"Time to go!" he yelled back.

At his feet the Auctioneer grabbed his leg. Faolan slammed a foot into his chest, knocking him to the ground, and leaped onto the platform.

"Help me with Immari," Araylai said as she wrapped her arms around the beaten female and helped her to the steps.

Legs too weak, Immari stumbled and fell to the floor. Faolan ran across the stage. Scooping her up in his arms in one swift motion, he leaped off the stage, and landed with an oomph. A jolt of pain ripped through his side, but he didn't slow down. Gritting his teeth, he pressed Immari to his chest, and took off. Araylai landed right behind him, and together they raced across the sand to the slave pens against the wall.

They ran past the last cage, and past a small army of carts until the stone face of the wall was exposed. As they approached the wall a blast of hot air hit them like a brick wall.

"Up ahead," Araylai said, pointing to a metal grate low to the ground.

They pushed through the heat and ran up to the grate that covered the hole in the rock. Faolan set Immari against the wall next to the grate, and whipped out his knife and furiously attacked the metal brackets that held it in place as the heat pummeled his face and hands. Araylai did the same, squinting her eyes against the plumes of thermal energy as she fought to free a bracket. The pile grew as one popped free, and then another.

Immari's weak voice reached their ears, "The guards. They come."

"Grab the grate," Faolan said to Araylai.

Together they wrapped their sweaty hands around the grate. With a leg each against the wall they pulled with all their might. The wall crumbled as the last of the brackets gave way. Araylai tossed the metal piece aside, and slid inside.

"Immari, hurry," Araylai called from the hole.

Immari crawled to the hole and dragged herself into the heat.

"You! Intruders! Stop!" The guards were almost upon them, spears and knives waving in the air.

The one in front raised his spear for the throw.

Faolan saw it and dove into the hole just as a rush of hot air brushed by his head. The spear hit the top of the entrance with a crack. It bounced off the rock and fell to the sand.

In the tunnel, Faolan rolled to a stop next to where Immari rested against the hard wall.

"Keep moving," he said, gritting his teeth against the pain in his side as he got to his feet.

"Leave me," Immari said. "I will only slow you down."

"No one gets left behind," Araylai said.

"You won't make it with_"

"This is not the time to argue," Faolan said, cutting her off. He lifted Immari up into his arms just as a shadow filled the tunnel entrance. "Run."

They took off, leaving the last of the light from the entrance behind as they headed into the oppressive heat. Araylai led the way, following the bend of the passageway with her outstretched hands. Faolan ran blindly behind his partner with his burden in his arms, staying as close to her back as he dared to in the dark. Two hundred feet in the passageway widened at a branch, and the darkness shifted from black to grey to a putrid green. Tiny lichen plants glowed from nooks and crevices in the ceiling, getting thicker and thicker the deeper they went, until it became a solid mass of living light.

Without hesitation, Araylai veered into the left tunnel. They raced ahead into the relentless heat, turning right and left, then right again, until Faolan lost all sense of direction. The hot air burned their mouths and lungs, but they didn't dare stop. Sweat beaded on his forehead, soaking his hair, and ran down his face to his chin. He blinked the saltiness out of his eyes and glanced at the dead weight in his arms.

Immari's bruised and broken skin glistened in the eerie light as a film of sweat covered her body, soaking what little remained of her clothing. Her face glowed an eerie green. Shadows from the bruising mixed with her pale skin and the light of the cave. Like death her eyes stayed closed, her mouth open and loose.

"Araylai, we must stop," he called out.

He stopped and laid Immari in the middle of the floor. Dragging his robe over his head, he bunched it into a rough pillow, and slipped it under her head. Araylai set the sack on the floor and crouched down next them, and touched the dark stain on the robe.

"Blood," she said.

"It's mine," Faolan admitted. "Just a scratch. Help me with Immari. She doesn't look too good."

"Immari, can you hear me?" Araylai said.

Immari moaned as her eyes remained closed.

Araylai looked across at Faolan, her eye rings flashed with worry. "She is too weak for this heat. We do not know how far off course we are."

"I can fix that," he said.

He slipped the tagfinder from its clip on his uniform and checked the readings in the pale light. The green dot beeped reassuringly inside the grid. He touched the screen and pulled up the hologram.

"According to the diagram, we have turned west. Sharra is a mile and a half in that direction," he said pointing to the wall behind her head. "It's not straight going either."

"Immari will not make it to Riff in this heat."

"We can't go back. Our cover has been blown. We can only go forward."

"There is another option," she said.

"No," he said, shaking his head. "What are you thinking? Maitland would never go for that."

Araylai looked down at the still figure between them, at the fresh marks that covered her body. "I will not leave her here to die."

"Who is she?"

"She was my closest friend. My mother must have seen her as a threat to have done this to her." A tear dropped from her eye, and then another, mixing with the sweat of her face.

"Your mother did this?

"If I would have left her on the auction block, it would have killed her for sure. An easy way for my mother's hands to remain unconnected. I cannot leave her here. I must take her home."

"What about Lazarus?"

"He will understand. I will not have her death be on my hands, if I can help it."

"Go, then. I will find Sharra on my own."

Faolan helped lift Immari into a sitting position. Crouching next to her, Araylai wrapped her arms around her friend and leaned her into her chest. He set the sack on Immari's lap.

From the bundle, Araylai pulled out his boots. "You'll need these now."

"Thanks," he said, taking them.

"And this," she said handing him a flask. "Water."

"How did you…"

"I pilfered it in the markets," she said. "Be careful. I will meet up with you in Riff."

"I'll keep my Link open. Let me know when you're back."

Her eyes grew vacant as she prepared for the shift. A moment later the two Arderian women disappeared. After they left he put his boots on. Ripping a strip from the robe, he wadded it into a ball and tucked it into the slit in his uniform below his ribs. With the rest he wiped down his head and neck, knowing it was a futile exercise. Checking the tagfinder, he set a new course alone, into the maze.

Chapter Twenty-One

———

A commotion in the hallway jarred Sharra from her glazed stare into the sea. The door opened and Caetus walked in, his aura close to indigo with concern as she got up from her bed of pillows.

"They have caught the hu-man," he said.

"Already?" Her hand reached for the knife tucked in the belt at her waist.

"He is alone. Nayada will not let him hurt you."

She nodded, but did not remove her hand from the blade.

"They bring him to you now. I thought I should warn you first."

With a silent thought, he motioned the hunting party in.

Through the door, Calyx and Cael half-carried a man between them. His Vault uniform was torn and bloody. His dark hair was plastered to his head. Sweat dripped down his face and neck, and into the collar of his suit. With his hands tied behind his back, he struggled to get away as soon as they had crossed the threshold. The Umbra scouts pulled him up and held him firmly.

Nayada grabbed him from behind and pressed her blade between his shoulders. "Stop. Or do you want to feel my knife in your back."

The man stiffened. "I'm telling you that I'm not a threat to your kind. I'm here on a rescue mission, for one of my own, another human."

"We will see about that," Nayada said as she pushed him further into the room.

Through a rip in the left side of his black uniform peeked a cloth of crimson red, turning dark where it had smeared onto the outside of his uniform. On his forehead below his unruly black hair, a fresh wound oozed a rivulet of blood. It mingled with his sweat and ran down the side of his brow to his chin and dribbled down into the neck of his collar.

Sharra froze at the sight of the man. "Faolan! Faolan? She shook her head and backed away. "No. Not you."

Faolan turned at the sound of his name and saw her. "Sharra. You're safe. Thank god."

She eyed his tattered uniform with dawning understanding. "You've been working for the Vault all along. I should've known. The night you helped me with Tanner, and then the Ball... you were playing me, weren't you. Why?"

"No. It's not like that," he said as he twisted

between Calyx and Cael with renewed energy.

"Stay away," she said, raising the knife between them. He stopped at the sight of her fear. "On the balcony, why didn't you kill me then? You had me alone. It would have been so easy. Why go through the trouble of dumping me on this planet?"

"I'm telling you, I'm not the one who did it. I've come to rescue you."

"Rescue me? The only person who knows I'm on Ardus is the one who tried to kill me."

"Let me kill him for you," Cael snarled. His crested fin flicked in agitation while the rings of his eyes flashed bright. "It would be my pleasure."

"Wait," Faolan said. "Let me explain."

Sharra sent Cael a silent no. Out loud she said, "Thank you, Cael, but no. I want to hear what he has to say."

"Explain hu-man," Nayada said, pressing the blade through his uniform, breaking the skin on his shoulder blade. He hissed with pain. "How did you come to find her then?"

Faolan gritted his teeth against the pain, but kept his eyes on Sharra and said, "Lazarus commissioned a tag to be placed inside you shortly after Dash's death when we realized you were still in danger. When I lost you on the grid, and you didn't return to the Vault, we started a search party. A lead came in a few days back that you were on Ardus. The tagfinder picked up your beacon as soon as we hit the atmosphere. We knew you were still alive, but down in the city underneath the water. We came as soon as we could arrange a way down."

"You speak of a 'we'. Where is this other 'agent'?"

Nayada asked.

"Araylai," he said, keeping his eyes on Sharra's face. "She was our only way to shift into the city."

"Araylai is here?" Caetus said in alarm as the aura's in the room bursts midnight blue at the news.

Faolan shook his head. "She shifted back to the Vault as soon as we made it to the thermal tunnels down at the edge of the market place."

"Which market?" Nayada said.

"I think she said it was the Sand Markets. Or something like that."

Sharra could see the others relaxing, and didn't like it. She had no reason to trust him. He had been nothing but deceitful since their first encounter, using her, and manipulating her. Her knuckles whitened as she gripped her knife and inched her way towards him, keeping her eyes glued to his handsome face as she pushed the feelings in her heart aside.

"You could be making this all up," she said as she touched his chest with the tip of her blade.

"I can prove it," he said. "I wear a Link. Take it, and contact Lazarus. He's waiting for news."

"I can't use it, nor can I shift. You saw to that."

"Please, Sharra, believe me." His silver eyes pleaded with her. "I would never harm you, or put your life in danger. I asked Lazarus for this mission. I only wanted to bring you back home… safe."

Caetus set a webbed hand over hers, staying the knife. "His faint aura speaks the truth. He is not the one you are looking for."

The blurred face of her brother swam before her eyes. As quickly as it came, it disappeared. Sharra knew the answer, but didn't want to believe it. It was easier to keep thinking it was someone else. That it was her brother... well, it just couldn't be. Caetus assurance that Faolan was innocent wasn't enough. She had to see it for herself. It would mean breaking her own rule. It was the only way to know for sure. Her conscience pricked her for a second. She pushed it quickly aside. Faolan would just have to understand.

With a delicate touch, she reached out and entered Faolan's mind. A veil of pain from his wounds colored his thoughts. Yet, the truth was there. It hit her like a fist to the face. She could not deny the strength of his determination to prove his innocence, nor ignore the underlying emotion behind it.

It was love, pure and simple love.

Not the love of a fellow comrade in arms, even though that was there too. The Vault tied all the agents together, mentally and emotionally, as she had already experienced.

No, this love went beyond that. It was the kind that she had always dreamed of finding, the kind that bound two people together- forever. That love crept into her mind, caressing her with unspoken promises, uninhibited by any barrier of fear or rejection.

She sucked in her breath and slammed her shield down, breaking the connection with the swiftness of a guillotine. His feelings for her swamped her brain, and seeped down to her heart. It responded, thudding hard against her ribs. His strange eyes bored into hers, and she flushed. Unable to bear it any longer, she dropped her gaze as she lowered the knife and stepped back.

"I believe you," she said. "Untie him."

Cael and Calyx held Faolan steady while Nayada cut the bonds around his wrists. The rope fell to the floor. The Umbra guards let go of him, but kept a wary eye as he rubbed at the red marks on his wrists.

"Thank you," he said as he pressed a hand to his injured side. "I should contact Lazarus. Let him know that you're safe."

He dragged himself over to a chair and sagged into it, at the same time pulling the wire of his Link down to his jawline. After a brief conversation with the Head Director, he next contacted Araylai.

"Yes," he said into the mike, "I've found her. She's safe in the care of the one called Caetus in Riff. Where are you?" He listened for a moment. "Yes, we will wait for you. Be careful, your friends don't think it safe for you in the city."

He flipped the mike back up. "Araylai says she is in the Blue Corridor of the Upper Knoll."

"That is a couple hours away," Cael said.

"She should not have come back. Ardere is no longer safe for her," Caetus said.

"Whether you like it or not, she's here and on her way. You can try to talk some sense into her when she gets here. I've tried already. Maybe she'll listen to you," Faolan said with a sigh and winced in pain.

Sharra knew that he was in more pain than he was letting on, and sent a silent request to Caetus.

"Cael, help Sharra take the hu-man to her quarters, and give him what he needs for his wounds. In the meantime, Nayada, you and Calyx can scout for Araylai. We need to get to her before she is spotted by one of the Queen's consorts."

Faolan got up and swayed. Sharra rushed over, but Cael beat her there, steadying Faolan with a hand as he took his arm and swung it over his shoulder. They left the others to their duties as they headed through the quiet outpost to her room in the guards' quarters. Once there, Cael gently deposited Faolan onto the edge of her bed.

"I will go get my kit," he said, and shot out the door.

Faolan reached up with his free hand and began undoing the zipper to the tight-fitting jacket of his uniform. Underneath, the once white t-shirt was soaked crimson with blood. Sharra gasped at the sight as the smell of rusty metal hit her nose.

"Oh, Faolan," she said. "You should've said something. How bad is it?"

He let go of his side, and with a groan pulled one arm out of the jacket. Breathing heavily, he stopped and grabbed his side again, unable to finish the job.

"Bad enough," he said.

Sharra took the other sleeve and slipped the jacket off, and tossed it aside. A rolled up pad soaked with blood fell away. With another groan he lifted his arms one by one as she eased the t-shirt over his head, exposing the puncture wound in the left side a few inches below his ribs. Fresh blood oozed from the one-inch opening and ran down his side. She quickly made another pad from the ruined t-shirt and pressed it against his side, and pushed him down onto the bed. With a sigh, he laid down and shut his eyes.

"We need to get you back to the Vault," she said as she kept pressure on the makeshift pad.

"I promised Araylai I'd wait for her."

"She'd understand. Link with her."

She didn't get any further, for after a brief knock on the door, Cael came in carrying a tray of supplies and a carafe of water. He set them on the chest by the bed and took Sharra's place, removing the pad to examine the wound.

"A knife wound," he said. "They are common here. It looks clean. No signs of poison. You are very fortunate."

He took a clean cloth and wet it with the water from the carafe, and cleaned the blood away. He then pressed open the cut with his fingers and poured a foul-smelling liquid into the hole. The muscles around the angry flesh wound rippled with spasms as Faolan's body tensed with renewed pain. He groaned, but Cael held firm as he pressed the wound together and squeezed a thin line of clear substance along the cut. The glue-like material held. The bleeding stopped.

Faolan grunted, and said, "Hurts like hell. What did you put in me?"

"Fireweed. Kills everything."

"I believe it."

"Here, drink this." Cael handed him a cup of brown liquid. "It will dull the pain."

Faolan downed it in one swift gulp and handed the cup back. Sinking onto the bed, Faolan sighed in relief as the medicine hit his blood stream.

"That's as good as a Vault pen. Very effective. What's the drug you use? I bet Cam would be interested," Faolan said.

"It is only good if you remain quiet." Cael gathered the discarded clothes, and headed to the door. "I will see what I can do with these. Rest for now. And listen to Sharra."

Chapter Twenty-Two

The door shut behind Cael, leaving the two of them alone. Neither said a word. Sharra picked up a fresh cloth from the tray. After wetting it, she sat on the edge of the bed and gently wiped at the stain of blood on Faolan's stomach where Cael had finished off. Though it was clean where the knife had gone in, the blood had run down the front to his lower belly to the edge of his beltline. She worked in silence as she grappled with her emotions. Her nineteenth century man, the man she had tried so hard to forget was with her in the flesh once again, hurt but alive. It had to be fate… or someone's idea of a bad joke. She didn't care. He was there. He was a Vault agent. And he loved her. All the feelings she had worked so hard to suppress came flooding back.

She ran the cloth back and forth over his skin below the wound, and across his stomach, watching the hard muscles in his abdomen ripple as she wiped the drying blood away. The cloth soon turned red. Grabbing another one, she wet it and continued wiping the trail of blood to where it collected in his bellybutton. His stomach jumped underneath her fingers as she dabbed it clean. It made her heart flutter. Her breath turned shallow as she followed the trail of blood down the line of dark hair that led to the rim of his pants. The silver Vault logo on the buckle of the belt that he wore around his lean hips shimmered under a film of dried blood. It caught her eye. Her hand stilled at the edge of his beltline for a tantalizing few seconds as the flat metal of the insignia came to life before her eyes. Like the liquid metal of the pylons it flowed within its set form on the buckle, teasing her, goading her. And then it passed, turning back to the flat metal of before.

She blinked not believing her own eyes, and shook it off as she had when the Vault business card from the job fair had done the same thing. She had forgotten about that, the business card, until now. She had always meant to ask Lazarus about it, and never got to it. There had been bigger problems to worry about since then, like the double agrylium in her head, and, oh yes, someone was out to kill her.

The strange feeling passed. When it did, her hand began to move again. Following the edge of his pants where most of the blood had collected, she wiped back and forth with a fresh cloth smearing it as she concentrated on getting it all off. So caught up in what she was doing, she didn't see his hand until it grabbed her wrist and held her still.

"I think that'll do for now," Faolan said in a tight

voice. "I may be hurt, but I'm not dead."

Her eyes flew to his face and caught the intense look in his eyes. She flushed red as she realized her administrations had affected him as much as it had affected her. She jumped up and turned her back to him as she grabbed another cloth and began to wipe her hands clean.

"I don't make a very good nurse," she said, feeling his eyes on the bare flesh of her back as she wiped her hands.

"On the contrary. I think you're a wonderful nurse," he said. "Very thorough."

"I should have left it for Cael."

"But you're much prettier," he said with a smile as he pushed himself up onto his elbows. "Plus, I don't know if I trust them. How much do we really know about this alien race?"

She threw the cloth onto the tray, and whipped around to point a finger at him.

"You're one to talk. You're wearing a Vault uniform, and have an agrylium mark behind your ear. I don't know why I didn't spot it before. Why did you hide it, that you were an agent the first time we met? Tanner almost died that night. You knew we were in trouble. You could've shifted us back then and there. But you didn't. Why?"

The big gash on Tanner's forehead, the knife wounds on his body, the strong smell of blood, and the fear of death still haunted her dreams. Hands on her hips, Sharra glared at him as she waited for an answer.

"I couldn't shift you and Tanner. Believe me, I wanted to. Tanner was a friend of mine... is a friend of mine," he corrected. "I could see his injuries were serious, and I knew you were fresh in the field. But once I figured out that you were off to get Lazarus, I knew I had to disappear."

"Why?"

Faolan lay back on the pillow, and sighed. "It's complicated."

"Everything at the Vault is complicated."

He smiled. "Let's just say, Lazarus and I didn't see eye to eye on some fundamental issues a while back, and I thought it best if I vanished for a time."

"What made you choose eighteen twenty-five London?"

"It seemed as good a place as any." Faolan shrugged his shoulders. "I still would've been there if I hadn't stumbled upon the plot that led me to you."

"So it wasn't a chance meeting after all."

"I couldn't stand by and do nothing, knowing Dash was up to no good. So I placed a tag on one of the thugs he had hired and followed him, but by the time I got there... I'll never get over that sight. You were like an avenging angel in the mist, standing over Tanner's body with just a piece of splintered wood in your hand."

Sharra looked at the thin white scars on her palms where the bigger splinters had left their mark. "That night changed me."

He reached for her hand and pulled her down, and cradled her next to his body. She wanted to resist him, but her body betrayed her. And so she gave in and sank next to his side.

"The Vault changes everyone," Faolan said. He turned her hand over and traced the thin lines with the pad of his thumb. "You shouldn't have battle scars."

His thumb left the scar and slowly circled the sensitive skin of her palm. Shivers ran down her spine. She tried to focus.

"What about the Ball? Was that planned too?"

"Lazarus knew that your troubles hadn't ended with Dash's death, that there was still a traitor loose in the Agency. Placing the tag on you was my idea. Since I had been out of the picture for so long, I was the logical choice to keep an eye on you. The Ball in London was chosen because we knew you wouldn't question my presence there."

"So the kiss was just a diversion," she said, disappointed.

His thumb stopped its torturous circling, but he didn't let go of her hand. Instead, he placed it on his chest, folding his hand over it, and closed his eyes. His voice softened as he said, "It took all my strength not to take you into my arms the first time we met. You were like a scared doe, all big-eyed. I still can remember the smudges on your one cheek, and your braid all eschew. I wanted to kiss you right then, but you had just been attacked, and were in a vulnerable state." He paused and smiled behind his closed eyelids, and whispered. "No, the kiss we shared at the Ball was real."

Her heart fluttered at the words as she remembered his lips on hers as if it were yesterday. The power of his touch scared her and thrilled her at the same time. And now they were together with no more pretenses. Under the warmth of her hand his heart beat steady as his breathing slowed.

"I didn't lie that night," he said in a soft whisper.

"You are beautiful, and... desirable, and... and... I think Cael spiked my drink."

His words died away as his body relaxed into a drug-induced sleep, leaving her alone with a warm glow in her heart.

He loved her.

As strange as that was, she knew it to be true. She bent over their clasped hands and gently kissed his lips, and pulled the sheet over his body before stretching out next to him on the narrow bed. Now all she had to do was wait for Araylai to show up, and they could go home.

"Home," she said, with a mixed sense of longing and dread. For back at the Vault was Tanner, the other man who was in love with her. If that wasn't bad enough, she had a much bigger problem waiting there.

Her brother.

How that was possible, she didn't know. And yet, it must be, for how else could she explain all this.

Chapter Twenty-Three

The cavern ceiling that made up the small outpost town of Riff dimmed with the setting of the sun. In the darkening light the shallow photophore lamps like flattened paper lanterns came to life. Soon the cavern was filled with a glow that would have been romantic if it weren't for the balky Guard House that stuck out of the far end. The smell of spiced kelp floated through the empty tiers of streets. Inside their carved-out homes of translucent rocks, families gathered for their evening meal all the while unaware of the two scouts watching the main street with eagle eyes from their vantage point at the post.

Like clockwork the sweet sound of reeds floated down from the third tier from old Duris's home to serenade the town folk as they ate. It played a duet with the ever-flowing fountain that spilled from the ornamental fish head in the wall in the center of town, creating beautiful music that soothed even the hardened spirits of the aged.

Nayada smiled a small smile glad to have a chance to be out of the barracks to hear the blend of water and music. Even where she stood on the balcony of the Guard House, the ruckus from the dining hall could be heard through the archway behind her. Dinner was always a noisy affair inside the Guard House. Caetus said it was good for morale for them to have a place to relax and be free. She disagreed. Being an Umbra was about discipline, honor, and loyal service, not about having a good time. That was for when they went home to their pods.

Ignoring the noise behind her, she scanned the cavern from her vantage point on the balcony. From there she could see the whole town, all four tiers. Unlike the main caverns of the city, Riff was deemed small in comparison. Everyone here knew everyone else. The habits of the locals were noted- good and bad. For the most part, the outpost used that to their advantage, like tonight. She could dismiss the every day things without a thought. It was the unusual that she was looking for, the thing that was out of place in a place of repeated sameness.

On the ground level a lone figure stepped out of a doorway. Nayada spotted her right away. With knees bent, the female crept down the broad street, hugging the shadows cast by the decorative canopies that hung over the row of shops that lined the ground floor. Out of the night, a noise of metal on metal resonated through the cavern over the top of the melody of reed and water. The female stopped at the sound. Head tilted she searched the opposite staircase of streets to the top level, but nothing moved. The echo died away. She turned back to her intended path, and continued cautiously down the street.

"Now, that is something unusual," Nayada whispered.

Before the stranger saw her, she crouched low behind one of the thick banisters of the parapet that protected the outer edge of the balcony. Above her head, resting on the top of the banister was a large disc of photophore. From its shallow bowl burned a cool light out into the night, casting her in shadows.

She peeked between the banisters and watched the figure slowly glide up the street. Below on the ground level, Calyx waited from her vantage point off to the side in the shadows behind one of the right outward pillars that supported the large curved balcony.

Nayada reached across the short distance and connected with Calyx's mind.

A stranger comes. Left side of street.

Hugging the pillar, Calyx leaned one eye out and sighted the Arderian before tucking away again. *I see her. What do you think? Is it her?*

Too far to tell yet. We are not to take any chances. Wait until she passes you before you move. Dorsal position. I will take lead.

The stranger reached the end of the protection of the shops, and ran across the lighted ramp that led to the next level. Reaching the other side she pressed her body against the shadows of the retaining wall of the ramp and searched the lighted entrance of the Guard House. Deeming it safe, the female left the ramp, and still hugging the wall, reached the first set of pillars and headed to the center to the open archway.

Now, Nayada said.

She leaped from her hiding place and jumped to the floor below, landing in a crouch in front of the stranger. In one swift move her knife was out and pointed at the female's heart. At the same time Calyx slipped behind the startled Arderian as silent as a ghost, her knife drawn and poised.

"Hold," Nayada said. "State your business here."

The female raised her hands palms out. "I mean no harm. I have come on an errand, from the city."

In the dim light of the overhead photophores the birthmark on the female's right palm stood out like a beacon against the luminescence of her skin. Nayada's crest flicked in surprise at the sight of it. In her mind she saw an identical mark hidden in the palm of her own knife hand. Doubt crept into her aura as she stared at the raised hand of the stranger. She flicked her gaze to the stranger's face, and caught the surprised look in the identical eyes staring back at her in a face all too familiar to her.

"How can this be?" Nayada said.

The cool orange of the stranger's curiosity shimmered in the air around her, but she quickly hid it. Instead, she said, "I was informed that Caetus is stationed here. He is holding something safe for me, and I wish to... collect it."

"I know what he holds," Nayada said.

"If you know what he holds, then you know who I am," she said.

As she spoke she lifted her shield and sent an

invitation across the breach between them.

Having never seen the princess, Nayada had no clue what the royal Arderian looked like. The female before her could be anyone. And that she looked identical to herself confused her even more. It could be a trap. Taking no chances Nayada entered the female's mind cautiously. Her Umbra senses were heightened, ready to cut the connection at any signs of a mental trap as she traversed through the first layers of the Arderian's consciousness until she came to the truth that the female's mind revealed. The evidence of it stood right before her, in mind and body. Until then she didn't believe it.

She quickly withdrew and lowered her knife.

"My Heres," she said, bowing her head. "I meant no disrespect."

"Please, do not show me such honor. It is unsafe for you to do so, especially in public," Araylai said as she scanned the tiers of the cavern in case it had been witnessed.

Nayada lifted her head and sheathed her knife. "Calyx put your knife away." To Araylai she said, "We must get you off the street. We can talk inside. There are too many eyes in your mother's service."

"And too many rumors," Calyx said.

Nayada snatched a cloak from a peg from the front sentry room as they passed by, and gave it to Araylai.

"Just in case someone on duty at the post knows what you look like," Nayada said.

Araylai slipped it over her shoulders and raised the hood over her head, and followed Nayada through the open courtyard to the large metal doors of the main building. Once inside, they passed through the main conclave, avoiding the open doorway to the dining hall where a regiment of Umbra guards chatted good-naturedly over their evening meal.

As they entered the back hallway, Nayada pointed Calyx to the sleeping quarters. "Find Cael and have him bring our two guests to the conference room. We will meet you there."

Ten minutes later in the conference room, Caetus stood before the princess and bowed.

"My Heres, you honor us."

"Praemin Caetus, it is I who am honored. You risk much, not only in seeing me, but also for hiding my hu-man friends."

"It is Nayada you need to thank. It was her quick mind that saved the hu-man called Sharra from too long on the open water."

Nayada's aura glowed yellow with the unexpected praise. "It is the reflection of the wisdom handed down to me by my guardian and mentor."

Caetus's eyes beamed with pride. "See how humble she is? She does all the work, and yet, she gives me the credit when I had nothing to do with it."

"There are those that are still loyal to you, Princess," Nayada said, changing the subject. "Not all believe the propaganda spread by the Queen's cohorts."

Araylai touched the Link behind her ear, and listened for a moment, and said, "My partner says that someone called Cael brings them."

As soon as she said it, a knock sounded on the door. Nayada cracked it opened and peeked out. Seeing her pod mates, she swung it open and gestured them through.

"Hurry. The dinner bell will be ringing any moment now," she said.

Calyx rushed the two hu-mans into the room with Cael bringing in the rear. Once safely inside, Nayada shut the door and locked it, and took up station next to her guardian. Araylai moved to the female hu-man and hugged her, her happiness written in the yellow of her aura. Nayada studied the princess while she talked with the hu-mans, seeing the same facial features as her own, the same amber-colored eyes, down to the deep green rings that framed them, to the many-faceted dorsal fin that ran from her head and down her back. She looked down at the mark in her palm and then at the princess.

At her side, Caetus stirred. Feeling the touch of his thoughts, she opened the private channel.

Do you see it? she asked, and read the hesitation in his aura. *You must.*

Resignation colored his thoughts as his shoulders sagged with some unknown weight. *I had hoped this day would never come, that you would be spared.*

Spared from what? What can be so bad that your aura mourns?

The truth.

Chapter Twenty-Four

As soon as Sharra saw Araylai she rushed over to greet her. A smile lit up Araylai's face. It was as bright as the yellow aura that surrounded her like a shiny sun.

"Lazarus and Tanner will be relieved to know that we have found you," Araylai said hugging her.

Sharra returned the hug, careful of the delicate fins on her friend's back as she tried not to think of Tanner. "Faolan has already been in contact with Lazarus. We were just waiting for you."

"I see you have gone native," Araylai said.

Sharra glanced down at her halter-top garment and thigh-length shorts, and laughed. "Yes, well, I thought it might help to blend in with the locals."

"I think it suits you," Araylai said. "Shows off your legs."

"And other parts," Faolan said softly from the side

with a gleam in his eye.

Sharra heard him and averted her face from their view as she felt blush steel up her neck and blossom on her cheeks. Renewed hope sprang up in her heart. Since he had woken up from his drug-induced sleep and had found her cradled in his arms, he had pushed her away. From then on he had kept her at arms length to the point where she started to question the emotions she had glimpsed in his mind.

And now, in front of everyone, he had to go and say something like that. She blamed it on the loss of blood from the knife wound, or residue from the drink Cael had given him. Whatever the case, it was enough to give her hope. She just needed to get him alone again so they could talk.

"But you'll need more than a skimpy outfit to blend in, or haven't you noticed that the locals don't look like us," Faolan said, snapping her back to the present.

Both girls ignored the comment. Instead, Araylai asked, "Have you been treated well?"

"Caetus has been a very gracious host, and Cael has been helpful, too."

"Do not listen to her. I have done very little," Cael said from behind them.

"You have done more than your duty called for," Sharra said to him. "That goes for Faolan, too. And you. I can never repay you."

"You would have done the same for me," Araylai said.

"But you have risked so much coming here."

"Friends help friends, at whatever the cost. Is that not right, Faolan?"

"You know I would do anything for Sharra," he said, and stopped. "But you're not talking about me, are you. This is about the female you saved, Immari."

"Immari?" Caetus said from across the table where he stood in conversation with Nayada. "Was not she one of your Hera maids?"

Araylai nodded, and said, "I have left her in Cam's capable hands, our healer at the Vault."

She then explained how they had come across Immari in the Slave Markets, and how Faolan caused a diversion, getting stabbed in the process, so that she could free Immari from her bonds. And then she told of their flight into the thermal ducts where she had left him to find Sharra on his own so that she could shift her beaten friend back to the Vault for medical treatment.

"I wonder how Lazarus is taking it," Faolan said, "having another alien on board."

"He will understand."

"And your friend, being torn from her world cannot be easy for her."

"Immari will adapt, like I did. All that matters is that she is safe."

"How does a Hera maid end up with the slavers?" Nayada said, getting to the question that was on everyone's mind.

"Queen Aniani does not like to leave loose ends," Caetus volunteered, and paused as he looked at Nayada. "Immari was a loose end."

Cael's aura flashed red with anger. Crest flicking, he said, "What are you saying? That it was only because Immari was a friend of the Princess that it made her a loose end?"

"Not just a friend," Caetus said, "but a close connection, someone who, if she so chose to, could influence others in the court against the Queen."

"Or have damning information, like Praemin Rue," Cael realized. "If word gets out that he is hiding evidence, or that we are looking for it…"

"Loch knows what he is doing. He will find it." Nayada said with confidence in her aura.

By her side Sharra felt Araylai stiffen. "What is this evidence you speak of?" she asked.

"It is a receipt connecting your mother to your disappearance. We are hoping it is enough proof to clear your name and restore your honor," Nayada said.

"Is this true?"

"Loch is with Praemin Rue as we speak."

"To have my honor restored… I never thought it possible."

Caetus came around the table and bowed, hand on the hilt of his dagger. "There are many still loyal to you, My Heres, those who never believed the lies spread in your name. I tie my honor to yours, and pledge my knife to you. If you choose to challenge your mother against this insult, I will stand with you."

Around the table, Nayada, Calyx, and Cael followed suit, bowing to her with their hands on the handles of their daggers, united in their show of allegiance, each pledging themselves to her without reserve.

She repeated the vow. "My honor is tied to yours."

With renewed energy Caetus said, "We cannot move until we have the evidence safe in our possession. Until then we must keep you hidden. It would not be good if your presence here gets back to the Queen."

"I hate to interrupt you," Faolan said, "but we were all over the Harena Market yesterday. It would be nearly impossible for someone there not to have spotted her especially after the scene we created rescuing Immari. By now those guards would have gone straight to your Queen. My guess is that the search is on. Proof or no proof, Araylai is not safe anywhere on this planet. We've stayed too long already. We should leave for the Vault now."

Sharra read the conflict in Araylai's aura. Touching her arm she reminded her, "The Vault can be a powerful ally. We can go back and work something out with Lazarus."

"I have heard a saying from your world once, and it stuck with me," Araylai said. "It goes something like, 'the good of the many outweighs the good of the one.' It is true. I know my mother better than anyone. Power means more to her than the sanctity of life. If I stay, I know more will die in her search to find me. But if I leave, she will win, and the suffering of the people will continue unhindered, for there is no other of the blood to challenge the throne."

"What do you wish to do then?"

"I… I do not know. I need to think." Araylai turned to Nayada and asked, "How long have I been gone?"

"Two years," Nayada said.

"Two years…" Araylai repeated in shock.

"No decision has to be made tonight, My Heres," Caetus said. "Please, accept our humble hospitality, and stay the night. We can retire to the interior of the stronghold, in the Otior, where you will be undisturbed."

Faolan shook his head and pulled the two girls aside, his voice low with urgency as he said, "We should go. Our mission was to find Sharra and bring her home. You can do your thinking back at the Vault, where it is safe."

"You do not understand," Araylai said just as fervently. "My mother... I have always seen the blackness of her aura when others could not. I know what she is capable of. This new situation... it is not that easy to walk away from. I need time to learn more."

Sharra didn't like it any more than Faolan, but understood Araylai's need. Some day soon she would be in the same position. Greyson was still out there. And she was learning the hard way that he had turned into a dangerous man.

A killer.

And so she provided a compromise. "One night. What's the harm of staying one more night, especially after all that has happened. It won't cost us anything. Unless you need to get back to the Vault for some reason."

Faolan stared from one set of pleading eyes to the other, and sighed.

"One night," he said. "And then we go."

It was something. Sharra hoped it would be enough.

Chapter Twenty-Five

An urgent knock jarred Sharra from her sleep. From under her pillow, she grabbed her knife, and sat up, eyes glued to the bedroom door. Faolan heard it too and jumped to his feet from his bed on the floor. Knife in hand, he plastered his back against the wall next to the door.

Their eyes met across the room.

Faolan pointed to his chest and then to her, finishing with the tattoo behind his ear, signaling to shift.

She shook her head and mouthed, "Wait."

He frowned, his silvery eyes hooded, but he didn't move from the wall. Faolan's muscles tensed as the door opened a crack. Sharra jumped off the bed and spread her arms out, knife in hand.

From the crack came a voice, low and urgent,

"Sharra, it is I, Cael."

Faolan lowered his weapon, and pushed the door open to let him in. "What's happened?"

Cael entered crest flicking. "The princess is gone! They have taken her away!"

"I knew we should've left last night," Faolan growled.

Sharra's breath caught in her throat. "Who's taken her?"

"Come, we must help Nayada," he said. He thrust a cloak in each of their hands. "Hurry."

She threw it around her body and clipped it at her throat as Cael waited impatiently by the door. Once they were covered he turned and disappeared out into the hallway.

Sharra gave one look at Faolan, and whipped the over-sized hood over her head, and took off after Cael.

"Sharra, wait," Faolan said a few seconds later, adjusting the hood as he caught up to them, "you don't know what you're running into."

"Didn't you hear him? They took Araylai."

"This isn't our fight."

She shot him a look from under the rim of her hood.

"'Never leave a partner behind,'" she quoted. "Or have you been gone so long that the handbook means nothing to you anymore?"

"This is different, and you know it. She can shift whenever she chooses."

"Do you know that for sure?"

"Look," he said, his brogue thickening with exasperation, "I'm not her keeper."

His words struck her like a hand. "But you're mine,

and that's okay."

A heavy sigh escaped from the recesses of his hood.

"Point taken. I'll Link with her as soon as we stop."

An oppressive undertone of doom hung in the early morning air as they ran through the dark conclave. Their bare feet slapped on the warm stone floor as they hurried through to the far entrance that led to the outer wall. Like an unwanted yoke, the feeling of dread hung around their necks, carrying the weight of uncertainty and danger with every step they took. Yet they kept moving, hugging the shadows cast by the photophores pans until they left them behind, and entered the private section reserved for the Umbra Elite.

Cael led them into Caetus' quarters, and through the partially opened door of the Otior. Sharra pressed a hand to her mouth in shock. Gone was the beautiful sitting room. Upturned furniture and scattered pillows littered the sea-foam rug as if a massive wind had come through and stormed the place. The sea creatures of ivory and greenstone had been knocked off the low tables and were now strewn on the floor like unwanted trash. A glass table lay shattered in pieces in the center. On the other side of it amid the wreckage of broken glass kneeled Nayada over a body on the floor. As soon as they had entered her head popped up, crest flicking. Her proud posture was gone.

"It is Caetus. I cannot stop the bleeding," she said, pleading with her eyes.

Blood oozed out from between her fingers from where she pressed down on his chest. It covered her hands, staining the thin material of his shirt. Her aura turned deep violet with the grief she was unable to hide

243

any longer.

Sharra dropped to her knees, pushing an ivory statuette aside to cradle the dying Arderian's head in her lap while Faolan stood sentry over them. A sheen of perspiration glistened on the old Arderian's pale face. The once bright aura around his body fluttered and dimmed. Sharra saw it, and grew frightened.

"Where is Calyx?" Cael said.

"I sent her to get the Healer."

"We do not have time to wait for her to come. Please, Nayada, let me help."

Cael leaned over to take Nayada's hands away, but she stopped him with a shake of her head.

"If I take the pressure off, he will die," she said.

Caetus stirred under her hand. With great effort his eyelids fluttered open. He searched the air above him until he found her face.

"Nayada…" Caetus said, his voice rough with pain.

A lone tear slipped down her cheek and fell to his chest. "Please, do not speak. You must conserve your energy."

"You must… go after Araylai. If Queen Aniani…"

"We will find her. I promise."

"There is something I must tell you… in case Aniani… succeeds."

"Shhh… save your strength."

He turned to Cael who had crouched low by his side. "In my room… under the mosaic… there is a box."

Cael bowed his head. "I will get it for you."

Cael jumped to his feet and flew over the pillows, and disappeared through the far door.

"Is he gone?" Caetus said.

"Yes," Sharra said.

With great effort Caetus dragged a hand over Nayada's where they held his lifeblood at bay.

"Have you ever wondered why I made you hide the mark on your palm from others?" he said. "It was to keep you safe. Your mother... she had the same mark, as did her mother. It is a mark of glory... and power... and death."

"Please, it is not important now," Nayada said.

"It is more important than you realize. We did what we had to do, your grandmother and I... to protect the royal line. Queen Arwynn had already lost one daughter by the treacherous hand of her firstborn... and could not risk losing another. That is why she hid her pregnancy and had your mother in secret... here among the commoners of Riff, so that Aniani would not find out, and destroy that child too. After Queen Arwynn died... only I knew of your mother's true heritage... your heritage."

"I do not understand. What are you saying?" Nayada said.

"I think you know, my child. I see it in your eyes."

Sharra looked at Nayada and remembered when she had first seen her in the sea; how at the time she had thought it was Araylai. She followed the genealogy in her head, and understood.

"Queen Aniani and your mother were sisters," Sharra said. "That makes Araylai your cousin, and you... a princess."

"The mark on my palm..." Nayada said.

"Is the mark of royal blood," Caetus said. "You were born Princess Aliya... the daughter of Adaylai, the third daughter of Queen Arwynn of the royal house of Ardere. I tell you this… because I cannot…"

"No," she said. "I do not want this thing. Only you. Stay. Please."

"The box. It is important. It holds your mothers' papers, and your birth line. Your father's, too."

"My father. You knew my father?"

"I am sorry. I meant to tell you, but the time never seemed right. Keep the box hidden… until you need it. You have good people around you… Trust them…"

"I will."

"Nayada… you are my best Umbra," he said with a weak smile.

Her lips trembled as fresh tears spilled from her eyes. "I had a good teacher."

"The sea… she calls me home… I can feel the cold of her touch…" he whispered as the last of his strength seeped away. His aura once red with pain dimmed lighter and lighter until all that remained was a blush of pink. With his last breath he whispered, "My honor is bound to yours…"

"As mine is to yours," she said through her tears.

The last of his aura dissipated away as the light faded from his eyes until there was nothing left but the cold stare of death.

No one moved. Only the sound of Nayada's heavy breathing could be heard in the stillness of the room. Finally she raised her bloody hands from his chest. With the pads of her thumbs she gently closed his eyelids.

"Find peace," she whispered.

It was thus that Cael came upon the group. His steps faltered at the sight of their dead guardian. He dropped to his knees on the floor next to Nayada, the shallow box within his hands all but forgotten as his aura flared violet in grief.

A few feet away where he kept sentry, Faolan caught Sharra's eye with a jerk of his head to come over. She frowned, but obeyed. Lifting the dead guardian's head from her lap, she slipped a pillow underneath and got to her feet, leaving the Arderians to mourn their fallen mentor.

"I've linked with Araylai," he said with a frown as she approached him. "She says the Royal Umbra have her."

"And?"

"And… she's not shifting out. Something about honor, and duty, and such."

"Did she say where they were taking her?"

"To the Queen," Calyx said from the doorway, answering the question before Faolan could reply. Towing an ancient Arderian behind her, the right Pectoral pushed her way through the pillows, making a trail for the elderly Healer. "The sentry guards out front are dead. Whoever did this did not want their presence known. Everyone else is still asleep…"

Her voice faded away when she saw their auras.

The Healer bent down next to the body. With gentle hands, she touched his neck and held it there until she was sure. "I am sorry. I am too late."

The room was silent as the finality of the words sank in. No one wanted to hear them. Calyx reached down and dragged Nayada away from the body. Cael followed with the box in hand.

"Come, Lead Umbra," she said. "We cannot stay

here. It is not safe anymore. The time for grieving will come later."

Nayada looked at her palms red with the blood of her mentor. The damning mark was there on the pad of her thumb, darker than the blood that stained her hands. The Healer saw it and draped a white cloth over her hands, hiding it from the others.

"Clean them, and remember the spilt blood of your guardian. Your future is what you do with your hand," she said with the wisdom of years shining in her eyes. "I will see to his care. The sea gives as the sea takes."

"And the Queen...?" Nayada said, staring into her knowing eyes.

"She is not the sea," the old healer said. "Now go."

It was enough to shake Nayada free from her despair. With water and a cloth, she rubbed the blood of her beloved guardian from her hands. When they were clean, Cael handed over the wooden case. With a nod of her head she led them out of the Otior without a backward glance. In the darkened corridor, they moved on silent feet through the quiet conclave. The sun was not yet up to lighten the reef walls, making their passing easier.

But the darkness did not quell the fear in Sharra's heart. Caetus was dead. Araylai taken. And now they were on the run. Maybe Faolan was right and they should shift away, and leave the Arderians to their fate. They didn't belong in their world. They were two humans caught in the middle of an alien family feud. What could they do?

She shoved that line of thought away as quickly as it had come. It was her fault that Araylai was in this situation to begin with. There had to be something they could do.

"Faolan, try the Link again," she said.

He slid the mike down, and did as she asked. After a few tries, he gave up and put the mike away. "Either she's too stubborn to respond, or something is stopping her."

Sharra pressed her lips together with resolve. Friends do not leave friends behind.

"Or they may have found the device. We have to keep trying."

Nayada gestured them inside the sentry house at the entrance of the outpost. Outside, the dead body of a sentry lay sprawled face down on the ramp. A puddle of blood seeped out from under her body. Gravity pulled it so that it trickled halfway down the ramp. Sharra shivered at the sight. Beside her, Faolan gripped his side where the bandage covered his wound as if feeling the dead sentry's pain. They turned away from the body, Faolan taking her hand, and followed the others into the guardhouse.

"We have to hurry," Nayada said.

She grabbed a long knife from the cache, and slipped it into her belt. A slim one found a place under the medallion of her armband.

"The next change of guards will be here with the first morning bell. Once they see the dead sentries, the alarm will be raised. Take only what we need without it being missed."

Faolan stepped over and helped himself to a knife. "What do you have planned?"

"This is not your battle. Take Sharra, and go home."

"Sharra reminded me not so long ago of a basic truth: Never leave your partner behind. So, unless you want us to strike out on our own to search for Araylai, you had better make room for us somewhere in your plans."

"Cael, talk some sense into these hu-mans."

"Sharra_" Cael started, but Sharra cut him off.

"You hold honor high," she said, as she joined Faolan at the armory. Choosing a slim blade from the cache, she weighed it in the palm of her hand, testing its balance. It felt good. "So you will understand when I tell you that Araylai and I are honor-bonded. I cannot go home and leave her. What good is my honor to her then? I must help her."

"She has made a valid point, Nayada," Cael said as he handed Sharra a thigh sheath. She strapped it on and slipped the blade in. Another knife went under her belt.

Amber eyes stared at them.

"I see I will not win this one," she said. "All right, I do not have time to argue with you two. You may join us. Do not make me regret it."

Faolan smiled. "You won't. Araylai said that the Royal Umbra have her. The way I see it, we have two immediate objectives. One is to find out where they have taken her, and what they plan on doing with her. The other is to get our hands on that document before your enemies do."

"Loch should have it by now," Calyx said. "Praemin Rue will only be too happy to pass it on in order to save his own fins."

Sharra shook her head. "I wouldn't be too sure about that. Does anyone else feel it's a bit suspicious that they found Araylai so quickly? I mean, it's Riff. Why would they look here?"

Nayada's whole body stiffened as the meaning behind the words sank in. Auras flared black around the room as she broadcasted her thoughts.

"A worm," Cael said in disgust, "planted right under our own noses."

"At Riff?" Calyx asked. "But why? We are an insignificant post where all the dross is sent. What could interest her here?"

Sharra looked at the case in Nayada's hand.

The Lead Umbra followed her eyes to the forgotten box. Understanding flashed in her eyes, and with it returned the pain. Her knuckles whitened as her grip on the box tightened in her despair.

"Me…" Soft as a whisper she breathed the word, but Calyx was close enough to hear it.

"You cannot blame yourself for any of this," she said as she tried to console her friend. "Caetus' death was…" Her words faltered and stopped.

Feeling Nayada's distress across the short distance between them, Sharra reached out and touched her mind with gentle care. *It wasn't your fault. She didn't know about you. Otherwise, you would've been taken already, or worse. Caetus was a good man, and protected you with his life. It is right to grieve for him. But your pod needs you to be strong, especially now.*

The box…

It is best to keep it to yourself for now, for your safety, and for the safety of your pod. It is a weapon as sharp as any knife. There may come a time when it will save your life.

Or kill me.

Then do what's right.

You are wise, land-walker. Nayada glanced at the box for a few precious seconds before passing it to her through the small space between them. *Take it, and keep it safe for me until I find a place for it.*

Sharra took it, and hid it in her cloak. *I'll guard it with my life.*

Clear-eyed once again, Nayada turned back to her friends. "Caetus lived and died by honor. His death should not be for nothing. Faolan has it right. We need information before we can do anything, and it needs to be done discreetly. We are scouts. This is our specialty. We will split into two groups. That will make us less conspicuous."

"Have you forgotten about the hu-mans?" Calyx said.

"We are used to blending in," Faolan said. "That is our specialty. Plus, we can use the thermal ducts to get around unseen, if it worries you that much."

"Cael, take Sharra and Faolan, and find Loch. We need to know if he has the document or not. Calyx and I will go after the princess."

"Won't they kill her right away?" Sharra said.

"No," Nayada said. "Queen Aniani will do it right this time, and make it public. No loose ends. That gives us some time. Cael, do you remember the Helix House where we first found Loch?"

"How can I forget it? The poor guppy was so deep into the juice after he lost his eye I did not think we would ever get him out of there."

"You have until the evening bell to find out what

252

you can, and meet us there. If things go wrong, I want you to head across the kelp fields to the Outcrop, and wait for us at the east end."

"The sun is coming," Sharra said feeling the air-pressure build behind her ears. Faolan nodded in agreement, stretching his jaw open in a yawn. She did the same, relieving the pressure with a pop.

Outside the sentry room the cavern walls began to awaken with the touch of the morning sun as it crested the unseen horizon of the planet. The fluorescent plant life that grew on the ceiling came alive, adding a soft glow to the warm air. It was their signal to leave.

"Do not trust anyone," Nayada said.

Sharra slipped the box into a sack. Tucking it under her belt with the knife, she followed Cael out the door with Faolan at her heels. Hugging the shadows underneath the balcony, he led them down the ramp to a passageway cut in the stone embankment.

Behind them, the two female guards took off down the street on light feet, taking a different route. Sharra stopped at the entrance of the passageway and turned to watch their backs fade away into the rising light.

"Sharra," Cael called from somewhere inside.

"Coming," she said, and entered the darkness of the tunnel.

Chapter Twenty-Six

———

A row of photophore bowls waited on a shelf just inside the tunnel. Cael took one down and activated it with the pass of his hand, and gave it to Faolan. "The rock is thick through here," he said as he took another one down. "We will need these to show us the way."

As Faolan passed the light onto Sharra, he said, "We'll need more than that. We'll need water, too, if we are to survive in the blasted heat. I hope you know your way around the thermal ducts, because I won't have a marker this time to lead the way through, and I sure as hell don't want to get stuck down there. I saw too many skeletal remains on my way to Riff to want to chance that again, poor souls."

Cael handed him the lighted bowl, and took another for himself.

"We are taking a different route."

"That's the best news I've heard yet this morning."

"Don't you fancy another tour of our wonderful city's understructure?"

"One time down there is enough for me, thanks."

"You may change your mind when you see where we are going instead," Cael said with a secret smile.

"And where would that be?"

"Into the belly of the beast."

A flash of a toothless gaping mouth broke through Sharra's memory. Her eyes widened in the dark. Not from the photophore light in her hand, but from the fear of being swallowed alive again. In front of her, Faolan caught the look on her face before she could hide it.

"Sharra?"

"It's nothing."

Holding his photophore above his head, Cael led the way down the passageway. Strange shadows bounced on the rock walls as he went. Sharra followed, and then Faolan, both holding their bowls high as they formed a line behind Cael. Deeper into the rock they travelled, away from the natural light of the outer walls of the outpost. Not even a speck of the native fluorescent lichen that grew everywhere was to be seen.

After a distance Cael turned left and led them up a narrow row of steps, thirty high. Their feet slapped on the stone as they climbed, rising above the second story of the outpost in no time. Up ahead, Sharra could see a light shining out of a doorway, illuminating the last few steps of the climb.

At the top, they stepped into a large stone chamber. Hanging from the ceiling by three twisted ropes of metal was a shallow bronze pan of photophore. The metal chandelier shone down upon the floor, casting shadows into the wide entranceways of three adjacent tunnels in the other rock walls, each large enough for a thick four-wheeled cart to easily fit through. Sharra could only guess where they led. It was too dark to see down them to know.

Without stopping, Cael veered left across the junction with Sharra right behind, and entered one of the tunnels, holding his pot above his head like before. Faolan quickened his pace and caught up to her. Matching his stride with hers, they followed the Arderian guard into the unknown, side by side. The light from the chamber disappeared behind them, and they were back to seeing only a few feet in front of them. The darkness stretched on for what seemed like an eternity. Sharra slipped her hand into Faolan's warm grasp. He squeezed it, sending her an unspoken message of support.

Before long the smell of salt drifted through the warm air. They came to another junction. To the left was more tunnel. But from the larger tunnel on the right came a beacon of light a hundred feet in, illuminating the edges where the tunnel ended and another cave began. They turned in that direction. The smell of salt became stronger with each step.

Cael slowed as they approached the opening, motioning for them to stay behind him. Sharra peeked over his shoulders to get a glimpse of the cave. A stack of crates on the other side of the cave entrance blocked most of her view, but the transparent wall beyond them told her that they were back at the outside wall of the reef. Through the strange wall of sheer material the ocean water glimmered with the rays of the early morning sun. The sound of water lapping fell on her ears. Faolan heard it too, and frowned.

At the lip of the cave entrance, Cael shelved his photophore pot with the others that were stacked there.

"Where are we?" Faolan whispered.

"Riff Porthole Station. Wait here," Cael said, and disappeared around the crates. By the time they had set their pots on the shelf, he had reappeared. "It is clear. Come."

They stepped around the crates blocking the entrance and walked inside the cave. More crates were stacked against the walls along with heavy woven-lidded baskets. One wall was left cleared. It was the window to the outside. The blue water on the other side was full of life. Everywhere tiny sissorback fish teemed over the glass, scouring it clean in their endless effort for food. Where the ceiling curved into a dome of glass, large shelled creatures moved languidly upon the uneven surface on thick tongue-like appendages. Into the sea at the base of the window jutted out a wide shelf of living reef. On it grew smooth mounds of charcoal coral-like round carpets between the random outcrops of coral and stalks of baby kelp. Bright colorful fish teamed all over the reef as they went about their early morning feeding rituals unaware of the observers on the other side of the glass.

"It's a dead end," Faolan said as he looked around.

"Maybe to us it is, but this is Ardus, their world, not ours," Sharra said as she left the flat part of the floor where the crates were stacked, and walked down the shallow incline to the source of the smell of the salt and sea.

In the sloping floor near the transparent wall glistened a large pool of clear blue water.

Cael joined her at the edge. "Keep one eye on the tunnel while I sort out transportation for the two of you," he said to Faolan, and dived into the water.

Sharra watched his strong legs kick him down, down, down, until the back of his feet disappeared into the depths of the pool. "He's gone."

From the crates near the door, Faolan said, "This is no time for a bath."

Sharra frowned. "Stop thinking like a human. They are born to survive in this world of water, gills and all. Didn't Araylai tell you anything about them before you came?"

"She kind of skipped that part."

"You must have figured some of it out by now. Look."

Faolan turned to where she pointed, and stopped short. On the other side of the glass wall Cael popped up in the open water on the far side of the coral shelf and swam towards one of the huge mounds of grey coral. A few firm kicks of his webbed feet brought him above it in no time. He righted himself with a splay of his webbed fingers and toes, and hovered in the water. The spinal appendages that held the long dorsal fin flat to his body snapped opened. A sunbeam shone down through the water and bathed him in shimmering light. His luminescent skin became alive under the ray of light, glistening with a dusting of pearl flecks making the rich colors of his fins stand out against his skin. Sharra marveled at the beauty of the alien creature. Beside her

Faolan stood frozen in place.

"Who would've dreamed such a creature existed," Faolan said under his breath as he stared out the window in awe.

"We're not alone. Makes you wonder what else is out there in the universe," she said in agreement.

"What's Cael doing?" Faolan said.

"He's waking up our ride."

As they watched, the mound quivered, raising a cloud of sand around its edges as it rose from the ground like a great beast. The fish that had been feeding off it shot away in fright. Slowly it unfurled the tips of its thick blubbery wings as it floated up to meet the waiting Arderian scout. When they were face to face, Cael pivoted with a flick of his fins and swam back the way he came. His strong legs carried him quickly over the short distance to the edge. Without a backward glance, he disappeared over the ledge. The huge winged animal followed, sailing gracefully to the edge of the reef, and dipped out of sight.

A minute later Cael surfaced in the pool at her feet.

"Stand back," he yelled as he pulled his body out of the water and ran to the wall.

Sharra ran with Faolan to Cael just as the water split open and the giant beast flew up out of the water. With a behemoth splash it thrust itself over the edge of the pool and onto the floor with a smack, missing them by inches. Half of its body hung out of the pool, and laid at their feet. Rivulets of water slipped off its smooth skin and ran down the slope of the cave floor and back into the pool.

"What the...?" Faolan said as he stared at the

mound of living flesh.

"Our ride," Sharra said.

An eyebrow rose above one of his silvery grey eyes.

"It's a bladderbird. Used for hauling cargo underwater."

He shook his head, still not understanding.

"Kind of like a pelican. You'll see."

"I don't like where this is going."

"Hey, you two, help me move these crates," Cael said.

With his fins tucked tight against his back once again, he grabbed a woven top off a crate, and began to throw bolts of homespun fabric off to the side. Faolan quickly went to another one and did the same. When both were empty, Cael hefted his up and directed Faolan to follow him with his. As they carried the crates over to the bladder bird, it opened its mouth on cue. Wider and wider it stretched until they could walk inside with plenty of room to spare.

Cael set his basket at the back of the beast's mouth, near the fine hair-like sieves of cream flesh that stretched over its gullet. Faolan did the same. Sharra picked up the lids, knowing what Cael had in mind. She didn't look forward to it, having ridden in a bladderbird once before, but knew it was the quickest way to the other side of the reef where the wealthy Praemin resided. Loch was there somewhere, and so was the precious document.

Sharra passed the lids to Cael, and hopped into a crate. Understanding flickered across Faolan's face.

"You've got to be kidding me," he said.

She raised an eyebrow at Faolan. "Afraid?"

"Hell, yes."

"Don't worry. You won't drown."

He peered at her through half-closed lids, before stepping into his crate. She sent him a reassuring smile before ducking out of sight. Folding her body, she rested her butt on the bottom as comfortably as she could. Nayada's box of precious documents pressed into her stomach. There was no room to move it, for her legs were in the way. So it stayed there jammed into her ribs in an uncomfortable position along with the rest of her body.

Cael peeked his head over the top and said, "It should take no more then twenty minutes. It is still early morning, so the service porthole station on the other side should be clear. Do not leave the crates until I open them... just to be safe. It would be too hard for me to explain away your presence if we are caught."

"Twenty minutes is a long time," she heard Faolan grumble as Cael set the woven lid over her head.

The world went dark as the bladderbird closed its massive mouth. The crates jostled together as the muscles of its mouth tightened around them as it slipped back into the porthole. She braced her limbs against the sides, and readied for the drop. The sensation of falling hit her. Bile rose into her throat. She swallowed and held her breath. A moment later the feeling passed, and she knew the bladderbird had reached the bottom of the tunnel to the outside water. Her crate settled back onto the floor of the bladder bird's mouth as it relaxed into the swim. The sensation of motions smoothed out into the rhythm of gentle waves as the beast flapped its great wings.

She wondered how Faolan was faring, but didn't

dare open her mind to him to find out. It was wrong to breach his privacy without his knowledge, and she knew it.

Yet she had no qualms about connecting with Cael. It was their way, after all. Otherwise, it was going to be a long twenty minutes. She reached out through the bladderbird, and felt the electromagnetic field of the male Arderian swimming along its side. He felt her gentle inquiring touch, and opened his mind.

Chapter Twenty-Seven

Twenty minutes later the mouth of the great beast tightened around the crates as it headed upward. Inside Sharra gripped the sides as her stomach rolled at the sudden change of course.

Brace yourself, Cael said through their connection.

Forewarned she pressed her limbs tight against the walls of her crate, and waited for the impact to come. Up, up, up they went, gaining speed as the bladderbird pumped its wings until with a final burst of energy it lunged out of the water and landed with a heavy thunk onto the hard floor. A great whoosh reverberated from outside as a tidal wave of water washed over the Portal Station floor. Inside the bladderbird, its muscles relaxed as it settled its precious cargo onto the floor of its mouth before stretching open.

Sharra pried her lid off, and stepped out onto the

damp floor of its mouth. The crate holding Faolan was silent. Tugging on the lid, she pulled it free, and peered inside at the body wrapped in a fetal position.

"Faolan?" she said with worry.

Faolan raised his head from his knees. His face was pale green. His lips were pinched. He took a breath of fresh sea air into his lungs through his nostrils, and slowly released it, bringing some color back into his face.

"A little warning would've been nice," he grumbled.

Sharra hesitated before she spoke, knowing exactly how he felt, though he did have some warning. Maybe it wasn't much, but it was more than what she had received on her first trip.

"You said that the thermal ducts were out of the question."

His eyes threw sparks at her. "That's before I got swallowed by a big fat fish." Grabbing the edges of the crate, he hauled his trembling body out, and leaned against it for support. After another fresh breath of air, he said, "I want full disclosure from now on. Agreed?"

"I'm sorry. I should've told you more. But there wasn't time."

"I'm not mad at you, Sharra. It's just that you've been here longer than I have, and know more about their ways. We need to work together as partners if we are to get Araylai back, and not get ourselves killed."

Cael came into the bladderbird's mouth wiping his body down with a cloth, unaware of the tension flowing between the two. Done with the cloth, he tossed it out against the wall. Grabbing the lids out of their hands, he threw them outside. They landed on the floor near the cloth.

"The morning crew will be here soon," he said as he took Sharra's crate and carted it outside. "We need to move the crates out, and get the bird back into the water."

Sharra left Faolan with the other crate, and followed Cael out of the mouth of the bladderbird. When both crates were stored against the wall of the station, Cael dismissed the big sea creature. Closing its tremendous mouth, it slipped back into the porthole and disappeared down into the deep, leaving the three alone.

The sea outside of the Praemin station window shined bright with the rising sun. Warm air flowed in from the two service tunnels and circulated around them. Cael started towards one.

Sharra flipped her hood over her head and wrapped the cloak around her body as she stepped behind him. Faolan did the same, taking up the rear. Eyes alert, Cael led them into the smaller of the two tunnels. Overhead the ceiling was covered with algae. It glowed with life, lighting their way. The smell of salt dwindled as they moved deeper into the reef.

Tucked under her belt and hidden from view, Nayada's box dug into her ribs where deep impressions were left behind from her scrunched ride in the crate. She shifted it to the front as she walked, careful to keep it hidden from the men, wondering what she was going to do with it.

For now keep it safe, she told herself.

She glanced back at Faolan glad to see his color restored. Faolan caught her look and sent her a lopsided smile before returning his eyes to scan the way ahead.

"So, what's the plan?" he said to Cael's back.

"I thought we could start with some of Loch's favorite hangouts," Cael said. "Poke our noses around a bit. Ask a few discreet questions."

"Why not go directly to this Praemin Rue's place and see if he's been there? It would save us time."

"Loch is an Umbra scout," Sharra said. "If he had been there, he surely wouldn't leave any evidence for others to find. Just like we wouldn't, or is that another rule you've forgotten about."

"I haven't forgotten any of those damn handbook rules, Sharra. They've been burned into my head right along with the agrylium. I just don't like going into a mission blind, that's all."

"You should trust that Cael knows what he is doing."

"I appreciate your vote of confidence," Cael said, "but I have to agree with Faolan. If our positions were reversed, I would feel the same. In a way it is true. We are swimming blind, not knowing where Loch is, or even if he has the document. We cannot help Araylai until we have something to work with."

"So what should we do?"

"While on the way over, Sharra suggested that you two can take Loch's place... be the eyes and ears of our pod. If the Queen has spies on Riff, then_"

"What do you mean, while on the way over?" Faolan cut in. "In the bladderbird? I can tell you right now that there was no conversing going on in there."

"Your aura is weak and your mind is difficult to read. While Sharra is_"

"It's okay, Cael," she said, her voice rising in alarm. "Faolan doesn't know your ways yet. We can save it for later."

Sharra didn't like where this was going. She never thought to tell her Arderian friends to keep her ability to connect with their minds a secret. For all they knew, all humans had this gift.

Why didn't she think of it before?

Maybe because it had become too easy for her, slipping back and forth between verbal and mental speech with them. Though that was no excuse. She had to stop Cael from saying anymore before Faolan learned the truth. To explain it to him would mean revealing more than she wanted to at this point. Even she didn't fully understand the connection between the agrylium and the marble-size ball of energy present in her mind. How could she explain it to someone else…

"No, go on," Faolan said. "Let the man speak. I'd like to hear this… what I cannot do… that you can do."

Crap!

Her mind spun as her brain worked for a quick reply. "That's not important right now. Right now we need to keep focused on the mission, and on Araylai."

She could feel the heat of his eyes boring into the spot between her shoulder blades as she held her breath, hoping it was enough to hold him off.

He paused as if wanting to say more, but held back. Instead he changed his mind, and said, "You want us to be your eyes and ears… Tell us what you have in mind."

Her body relaxed as she breathed a sigh of relief.

Cael pointed ahead. "This service tunnel leads to the main center of the Praemin district. Somewhere among the head houses of the district is Praemin Rue's estate. That is where Loch would have gone first."

"But, not us," Faolan said.

"No, the market is where we want to go. The night catch should be in by now. Rue's servants will be heading that way to buy their master's breakfast. The Praemin are known for liking their food fresh. Let us hope he is the same. It is as good a place as any to start."

He unclipped the medallion band from his arm, and passed it back to Sharra. She took it, the question burning in her eyes as she slipped it under her belt next to the box.

"It bears my status as an Umbra guard. No need to stir up any unnecessary curiosity," he said. "The same goes for the two of you. Try not to draw any focus to yourselves. Just listen and watch for anything out of the ordinary. Whatever you do, do not remove your hoods. Any glimpse of your hair, and we are done for."

"What about our feet?" Faolan asked.

"No one will look at your feet, unless you plan on kicking them in the face. I suggest that you refrain from that if at all possible."

The smell of cooked fish wafted up the tunnel.

"We are close to the entrance," Cael said sniffing the air. "Remember what I have told you. Stay close."

A hundred feet more and they were out of the service tunnel. Outside was a cavern ten times the size of Riff. Its wide floor spanned out in all directions. Close to the wall of the service entrance was a small city of canvas tents spread out in rows. Though there were many they took up a small corner of the cavern floor. Bright flags that hung from ropes and strung between tent poles fluttered in the light breeze that swept out of the great tunnel on the other side of the market. The voices of bartering carried over to where they stood.

Sharra stepped into the cavern and looked around. Where Riff felt compact with its four tiers tight against the wall and room for only one smallish building at a time along its lanes, this cavern's tiers were broader and more spacious with enough room to hold the grand homes two to three deep. Leafy gardens rose above the tall rock walls that surrounded the grand houses. Specks of red, yellow, and white dotted the tops of the greenery that grew high enough to be seen over the rock boundaries. Here and there some type of bushy vine cascaded over the walls in an array of color. It was the first time Sharra saw vegetation that wasn't growing on the cave ceilings. Like Riff there was a waterfall at one end feeding the township through the many Arderian-made waterways. It splashed from one pool to another as it descended down the tiers to the floor and joined the river that ran lazily through the cavern.

"Welcome to Decus, named after it's founding pod," Cael said. "They pride themselves on being the first to have brought living vegetation to Ardere. The many gardens you see are in honor of that memory."

"It's beautiful," Sharra said.

"It may be, but the beauty comes at a price."

"What do you mean?"

"A blood price. There are no nutrients in the sand. So in order to keep them fed it has to be added. My people, the Harena, pay that price with our flesh, blood, and bone so that the beauty here can live on. That is how we got our name: People of the Sand. It is the price of

269

our birthright."

The more Cael explained the more Sharra's eyes widened in horror.

"That's barbaric!" she said. "To be sacrificed for a plant. How can your people allow it to go on? Can't you stop it?"

Cael shrugged his shoulders. "Everyone has their place, from the highest to the lowliest. It stops chaos from taking over and keeps order. It is our way."

"Your way needs to be better."

"Sorry to butt in," Faolan said, "but now's not the time to talk politics. We need to keep moving before people wondered what we're doing dawdling here."

The many tents hid them as they worked their way to the fish stalls. It was easy to find, for the smell of fish led them straight to it. Fish of all sizes filled row upon row of wooden crates, from the half-ton Bluefin tuna laid out on a long slat of wood, to the thousands of tiny whitebait that packed the clear glass bins. All colors of the rainbow were represented, from plain brown to fluorescent purples and yellows. Stripes, vertical and horizontal, decorated their bodies, along with circles of all sizes.

Sharra and Faolan wandered around, examining one fish after another, all the while keeping a keen eye on Cael as he talked the trade with a gnarly vendor like a seasoned fisherman. Soon he had the information he was looking for.

After leaving the vendor with a nod, he came to them and said, "The House of Rue bears an insignia of sea-grass twisted through a twig of red coral. Look for it on their upper arm. It will be tattooed in green and red, the colors of Rues' House. Should be easy to spot. Stay in earshot while I keep working the vendors in this area." Out of a small pouch tied to his belt, he poured out a few baby pearls into Sharra's hand. "I do not know about you, but I'm starving. If you can find us some breakfast, that would be great."

"What about my hands?" she said as she took the pearls.

"Their eyes will be only for the money, and not on you."

She closed her hand around the pearls, and nodded with a smile. "Fish it is," she said and took off towards the smell of fried fish that drifted down the lane.

Soon she came back carrying three steaming parcels wrapped in broad kelp leaves. After passing one to each of the men, she peeled hers open. Her stomach growled. She tore off a piece of hot fish from the bones and popped it into her mouth, only then aware of how hungry she was.

With the fish in hand, they went back to work, searching the growing crowd of house servants and town folk for any sign of the Rue insignia.

From under her hood, Sharra scanned for any suspicious behavior, not really knowing what out of the ordinary meant to an Arderian. She assumed it was the same as a human. That is when she spotted it, a green and red twisted tattoo on the upper flesh of an arm.

She sent a thought over to Cael.

Over there. By the speckled fish.

He turned towards the booth.

I see him. Out loud he said, "You two spread out while I go talk to the Rue servant over there. See if anyone else is watching him. When I am done, wait a few minutes to meet up."

"And what if you're followed?" Faolan said.

"We will have no problem spotting them. Their auras will give them away," Cael said. "Only the elite can cloak their auras for long periods of time."

Around Cael, the green of his aura deepened as tendrils of darkness oozed out from his skin like swamp mud. In a matter of seconds the murky ink ate away the goodness of the green, leaving no hint of his former aura behind. Instead, blackness as vile as death hung around him like a shroud. Sweat beaded his upper lip and forehead as he concentrated to hold the evil color, until the effort proved too much. He let it go on a shaky breath. The black melted away, and his aura returned to green. His hand trembled as he reached up and wiped the sweat off his brow.

"I could not fake that even if I had wanted to," he said.

"You didn't have to do that," Sharra said.

"Do what?" Faolan said. "What did I miss? And what's all this about auras?"

"I'll explain later," Sharra said.

"Along with a few other things, I think," he said. "All right, Cael, whatever you two have going on can wait. Right now, let's stick to the mission before your guy over there disappears into the crowd."

Cael nodded and took off into the crowd. Sharra wandered away pretending to shop while Faolan left for the other direction. Three stalls down from where Cael and the servant were talking, she stopped and pretended to examine the day's catch from under the hood of her cloak while stealing furtive glances at the market-goers. Nothing. No sickly auras, no odd behavior, no stray thoughts of malevolence crossed her perceptive mind.

By the stall of speckled fish, the conversation ended, and the Rue servant moved on. Cael turned and scanned the crowd. His eyes quickly found her.

Find Faolan, and meet me at the south ramp. He flicked his hand, hiding the movement close to his body, as he pointed the direction he wanted her to go.

What did the servant say?

Not here. Find Faolan.

Cael melted into the crowd and was soon gone. Sharra left her spot and headed in the direction that Faolan had taken. He spied her before she did, and met her in the lane, matching her casual stride as he fell in step along side her.

"That was quick," he said. "Where is he going now?"

"South ramp."

"How do you know?"

Not knowing how to get around it, she said, "Cael told me."

"I didn't see him talking to you, unless I am missing something."

"Just leave it for now."

"Just like I'm to forget about what happened between you and him on the way here? I get it. I guess I was too stupid to see it before."

"What do you mean?"

"You and him. That's why you don't want to leave. You've a thing for that Arderian fish."

"No," she laughed. "It's not like that at all. Besides,

how can you think that, after we… after we kissed." Her voice faded away in confusion, until it hit her like a bolt of lightning. What more proof did she need that he loved her? Not that she needed proof, having seen it in his mind for herself. Her heart soared in her chest. She couldn't help the smile that came to her face, glad of the hood that hid it from him.

"You're jealous."

"Me? Jealous of a fish?"

"You must admit that he is handsome with his pearl skin and intricate webbing. And his eyes…" she said goading him on.

"I admit that their eyes are quite startling, but handsome? You've got to be kidding. Think of what your kids would look like."

"Maybe they would have the best of both species."

"Schools of auburn-haired fish." he shuddered beside her. "It's not right."

Laughter erupted from her lips. She quickly caught it and smothered it with a cough.

"Oh, you find it funny?"

"I do." Sharra lips quirked as she grabbed his arm and pulled him into the next cross lane. "The mission, remember? Let's go see what Cael has found out."

"This conversation is not over yet," he grumbled.

"I know."

Chapter Twenty-Eight

Praemin Rue's house sat within the second tier. The green and red markings of its colors were carved into the corners of the stone wall that surrounded the property. Cael pointed it out as they approached the grand door that led to the courtyard in front of the sprawling two-story house. On the street side of the stone wall grew fern-like trees in boxes constructed from crushed white coral. The fronds spread out like umbrellas under the stone sky, a strange sight in a world of sand, shell, and water. Into the door was carved the Rue insignia of coral and sea-grass.

Cael pulled the cord. A bell rung deep within the house.

From around the corner of the street came a worker pushing a cart. Sharra caught the movement from under her hood. At the first tree, he stopped and fiddled with a basket inside the cart before lifting out a large animal skin pouch. Hefting it to the tree, he released the spout and began to pour a thick dark liquid around the base of the plant. She knew it was blood by Cael's own words. In horrified curiosity she watched it disappear into the sandy soil. It was soon followed by a sprinkling of white powder that she could only guess was bone. A shudder ran through her as she counted the trees around the perimeter, twenty-four, not counting the ones out of sight. She swallowed hard and tried not to think about the lives that were sacrificed to feed them. There were so many plants in Decus. It made her sick.

The handle on the door moved as someone from inside answered the bell. Sharra dropped her gaze as a young servant poked her head out of the crack.

Before Cael could speak, she said, "The Praemin is not home."

The young housemaid's spiked webbing flicked in nervous agitation as she peeked out from around the corner of the door to eye Cael. The blue of her aura deepened in fear. As soon as she delivered her line her head disappeared behind the door, and began to close it, dismissing them without another word. Cael shot a hand out and caught the edge of it with a slap.

"We are aware that Praemin Rue is not here. I am an Umbra. Show respect, or it will not go well for you either," he said through the gap.

Sharra and Faolan stood to the side as they waited in silence while Cael handled the maid. From under his cloak, Faolan's stiff posture oozed tension. She couldn't blame him. Like him, she was starting to think this was a bad idea walking boldfaced up to Praemin Rue's front door, especially after what Cael had learned from the servant down at the market. Why Cael thought it was a good idea to reveal his status now, she didn't know, especially after all the warning he'd given about avoiding the House. Yet, here they were, right on the doorstep, asking for trouble. Cael had better know what he's doing.

The seconds ticked by until finally the door gave way a few inches. Cael didn't wait, but leaned in and presented the medallion band on his upper arm to the maid. Behind the metal insignia was sheathed a small blade. Her eyes blinked wide at the sight of it. The deep blue of her aura thickened around her.

"Your kind were already here." she said.

"We will not disturb the House any more than necessary. Our business is not with Praemin Rue. It is on a different matter, concerning any visitors that the House had received earlier yesterday," Cael said.

The housemaid opened the door a fraction more. Unshed tears glistened in her eyes. Her lips trembled as she replied, "Praemin Rue is a most gracious host, and has entertained many guests, or at least... he did. Once the other Houses hear of how he was taken... oh, the dishonor... What will happen to us now?"

"Rue is one of the Great Houses, as old as the reef Ardere itself. It will survive this... upset," Cael said gently. "If you want to help your master, then help us. Did your master have any guests yesterday morning before he was taken away?"

The maid sniffed and wiped her eyes as she thought.

"There was one, a young Herus. Rather handsome

he was if it was not for the missing eye. He stood right here, and would not budge until he had an audience with the Master. Even charmed the Headmistress into letting him in."

"And did he get to see Praemin Rue?"

"Oh, yes," she said, nodding her head, "After the Master was informed that the youngling had brought fresh news about his holdings from across the Kelp Fields, he took him right into his private Otior. It has been months since we have heard anything from the outer holdings. With the uprising and all... Praemin Rue has not dared risk sending any more servants. Too many have already gone missing."

"Was the young Herus still here when your master was taken?"

"No. He left right after morning thea. His news must have been good, for the Master came out looking much relieved. He has been walking under such a heavy aura of late, especially since his youngest son's death. The poor soul."

Sharra released her breath through her lips. At least they knew now that Loch had been and gone, and not taken with Rue when the Queen's Umbra had stormed the house yesterday afternoon.

"Did you happen to hear where he was going next?"

The maid lowered her eyes. "It is not my business to pry. I am just a servant." The aura around her swirled in an array of colors as indecision made her pause. Finally it settled when whatever internal battle she was fighting came to an end. She raised her eyes, and said, "I lied. I do know something. I will tell you because you are not like the others. I was on the second floor above the inner courtyard on my way to the balcony. The thermal ducts were running hot yesterday. Makes for quick drying of the laundry. But you don't care about that. Anyway, I was about to hang another load when I saw the Master come out of the main house with the young Herus. From my vantage point on the balcony I overheard him tell my Master that he was to meet friends at a Helix house by the mid-day meal."

"Did he say which one?"

"That was all I heard." She blinked once as she studied the darkening blue of Cael's aura in the silence of his disappointment. And then she said, "But I did see which direction he was heading, if that helps. The laundry balcony has a good view of the lower tiers, and I could not help myself but watch him as he made his way down the ramps to the first tier road. That is when he turned towards the guild shops, you know, the fancy ones where only the Praemin go. After that I lost sight of him."

"Thank you for your assistance," Cael said, letting go of the door. "Praemin Rue would be pleased with your cooperation."

"My Master is gone, taken in front of everyone like a criminal. He did not deserve the humiliation. He is a good citizen… a good Master. What are we to do?"

"Honor is not dead yet. Do not lose hope."

A tear rolled down her cheek. "What honor. There is no honor. Go. Find your comrade, and warn him. I am not the only one that knew he was here. They will find him first, if you do not. Go."

As soon as the servant girl shut the door, Cael slipped the insignia armband off his arm and put it into the pouch at his belt. They left the house and took the ramps down to one level above the ground floor. Sharra and Faolan fell in step behind Cael as he had instructed earlier. On the first tier they turned and headed to the shops.

"Do you believe her? Are we too late?" Faolan said as he walked close to Cael's back.

Cael kept his head forward as he answered him. "Loch is in extreme danger, this is true, especially now that he carries the document."

"How do you know that he has it?" Faolan said.

"It's because of what the maid said," Sharra said thinking back to the conversation between Cael and the maid, "about Rue, that he looked relieved after the visit with Loch."

Faolan frowned under his hood, and shook his head. "But that was because of the news Loch brought him of his holdings."

"Loch did not have any news," Cael said as they entered the shop area.

Around them the stores were just awakening as a few early risers opened the front shutters to their shops. One of them, a garment-maker, paused and looked at them over an armload of colorful fabric. Sharra ducked her head and stayed on Cael's heels, hoping the shopkeeper would forget about them and go on with his business. She wanted to rush through the district, but Cael kept a casual pace and a neutral aura.

When they were out of earshot, he continued to explain, "That was just a ruse to gain a private audience with Rue. No, I am sure that he talked the Praemin into giving him the document, especially with the prior knowledge that Rue had tried to pass it onto Praemin Minnowmen. That was why Rue was relieved. He probably thought it was the end of his troubles, getting rid of the damning evidence."

Sharra didn't like where the thought was leading. "But the Umbra took him anyway. That means they must know something."

"And when Rue talks, which he will, Loch will be next," he said. The delicate dorsal fin that ran down his back shuddered in a wave of agitation. It was a small movement, but enough to express his fear for his friend. Faolan confirmed it with his next words.

"I've seen first hand what the Queen's people do to their own kind. It's not pretty."

Cael pulled himself together, and said, "Loch is an Umbra Scout. If it had been safe, he would have brought the document back to Riff. He must have known he was being followed. We need to find him, before they do."

"It's been twenty-four hours since he was last here. He could be anywhere," Faolan said.

"I think he left us a clue. The maid said he was to meet friends at a Helix House," Sharra said.

"Yes, but which one. He has many that he… visits," Cael said.

"A drinker, is he? You're not so different than us humans after all," Faolan said.

The rings of Cael's eyes flashed bright for a second. "Do not judge what you do not know."

"Sorry, buddy. Just making an observation. No insult intended. He's your partner. Just think like him. If you were him, and knew you were being followed, what would you do?"

"I would quickly find somewhere to stash the document in the most unlikely of places."

"Like one of your Helix Houses?"

"Yes… just like a Helix House."

Chapter Twenty-Nine

The day was ending. The reef began to darken with the setting of the sun. Above on the jagged ceiling of the latest cavern the lichen that grew everywhere paled with the loss of the sun, casting the small town below into shadows. On the street a servant was busy waking the photophore street lamps one by one with a flick of his long pole. Sharra watched as he came down their street and jostled the next large copper pan high above his head. Stimulated, it began to brighten. When the photophore was fully awake, the servant moved on, weaving through the foot traffic to the next one. Soon one tier and then the other came alight with a soft glow, illuminating the tired faces of those returning from a day of drudgery under the cast system of the Arderian people.

A hand-drawn wagon pulled by four half-naked

slaves, and carrying a heavy load of coral rock, clattered down the street. They looked neither left nor right, but trudged straight ahead. A whip snapped at their backs. The sound echoed in the air. It drew neither a flinch nor a curl of a shoulder. The driver lashed the back of the closest and hurled curses at them, but they moved no quicker. None of those nearby lifted their heads in anger. No one raised a voice in protest. Instead they averted their eyes, and kept on moving.

Cael led them past a group of dirty children playing at the cave entrance, and down the center road to another line of storefronts. Years of neglect was evident everywhere. Faded awnings hung down in tattered pieces over the storefronts. The poles that had held them up were long gone. Those that still had windows were lucky. Most were boarded, or replaced with stone. The windows that survived were encrusted with a fine film of salt like ice crystals too thick to see through. Sand brought in from years of foot traffic had been carelessly brushed against the buildings, making for odd sand-drifts in the dry cavern. Mixed in it were discarded bits of trash and other things Sharra didn't want to think about. The smell wafted up through the opening of her hood, and made her gag.

She pressed the material of her hood against her nose and mouth. "It reeks in here. What is it?"

Cael's nostrils were pinched closed. "You don't want to know. Drop your body posture, both of you. We don't want to draw any more attention to ourselves than is necessary."

Sharra looked around the fold of her hood. "Are you sure Loch would come to this… this hovel? All the other settlements seemed more…"

"Clean?" Faolan offered through his pinched nostrils.

"The Royal Gold is here. It is his favorite Helix House."

Faolan's hood twitched. "You're talking about Loch? Our Loch? Isn't this a wee bit below his standards? The rest of the Houses we visited, I can understand him patronizing. Nice neighborhoods for what I know of alien neighborhoods: clean establishments, respectable clientele. Right up his aristocratic alley. But this… whoa… the smell's enough to put anyone off.

"Maybe we'll luck out, then, if it's his favorite hangout," Sharra said ever hopeful as she looked at the lichen-filled ceiling. "The sun has set. We need to hurry."

Up ahead a gold-painted metal crown dangled from a pole over the door of a storefront.

"There it is," Cael said. "We do it like the ones before. You two stand respectfully to the side while I talk. Faolan, mind your posture. And please, do not make eye contact. Not in this House."

"Fine. Just don't force me to test another drink of yours. Eight is enough. Any more and I'll be no use in a fight," Faolan said. He shook his head, and said in a low voice, "Knives… why knives."

"I'll drink it," Sharra offered.

"No, Sharra," Faolan said. "I won't let you risk it. I'll drink it."

"It's okay. Let me help. I'll drink it."

"No. Cael gave me the job. I'll drink it."

"Really, I want to."

Cael held up a webbed hand. "Stop it, you two. No one will have to drink it. I need you both to stay sharp. We already stand out as different."

"That's because we're clean," Faolan whispered to Sharra.

"You can be so stubborn sometimes," she whispered back.

"So can you."

The Royal Gold was a contradiction of names. Neither noble, nor wealthy, the Helix House sat unobtrusive in the long row of buildings. Wood, metal, paint: it all bore the signs of the relentlessness of the salty air that pummeled the town. Over a salt-encrusted picture window, one of the few on that side, was painted its name in large bold lettering. At one time it had advertised the establishment with gleaming color. Now, though, the red paint had faded and chipped, exposing the paler color of the wall underneath. On the ground, specks of old red and yellow paint gathered like snow and mixed with the sand pushed against the building.

Cael led the way in, but they got no further than the other side of the door. When Faolan shut the door behind them a burly female broke away from the wall and slapped a web-tattered hand onto the middle of Cael's naked chest, halting the group. An old crescent scar ran down the left side of her broad face and through her lips causing them to pucker where they had healed back together. Hard eyes looked down on him. Her lips twisted into a zigzag. Sharra could only assume that it was a smile. The scars made it hard to tell.

"Knives are left at the door," she said. "House

policy."

Cael peeled her hand off his chest. "No need to get testy. Just here for a drink."

"I do not care the reason. Remove your weapons, or get out."

Their eyes locked. Cael reached down and unstrapped the sheath holding his fighting dagger from his thigh, and slapped it into the palm of her outstretched hand. Without breaking eye contact, she pulled out a wooden box from the wall of boxes next to her, and transferred the weapon from one hand to the other and into the box. Though he had given her it, her hand remained out and her stare no less fierce. From his belt he pulled out a long blade and laid it on her palm. After that followed two throwing knives from the back of his belt, three shards of crystal from the strap that hung across his chest, and a pin-needle knife from the hidden pocket in his shorts. All ended up in the box.

The large female bouncer narrowed her eyes, and said, "All of them."

With his eyes still locked with hers, Cael reached behind his back and pulled another shard of crystal from the strap, and gave it to her.

"That is all. I swear. You can check if you want." He lifted his arms away from his body, palms out, and smiled a lecherous smile.

With a humph she turned and dumped the shard into the box and slid it into the cubbyhole in the wooden wall of boxes.

"Your key." She dropped a small bit of metal into his hand. "Now for your servants."

Sharra's breath caught in her throat. The box of

precious documents lay heavy against her skin. Beside her she felt Faolan stiffen under the huge cloak. He slipped a hand out and grabbed her arm. They both carried knives, but that was the least of their concerns.

Cael knew it too.

A sharp laugh fell from his mouth. "Give them knives? And risk one sticking out of my back? They had better carry only thoughts of good intentions for my health and safety."

Sharra took her cue and bowed her shoulders even more.

Beside her, Faolan mumbled, "Yes, master," and hunched his body in submission.

"See?" Cael said. "Obedience. No need for weapons. Now, I am thirsty. Or are you so wealthy you don't need anymore customers than the few I see sitting inside?"

"Humph," she said with a twist of her lips. Over the din of conversation she called out to the man behind the bar. "Boss? What do you think? Should I let them in?"

Instantly the place went quiet as all the heads turned to see what was causing the commotion at the door.

The bartender threw down his rag and said, "Quit harassing the customers, Della. I don't give a worm's fodder about the Harena he owns. The man is thirsty. Let him in."

Della looked them over long and hard before reluctantly moving aside. Faolan let go of Sharra's arm, but did not relax.

At the bar Cael dismissed his 'Harena' with a wave of his hand and took a stool. On cue Sharra and Faolan bowed and moved to the sidewall. Through the opening of her hood, she scanned the patrons while Cael ordered a drink.

The usual type was there. The regulars sat around tables talking loudly over pitchers of ale like every other place they've been to that day. Around them sauntered females dressed in barely a stitch, leaving very little to the imagination. Tattoos of intricate designs of color covered their pale skin. It drew the eye to their forms in more ways than clothing could ever have accomplished. Exotic. Intoxicating. Some were sitting coyly on the male patrons' laps brushing a seductive hand over the webbing of their backs. Though they said very little the body language of the alien females was obvious to Sharra of what they were there for, having seen movies portraying prostitutes in the same manner. Even the helix addicts that sat tucked away in the dim corners hunched over their juice of choice reminded her of drug addicts from her home world.

Through the ruckus of the busy establishment an invisible heaviness hung over the place, as if an evil spirit lived there.

She reached out a channel to Cael. *Do you sense it?*

The bartender put a heavy tumbler of dark ale in front of Cael. "Best Helix Ale of the House," he said.

Cael answered Sharra as he slipped a small pearl off a string of the same size pearls. *Yes. The room is thick with it. I will be quick.*

He dropped the pearl in the bowl, and took a swig of the thick brew while the bartender watched intently. He swallowed. A shudder passed through him as he tried to suppress a gag.

"Good," he choked out as he wiped his mouth. He

took another mouthful and swallowed, this time suppressing the shudder. "Yep. Good stuff."

The bartender laughed as he resumed wiping a glass. "Go easy there. Drink too fast, and the pleasure will be over before the hallucinations can even begin their merry dance in your head."

"It has been a while since I have had a good trip."

"The Royal Gold offers the best." The bartender put the glass under the bar, and began on another. "You drink like a brave man. Or maybe you are just ignorant."

"What do you mean?"

"Bringing Harena to this part of town is asking for a knife in your back. If you haven't noticed, folks around here can be a little touchy, seeing how half their families have been forced into the slave markets."

"I have been told by a patron of yours that your House was worth the risk." Cael raised his glass, saluted the bartender, and took a careful sip. Lowering his voice, he said, "You might have seen him recently... a one-eyed handsome sea-devil... likes trouble."

As soon as Loch's description left his mouth, the bartender's aura shifted a fraction before he got control of it again. He flicked a look over to his left as he ran a hand down the crest of his head. At a table against the opposite wall was a nondescript female nursing a drink in her hand. Head down, her aura was neutral as if the only thing that interested her was the color of the ale in her glass.

Watching the exchange, Sharra knew something was wrong. The aura of the female had no substance, as if muted. From what she knew of the Arderian race, that wasn't normal. Neither was the heaviness of the air around her. The white ball of energy in her brain tingled. She mentally agreed with it. They had stayed long enough. The private warning that came soon after from Cael told her she was right.

A Grex, he confirmed.

We should leave.

Not yet. The bartender knows something. It is in his aura.

Hurry, then. The heaviness is coming from her.

The bartender laughed. "Trouble. Is that what you males are calling it these days. Well, I guess that is one way of looking at it."

"Loch does like the females."

"And... other things..."

Cael smiled, "That he does. Has he been in lately?"

"That is for the House to know."

Cael let some pearls drop into the bowl by his hand. "Just trying to keep him swimming straight. We are honor-bonded. You understand."

"Ahhh... if that is the case..."

The bartender's hand disappeared underneath the bar. Shifting on his stool, Cael moved for the knife at his thigh, but his hand met the flesh of his leg.

Sharra saw it, and whispered to Faolan, "Cael's reaching for his knife."

"I see it."

"Be ready."

"Always."

From inside her cloak she slowly pulled the wooden case from her belt, and passed it through her sleeve to Faolan. He covered it with the flap of his cloak sleeve, and slipped it inside.

"When did you get this?" he whispered.

"Back at the guardhouse. I think it'd be safer with you. If things should go bad, you can shift it to the Vault."

"I'm not leaving you behind."

The bartender brought his hand up and laid something small in front of Cael. When they saw that it wasn't a blade, they all relaxed just a fraction. "He gave me this to hold onto, until… well, until… how did he put it? Someone minnow-faced showed up and asked about him.

A key, Cael told Sharra. *Loch must have left something in one of the wooden lockers.*

Cael moved to take the key, but the bartender laid a webbed hand over it before he could touch it. "For a small security fee, you understand."

The bartender touched the bowl with a finger. More pearls left Cael's string. They clattered on top of the small pile at the bottom like tiny pebbles. The bartender nodded once and took the bowl away with the hand that had covered the key. Cael finished his drink in one big gulp and set the tumbler down next to the key.

"Thanks for the brew," he said as he slid the key into the palm of his hand.

"Tell Loch when you see him to watch his back. You are right about the trouble. Usually it stays within the House, girls and such, but this time he has drawn interest from the outside, and not the kind I want here."

Cael left the bar and motioned for Sharra and Faolan to follow. As they did Sharra caught the female glance at Cael's back under the guise of sipping her drink. The green of her aura turned muddy with a flicker of tangerine, the color of triumph. And then it was gone. Neutral again. So quick was it that Sharra didn't trust her eyes.

The Grex watches you, Sharra warned Cael.

I know. We will get what Loch left in the box, and leave. Hopefully she is not here for us.

I don't know. It seems like too much of a coincidence to be random. Maybe we should leave it, and come back later when it's safe.

We may not get another opportunity to get it. I have to chance it.

The big female called Della waited at her post against the wall of cubbyholes. Arms crossed, she watched them with half-disguised malcontent in her eyes. Cael ignored her as he searched for the cubbyhole that matched the number on the key in his hand. Finding it he inserted the key, and pulled out the box. Inside was stashed nothing but Loch's thigh sheath. The dagger was gone. Cael scooped it up, leaving his own box untouched.

"Wonderful House, Della," he said with a smile as he handed the empty box and key over. "I will have to come back with my pod mates, and sample some of the other... pleasures of the House."

With that he walked out the door without a backward glance. Once outside he led them down the street away from the Helix House. Sharra glanced back at the door, but the Grex was nowhere to be seen. After a good distance Cael stopped to examine the leather sheath.

"This makes no sense," Cael said. "Why leave us his sheath?"

"At least we know we're still on the right track," Faolan said.

Sharra looked at the sheath. It was long, long enough to fit… "Did you look inside?"

"No."

Cael stuck his fingers in, and pulled out a rolled up piece of paper. Unrolling it, he quickly scanned its contents.

"He got it. It is all here; the contract, the parties involved. Even the Queens' signature and seal." He rolled it back up and shoved it into the sheath, and looked around. "It is almost the evening bell. We need to find a place out of sight to wait for Nayada and Calyx to show up. She will know what to do with it."

"I will take that, thank you."

Behind them stood the Grex. Hand outstretched, she motioned for the sheath with her webbed fingers.

Cael's aura flashed in surprise, and quickly turned dark in anger before he could suppress it. "Why would I give you anything?"

"Because you know who I am. I see it in your aura. You are wise to be afraid." She smiled and took a step closer. "You left your weapons back at the Royal Gold, traded them for that empty sheath. Now I am thinking, what kind of Arderian would leave all his knives behind, and walk out into the street empty-handed? That sheath must be worth something."

His hand clenched around the sheath. Tight-lipped he stared back at the Grex.

Cael… Sharra warned.

He blinked one slow blink. With his face to the Grex, he answered her through a compressed channel of color.

Remember how you told me Faolan could get you home?

*Yes, but_*

I'm going to toss the sheath to you. Take it to your world. Keep it safe.

Cael, no.

They are gathering around us, and I am unarmed.

Sharra scanned the street through the slit of her hood, looking for a way out. As her gaze lit up on an alleyway beside her, a male stepped out from it and sauntered over to stand off to one side of the female. Though he looked no different than any other Arderian, his eyes said otherwise. So did the massive amount of knives that decorated his body. Hard and relentless, his gaze bore into Cael as he fingered a long sharp knife on his chest belt. Another one approached from the other side of the street, knife in hand, and took his place within the semi-circle.

The locals gave them a wide berth as auras flared in various shades of indigo. Sharra knew it was the sign of fear. On the street pushcarts bumped and jarred as their owners hurried away. Feet slapped on the stone floor in a mass exodus. Doors slammed shut. The echo of movement continued for a few seconds, until all that was left was the sound of her breathing.

Three more behind us. That makes six. There are too many of them, Cael said.

The female leader narrowed her eyes as she stared back at Cael. "You are broadcasting." She skimmed over the locals, but found no sign of communication. "Whoever it is cannot help you. It is pointless."

Cael did not answer her. But to Sharra he said, *She is right. There is no other way out of this. Promise me you will come back and save Araylai.*

On my honor.

To the Grex he said, "It is only an empty sheath."

"If that is the case, why cause such a scene over it? Just hand it over."

"Find someone else to harass. I have no time for you and your kind."

Are you crazy? What are you doing? Sharra said to him.

Causing a distraction.

Why?

To buy you time. Be ready.

The crest of the Grex flicked in agitation. "Make the time, or your Harena will change ownership, as payment, shall we say, for your procrastination."

"Over my dead body," Cael growled.

"Heard and witnessed." Her eye rings flashed as a cruel smile spread over her face.

Now! he cried as he threw his arm out to toss the sheath to Sharra.

But the sheath didn't make it to her, for when he raised his arm into the air to throw it, a small knife sank into the back of his hand, and out through his palm, throwing off his aim. The sheath arched through the air in slow motion, and landed ten feet off to the side between her and a Grex. Cael cried out in pain and grabbed the wrist of his injured hand. Blood poured out around the knife and ran down his arm, but before he could pull it out, another knife thudded into his chest close to his heart. In that instant his aura turned red.

Eyes wide with shock, he grabbed his chest where the knife protruded with his good hand. Thick crimson liquid oozed out from around his fingers and ran down his torso. His aura faded. He stumbled where he stood.

The sheath, he said, his voice weak with effort. *Get the sheath.*

It was enough to break Sharra free from the shock that had overtaken her. She dove for the sheath in a flurry of grey cloak, and slammed into the hard road on top of it. Something hard hit her in the left shoulder. It stung, but she ignored it. From under the cloak, she pulled the slip of paper out of its hiding place from within the sheath, and crammed it into her belt just as a hand grabbed her by the waist and jerked her off the ground, and away from the sheath.

Across the way, Cael's knees gave out as his precious blood drained from his body. Before he could crumble to the ground, Faolan caught him around the waist, and held him against his chest.

Sharra, Cael whispered through the channel that was growing weaker with every second.

I've got it! Cael, I've got it!

Your back... You are bleeding. I am sorry. I have failed us both.

"It's ok, Cael. I've got it. Cael...?" she said, but he had no strength left to answer.

Fifteen feet separated them. It could've been a mile. It made no difference. The Grex were closing the noose of a circle around them. Though they'd thrown her to the side, there was no possible way she could make it over to Faolan in time to shift even if she ran.

Her shoulder began to throb. Cael was dying as she

watched.

Cael, don't give up.

Sharra's eyes met Faolan's across the way and read the desperation in their silvery depths. In his arms Cael laid lifeless. The seconds were ticking away.

Cael, she screamed across the link, *Wake up! I need you to wake up!*

His eyes flickered open. The once bright amber of his iris's were now a shadow of their former color. The electromagnetic energy of his aura was fading. Time was running out.

Tell Faolan I said to take you to the Vault. He can find me again. Tell him to bring the case back. Tell him… I'll be okay.

Her desperate words got through just as the connection broke. Faolan ducked his head as Cael whispered the message with the last of his strength before collapsing back against his chest. Faolan stiffened when he heard what she wanted, and shook his head.

"Yes," she whispered back. "Please."

A whirl of emotion flowed across his face as he stared back at her over the head of the fallen scout. Then a calm set in. It was the look of a shift.

"Just hold on," he ordered, and disappeared with his burden, and the hidden case.

Sharra huddled on the ground. Her shoulder hurt like mad, though that was the least of her worries. Left alone with the enemy, she braced herself for what was sure to come, knowing in her heart that her chances of getting out alive were slim.

The case of documents was out of their reach, safe at the Vault with Faolan. Cael was most likely dead.

Another casualty in the fight. She didn't want to think about it, or she'd cry.

At least, Faolan was safe. That gave her some consolation. And she was still alive... for the moment.

Chapter Thirty

———

The two male Grexs were closing in on Faolan and Cael, and jumped back in shock when their intended captives disappeared before their eyes. A whoosh of cool air came from the vacuum and ruffled their clothing before dissipating into nothing. Gasps of surprise and fear came from all over.

"What trickery is this?" cried the Lead Grex. "Jury, explain."

Jury, the male standing closest to where they had been, looked around helpless. "I do not know, Mistress Jaard," he said. "They were standing here just a moment ago. We all saw them. I swear by the Sea Mother of us all, the air, it swallowed them up."

"The air cannot have done this."

"I swear by the mother of us all, it's true. You saw it, too. It is the work of Aeris, the sky god himself."

"Shut up, you worm. Keep your superstitions to yourself, or I will kill you right now and be done with it. They must be around here somewhere." She pointed a finger at two of his companions. "Jalen. Lede. Search the neighborhood. Find them."

Jalen, the male nodded to Jaard, and moved silently off to check the nearby buildings. Lede, the female, followed suit, and took the other side.

Through her hood, Sharra stared at the empty spot where Faolan had supported Cael's body. The only evidence that they had been there was the small trail of blood left behind on the dirty stone road from Cael's wounds. The image of Cael's limp body and the knife buried into his chest was burned into her brain.

Jaard called out to the male standing over Sharra. "Kaden, bring me the slave."

Kaden reached down and dragged Sharra unceremoniously off the ground, jarring her shoulder as she was set roughly on her feet. Pain shot out from the spot on her back. A cry escaped from her lips. She could not stop it. Her hand reached for the spot, but her arms were held tight to her side.

"Shut up," Kaden barked.

Something warm and wet ran down her back. At the same time a wave of dizziness came over her. If it weren't for the hands clamped on her arms, she would have fallen over. In her good hand, she clutched the sheath to her chest as if it could shield her from what she knew was to come.

Underneath the hood of her cloak, she could feel the

301

circle tightening around her. The one they called Jaard came up and stood before her. Sharra hunched her shoulders and hung her head, hoping the pose of submission would delay the inevitable. Fear coursed through her. Once they found out that she was human, and they would, her chances of getting out of this before Faolan shifted back for her would be very slim.

"A slave willing to take a knife for your master... How original. Too bad that he has deserted you, the coward."

A surge of dark energy touched the shield around her mind. It terrified her. Trembling within their grasps, Sharra held the shield tight with all her might. When Jaard found the barrier, she pushed harder searching for a way in. The ball of alien light in her head awoke as it felt the dark presence of the Grex on the other side of the shield. It pressed against the inside of her shield begging for freedom to feed. Though it was tempting to let it go, hurting the Grex leader would only make things worse for her. So, she hushed it, and sent it back to the recesses of her mind to wait.

"You are closed to me," Jaard said surprised. "Strange for a slave to be so strong-minded. But that is not my concern. I want what you have."

As Sharra heard the words, the sheath was torn out of her hand. A moment passed. And then another. She stood there hunched over; fighting the fear of what she knew was to come, forgetting for the moment about the knife in her shoulder.

"Nothing," she heard Jaard say. "She must have removed it. Search her."

More hands converged on her body as Kaden held

her arms. Instinct took over as she struggled to get away.

"Hold still, or you will feel my knife in your side," Kaden said close to her ear.

Someone grabbed her hood and tore it off her head. Down came her hair in a tumbled mass of reddish brown. A gasp went up among the Grexs. Sharra raised her eyes and saw the rings around Jaard's eyes flashed bright in alarm.

"A land-walker," she said, quickly recovering. "Then the rumors are true."

"It must be the one that was spotted in the Sand Market a few days back," Kaden said.

"A land-walker and the Princess in the city at the same time. It cannot be a coincidence."

"Shall I kill her?"

"No. She may be valuable. Plus, she knows something. Look at her eyes. Remove the knife from her shoulder, and strip her."

Sharra gasped in pain as the knife was pulled from her body. With it out of the way they dragged the cloak off of her with a whoosh of material. While Kaden held her arms, the others removed the knives from her belt and leg sheath, before unclasping the halter-top from her neck and stripping it off her body. It landed on the ground next to the cloak. From the folds of the halter-top fell out a sheet of crumpled paper.

Half naked, Sharra struggled between her captives. Uncaring that her breasts were exposed, uncaring of the knives all around her, she glared at the Head Grex as she watched her pick it up and smooth out the wrinkles. Jaard's eyes darted over the page. As she read, a strange light appeared in their depths as understanding of what she held reached home. A smile touched the corners of her lips.

"Well, well. Now I see what all the fuss is about." Jaard carefully folded the sheet and tucked it into her waistband.

Sharra twisted in Kaden's arms, but he held her tight. "I have powerful friends. If you hurt her, they will come. You cannot stop them."

"You do not include yourself. Will they not come for you too?"

"Araylai and I are honor-bound as I am to the rest of my pod. My pod knows this, so be warned. We humans don't react well when one from our pod is threatened."

A short laugh burst from the Grex. "Is that the case? Then why are you still here, and your pod member gone? I think you lie."

"He will be back, and with more. My partner marked you while you were not looking. There is nowhere you can hide on this world. You will be found," she said, hiding the lie behind the shield covering her mind.

"I only see you. Therefore, it is you that I must deal with. And since you say you are honor-bonded to the Princess, then your fate is with hers."

As she spoke Jalen and Lede came running back from their search. At the sight of the alien human held captive in Kaden's hands, they stopped short. Their eye rings flashed in shock as Jaard's had done before.

Lede recovered first. Her crest flicked in agitation as she gave her report. "We searched the whole area. Nothing, Mistress, not even under the threat of a knife."

"They are not here," Jalen reaffirmed, before turning back to stare at Sharra's hair. "What is that?"

"A land-walker," Kaden said.

"So that is what they look like. That stuff hanging from her head, is that a growth, like the sea-grass that attaches to the wandering shellcrabs? I assume it is a female by the look of her_" Jalen's eyes fell to her chest.

"Yes," Jaard cut in, "it is a female. So what."

A blush crept up Sharra's neck as she glared at the Arderian male staring at her naked chest. Finally he lost interest and went back to her hair.

"It looks like brown sea-grass, but finer," he said reaching out to touch it.

Lede jerked his arm back. "Get over it, Jalen. We still do not know where the other two are."

"No matter," Jaard said. "We got what we came for, and more. Lede, you and Jalen stay here for a few days, just in case they show up looking for their 'lost slave.'" Jaard signaled Kaden. "Cover the prisoner, and bring her along. We have some business with the Queen."

Her halter-top was tossed over her body and clipped back around her neck. The discarded cloak was next. Pain ran down her arm when they grabbed her shoulder as they forced it on. She cried out in pain.

A hand grabbed her good arm and jerked her close. It was Jaard. Her eyes were hard as granite, like the stone of the cave floor.

"Quiet, land-walker, or I will show you the meaning of real pain," she said before shoving her back to Kaden.

Kaden caught her and jerked her around to face him. She pressed her lips together and swallowed down the pain as he pulled her hood over her head and down to her chin. Once her hair and face were hidden behind the garment, Jaard gave instructions to the rest of her pod. Dressed as a Harena slave once again, they marched her down the street, a Grex on each arm.

As they left the Royal Gold behind them the street once again began to fill with people. No one paid attention to the small group as they led her away. Either that, or they knew better than to interfere. Blinded by the hood, her nose told her when they had left the town and entered the extended tunnel, for the smell of salt and decay that permeated the cavern no longer filled the space inside her hood.

The reef system of the city of Ardere was extensive, with multi-levels of cave systems connected by complex tunnel ways. She did not know how long they marched. Tunnels turned into caves, caves into more tunnels. Some smelled strong of fish, while others of dried grass. Still others smelled of things she couldn't identify. The noise around her ebbed and flowed as the traffic, foot or wheeled, left the tunnels and dispersed into the next cave system.

Hours must have passed for she felt her body growing weaker with each step as the injury of her shoulder took its toll. Her feet grew heavy, and she stumbled. Kaden jerked her back onto her feet. By the fourth time, he called a halt to the group. Jaard didn't like it, but agreed. Grateful for the reprise, Sharra sagged between them.

A discussion ensued around her. It quickly turned heated. Words of "too many eyes this route," and "she won't make it," were spoken in low harsh voices. She knew it was about her, but didn't have the strength to care. It was only when they thrust a cup to her mouth and told her to drink that she knew they had come to some kind of decision.

She didn't resist, but drank the tart liquid, knowing there was no other recourse for her. She would be dead soon anyway. Warmth flowed down her throat and settled in her belly. Soon it spread out from her torso to her limbs, dulling the pain in her shoulder. Her body felt lethargic. It was a feeling she had felt before.

Her brain became fuzzy as her vision blurred inside the hood. With no will left to resist, her knees buckled, and she sank to the ground between her guards, and let the darkness come.

Chapter Thirty-One

It was the sound of liquid being poured out nearby that brought Sharra back from that dark place where nothing existed. Consciousness returned to her slowly as if pushing through row after row of heavy black drapes. At the other end, a dark shade of grey registered behind her eyelids. A dull ache filled the back of her head like a bad hangover. As her senses returned so did a pounding pain in her shoulder. The smell of urine, body waste, and death burned her nostrils. She opened her eyes to a lighter shade of dark. Lichen must be growing on the ceiling. It wasn't much, but it was enough to see the hard stone beneath her cheek and the matching wall a foot from her face.

Someone had removed her cloak and covered her legs. She moved her bad arm, and groaned.

Something wet touched the flesh of her bad

shoulder and swept down her back. She jerked, and tried to rise, but a firm pressure stopped her.

"Lie still. It will only hurt worse if you move."

The voice was familiar even with her fogged up mind. "Loch? Is that you?"

"Yes," he said. He sounded tired.

"My shoulder__"

"Needs tending."

She rested her head back on the floor and closed her eyes. Somehow Loch was there. She was not alone, and for the moment that was enough.

"Where are we?"

"In a holding cell." Loch rinsed out the cloth in the bowl and returned it to her back. After a while he said, "Who did this to you? The male hu-man? Why did the pod not protect you?"

"The human turned out to be a friend, a part of my pod. He was brought here by Araylai to rescue me."

"Then the rumors are true. The Princess is here." The words were said on a soft whisper as if something finally made sense to him.

"Yes. You had already left for Praemin Rue's house by the time they made it to Riff. Faolan wanted to take me home right away, but Araylai, when she heard the news about the document and her mother, wanted to stay longer to take more council. We should've made her leave. We were stupid."

"What happened?"

"The Queen's Umbra stormed the outpost during the night, and took her away."

"How could they have known so quickly that she was there?"

309

"Nayada thinks there was a plant, a worm. They…" Sharra paused as the events of the last day caught up with her. Her eyes filled with water. "Caetus is dead."

"Caetus."

Loch sat back in shock.

"Loch, it's all a mess." A tear escaped down her cheek and dropped into her hair. "Cael…" She couldn't say it.

"No, not Cael, too," he groaned.

"We knew we needed to get that document in order to have any chance of saving Araylai. So Nayada sent us out to track you down. We followed your trail all day." Her voice wavered. She took a shaky breath and continued, hating the words that were to come. "Cael knew you well. He led us on a trail of Helix Houses until we came to The Royal Gold. He found the sheath, but so did the Grex. Cael… he… he…" A sob bubbled up her throat. She tried to catch it, but couldn't. "I tried. We were surrounded. I saw the knife in his heart. He went down."

"No."

It was too dark to see his aura, but Sharra didn't need it to feel his deep anguish.

The next bit of news was just as bad. "They've got the document, Loch."

She waited for a response, but none came. Dragging the cloak off her legs, he ripped a long strip from the bottom, before placing the cloak back over her body. With the strip, he slowly wrapped it around her shoulder and underneath her arm, and tied it tight, covering the wound. It was only when he moved away that she realized that he was also hurt.

Half-crawling he dragged his body to the wall next to her, and leaned back, slow and deliberate as if each movement cost him a bit of his soul. The sound of his tortured breath pierced her heart.

Pushing up onto her elbow, she peered up at him through the greyness. His dorsal fin hung limp down the side of his face and over one shoulder. Even in the dark, she could see the swellings that covered his once handsome face. Deep patches of color marred the pale skin of his arms, chest, and legs where he had been beaten. There was no telling what injuries were hidden underneath.

"Oh, Loch."

"Don't worry about me. I have been through worse."

He pushed the webbing away from his good eye with a tired hand. Down the inside of his arm ran a line of fresh cut marks like someone had ticked off the days on his flesh. She saw it and wanted to cry, cry for him, cry for Cael, cry for herself.

Loch leaned his head back against the wall. Silence stretched between them. Sharra didn't know what to say to comfort him. It was all too raw, even for her.

Finally, he said, "The funny thing is, they asked me nothing. Nothing. I guess they did not need to after all."

"I'm so sorry."

"It is not your fault. We all knew the risk. Even Cael…"

He floundered on his friend's name. Sharra reached out and took his hand that lay lifeless on the floor. Wrapping her fingers around his, she settled back onto her side on the floor and pressed his hand to her face, sharing what little comfort she could give.

After a moment he swallowed and continued, "At least he died with honor. I can only hope to do the same."

"You are not going to die. Do you hear me? Don't you even think it."

A soft snort came from his direction. Sharra felt the pained smile behind that small effort.

"Are all you hu-mans so stubborn?" he said as he settled down on the floor next to her.

Sharra thought of Faolan, and smiled. "No. Just me," she lied.

Holding his hand, she curled into a ball, resting her head onto her good arm and closed her eyes. Her shoulder throbbed, but it was nothing compared to the pain in her heart. If she was feeling this way, she couldn't imagine what Loch was going through.

In the quiet he whispered, "I hope you have enough stubbornness for both of us. We will need it."

So quiet was it said that she had almost missed it. In some ways she wished she had, fearing what it meant.

It seemed like she had just fallen asleep when the sound of the clicking of the lock in the door awoke them both. A photophore pan was thrust into the room on a long pole from the opening in the door. The light bounced off the ceiling of the small cell, for that is what it was now that she could see. No windows. No bars. No furniture, only a bucket in the corner for a toilette. It was a box cut out from the rock of the understructure of the reef. No light could reach it for it was too deep, too far from the warming influence of the sun's rays. It was a tomb made for the condemned. And there was no doubt that's what they were.

Two large guards dressed in purple, black, and gold, the colors of the Royal Guard House, stepped into the cell brandishing long swords. One of them held the light up while the other went over to Loch where he laid and kicked him in the side.

"Get up," he said as he trained the point of his blade at Loch's chest.

Loch ignored the blade as he got painfully to his hands and knees and lifted himself off the floor onto his feet. He tottered where he stood but didn't fall. His dorsal fin folded back tight against his body with effort.

Needing no prompting, Sharra rose to her feet next to him. Grabbing the cloak as it slipped off her body, she pressed it to her chest like a shield.

Once they were up the guards moved aside as an older female stepped in between them and looked over the two prisoners. Wearing a long flowing dress dyed in the deep Tyrian purple of the House of Ardere, she stood as if the world answered to her, and to her alone. Maybe it did. With her webbing crested high above her head and down her back through the slit in her gown like a sailfish, she could've been the Queen for all that Sharra knew.

The Arderian cast her eyes over the tiny room missing nothing. When they landed on Sharra and stopped, a shudder of cold went through her. The deep rings around the alien's reddish-brown irises flashed bright under the light of the photophore pan as her gaze took in Sharra's form. A flash of orange colored the aura around her. Just as quickly it was gone. Why the Arderian was caught surprised, Sharra didn't know.

Surely the guards had informed their superiors about her. The Arderian female must have found her wanting, for after her curiosity was satisfied, she moved on to Loch who stood stiffly beside her.

"Praemin Loch," she said, "of the House of Ayu, a highborn from the line of Lana of Ayu, your mother. Accepted to Bellicus Academy at the age of ten. Taught by the finest educators of the Queen in the art of war and strategy. Commissioned as a Spike at the age of twenty-five, youngest ever on record. Born to privilege and power, with a full life of prestige and adoration in front of you. Is this you standing before me?"

"High Councilor Larua," Loch acknowledged with a bow of his head. It was a small movement, made difficult by the injuries he had suffered.

The High Councilor looked him up and down, shaking her head at the condition of his beaten body. "How far you have fallen. And the dishonor... How your mother must be hiding for the shame of it. And for what? For misplaced loyalties?"

Loch lifted his chin, and said to her, "Loyalty is not a birth right. It must be earned, not with money, or threats, or devious planning, but with honor and truth."

The aura around the High Councilor flared red as his words hit their mark. She slapped him across the face jerking his neck with the force of her anger.

"How dare you speak of honor, you who has lost everything for a principle. Are you in such a hurry to die?"

Loch stared at her, his aura dark with controlled anger. Pressing his lips together, he refused to rise to the bait.

Larua pursed her lips, as if disappointed. "No, I suppose you do not. It is a shame to waste such a strong sense of loyalty. It is a rare thing to find these days. If only you had used that for the Queen, your future would have been set. But since you have tied your loyalty to one who has been proven dishonorable... well... you have given us little choice."

Loch stiffened even more. Clenching his fists to his side, he said, "Araylai is not guilty of the crimes that have been levied against her, and you know it. The signatures on that slave trader's receipt shows the ones who are guilty of betrayal. And that makes you worried. Or why else would you go to such lengths to get it back. It is because you know who is behind it all, don't you. And you need to keep it from the Houses of the High Court. This isn't about honor. It's about power. And no matter how hard you try to suppress it the truth will always be revealed. I have read the document. So have others. The truth is out there now. You cannot stop it, nor the Queen."

"You speak bravely. Yet this is all speculation with no proof."

"We do not need the document anymore. The proof is in the aura of the people."

"The people are no better than the slugs that lick the reef clean."

"They are not mindless animals. The people of Ardere, from the Harena all the way up to the Highborn, are what make us one of the greatest Houses of Ardus. The truth will reach them. The Queen's hold on the people has weakened. The people will rise up. It is inevitable, because honor is what drives us, feeds us. We cannot deny who we are."

"You seem so sure of this 'truth.' Then you will be interested to see which 'truth' the High Court will pronounce today when the captured princess is brought before them for her crimes."

Sharra's breath hitched at the news. Beside her, Loch's body twitched. She grabbed his arm, stopping him from doing something stupid.

The guards, she warned.

Larua missed neither movement. Neither did the guards. At the first sign of defiance they took a step and raised their swords ready to protect the High Councilor. Larua stopped them with a graceful lift of a hand. Though they stopped, they kept their swords pointed at the prisoners' chests. Larua smiled. It was not a friendly smile, but a knowing smile, as if she learned something new, something useful from the physical interchange between the two prisoners.

"I see the hu-man knows her place."

The muscles in Loch's arm tightened under Sharra's hand. "She has nothing to do with this."

Loch, stay calm. Or you'll make it worse for us.

But Larua had already answered him, saying, "There I believe you are wrong. This interview is over. Guards, bind her hands, and bring her."

With that she swept out of the cell without a backward glance. The guards shoved Loch away, throwing him against the wall. He cried out and slid to the floor where he remained bruised and broken.

"Loch!" Sharra said as she lunged to him.

The guards were on top of her before she could move to help him. They grabbed her arms, and bound her wrists in front of her body. At their touch the ball of energy moved to spring free to defend her, but she held tight, waiting for the right time. Sharp pain radiated out from her shoulder as they dragged her away from Loch. Twisting her body, uncaring of the pain it caused, she reached out to Loch with her eyes. When their eyes met, the spark that once brightened his was gone. All that she saw was sad defeat in their dulled depths.

I am sorry, he whispered.

"Loch!" she screamed as the guards dragged her out of the cell. *Wait. Don't give up. All is not lost. There is_"

The connection was broken before she could finish. He was too weak, his electromagnetic energy almost spent. The guards slammed the door and locked it behind her. Loch was left in the dark cell, still alive, but for how long, and with little hope. For all he knew everyone of his pod was dead, or soon to be dead. She wished she had told him about Nayada. Then again, maybe it was best that he didn't know. He wouldn't survive the torture.

The guards led her past other cells. She probed them one by one, sending out questioning tendrils of energy, but nothing came through their thick walls. Hopefully Nayada and Calyx were not in one of them. The High Counselor did not mention them, only Araylai. Whatever was going to happen was going to happen today. Time had run out. Araylai's honor would not save her. Sharra was sure that the High Councilor would see to that.

Yet there was another option open to Araylai, if only Sharra could get to her and talk some sense into her. There had been too many sacrifices already: Caetus, Cael, Loch, even the oppressed people of the city. Sharra's personal tragedies seemed minute stacked against the overwhelming loss to Araylai and her people.

She had to help. She would never forgive herself if she didn't try. Her own problems could wait. Greyson could wait.

Faolan was the key.

She was tagged.

He was probably in the city right now tracking her movements. He would've discussed the situation with Lazarus first. They were smart, her friends, very smart. She depended on that, and hoped that they saw the value of the information in the case she had given him to keep safe. Now that the slave trader receipt was lost to them, that information was all they had. And it was powerful, powerful enough to overthrow a wicked Queen.

Chapter Thirty-Two

They had left the darkness and the stench of the prison behind, climbing ramps and stairways one level at a time until they reached the barracks. Sharra was marched through them, past training arenas, and more tunnels. Soldiers were everywhere, cleaning, working, training, doing things that Sharra could only guess with weapons other than the knives strapped to their thighs. Though she was noticed, discipline remained tight, for they were the Queen's chosen and knew better than to disrupt the small party with their curiosity. It was only after they passed that the whispering started.

Though she looked neither right nor left, Sharra could feel their eyes upon her back, hear their whispers, and feel how alien she must look to them with her strange hair, eyes, and skin. Marched through the barracks, she felt like a spectacle, an animal. Her clothing was torn in places and covered in blood and dirt. More dirt was on her hands, feet, and legs. She tried to lick her dried lips, but there was no moisture in her mouth. She needed water, and yet dared not ask for it. Her stomach churned with hunger and fear.

They entered another tunnel that was wider than any of the ones they had traversed so far. A squad of foot soldiers trotted passed them on their way back into the city, each with a spear resting upon their shoulder. In the opposite lane was a caravan of wagons piled with goods to the point of overflowing. Tied to the tongue like horses were four slaves per wagon, two on each side. With their hands on the crossbars, they pushed, dragging one foot after another, drawing their heavy burden behind them with tired feet as they crawled towards the barracks.

In the tunnel wall was another tunnel discreetly dug out with its own nook-like foyer. Though smaller it was well lit, and more strangely, protected by two guards wearing the Queen's colors. Over their backs were draped cloaks made of gold cloth, much different than any other guard that Sharra had seen so far. On their upper arm they wore the insignia of the Queen welded onto a band of twisted metal: a medallion of a slender scepter crowned with a black pearl over a thin slice of nautilus shell. It was the same band the Umbra Scouts wore, but made of gold.

Without hesitation Larua drew her party into the nook. The guards crossed their wicked spears, blocking the way. Larua held up her hand, signaling the guards behind her to halt with their prisoner.

"I am sorry, High Councilor, but it is the Queen's

orders that we stop everyone," a guard said.

"I am glad to see that you take your position seriously," she said as she passed over a document. On top was a seal of the scepter medallion.

"We cannot be too careful. Those opposed to the Queen have become more cunning." He broke the seal, and read it before passing it back. "All is in order."

She took it and tucked it away. "Queen Aniani appreciates the loyalty of those who serve her. I will tell her of your fine obedience."

He bowed his head, and said, "Thank you, High Councilor," and waved her party through.

The short tunnel led them to a strong metal door and another set of guards. Again Larua handed over the document before they opened the door and let them pass. Sharra blinked in surprise as she was led out of a towering wall and into a cavern of gigantic proportions. All at once light, noise, and space assaulted her senses. She stumbled in their grasp, overwhelmed. The guards hardly noticed as they dragged her across a quiet courtyard to another wall shorter than the one at their backs. Somewhere down below her feet buried in the layers of rock was the prison where Loch remained closed off from space and light. It seemed so far away. She didn't realize how claustrophobic it had felt until now when she was free and the sky was high above like a radiant shield.

As they crossed the courtyard, a pleasant breeze touched her face. Sharra raised her head to it, soaking it in, appreciating the simple thing. With the sensation on her skin her senses calmed down, and reasoning returned. So did her determination. She needed to stop wallowing in despair and work on a plan. How many times had Tanner drilled into her during her training that information was the key to a seamless mission. Information she could get. If they wouldn't tell her, then she'd have to use other means.

"Where are we?" she asked a guard as they entered an archway in the wall.

Pride covered his face as he informed her, "You are in Ardere, the central city of the House of Ardere, the most powerful House of Ardus, and the home of the Sea Mother herself."

"The sea mother?"

"Queen Aniani."

At the pronouncement they were through the wall. The guard swept his free hand in a grand gesture across the expansive courtyard to the vision across the way.

"The Palace," he said.

Carved out of a wall of crystalized rock, the palace rose above the central city like a huge nautilus shell, curving ever smaller until the tip ended at the top of the crystal where it met the grey stone of the reef. Cut to a many faceted jewel it shimmered with a thousand colors as its facets caught the rays that burned down from the source high above on the ceiling. From the facets were carved out balconies and windows one level after another. In the openings the sheer draperies of the palest of pastels were pushed aside, and fluttered in the warm airflow that circulated throughout the central city. Half buried in the surrounding granite, the palace shone like a monstrous jewel, lighting the city like a giant nightlight. Though the city needed no help. Light was aplenty. The source, whether lichen or some other, was stronger than any of the other caverns that Sharra had been in so far.

Sharra's eyes widened in awe at the sight of the jeweled palace. It looked as alien as it was beautiful. Its beauty reminded her of Araylai. Not only her physical appearance, but also more importantly, that this was taken from her friend: the wealth, the privilege, and her heritage, not to mention her honor. Life at the Vault was nothing compared to what had been stolen from her friend. All because of the greed, treachery, and deceit of her mother.

Two weeks ago Sharra wouldn't have understood that such treachery could be possible. Now, she wasn't so sure. All she had for family was Greyson, even if he sucked as a brother. Yet could he be the one behind her troubles? Why would he want her dead? It made no sense. And if things kept going as they were, she may not live long enough to find out.

They did not cross the marble courtyard to the palace. Instead, they marched along the inner wall, past more doors until Larua found the one she was looking for. Inside was another long hallway. Tired and weak, Sharra gave up trying to keep track of where they were going. As long as the transmitter Faolan held picked up the signal of her tag, there was hope. Finally the guards dumped her in a room and shut the door.

A photophore pan hung from the ceiling. Against the wall was a narrow bed next to a table. Other than that, the room was bare. No windows, only the door, and the light above her head. She fell onto the bed, exhausted, and thought of Loch in the cold dark cell somewhere deep below. The look of despair on his face was burned into her brain. All hope had left him.

Please, hurry, she begged Faolan, *before it's too late for both of us.*

She didn't know how long she slept. It was the footsteps outside the door that woke her. She sat up with an effort and got to her feet as the door opened. The same guards came in and stood at attention just inside the door. Larua flowed in on a breeze of purple robes, and stepped to one side. Behind her came another female dressed in a white gown as pure as new fallen snow. Around her slim waist was knotted a twisted belt of gold. A matching bandlet was wrapped around her left arm. On her high forehead rested a tiara crown of the finest of gold. The gold had been bent and folded into an intricate pattern of swirling sea creatures that played among the many set stones of diamonds and pearls. They met in the center, and twined around a large white pearl that glistened with an internal luminosity. It was the largest pearl Sharra had ever seen.

Golden crest high, the beautiful Arderian stopped next to Larua. Green-rimmed amber eyes stared at her out of a familiar face. For a moment Sharra thought it was Araylai, and almost cried out in relief. But she stopped herself for the green aura of the Arderian felt wrong, as if controlled, and not real. Where there should have been a sense of goodwill behind it, there was none, only darkness, and something deeper, more menacing. The ball of energy in her head agreed with her for it had awoken as soon as the Arderian had entered the room, recognizing the strong electromagnetic energy source that radiated from the alien's body. As soon as Sharra felt it stir, she suppressed it and tightened the mental shield around it.

Aniani, Sharra thought.

The softening flesh below the queen's chin coupled with the fine lines around her eyes and mouth confirmed her suspicions. And when the Arderian spoke, she knew for sure. Underneath the bell-like quality was a harshness that Araylai's voice never possessed.

"Larua, step outside. I want to speak to the hu-man... alone."

"My Hera, she is dangerous."

"Look at her. She is ready to fall over. I doubt she has the strength to swat a rudbug let alone dodge the knives of my Umbra. Besides, her hands are tied. Now go."

Larua pursed her lips, but bowed, saying, "Yes, my Hera," and left the room in a swirl of robes, leaving the guards with the Queen as she closed the door behind her.

The room darkened a fraction. At first Sharra thought it was because the brighter light of the hallway had been blocked with the closing of the door, but it wasn't that. For as soon as Larua left the room, the green aura that had surrounded the pale flesh of the Queen darkened until it was blacker than the deepest abyss. Not realizing that Sharra with her extra agrylium could see her aura, Aniani unwittingly exposed her true thoughts to the enemy. No light, love, or compassion shone from her being.

Sharra stiffened at the sight of it, and feared for all of them.

"So, you are the hu-man responsible for the trouble in my reef. Injuring a guard, and killing an auctioneer while abducting one of my citizens is a great insult to my people, and deserves punishment. Though you have done more than that. Conspiring with insurgents to commit treason against the throne, that is a very serious charge. Do you know what the penalty is for that?"

As the Queen spoke, Sharra felt a tiny surge of energy touch the shield around her mind. Finding it blocked, it grew stronger, spreading out like fingers as it searched for a breach in her defenses. Sharra had been prepared. Larua had used the same tactic before. Though the Queen tried hard to break in, the shield held firm. After a few seconds the Queen withdrew.

"Interesting. I have never met a female of your kind."

"Sorry to disappoint you."

"On the contrary. I find you more fascinating than the male of your species. They are too... predictable. You, on the other hand, are a contradiction."

"How is that?"

"I have found that your species, when given the choice and the means, would rather save their own life, especially when the cause has nothing to do with you. Greed, and lust for power drives your kind. That I can understand. Yet here you are, a hu-man with nothing to gain, caught in the middle of something that does not concern you."

"There you're wrong. It does concern me."

"Then someone must be paying you a high price. Tell me, what it is. Maybe someone is holding something against you to make you come here and prove yourself. No, you are the superior sex. I cannot see you letting anyone control you. Power, then, or working for a higher position in your ruling party. That must be it, for what else would drive you?"

"Something that you would not understand."

"No? Indulge me."

"Friendship. The kind that is given freely. And the only gain or profit, is not for selfish reasons, but is based on mutual respect and love."

"That is an ideal that is wasted on the weak."

"No, it is the weak that fear it for it takes strength of character to commit your soul to another."

"Is that so? And you are willing to die for this… commitment?"

"Never leave a partner behind. That is our code of honor. Araylai is honor-bonded to the Vault, as we are to her. You forfeited that when you signed her away to the slave traders. She belongs to our pod now, and what is ours we protect."

"My daughter is of the House of Ardere, royal by birth. She would never give up that honor. That is why she has come back, to fix the breach between us, and heal the wounds of her betrayal."

The blackness swirled around the Queen. In it Sharra felt the lie. Clenching her fists between the bindings of her wrists, she called her on it, knowing it was probably a stupid thing to do. But Araylai needed her, even if all she could do was defend her with words.

"You lie. Araylai knows you were behind her abduction, and the subsequent besmirching of her name. Treason, you call it. It's you, her own mother, who is the betrayer. She has seen the proof in your own handwriting, and soon the whole city will know. You cannot stop the truth. It is stronger than you, Larua, or any of your henchman."

"Where is your proof? It is your word against mine.

Who do you think my people will believe? You underestimate my power. And so has Araylai. I had come willing to pardon you of your crimes against this city, deeming it as ignorance on your part. But Larua is correct, you are a dangerous creature, and must be dealt with accordingly."

The Queen tilted her proud head as she took in Sharra's defiant posture. Unblinking Aniani stared coldly at Sharra through eyes so similar to Araylai's it shook Sharra, except they were not the gentle amber of her daughter's, but hard, like steel.

"You never answered the question that I first asked you, of what the penalty for treason is. The answer is death. Since you say that you are bonded to Araylai, then it is only fitting that you share the same fate as her. My House will stay in my control. No weak Arderian or human will take it from me. I will see to that!"

Sharra's heart pounded in her chest, knowing it was not an idle threat. Fear rose up her throat. She swallowed it down, but not before the ball of energy caught it. Feeding off her fear, it pulsed against its restraints. Aniani saw the fear in her eyes and smiled.

"Oh, and another thing, if your pod is as loyal as you say, and they do show up in Ardere... they will be deemed a threat, and killed on sight. Their deaths will be on your head, not mine. Unless you wish to change your mind. It is still not too late. All you have to do is deny everything before the court, and I will make sure you get home."

"Unlike you, I believe in honor and loyalty. So, no. I'll pass, and let justice decide my fate."

"So be it."

But the Queen wasn't done. She stepped closer and opened her hand. On her palm rested a slim piece of metal. It was a Link.

"My daughter was wearing this. Do you know what it is?"

"She didn't tell you?"

"She was not in the mood at the time."

I bet, Sharra thought. But it told her something: Araylai was not talking.

"Yes, I know what it is," she said. "It's a gift from our pod leader, a symbol of who we are, who we support, like the crown you're wearing."

"Then it is of some value."

"Not any more."

"No matter," she said as she closed her fist around it. "I have something of greater value. You. It will be interesting to see if Araylai finds you as valuable as you do her."

With those words the Queen motioned to the guards, who had remained by the door in quiet attention. The interview was over. As they opened the door, she said to the nearest one, "See that the prisoner gets some water, but nothing more."

When the door shut behind them, Sharra sank down onto the bed. Uncontrolled tremors ran through her limbs and shook her torso as she gave into her fears. She had learned a few things, and they scared her: first, Araylai hadn't shifted out, and second, her mother was out for blood. Whatever Queen Aniani had planned was going down that day.

Good. I will not last much longer.

This was much worse than the confrontation with

Dash. The woman was pure evil. Even her pretense of an aura could not hide the fact from Sharra. Her words confirmed it. Loch was right to be afraid. They were all in mortal danger. Faolan was their only hope, and time was running out.

Chapter Thirty-Three

After the water came, Sharra lay down on the cot. Though her thirst was quenched, sleep would not come. The thought of dying was heavy on her mind. No matter how she tried, she could not see a way out of her predicament. Nothing had been said about Nayada and Calyx. Nayada was smart. Sharra was banking on that. As trackers, they'd be cautious, or so Sharra hoped. The Royal Gold was where they were to meet. Once Nayada and Calyx had discovered they'd been taken, for surely the ugly bouncer called Della would've been only too eager to exploit the knowledge, then the two scouts would've known to abort the mission and flee, and not let the honor they hold so dear get them killed for nothing. It would break her heart if they were somewhere in that horrid prison. Loch was still alive down there, for now, and Araylai, too. That brought her some consolation. If Faolan didn't make it back in time… her fate would be sealed with Araylai's. She couldn't bear it if Nayada and her pod were also killed.

"Cael," she whispered, and silently wept for the loss of a friend.

He did not deserve to die. None of them did.

She touched the melted agrylium spheres behind her ears. If only they worked, then none of this would have happened. She could have shifted home from the start. Araylai would still be at the Vault. The domino effect of death and betrayal never would've started. That would've meant that Cael and Caetus would still be alive, and Loch not imprisoned in the bowels of the palace awaiting his fate.

The Vault could not help her. It all depended on Faolan, and the precious information he had carried back to the Vault. If they could show what was in the case to the High Court, the information could save Araylai. Sharra did not know how, but Nayada seemed sure of it. All she knew was that she had to try.

Faolan, please find me, she pleaded.

When the guards came for her, Sharra did not protest. The loss of blood from the knife wound had taken its toll along with the emotional distress of the last twenty-four hours. As the three came in, she stood up to face them. She swayed on her legs as they shook from weakness and fear.

The head female Umbra looked her up and down, and said, "Take her before she falls over."

The two male guards stepped forward, and grabbed an arm each. Sharra sagged against them, letting them carry most of her weight between them. With her wrists still bound, they led her out of the cell. On the other side six more guards waited. They surrounded her, front, back, and sides. The lead Umbra gave the order, and the unit marched forward down the wide hallway.

They went through several checkpoints until they came to a set of doors. Papers were passed and checked before the go ahead was given, and the doors were opened. Once through the guard shut them again, leaving her alone with her escort.

The walls around them were no longer rock, nor the hard coral substructure so often seen used as building material. The walls were something different, something Sharra hadn't seen before in the rest of the reef. They glowed, not with the lichen that grew everywhere, but with its own internal luminosity like a light bulb shining through a lampshade of white glass. It reminded her of the outside walls of the palace.

The walkway opened up into a magnificent grand hall. They were inside the palace.

The thick outside wall of the palace arched overhead four-stories high. Sharra had to stretch her neck to see where it came to a point high above against the inside wall of the massive hall. Long walkways were carved out of the white crystal of the outer wall one level after another. They travelled across the whole length of the outer wall like the lines inside a shell only to end at the arched entrances where the outer wall met the inner wall. Banisters of the same luminescent material lined the inside exposed side of the walkways, for it was a long way down to the ground if someone should fall. At regular intervals wide balconies had been cut through the wall and jutted out into the air to overlook the splendid view of the courtyard and the city beyond.

A warm breeze flowed through the openings stirring the long strips of sheer fabric that framed them, and over the few Arderian courtiers who strolled along their paths. The breeze caught their exquisite dresses of silk and gauze, making the material dance around their legs and around the proud webbing of their dorsal fins. More windows were carved out of the four-story inner wall. Some were closed while others were open to the breeze. The grand hall curved around the slope of the inner wall like the inside of a giant seashell. More courtiers, male and female, wandered through the hall as if they had no place to be and no constriction on time.

All was spacious and light. It was meant to impress, and it did.

The guards' webbed feet slapped against the white floor as they marched their prisoner through a group of elegantly dressed courtiers. Hearing them coming, the courtiers moved out of the way to let them pass. Upon seeing the alien human in the midst of the squad, they stopped to stare, unabashed by their obvious curiosity, and started to whisper to each other behind their webbed hands. The guards looked neither left nor right, but kept a tight circle around Sharra as they passed one group after another.

From an entrance further up and off to the side emerged another squad. A space between the guards opened for a brief moment as they marched along. In the middle, trussed up between two guards was Loch. Sharra got a good look at him and sucked in her breath. His once bright aura was muted, the color dulled by pain and injury. His pale skin gleamed with dark bruising. Legs, arms, torso, and face: no part of his body had been left untouched in their search for information. Multiple cuts riddled his arms and legs. His good eye was a slit in his swollen face. She wanted to cry for his pain, for the torture they must have inflicted on him. It made hers feel insignificant in comparison. And yet, though he was suffering, he'd cared for her wounds back in the cell that they'd shared, and given her comfort when he had needed it even more than she.

Half naked, he stumbled as she watched. They yanked him back to his feet with no mercy on their hard faces. Pain washed over his face and darkened his aura as he righted his body and struggled to move his feet.

Loch, she groaned inside as she reached out to him across the hallway.

His head twitched in surprise at her mental touch before he could stop it. And then she felt his relief as he quickly let her in.

I thought you were… Are you okay? he said.

The two squads met and merged as they spoke in the silent link. Loch was pushed in front of her. Finding hidden strength in her presence he stiffened his spine as they marched them forward. His back was covered in fresh welts. They crisscrossed like thick red ribbons over the webbing that hung loose down his spine, shredding it where it dug the deepest. At the sight she wanted to cry even more.

Why did they do this to you? she said.

To teach me a lesson. There was a pause, and then the electromagnetic energy turned hard. *They did not ask me anything. I guess Rue had already given them what they wanted. I am to be made an example of. No position, Praemin or otherwise, is unaccountable.*

I'm so sorry.

It does not matter anymore. Soon, it will be over.

No. There's still hope.

Hope? Loch scoffed. *Hope was taken away when Aniani became queen.*

They came to a halt in front of a pair of high arched doors carved in white ivory. With long crossed spears two guards blocked the entranceway. Dressed in the full uniform of the Queen's Umbra, they held the squads there as they waited for a report to return from the inside. Permission was soon granted. The guards uncrossed their spears, and pushed the doors open. As one unit the squads moved, taking their prisoners with them through the ivory doors. They crossed another hallway to an identical pair of doors guarded by more of the Queen's Umbra.

Sharra saw Loch's back stiffen with tension as the squads waited again for clearance.

The throne room, he informed her. *The High Council will be inside. Stay brave, my friend, no matter what happens. If nothing else, let us be remembered as ones who hold onto to our convictions and die with honor.*

It's not too late. Faolan will come back. And he will bring help. I'm sure of it.

I hope you are right, for we will find no help from those inside without some kind of proof.

Their wait was short for the clearance came as soon as they stopped. As they started forward, Loch's link tightened with urgency as he warned, *Once inside, I will not hear you. There is a device in the ceiling that blocks all who stand within the arena.*

336

Her heart quickened as they approached the threshold of the door. On the other side lay the vastness of the throne room.

*Loch, listen. There is something you should know. It's about Nayada_*

But that was all she got out. As soon as she crossed the threshold and entered the throne room the connection was severed, and her mind went silent. Loch was gone. Not only Loch, but also all residue of electromagnetic energy that the Arderian people put off was silenced. Having dealt with the anomaly for several months since her assimilation, she had gotten used to it. Now, when it was abruptly taken away, the emptiness felt strange as if she had somehow gone deaf. If it affected her that way, it must be much worse for the Arderian's for it was an integral part of their being. It really did make them deaf, that is, in the mind. They could still verbally speak, though Sharra didn't think that was their first choice. By the tight looks on the faces around her, she believed her assumptions to be true.

She scoffed at her own musings. None of that was of any use. What really mattered was yet to happen.

The throne room opened out around them in a vast sea of space. Where the rest of the palace was white like pure snow, the seat of power was different. Inside the throne room it was alight with the colors of the sea as it should be, for the Queen represented the Mother of the Sea, their goddess whom they worshipped. Twelve stunning pillars of aqua-blue encircled the outer rim fifty feet in from the throne room walls. Evenly spaced they curved up re-enforcing the immense arched ceiling. Another row of twelve pillars looped around halfway in, taller than the first as they supported the highest curve of the ceiling. Carved into them were life-like sea creatures. They danced up and down the pillars in poises of play among the sea grasses of ivory and schools of colorful fish that swam in the waters of Ardus.

Embedded into the floor was a large replica of the medallion that the Umbra wore on their armband, minus the scepter. Where the medallions were made of metal, the emblem in the floor was made from polished stones that matched the colors of the sea. Brilliant blues, fluorescent greens, and vivid yellows shimmered like jewels in the nautilus shell mosaic that curled around the floor in a wide path that started at the outer pillars, becoming thinner and thinner the closer it came to the middle of the chamber until it closed in the center in a tiny swirl of gems.

Sharra's eyes widened at the sight of such alien splendor. It bespoke of power and of grace, and of a sense of agelessness. It bespoke of a oneness with the sea that encompassed their whole way of life. Her fear renewed in her chest, not just for herself, but also for Araylai and Loch. For this was the Queen's domain, and now that Sharra saw it first hand, she knew that Aniani's threats were real.

The squad marched them through the first ring, and across the mosaic in the floor. The metal fixtures of their leather armor clinked in the silence of the air.

A voice spoke out from somewhere up ahead, and echoed across the expanse of floor.

"Bring in the accused!"

Sharra recognized the voice. It was the one called Larua, the High Councilor.

Peeking around Loch and through the marching guards, Sharra searched the throne room for an escape route. Sentries were posted beside pillars and at the entranceways around the monolithic chamber. There was no way they could make a run for it. They'd be dead within seconds.

More importantly, there was no way Faolan could sneak in without being noticed.

Rule number sixteen in the Vault Handbook stated, "Never expose your identity as a Vault Agent in any time line (past, present, or future) unless recruiting."

Oh, why did she have to go and harp about that stupid rulebook to him? About obeying it? Of all the times to break one of its rules, it was now. Yet would they this time? She looked ahead, at the crowd waiting for them, and thought not.

Gathered around the inner rim of pillars, the courtiers waited draped in colorful silk and gauze garments. Like beautiful butterflies their dorsal webbing stood out in full sail, from the spine of their forehead down to the tip of their tailbone. All heads were turned inward to the twenty-four House Representatives that sat on tiered seating that fanned out on both sides of the throne, twelve on the left, and twelve on the right. They were the High Court, chosen from the major Houses of Ardere. In their ceremonial garments of Tyrian purple they sat like statutes upon the tiered seating. Most were older females, but whether male or female, all had the same haughty look that came with old wealth and privilege.

The chinking of the armor warned everyone of the squads' approach. As they reached the circle of bodies a pathway opened up as the courtiers backed out of the way. When they saw the prisoners a hushed whisper broke out.

After they had passed through the courtiers, the circle closed behind them. The Lead Umbra gave a signal, and the squad broke apart. Most left the inner circle to take up positions around the room, except for the four who held the prisoners. Sharra was trapped inside the circle with Loch. With her hair hanging around her shoulders in a knotted mess, and with the warmer color of her skin, she stood out in their midst like the alien that she was.

Between the High Court, and upon a shallow dais, sat a throne of extraordinary beauty and grace carved from the largest emerald Sharra had ever seen or dreamed even possible. Like other gems, the emerald corundum sparkled, casting green light around the room upon faces, gowns, floors, and wherever there was a surface. From the translucent trigon spikes was cut out a deep seat. Graceful armrests curved from the backrest of spikes and down both sides of the seat, each carved with scenes of playful sea creatures in the same design that the pillars bore. Even the lower portions of the emerald trigon bore the same mark of the master artisan as the seascapes continued to play upon the crystal.

Upon this magnificent throne sat the Queen overlooking the court like the Goddess of the Sea that she represented. A sheer gown of gossamer fell from her shoulders and crisscrossed over her breasts to drape softly over her hips and down to her bare feet. Low on her waist was a thick belt of gold that was tied to one side. Precious jewels sparkled on the crown that sat upon her brow and on the armband clamped to the fleshly part of her upper arm. From a gold chain between her small breasts hung a pendant of her House.

The whispering grew louder the longer Sharra stood there. Even the High Court was affected by her alien presence. The vaulted ceiling, like an amplifier, caught their muffled voices, along with the courtiers, and threw it around the pillars in a wave of sound, angering the Queen. Letting it go on long enough, her voice boomed from the throne in one command.

"Quiet!"

The throne room immediately went silent. Though they were obedient, their auras glowed in an array of shades of orange, as their curiosity remained high.

At the Queen's left shoulder stood a silent Larua as she watched the summoned Houses with an all-knowing eye. She bent down and whispered into Queen Aniani's ear, pointing to where the prisoners waited.

From her throne, Queen Aniani stared across the floor at Sharra. Disdain flashed in her amber eyes. It pierced through Sharra's defenses, making her tremble. And then her eyes moved away to a commotion behind them. Sharra turned in time to see the courtiers open to let another squad through. Once inside the circle, they deposited their prisoner in the center where the nautilus shell ended in a final tight curl, and marched back the way they came leaving another two guards behind with the new prisoner.

Held between them was Araylai. New bruises colored the pale skin of her arms, and on her left cheekbone where someone had hit her with a fist. Like Loch and Sharra, her hands were bound in front of her body. With her shoulders back, and chin tilted, she stared at her mother in silent defiance. Aniani stared back. No love or mercy was in the Queen's eyes, or in her aura. Her beautiful face remained cold, as cold as the stone palace around her. The aura around her body was suspiciously neutral.

Queen Aniani spoke to the High Court, saying, "We need no formal words. The accused stands before you. May the High Court begin."

From a lower tier of the High Court, an older Praemin stood, and opened a rolled parchment. Holding it out, she began to read it to the assembly. Her voice rang out, pure like a chime of bells.

"Heres Araylai, daughter of Queen Aniani, descendant of the great House of Ardere, Princess of the realm, Heir Apparent to the throne: you have been brought before the High Court to be tried for your crimes against the throne, and against the Goddess herself."

"Praemin Tegamen," Araylai said with a bow to the woman, "I know your House to be honorable. And I respect the office you hold as Speaker for the High Court. Please, tell me, what am I accused of so that I may make a defense for my honor."

The red accusation of Praemin Tegamen's aura flooded with blue for a moment as her eyes softened just a little, but the sympathy was short-lived, for Queen Aniani squashed it with a piercing look from her seat on the throne.

Taking a deep breath Praemin Tegamen held up the parchment, and read, "The crimes listed against you are as such: Breaking the honor-bond of your people, forming an allegiance with the enemy, exposing innocent Arderians to alien corruption, conspiring to commit treason against Queen Aniani and the city of Ardere. These are the crimes laid against Heres Araylai of the House of Ardere."

"Read my aura," Araylai said. "I have committed no crime. My heart has always been pure towards the people of Ardere. Where is the proof of these allegations?"

"You want proof?" The Queen rose gracefully from her throne and descended the dais to the floor. Her gossamer gown floated around her slim legs as she approached her daughter and stood before her face to face. Grabbing Araylai's head, she tilted it to the right and exposed the agrylium tattoo behind her left ear for the High Court to see. "Look! This is your proof. She has given up allegiance to her own people for this. The female hu-man carries the same mark. They are bonded. I have heard it myself from the hu-man's own mouth."

At her words, she pointed to where Sharra stood. All eyes followed. Sharra flinched under the hard gaze of the crowd. The twisted truth that the Queen fed the Court was working, and why not. They could see the mark on the skin of Araylai's skull as clearly as they could see her, the alien human, standing beside the accused. Anger welled up into her heart at the cunningness of the Queen. Helpless to do anything about it, she stewed silently between her guards.

"What have you done, mother?" Araylai said as she glared at the Queen. "This is between you and me. Sharra is not a part of this. Let her go."

"There is only one way the hu-man will leave here, and that is dead. Guards, kill her."

The two guards holding Sharra pulled out their swords and raised them for the strike. Beside her Loch pushed against the restraints of his guards, but it proved useless.

"Sharra," he groaned in apology, not able to stop them.

"No!" Araylai cried out. Her crest flicked with alarm as the guards' muscles tightened for the strike. "Please, no!"

Sharra's heart began to pound against her ribs. The guards' hands were on her flesh. In her head the ball of energy beat the wall of her control as it pleaded to be free. She knew what it could do, and was about to let it. The alien energy read her thoughts and grew excited. Just as she was about to release it, the Queen shouted, "Stop", staying the swords of the guards.

At the command of the Queen they lowered their weapons. Sharra sagged between them as her knees gave out. They hauled her unceremoniously back up to her feet. She closed her eyes in relief, grateful for the reprise no matter how small it was, but the expanding ball inside her head grew angry at the denial.

Wait, she said to it. *Wait for the right time*.

It listened. Backing down, it slowed to a bright simmer within the confines of her control, and waited. Sharra lifted her head to look at Araylai, and read the distress in her friend's eyes.

"Shift out," Sharra whispered.

Reading her lips, Araylai shook her head, and mouthed, "No."

"Why?" she mouthed back.

But Araylai only shook her head.

Meanwhile the Queen had turned to address the High Council. "It is obvious that there is a bond between my daughter and this hu-man. What other proof of allegiance do we need?"

"Friendship is not a crime, mother," Araylai said.

"When it is with the enemy, yes, it is. It is hard enough to keep the hu-mans off our waters, let alone out of our cities. There are strict laws in place to keep them from contaminating our world, our reefs. Your weakness of character has brought them down right into our midst, into the heart of our city. You have done this. You."

"No, mother. It is your greed for absolute power that has done this. They are not all evil like you say. It was a hu-man that rescued me from the off-world slavers that you sold me to. He showed me great kindness, freely gave me a home, and a pod when I had none. Yes, mother, I know it was you who arranged my kidnapping, and subsequent transfer to the surface. I heard them laugh, calling you a barbarian as they loaded me onto a shuttle. I saw your seal on the chest of blood money that came with me. You know the one. It guaranteed their cooperation. They could not help but gloat at how easy it had been to get you to give them the maps where they could rape our waters without interference. Your name was all over their lips."

"Silence!" she commanded.

Her voice echoed through the chamber above everyone's head, the bell-like sound harsh in her anger. All around them the courtiers, guards, and even the High Court crests flicked in agitation. Auras deepened in shock.

"Praemin of the High Court, witness how she

defiles the throne with her words. You see how she hates me. Her aura is bright with it. If these accusations are true, where is the evidence?"

Loch stirred again. Mustering up what little strength he had left, he raised his body erect and stood tall and proud before his peers, and said, "I have seen it: a slavers' sales receipt with your signature and the seal of the House of Ardere on it. I held it in my hand. It was real. Test my aura, and see."

"Praemin Loch, is it? Does not your mother sit with us on the High Court?" Praemin Tegamen said.

"She does."

On the second tier, a thin female with skin the same shade as Loch's turned her face away, hiding her shame under a compressed aura as she held her crest stiffly up.

"And yet you side with the accused," Praemin Tegamen said.

"I side with the truth. Is that not what the High Court stands for? Truth and honor?"

"Where is this receipt?"

"It is gone," he said, "destroyed, I presume. Arderians have died in discovering the real truth behind the disappearance of the princess, and subsequent whispers of treason. Praemin Minnowmen's son, Praemin Rue, Caetus of Riff, Cael of the Umbra Scouts of Riff, all died because the Queen knew that receipt would spell her doom. Even this hu-man that stands before you took a knife to bring honor back to our great city."

"These are fine words," she said, "but that is all they are... words. We cannot trust the shade of your aura. Anyone with a sense of control can contain their aura to reflect any emotion they wish. To come here without proof is ludicrous. We cannot afford to have dissension among ourselves. Order must start at the top. Heres Araylai has broken the law by collaborating with a hu-man. That we can see with our own eyes. Without proof, the High Court has to dismiss the complaints against Queen Aniani. Otherwise, there would be no justice for anyone."

"What about justice for the Princess?"

"I am sorry, Praemin Loch."

Sharra saw a small smile of satisfaction tickle the corners of the Queen's mouth at the finality of those words. Araylai saw it too.

"Why do you hate me so much? I am your only daughter, your flesh and blood," Araylai asked her mother.

"Because you are weak of character, and have shamed our House. Blood cannot protect you from the law of the Houses. Order must be maintained. It is the will of the Sea Mother and must be obeyed."

With those words Queen Aniani returned to her throne and sat down. Adjusting the folds of her gown around her legs she readied for the verdict. Her aura brightened in confidence as she read the answer in the auras of the High Court. Praemin Tegamen returned to her place on the tier. As the Speaker of the House turned to face the whole assemble, the High Court rose as one.

Her voice rang out cold across the whole assembly as she announced the verdict. "Praemin Loch, due to your association with the Princess and this hu-man that stands before us as evidence, we the High Court find you guilty of conspiring to commit acts of treason against the people of Ardere. And you, Araylai, daughter of the House of Ardere, we the High Court find you guilty of treason against the throne, against the people of Ardere, and against the Sea Mother of us all. The penalty for treason is immediate death. Let it be heard and witnessed."

With one voice the High Court said, "Heard and witnessed."

"Then it is done. Bring them to the dais. Let the Sea Mother look upon them as they die. And may the seas accept their blood in atonement, and wash them clean of their error."

Chapter Thirty-Four

The guards pushed Araylai to her knees in front of the dais. Sharra was dragged over and forced down next to her. Pain shot through her shoulder as she hit the ground, making her cry out. Then Loch was added to the line. He collapsed to his knees on the other side of Araylai. His dorsal fin hung loose down his back as he struggled to stay upright. All were bound. Three feet separated them from each other. It may as well have been a mile. Sharra didn't know how fast Araylai was at shifting, but she knew there was no way she could save them all.

Sharra leaned over and whispered to Araylai, "You must save Loch. All you have to do is shift."

"This is my fight… my honor. Loch understands this."

"It's your 'honor' that has gotten us into this mess

to begin with."

"You should be back at the Vault. Not here. Where is Faolan?"

"He's bringing a solution."

"He is late."

"Yeah, I've noticed."

"Silence!" barked the guard standing behind them.

From the throne, the Queen stared down at the three of them with cold eyes as the executioner was called for. Larua, who had remained stoic by the Queen's side, placed a reassuring hand on her shoulder. Their auras gave nothing away, not even a hint of mercy or regret.

Araylai stared back at her mother, and whispered to Sharra, "There is one more thing I can try."

"What are you waiting for? Do it."

Araylai raised her voice, and addressed the High Court, saying, "If I am to die, then I demand the bloodright that is mine by the birthmark on the palm of my hand."

As she spoke she raised her tied hands palms out to the High Council. The mark on the soft pad under her thumb was plain for all to see.

"I, Araylai of the House of Ardere, invoke the Blood Challenge against Aniani the Queen, for the right of succession, as my mother had done to her mother," she said.

Aniani stiffened in her seat. The rings of her eyes flashed bright in anger. She went to rise, but Larua kept a firm hand on her shoulder. She blinked a slow blink to cover the lapse, and was once again in control.

It was Larua who answered Araylai. Standing next to the Queen, she said, "If you would have challenged the Queen before your verdict was given, your request would have been honored. But according to the law, anyone found guilty of treason will be stripped of her House. That means that all rights reserved for the House of Ardere are no longer yours. Therefore, your challenge has come too late. Your sentence will be carried out, and you will die, Araylai, and so will your friends."

From behind the throne emerged the executioner. She bowed to the Queen and the High Councilor, towering over them like a large sea creature. Around the thick muscles of her arm was a red medallion armband of two crossed swords, matching the real ones sheathed at her back. Two more dangerous looking daggers were strapped to her thighs in easy reach of her large webbed hands that hung deceptively loose at her side.

Larua pointed a finger at Sharra, and told the executioner, "Start with the hu-man. It is only just that Araylai should witness the outcome of her actions before she dies."

"With the Queen's permission," the executioner said with a bow.

Queen Aniani nodded, "Granted. Keep it simple. No grand exhibition will be necessary. Blood will be enough."

"It will be done."

The executioner stepped off the dais. Fixing her gaze onto Sharra, she drew a sword out of the sheath from her back with a swish of metal against leather. Sharra began to tremble again. A few quick strides, and the sword was in front of her. In its gleaming metal surface her face stared back at her wide-eyed and pale.

Her blood pounded in her ears as she watched the

arm of the executioner draw the sword back. She closed her eyes, and stiffened her body as she braced for the blow. Her head was blank of thought. Even the alien presence in her head was forgotten. Seconds seemed like hours as she waited for the death stroke, but it didn't come, for it was interrupted.

From outside the throne room came the sound of muffled shouting, followed by two consecutive thuds. Sharra's eyes flew open. Above her the executioner hesitated with the sword as she peered over the courtiers in curiosity. Within a flash, the far doors burst open and slammed against the wall. Two guards fell through and landed on the ground with a thunk and lay there unmoving. A gasp went up among the courtiers as figures stormed over the bodies and spread out through the back of the vast room.

At the noise the Umbra guards unsheathed their weapons and charged. But they were unprepared for the high tech gear of their enemy.

Spurts of red energy flashed around the room as the invaders' hand held lasers found their marks. With military precision they picked off the guards one by one as they moved further into the room. When the red beam hit them, the guards stiffened as if electrocuted, and dropped to the floor.

"Sharra," called a familiar voice.

It was Faolan. He had come for her. Relief flooded through her in a wave of dizziness.

"Over here!" she yelled.

A flare of red energy beamed overhead, hitting the sword above her head in a spectacular flash of color. The sword turned into a conductor as the energy travelled down to the executioner's hand to explode into her body. Like the guards, her body stiffened under the assault of raw energy. Her sword hand slackened as she struggled to stay upright. Losing the battle, the sword slipped from her lifeless hand as she dropped to the floor like a stone at Sharra's knees.

"Umbra, protect the Queen!" Larua called out as the sound of more firing ricocheted through the throne room.

The guards abandoned the prisoners and rushed to the dais. Swords out they surrounded the Queen, shielding her with their bodies as they stared over the heads of the stunned courtiers to the fighting on the other side.

A foot away from where Sharra sat on her knees was the thigh of the downed executioner and the nasty dagger that was strapped to it. She dove for it, and wrenched it out of the sheath.

"Get the sword, quick," she yelled to Araylai as she crawled to Loch with the blade between her tied hands. "I've got Loch."

Araylai grabbed the sword between her bound hands, and took off towards the throne, dodging flying blades as she dove behind a pillar. In a matter of moments Sharra had Loch free of his bindings. He grabbed the knife from Sharra, and with what little strength he had left he attacked her restraints. Finally her bindings fell to the floor next to his. She took back the knife, and got to her feet. Grabbing Loch's arm, she pulled him to his knees. A low moan of pain escaped his parched lips, and made her stop.

"I am done," he said as he sagged back to the floor.

"Leave me."

"Haven't you learned anything yet? We never leave a partner behind," she said.

Adrenalin crashed through her veins as the fighting drew closer to the semi-circle of stunned courtiers. Ignoring his moans of pain, she pulled Loch to his feet. He swayed where he stood as he struggled to stay up.

"Lean on me," she said as she slipped her good arm around his body. "We're getting out of here."

"You are stubborn to the core," he mumbled, but did as he was told.

"Yes, I am."

Everything was happening so fast.

More blasts of energy ricocheted over their heads waking the courtiers from their shock. Screams broke out as panic set in. Auras deepened in fear as they ducked to the floor like falling butterflies of material. Some dove behind the pillars. While a brave few fled to the safety behind the tiered stands of the High Court.

At the dais the guards bravely stood over their Queen. With throwing knives at the ready they waited to spot the invaders. But the reach of the lasers outmatched them. And so like the other guards they fell one after the other as the invaders overpowered them. Their throwing knives clattered to the floor from their limp hands, useless against the superior technology, as their stunned bodies piled around the Queen's feet.

Faolan finally appeared from the recesses of the back of the throne room. Wearing the black Vault uniform, Sharra saw him immediately as he strode up to the outer edge of the quivering courtiers curled up on the floor. He dismissed them as harmless fluff as he waded through them to the cleared section in front of the Queen. In his hands he held two sleek guns of silver metal. Catching a movement near the throne, he fired without pause. A glint of steel blazed in his eyes as the last remaining guards on the dais went down with a flash of red.

Through the battle the Queen remained motionless like a carved statue of porcelain, powerless to stop the fray.

With the guards subdued, Faolan turned from the Queen to scan the area in front of the throne. When he did not find what he was looking for he expanded his search to the sides to where Sharra stood with Loch alone. Sharra knew the instant his eyes fell upon them that he was looking for her.

"I've found Sharra," he said into his Link as he finished the last few steps to where she stood holding Loch. "Secure the doors."

Tears sprang to her eyes at the sight of him.

"Faolan."

It was all she could say. Yet it said everything. The immense relief, joy, and most of all, love that she had for the man were mashed together in that one outburst.

Creases covered his brow as he ran a quick eye over her before positioning his body in front of them. Lasers up he turned them to the crowd and scanned the throne room as he stood guard over them.

"You're hurt," he said.

Sharra peered over her shoulder at the fresh blood seeping through the bandage Loch had haphazardly wrapped around her shoulder blade, and then to Loch, who leaned silently against her. His deathly pale skin hidden behind the swelling of his flesh glistened with sweat.

"Never mind about me," she said. "It's Loch. He needs medical attention, and stat."

"I just need some water... and some rest," Loch said.

"In a minute. We're not done yet," Faolan said.

On opposite sides of the tiered seating where the High Court huddled in their seats appeared Tanner and Viktor, also in Vault uniforms.

"No one move!" Tanner commanded.

Lasers out, they scanned the crowd holding everyone at gunpoint.

From behind the emerald throne materialized Lazarus cool and confident as usual. With casual elegance he rested a hand upon the cold crystal back of the throne and pressed a laser to the Queen's head. On the other side of the throne, Araylai held Larua restrained against a tall crystal spike, holding her hostage with the edge of the executioner's sword.

Praemin Tegamen stirred from her seat where she had taken refuge. Crest all a flutter, she faced Lazarus with righteous indignation, and demanded, "How dare you intrude into these proceedings, and take our Queen hostage."

"You hold some things that are dear to us, and we want them back," Lazarus said.

Queen Aniani stirred under his hand. Her angry gaze slid to where Sharra stood holding Loch up.

"Then take your hu-man friend, and go," she said before Praemin Tegamen could reply. "She has brought nothing but trouble to our city ever since she arrived."

"I will. And I will also take Araylai, if she will still have us."

Queen Aniani sneered. "That I cannot do. Araylai has been tried by our laws and found guilty. The punishment is death. It is our way. And she is too honorable to defy the laws of her people."

"You are the Queen. You hold the power of the people in your hands. Pardon her, and let her go. She is your daughter, for Christ's sake. Doesn't that mean anything to you?"

Sadness filled Araylai's face as she looked over Larua's head to where her mother sat. With a stiff neck Aniani faced the room, refusing to acknowledge the pull of her daughter's eyes. In the silence the assembly waited for an answer from their Queen. When it came, there was no hint of compassion in her voice. No familial love. Only the cold hardness of her heart, as hard as the emerald throne beneath her.

"The Ardere House has ruled our great nation for many a century," Queen Aniani said loud and clear. "By the grace of our illustrious Sea Mother the bloodline of the queens has remained strong. A strong Queen means a strong nation where under which the people can thrive and prosper, and our enemies defeated. Yet, weakness like an evil weed will find a way in. And if we are not vigilant to eradicate it, then it can dilute the bloodline, and make us vulnerable as a people. There can be no mercy. Action must be swift. For the good of our nation. For the good of the House."

The echoes of her ringing speech died away. The listeners stared at their queen who sat regally on her throne, crest in full sail. Moved by the conviction in her words the courtiers straightened their shoulders and stood taller. Crests rose, stretching dorsal fins out, as pride for their nation set their auras to light. The High Court was the first to agree, nodding their heads in approval. The Queen cast her eye over the assembly. A tiny smile of triumph tickled the sides of the Queen's lips. It made Sharra sick. How could a mother hate her daughter so much?

Queen Aniani wasn't done. Uncaring of the gun held to her head, she sat up taller, beautiful, yet terrifying, every inch the Sea Goddess that they worshipped. Her face turned cold again as she pressed on.

"The blood in my daughter's veins is weak. The proof of it has been given to the court this day. If she were of stronger blood, she would not have gotten into this position. The law is the law. The House cannot abide treason, my daughter, or not. So the verdict must stand. Unless there is evidence to prove otherwise, of course. That would change everything. I would not want be called unjust."

Lazarus made a noise beside her.

"Huh," he said. "Evidence. I'm glad you've confirmed that point. For you see, the Vault holds all in our family dear, mistakes and all. And though you may not agree, Araylai is a part of our family. So while you were busy conspiring to have your own daughter killed, I did some investigating of my own, for evidence, you see. And I've discovered something that I think you'll find very interesting." Keeping the gun to her head, he spoke into his Link, "Okay, Katherine, bring her through."

A murmur went through the crowd as it split open

and let in the newcomers. Into the inner circle with crest held high walked Nayada and Calyx side by side. Bringing in the rear was Katie holding a laser as she guarded their backs. No one paid attention to the human. It was the Arderian Umbra Scout leader that caught their eye. Fingers pointed and crests flicked, as the whispering grew louder. Her resemblance to the Queen and her daughter were plain for all to see. It was not only her face, or the pureness of her porcelain skin, but also in the identical patterns of color that laced through her dorsal fin. Royal fins. Nayada neither looked left or right, but kept her gaze focused on the High Court. Clutched in her hand was a wooden case. Without bowing to the Queen, Nayada went up to Praemin Tegamen and stood before her while Katie and Calyx guarded her back.

"Praemin Tegamen," Nayada said as she bowed to the elderly Arderian. "I wish to bring no disrespect to this Court. However, there has been a gross error of judgment done this day. You can find the proof in here."

As she spoke, she removed a stack of papers from under her belt and held them out. Praemin Tegamen stared at the papers with distrust.

"There is no honor in the spilt blood of the innocent," Nayada said.

"How do I know these are real?" she said.

"I would not dishonor the High Court with anything but the truth. Please, take them."

Reluctantly she took them and began to read. The top one was printed in block letters: Interstellar Trading Company. That was all Sharra could make out. The rest was too small. Praemin Tegamen read it and passed it on to the other Houses. One by one each member of the

High Court went through the papers as the assembly murmured among themselves.

On the throne, Queen Aniani fidgeted in her seat. With furrowed brows she stared at Nayada, at the features that were so familiar to her own as she tried to figure out what was going on. Her eyes fell on the wooden case in Nayada's hand. Her frown deepened.

Sharra saw the Queen frown, and followed her gaze to the box. It was the one she had given Faolan before the Grex got her. She smiled an internal smile in anticipation of the Queen's reaction when the secrets it held were out in the open. In her excitement she gave Loch a reassuring squeeze. The unexpected pressure made Loch groan in pain.

"I'm sorry," she said as she loosened her grip around his waist.

"Put me down," he said, "before I fall down. I cannot stand much longer, and you need to conserve your strength."

Faolan glanced at them, and agreed. "You two have done enough. Rest. We've got this."

Sharra didn't argue. The pain from the wound on her shoulder was getting worse. With her adrenalin spent, Loch's weight dragged on her body like a heavy stone. Gratefully she lowered him to the floor, and fell down next to him. Wrapping her good arm around him, she held him steady as she watched the scene unfold with growing understanding.

"What is Nayada doing?" Loch asked as he watched his Scout Leader.

"Changing policy," she said. "Shhh, now listen."

The papers were collected and given back to

Praemin Tegamen. After a nod from each of her fellow House Representatives, she tucked them into her robe, and turned back to Nayada.

"What is your name?" Praemin Tegamen asked.

"Nayada, Lead Umbra Scout of Riff."

"Nayada of Riff, the High Court thanks you for courage in this matter. It would seem that the Queen misled us. You have saved us from an act of dishonor." Praemin Tegamen then turned to the courtiers, and in a ringing voiced called out, "Due to the new evidence presented to the High Court by the Umbra Scout Nayada, the High Court has reconsidered their judgment and have found Heres Araylai innocent of the charges brought before the Court today. In so doing, all charges against Heres Araylai have been dismissed, and her honor restored. Hear and witness!"

As one the Houses of the High Court vowed, "Heard and witnessed!"

"Araylai, you are free," Praemin Tegamen said to the princess.

The murmuring of the courtiers grew louder as excitement built in the throne room at the pronouncement. Yet Nayada was not done.

Her eye-rings flashed as anger burned in her aura. "The freedom of the Princess is not enough," Nayada said. "How long will you do nothing? The honor of the House of Ardere has been blackened far too long under the rule of Aniani. Her cruelty runs deep through our city. How many more have to starve to feed her thirst for wealth and power, or die in the Kelp Fields in a civil war that is leading nowhere, or suffer by the hands of her Grex who have subverted our great city into corruption

361

with her permission? These are just distractions to keep the eyes off their true source. Our city has been under a black aura long enough. The people will not stand it any longer. The head of the eel must be cut off to stop the poisoning of the sea."

The sound of clapping came from the throne.

"Bravo. Bravo," Queen Aniani said as she clapped, mocking Nayada from her elevated position. "Such a passionate speech coming from a commoner such as yourself."

Nayada raised her chin, her face a picture of pride, and said, "There you are wrong. I am Aliya, the daughter of Adaylai, your youngest sister from your shared mother Queen Awynn."

Gasps went up through the room except for the Vault team who stood at the ready. Only Araylai reacted from out of the team, for the news had come as a complete surprise to her. Her sword arm dropped from Larua's neck for a moment, but she quickly recovered before Larua could move.

Queen Aniani's aura burst red as her eye-rings flashed in anger. "What blasphemy is this? I had only one sister, Anala, and she died as a young child from a wasting disease. There were no others."

"I have the proof in this case." Nayada handed it over to Praemin Tegamen. "It was kept safe for me by my guardian, Caetus, my grandmother's most trusted guard and friend. I have read what is inside. I think the High Court will find it… educational."

"Papers can be forged," Aniani scoffed.

"But the truth cannot. I know why my mother was born in secret. And when the Court reads the testimonies, and the letters, they will too. It is your blood that is weak, Aniani. You have been nothing but a pawn in the play for power. Think back to Anala. Who was it that fed your jealousy towards your sister, my aunt? Was it that she was stealing your light? She was only nine. And what about your mother, my grandmother? Was she in your way, too? Is that why you invoked the Blood Challenge, because she saw what you had become: the weakness in your blood, the weakness of your mind, and you could not stand it? Think, Aniani. Think hard. Who was it that helped you drive the knife into your own mother's heart? Through all the years someone was using you, and you did not even see it. Who was it that put you up to selling your own daughter to the Outworld slavers?"

The questions hit home, for the Queen glanced out the side of her eyes for a brief second to her trusted adviser under Araylai's sword.

"Ahhh," Nayada said. "The light of comprehension has hit you. Embarrassing isn't it, to discover that all these years you have been played for a fool. It is your blood that is weak, not your mother's, nor your sister's, nor your daughter's. It is you."

Aniani whipped her head around and glared at Larua. "You. You did this to me."

Larua raised a brow, and said over the sword at her throat, "Did I? You are the Queen. I am just an adviser."

"Too many have died for your lust for power. It must stop today," Nayada said.

"The Blood Challenge had been given once today, and had been denied," Praemin Tegamen said. "Araylai, now that your rights have been returned to you, do you wish to restore honor to the House of Ardere?"

"I do. More than ever," she said. "But I cannot take the same path that my mother has taken, no matter how much she deserves to die. I am a Vault agent. That is my House now, my pod, and my code of honor. Therefore, as my birthright I choose to abdicate my position as heir apparent, and give it to my cousin, Aliya of the House of Ardere. If she so chooses, let her take up the Blood Challenge, and avenge the people."

The faces of the assembly turned as one to Nayada as they held their breath and waited for a reply. She stood motionless in front of the High Court, her eyes wide with shock at the pronouncement. Slowly she turned to Araylai as if waking from a dream. Their eyes connected.

"My Heres, I am not worthy to carry such an honor," she said.

Araylai lowered her sword from Larua's neck, and came to stand next to her cousin. Nayada withdrew a knife from her thigh and cut the cords around Araylai's wrists. Once free Araylai took Nayada's hand and placed it over her own heart as the High Court watched in interest.

With Nayada's hand pressed to her heart, Araylai said, "You have already proven your love for our people when you did not have to. You are honorable, and trustworthy, and strong of will. Your pod follows you willingly to the point of death, because they love you. What greater quality could a leader possess? Blood does not guarantee love or inspire loyalty. The proof of this is in my mother. It has to be earned. And you have earned it."

"You honor me. I am humbled. But how can I ever fill that honor? It is impossible."

"No, it is not. Take my place... and do what I cannot." Araylai squeezed her hand, and looked across at Sharra, and said, "I am happy where I am."

Nayada followed her gaze with new understanding. "Sharra is the sister you never had."

"Yes. But now I also have a cousin."

She turned Nayada's hand palm up. On the soft part of her thumb was the birthmark that matched her own. She bowed over the open palm, and kissed the mark, before lifting it up in the air for all to see.

With a shout Araylai said to all, "My House I give to Heres Aliya. Heres Aliya is now the first, and thus stands as heir apparent to the throne of Ardere. Let the bloodline of queens come through her House. Hear and Witness!"

A loud shout went up from the assembly, as they proclaimed as one voice, "Heard and witnessed!"

Araylai released Nayada's hand, saying, "Take up the challenge, for the tide flows our way this day."

Nayada smiled, and said, "With pleasure," before offering the official words to the High Court, "I, Aliya of the House of Ardere, invoke the Blood Challenge against Aniani, the Queen, for the right of succession."

"The High Court accepts the Blood Challenge," Praemin Tegamen said. "Opponents, choose your blade, and enter the center of the nautilus."

At the pronouncement the assembly shuffled back, opening up the floor around the center of the nautilus to make a ring for the fight. Eye-rings flashed as anticipations grew. What courtiers had been loyal to the

Queen now stood divided among their peers. Tensions ran high among the Houses as they watched Araylai squeeze Nayada's arm reassuringly before leaving her in Calyx's capable hands.

As Araylai left the floor in front of the High Court, Katie came to join her. Together they went to Faolan to where Sharra sat on the floor holding Loch. Faolan helped Araylai lift the injured scout onto his feet, and passed him over to Katie. Between the two women, they supported him off the floor and eased him down to sit on the edge of the dais out of danger's way. Faolan watched them fuss over their charge with a shake of his head.

"I hope that Araylai and Nayada know what they're doing," he said as he assisted Sharra up.

"Nayada is strong and disciplined. Whereas Aniani has depended on others to do her dirty work for far too long, and is out of practice. This is the only way. Araylai did the right thing," Sharra pointed out.

"It's barbaric, that's what it is."

"Are humans any better?"

With an arm around her waist, he helped her to the edge of the High Court where Viktor stood guard. At the sight of her, the big blond giant jerked as if hit by a bat. Thick furrows appeared on his brow as a deep blush stole up his neck and flooded his face, making his blond hair look even blonder. His throat worked, yet nothing came out. Finally he swallowed and spoke.

"Sharra, I am so_" he started, but Faolan cut him off with a shake of his head.

"Later," Faolan said.

Viktor swallowed again, and nodded, though the furrows remained.

Sharra barely noticed the exchange for her attention was on Nayada and Calyx who had moved to the center of the circle. Nor did she notice the numerous glances Tanner shot their way from the other side of the throne where he stood guard in front of the tiered seating.

Queen Aniani sat like a white marbled statue on her emerald throne, cold and beautiful. No emotion showed on her smooth face, or in her wide amber eyes. Not a muscle moved as she stared off into the air. Only her knuckles, blanched white against the armrest that she gripped, gave any emotion away.

Lazarus removed the gun from the Queen's head, and left to join Araylai, Katie, and Loch. Calyx left Nayada in the ring and met up with them.

"Loch, handsome as ever I see," she said as she gently reached down and took her pod-mate in her arms and raised him up.

"Not funny," he said.

"Too soon?"

"How can you joke at a time like this? I cannot. My heart is too heavy."

"Then let me help lighten that load for you." She whispered something to him. Whatever it was, it perked him up, and gave him renewed strength.

On the floor Nayada waited alone in the circle. In her right hand was a long double-edged knife.

Finally the Queen moved, turning her head to look at the knife that Larua presented to her in the flat of her palms. She stared at it for a long moment as if it was a foreign object. Then her eyes began to glitter with a strange light. Slowly she lifted the crown from her head, and set it on the seat beside her. Taking the knife out of her adviser's hands, she closed her webbed fingers around the long handle, and smiled. Grabbing the skirt of her dress, she stabbed it near her thigh and ripped the thin material all the way around. Slowly she left the throne, dragging the gossamer piece behind her before dropping it on the dais as she stepped off to join her newfound niece in the center of the ring.

The Blood Challenge had been given. Only one would come out alive. Whoever that was would be crowned ruler, and no one could dispute it. Sharra begged whatever god or goddess was listening that it'd be Nayada, or else life in the city of Ardere would go from bad to worse, and all that they had tried to accomplish this day would be for nothing.

Chapter Thirty-Five

The tableau was set. The Auras all around were thick with emotion. Not an eye blinked as the assembly watched the Queen step gracefully into the ring. Her ripped gown showed off her toned legs as she walked to the center, testing the balance of her knife as she did. A calculated look covered her face as she watched her opponent sink into a slight crouch, and with arms out for balance, raised her knife. The Queen stopped a few feet from the reach of Nayada's knife, and sank into the same crouch. With blades up, their eyes locked in an intense stare.

All eyes in the throne room were on the center of the ring as the two opponents faced each other. The steel of their sharp blades caught the light as they started to circle, each one gauging the others reach.

At the sideline Sharra held her breath, and pressed

against Faolan's side. Wrapping an arm around her, he drew her into his body, and held her close. His warm embrace gave her strength. She didn't care who saw. She needed him. If Nayada failed... no, she didn't want to think about that.

All of a sudden, the Queen lunged at Nayada. But Nayada had been ready. She twisted her body to the left, and hit the Queen's knife to the side with her own. The sound of metal on metal rang in the air. Before it could dissipate, Nayada swung her knife around and caught Aniani across the thigh. The Queen's aura flashed red with pain. She jumped back with a hiss. A long line of blood appeared on the pale skin of her thigh as she flexed her muscles in a fresh crouch.

At the sight of it Praemin Tegamen called out, "First blood to Nayada."

Crests flicked and eye rings flashed around the room at the pronouncement. Auras flowed back and forth between one end of the spectrum to the other as emotions began to rise.

Inside Sharra's head the alien threads of energy grew excited as it felt the electromagnetic energy increase within the throne room with the alteration of the mood of the alien assembly. Hungry, it pounded against her mental restraints, asking to be set free. She shook her head, and held on tightly to the ball.

"Are you okay?" Faolan whispered, catching the slight movement of her head.

"It's nothing," she said.

Sharra turned back to the ring. A smile of pure malice spread over Aniani's face, but it was short-lived. Before she could settle into a crouch, Nayada charged with a thrust to her chest. As Aniani blocked it, Nayada swung her left fist up into the opened space between them and hit her underneath the chin. As the Queen's head snapped back, Nayada's blade ran a trail through the material of the front of her dress. The sound of tearing followed the blade, cutting another fine line into the Queen's flesh. But as she did, the Queen's knife hand swung around and across the halter-top at Nayada's belly. Again the sound of ripping material filled the chamber.

Sharra gasped, and hid her face into Faolan's chest. She couldn't watch. It was too much. Faolan was right. It was barbaric.

Faolan hugged her, and said, "She's okay. It just tore her shirt."

"I can't watch," she said.

He ran his hand down her hair, and pressed her face back to his chest. "You've done enough. I'll tell you when it's over."

"I hate this."

"Shhh, I know. It'll be over soon. Nayada is stronger."

Behind her she could hear the sound of another hiss. She wondered who got injured, but didn't dare look. The bodies came together with a thud. The sound of struggling filled her ears. A collective gasp went up, but still she kept her face averted.

Off to the side where Faolan held her sat the empty green throne. She focused on that as the battle raged at her back. That was when she saw the forgotten High Councilor. Half-hidden behind the crystalline back of the throne stood Larua. Unlike the rest who were focused on the fight, Larua was staring off to the side. Sharra followed the direction of her gaze. It ended on Araylai who stood watching the battle to the front of the small group protecting Loch.

Something felt wrong about it. Maybe it was the way that Larua's eyes narrowed, or the tightening of her jaw muscles, or the stillness of her whole body. Whatever it was, Sharra knew enough to listen to her instincts.

Disengaging from Faolan, she left him with Viktor, telling him that she needed to sit down. So engrossed in the two combatants, no one noticed her small figure as she crept along in front of the curved row of tiered seating where the High Houses once sat. Now they were on their feet, agitated, with auras flaring bright.

Sharra glanced over to the fight in time to see Aniani kick Nayada's knife out of her hand. Another gasp went up as it skittered across the floor. Without hesitation Nayada charged in and knocked the Queen to the ground. Weaponless she wrestled with the knife hand of the Queen as they rolled around in a jumble of arms and legs.

The energy held captive in her head caught the excitement of the crowd, and pulsed harder, waking Sharra back to her purpose. Again she turned away from the fight. She was almost to the dais when she caught a glint of steel in the folds of Larua's gown. It was a knife. Sharra was sure of it. Her instants were right.

With her eyes intent on Araylai, the elderly Arderian slowly slid the small knife up, using a crystalline to hide it until the blade was raised up over her shoulder. Her eyes were fixed on her target. Sharra watched in horror as her muscles stiffened for the throw.

Time slowed down to a crawl. Sharra looked for help. Lazarus was intent on the battle, too far away to help. Katie and Calyx were attending Loch on the floor behind Araylai. Tanner was on the far side of the other row of tiered seating, also too far away. When she looked at him, he saw her fear, and frowned. There was no time to warn Araylai, for the knife would be buried in her heart before Sharra's call would register the danger. It only took her brain a second to come to that conclusion. It took her another millisecond for her body to react.

Larua's hand went back for the throw. With all the strength she could muster, Sharra leaped forward and rammed into the High Councilor's body. They went down in a heap behind the throne.

Now! she said, and released the energy from its prison as she held the Arderian face down to the ground.

Freed at last, it coursed down her nervous system in a wave of excitement. Before she knew it, the threads passed through her skin where it touched Larua's, and attacked the aura of the High Councilor. Like the cloud of the Vault chamber, it spread out and surrounded its victim in a thin sheet of white. But unlike Sharra's first experience with the Vault cloud when it had entered her body and freed her from the hands of J.D. Dash, this time the feeling was different... primal... hungry... and angry.

And she was glad.

Underneath her Larua hissed as she struggled to get away, but the threads grew stronger the more they ate, draining her of the electromagnetic energy that made up the core of her aura, her life force. In a matter of seconds the blackness of her aura faded to grey, then white, until there was no color left, but the emptiness of air.

Sharra could feel Larua go still underneath her. With nothing left to consume, the cloud of threads broke apart and swarmed back across the connected skin and entered her body before she could move. Once in her nervous system it travelled quickly up to the nest in her brain. As it flowed, renewed power coursed through her veins. The hair on her skin stood on end as uncontrollable tremors shook her body from the alien effect. As soon as all the bloated threads were back between the agrylium in her head the shaking stopped and her body returned to normal.

"Sharra?"

Hands came down and lifted her off the fallen Arderian. Turning her around, Tanner held her steady. At their feet Larua lay face down, arms out, unmoving. The thin webbing of her dorsal fin covered her face like a peace of cloth, and lay loose over the slit through the back of her gown.

"Sharra," Tanner said. His eyes, dark with worry, searched her face. She lifted her eyes to his. At the sight of them he froze.

"Tanner," she said with relief, not noticing his shock. "She had a knife. I had to stop her…"

"Your pupils," he said as he stared into her eyes, "they're glowing."

"Are they?"

She slammed down the shield around the twisting threads of energy, encasing their light back within the ball.

Tanner frowned. "It's gone. I could swear it was there a moment ago. What's going on?"

"Never mind that. Help me with Larua."

They bent down and turned her over. On the floor hidden by her body where she had fallen was a puddle of blood. In her chest buried up to the hilt was the knife meant for Araylai. Tanner felt for a pulse, but shook his head.

"What happened?" he asked.

"She was going to kill Araylai. Everyone was watching the fight. It was happening so fast. I didn't know what else to do."

There came a shout of surprise from inside the ring, followed by a heavy thunk as bodies hit the ground. Then, all went quiet. Sharra stood and ran to the back of the throne afraid of what she would see. Tanner came behind her and held her steady. Neither said a word.

In the center of the ring Nayada straddled Aniani's body on the floor. Not a sound could be heard in all the assembly, but her harsh breathing. Head bent to her victim, Nayada pressed her knife into the chest of the fallen Queen in one final thrust. Underneath her Aniani's eyes bulged in a flash of color, and then went blank. Her head fell back to the floor with a thunk as the life left her body. Her once white dress was covered in blood. More was pouring out from around the blade buried between her breasts.

No one moved, not a flutter of webbing, nor a blink of an eye.

Nayada stayed like that, frozen for a moment in the silence of death as she fought to catch her breath. Finally she let go of the handle of the knife and rolled to her feet. With the Queen's blood dripping from her hands, she turned to face the High Court.

"Queen Aniani is dead," she proclaimed.

Praemin Tegamen stepped down from the tier and crossed the floor to where Nayada stood next to the motionless body of the Queen.

She took one brief look at the body, and then turned to the onlookers. In a loud voice she pronounced, "The Blood Challenge has been satisfied. The sea has decided. Queen Aniani is no more!"

She grabbed Nayada's arm and held it high, uncaring of the blood that was wet upon it. The mark of the bloodline of the House of Queens that was on the fleshy part of her thumb showed dark through the stain of fresh blood. She turned in a circle with Nayada, showing off the mark so that all could see.

As they turned within the circle, Praemin Tegamen cried out, "All hail our new Queen, Aliya, daughter of Adaylai, daughter of Awynn of the House of Ardere. May the seas bless her rule with justice and honor for the good of the people and for all of Ardere."

During the proclamation Calyx and Katie helped Loch to his feet. Nayada searched the crowd as she turned. At the sight of her pod, a smile of relief filled her eyes. From the sideline the two scouts smiled back at their leader. Pride was written in their stance and on their faces.

Their voices joined the assembly, louder than the rest, as all acclaimed as one people, "Hear, hear. All hail Queen Aliya!"

Praemin Tegamen bowed low before Nayada. The rest followed suit in a rustle of material as they gave homage to the stunned Umbra scout.

Around the room, the Vault team bowed along with the Arderians, Sharra more than the rest. It was over. Araylai was free, her honor restored once again among her people. But it had come at a heavy price. She hoped Araylai would not some day come to regret the decision that she had made today. She glanced over at her Arderian friend. She looked at peace. For now that was probably enough.

As for Sharra, this chapter was over, though there would be no rest for her. Her own demons still haunted her. Betrayal and treachery were lessons well learned on Ardus. They would come in handy, for she now knew that she faced the same type of treachery that Araylai had faced with her mother. The melted agrylium tattoos bore testimony to the reality of that fact. No longer was she in the dark. Fate had intervened. She had a face, and a name.

Ardus had done its job.

It was time to go home… It was time to find her brother.

Chapter Thirty-Six

———

The city was abuzz with the sound of excitement. Colorful pennants hung from every window, balcony, and pole in celebration of the day. Children with long streamers in their hands raced through the streets laughing and shouting. Dressed in their finest their parents followed at a slower pace as the crowds carried on to the city center. The sound of joyful music drifted over their heads. Stringed, horned, and wind melded harmoniously in a new song, lifting the hearts of everyone who heard it.

At ground level of the Arderian reef, nothing stirred in the large cavernous section that housed the Harena Markets. Aisle after aisle of the tent city lay desolate. Not a cart, or a wagon, or a house servant travelled along its breath. Wares that normally spilled out into the streets were tucked inside their stalls, the fronts closed tight.

The flags on the awnings flapped in the breeze. It was the only sound to be heard except for the music that floated in from the extensive tunnel systems.

Even the slave blocks near the wall were empty. In the fenced yards across the way the animals that were left to fend for themselves crooned for attention, but there would be none on that day.

Everyone that was anyone, from the wealthiest Houses to the poorest of slaves had other things on their minds. For it was a day long in the making. It was a day of new beginnings, of reconciliation… a day of honor.

That day the sea smiled down upon the great city of Ardere, gifting it with the full light of the sun through its calm waters, encompassing it in its warm embrace. The city glowed brightly as the lichen ate up the rays, bathing those who lived there in a radiance like never before experienced.

In the great cavern of the main city, the palace sparkled with light. Arderians from all over poured into its courtyard. Auras gleamed. Crests sailed high. Class distinctions were forgotten. On that day all were of the same mind.

Off the banisters of the balconies in the palace face, bright streamers swirled in the air. From the center one a small orchestra played a joyous tune. Yet they were not alone in the palace face, for a number of fancy dressed guests, male and female, crowded together inside the other balconies. Merrily they waved to the people below, all sharing in the joy of the day.

Inside the huge throne room, the mood was solemn. Royal Umbra guards in full uniform lined the curved walls of the chamber, and at each of the four huge double doors. At each of the two rings of pillars stood more guards. But it was the ones around the throne area that stood out. Dressed in the muted greens of the Riff Outpost with their medallion armband proudly displayed on their arms, the Umbra guards that had been under Caetus' command stood at attention inside the inner circle and around the dais of the throne in a special place of honor. The rest of the floor was so thick with guests that the shell mosaic was barely visible. Guests from all over stood silently as all eyes watched the scene in front of the throne. All the Houses were represented along with many from the township of Riff.

At the right armrest of the throne stood Calyx in a gown of Tyrian purple. Her Riff armband was gone. Instead she wore a gold one with the Queen's markings. But her former station had not been forgotten for the Riff medallion had been reworked and now hung between her breasts in a place of honor.

Loch too was there, on the left side just in front of the throne in a uniform of purple, black and gold. Bruises were on his pale skin, along with the half-healed cuts that ran down his arms, but he paid them no mind for he wore them as a badge of honor. With a hand on the hilt of his newly commissioned sword, he stood at attention. His good eye was clear of pain. His crest was high, and his aura bright.

Upon the dais of the throne, Nayada, or Aliya as was her royal name, kneeled on a small pillow and faced the silent audience. Gone was her scout uniform of muddy green. Instead she wore a gown of the color of the warm seas of Ardus, her home world. Her skin glowed with luster. In front of her was Araylai in a dress of white. Between her hands she held the jewel-encrusted crown of the Queens of Ardere. Slowly she lowered it onto Nayada's brow.

As she did, she said loud and clear, repeating the words said to all the queens before, "With this crown passes the honor of the House of Ardere. May the seas cleanse you this day, and fill you with wisdom. Let peace be your aura, and humble be your heart."

As her fingers slowly left the crown, their eyes met. They both smiled a smile of understanding, and of friendship. Around them the crowd waited in expectation.

Araylai raised Nayada to her feet and turned to the assembly, and said, "The blackness of the former Queen has passed away. Rejoice for honor has been restored to our great city. It shines once again as the jewel of the sea. It is a day of new beginnings. A ruler stands before you, chosen by the Bloodright of the queens before her. Let her name be praised with glory, and sung with honor. Hail, Queen Aliya, of the Great House of Ardere."

The crowd responded with a loud, "Hail, Queen Aliya!"

Afterwards a thunderous cheer broke out. It shook the great chamber with the force of their happiness.

Off to one side of the dais, the Vault team cheered as loud as their new Arderian friends. Sharra's heart rejoiced not only for Araylai and Nayada, but also for the friends that surrounded her. Lazarus, Tanner, Viktor, and Katie, were all present dressed in their finest, all there to support Araylai as a family who loved each other would.

Standing at Sharra's side, Katie clapped her hands, her face shining with excitement. Lazarus looked at his daughter's exuberance with indulgence, while Viktor hovered behind them like a big papa bear. On the other side of her Tanner stood tall and handsome in his crisp white shirt and black tuxedo. He caught Sharra's happy face, and sent her a wide smile. She smiled back, captured in the goodwill that filled the throne room. As she did Tanner looked down into her eyes, searching their depths for something.

"What?" she said.

"Nothing." Tanner tore away from her gaze, and turned to watch the newly installed queen hug her cousin. "I'm just glad you're okay."

Was she okay?

That was a debatable question one she struggled to answer. Pushing that dark thought aside, she readjusted the strap of her sling on her good shoulder where it wrinkled the material of her dress. The wound still throbbed, but was healing thanks to the skill of the court healer. The inner wounds, the ones the others couldn't see, still festered and hurt, and Tanner's next statement didn't help.

"I know a lot has happened recently," he said, "and this is probably not the place to bring this up, but I can't stop thinking about it."

"What is it? Is it something I've done?"

"You tell me. Twice now I've seen a strange glow come through your pupils: that time in the Vault when Dash died, and here when I picked you off Larua. I just need to know…"

"Know what?" she said.

Her brow furrowed as her mind raced to find an answer for the question she knew he was about to ask, dreading the truth. But he never got to finish for Katie touched her arm and drew her attention across the floor to where the crowd opened.

"Faolan's arrived," she said. "And he's brought a gift for the new Queen."

Through the aisle of joyful Arderians strolled in Faolan as if it were a ball of the haute ton of London of the nineteenth century. With his dark hair slicked back, and wearing a tuxedo like the rest of the Vault men, he looked like a black panther on the prowl, dangerous and sexy. A smile played on his lips as he went up to Nayada and bowed an elegant bow that came from years of experience.

"I apologize for my lateness," he said, "but I'm hoping the gift that I've brought with me from the Vault will make up for it."

From the throne, Loch gasped as he stared at the opening from which Faolan had come. "It cannot be. I am seeing things."

His aura flashed bright as his eyes widened into saucers. Crest flicking he started down the dais towards whatever was down there. Hitting the floor he took off with a cry.

"What is it, Loch?" Calyx asked.

"Cael! It is Cael!"

Through the opening appeared their lost pod member, healthy and whole. A huge grin covered his face as his eyes lighted upon his pod mate. Loch leaped the last few feet, and grabbed him, stopping him with the force of his emotions. He blinked and then blinked again, as he drank in the sight of his pod mate. Behind him came Calyx, and then Nayada. The humans didn't need their alien auras to tell them how they felt. Their happiness was blatant for all to see as they surrounded Cael with hugs.

Tears came to Sharra at the sight of Cael. Renewed joy filled her heart. She could not wait any longer and ran across the floor to join their group. With the energy tucked safely behind her shield, she hugged him as best as her good arm would let her.

"We thought you were dead," she said wiping a tear away.

"I would have been if you had not sent Faolan back to the Vault with me."

"When I saw the knife in your chest..." She stopped for a moment. The memory was still too raw. And yet here he was, smiling at her. "It was the only answer."

"I will not lie, it was touch and go for a bit, but Cam is an excellent doctor. And the medical chamber is... well... is..."

Sharra laughed. "Say no more. We've all been there. Anyway, I am so glad you're alive. It makes this day perfect."

Cael's aura saddened as his eyes fell on the bruises and half-healed wounds of his friend.

"It seems that I am not the only one who has suffered."

"We are fine," Loch said with a smile. "Since Queen Aniani's death, the people have rallied together to clean the dredge from the city. So thorough have they been that the courts are backlogged for months to come.

We have the Grexs swimming scared, which is a first. We even caught the worm planted in our barracks. It is a new city, Cael, a new city. And now that you are back, our honor is complete. And we all have Sharra to thank for this."

"Not just for my return," Cael said, "but from what I hear, for what she has done for our people. Having Faolan take the records with him, and removing them from the clutches of the Grex was a stroke of genius."

A blush stole into Sharra's cheeks at the praise. "I knew that if Aniani got them, it would mean the end of Nayada," she explained. "And I couldn't let that happen, not after what Aniani had done to your pod already. I had hoped that when Faolan read them in the safety of the Vault he would know what to do with them. And he did, saving us all."

"I couldn't let you have all the glory," Faolan said as he came up to stand close behind her. "Besides, Lazarus wanted his prize agents safely back. Who better to coordinate the rescue efforts than Cael and I?"

"I'm glad it worked," she said.

"So are we. And now, I have come back to find everything has changed. Nayada a Queen," Cael said, and bowed to his former pod leader.

"Rise, Cael," Nayada said. "I should be the one honoring you. And I know exactly what to give you. As my right as Queen I shall give you a Praemin House, the House of Cael, of the Harena."

"You honor me, my Queen," he stammered.

"Nayada. I will always be Nayada to my pod," she said with all sincerity. "Now, we should join the rest of our hu-man guests. As you are quick to point out, Sharra of the Vault, we are a pod, a family, and should never leave anyone behind, even at a celebration."

Curious, the crowd watched as the intimate group laughed happily as they moved across the floor to the other humans.

At their approach, Lazarus bowed and said, "Queen Aliya, on behalf of The Vault team, I want to congratulate you on your succession, and wish you a reign of peace and prosperity. And... to thank you for honoring our newfound alliance."

Nayada smiled over at Araylai. "Araylai will always have a place here if she so chooses to come back."

"My home is the Vault now," Araylai said. "And I am needed there."

Cael raised a webbed hand. "May I be so bold as to ask if you think that the Vault has room for one more Arderian?"

Auras turned red in shock as the implications of his questions hit his Arderian friends.

"Do you know what you are asking?" Loch said.

"Yes. I do."

"You would give up our pod to go live with the humans? Sorry, Sharra."

"No offence taken," Sharra said.

"Look at Sharra, at Faolan, and at the rest of her team. They are the same as us. I know our anatomy may be slightly different..."

"Slightly?" Tanner said.

An elbow slammed into his side at the jest. Sharra glared up at him, and said, "Be nice."

Cael smiled at the two, and continued to explain.

"Yes, we may be different on the outside, but, inside, here," he said, touching the spot on his chest where his heart rested, "we are the same. The same bond that our small pod shares is the same that Sharra, Lazarus, Tanner, and the rest at the Vault share. I am not saying they do not have problems, but I have had a taste of the Vault, and now understand why Araylai chooses to stay with them. If I could, I would wish for this also."

Nayada sent Lazarus a quick look. "It seems you were right in your prediction."

A knowing smile curved the lips of the Head Director of Vault Agency. "What the Queen is saying is that with the success of Araylai's integration into our elite society, we have agreed between our two entities to quietly, and I mean quietly, have a few join our group from this world. Immari, Araylai's friend, has already settled in nicely. And thanks to Sharra, who has been inadvertently recruiting during her stay on Ardus, Cael also has approached me on the matter. Well Cael, if your new Queen permits it, I'd say yes."

All eyes turned to the Queen. She touched Cael's arm, and searched his face.

"Is this what you really want?" she asked quietly.

"Yes. It is."

"Then… we will miss you. Go with them with honor."

The far doors of the throne room opened and a voice issued forth, "Honored guests, the banquet is ready. Please follow the Queen and her party into the banquet hall."

The guards left their posts and formed an aisle through the assembly to the double doors down the far

387

end.

"That is my cue," Nayada said. "Araylai, I will leave Cael in your care. He is your responsibility now. Come my friends. Let us not keep the hungry masses waiting."

Araylai hooked her arm through Cael's and said, "I will keep an eye on him, and make sure he does not dishonor himself in his new home."

"You insult me, Princess."

"Ahhh, but you do not know the hu-mans like I do," she chuckled as they followed the Queen to the banquet.

"Home," Sharra repeated as she trailed behind the Arderians with her teammates.

Lazarus heard her and stopped her with a hand on her shoulder.

"We need to talk about that," he said. "The Vault isn't safe for you to return to yet, not until we catch the man behind your attacks."

"About that." Sharra paused and took in a deep breath. "I'm always going on about the rules in our handbook to others without fully applying it to myself. Rule number fourteen in the handbook states that full disclosure must be given on all missions. I wasn't going to, but I've come to realize that I need you and your wisdom."

"Going to what? I'm listening."

"There's something I need to tell you... I know who it is... my attacker. I saw his face... heard his voice. But before I tell you who it is, I need to go back to the beginning."

The throne room was quickly emptying. She took the arm Lazarus offered. He led her through the guards to the far doors. Up ahead Tanner and Faolan walked side-by-side discussing something. She had no doubt that it was probably her. Both were handsome in their own way. Both were in love with her. It was a first for her, having two men fight over her. It felt good. Was that bad? She didn't think so. Though Sharra knew that she couldn't lead them on forever. That wasn't fair to anyone. Yet, her heart was torn. But they would have to wait because she had a bigger problem to deal with right now.

Greyson.

Beside her Lazarus waited patiently as she struggled with her thoughts. She needed help, and the only way to get it was with full disclosure.

She took another breath and plunged in. It was the only way.

"It all started with my parents' death…"

TIMELINE GUIDE

Antonio Rossi:
guild member, age 29 from Florence, Italy
Year 1658

Araylai:
heir apparent, age 24 from Ardere, Ardus
Year 2252

Faolan:
swordsman, age 28 from Rhinns, Scotland
Year 764

Cael:
Umbra scout, age 28 from Ardere, Ardus
Year 2553

Greyson Lane:
IT, age 23 from Chicago, IL USA
Year 1989

Grimm Hannay:
quarry worker, age 65 from Glasgow, Scotland
Year 1975

J.D. Dash:
sailor, age 31 from Boston MA, USA
Year 1853

Katie Hyde:
orphan, age 17 from London, England
Year 1789

TIMELINE GUIDE

Lazarus Maitland:
Earl, age 48 from Compton, England
Year 1741

Maxum:
centurion. age 47 from Rome, Italy
Year 1000

Sharra Lane:
accountant, age 24 from Charlotte NC, USA
Year 1996

Tanner Holmes:
Delta Force, age 33 from Bangor PA, USA
Year 1982

Tatiana Ivonovic:
ballerina, age 25 from St. Petersburg, Russia
Year 1895

Viktor:
shuttle tech, age 26 from Federal Ukraine
Year 2253

Zoe Fox:
model, age 22 from New York City NY, USA
Year 1987

THE VAULT
Book Three of the Vault Agency Series.

The hunt has started.

The prey is on the run.

Something is wrong with the Vault. Trouble has been brewing between longtime partners, and it's only getting worse. If Lazarus, the Head Director, doesn't figure out how to relieve the tension, his worst fear of mutiny may become a reality.

And then there is Sharra Lane's brother, Greyson. With her agrylium discs repaired, Sharra sets out to her past timeline to look for clues as to the origin of her brother's aggressive behavior, only to discover that Greyson's obsessive desire to destroy her runs deeper than she had thought possible.

When Sharra and the Vault team set out to stop Greyson, little do they know that their 'interference' will put in motion a wheel of events that will not only set her past on its fixed course, but ultimately, drive the future of the Vault to an unimaginable end.